STRIVERS ROW

During the 1920s and 1930s, around the time of the Harlem Renaissance, more than a quarter of a million African-Americans settled in Harlem, creating what was described at the time as "a cosmopolitan Negro capital which exert[ed] an influence over Negroes everywhere."

Nowhere was this more evident than on West 138th and 139th Streets between what are now Adam Clayton Powell and Frederick Douglass Boulevards, two blocks that came to be known as Strivers Row. These blocks attracted many of Harlem's African-American doctors, lawyers, and entertainers, among them Eubie Blake, Noble Sissle, and W. C. Handy, who were themselves striving to achieve America's middle-class dream.

With its mission of publishing quality African-American literature, Strivers Row emulates those "strivers," capturing that same spirit of hope, creativity, and promise.

PROMISES TO KEEP

PROMISES

TO

KEEP

a novel

GLORIA MALLETTE

STRIVERS
ROW

VILLARD / NEW YORK

Library of Congress Cataloging-in-Publication Data

Mallette, Gloria.
Promises to keep: a novel / Gloria Mallette.—1st ed.
p. cm.
ISBN 0-375-75744-9
1. Murder victims' families—Fiction. 2. Parent and adult child—Fiction. 3. Custody
of children—Fiction. 4. Divorced fathers—Fiction. I. Title.
PS3563.A4315 P76 2002
813'.6—dc21
2001046580

Villard Books website address: www.villard.com
Printed in the United States of America

2 4 6 8 9 7 5 3

First Edition

Book design by Jo Anne Metsch

Promises to Keep is dedicated to all the mothers, fathers, sisters, brothers, and children who are left behind when the life of a loved one is snatched from their loving arms. It is never easy. Keep the faith and stay strong.

ACKNOWLEDGMENTS

Without one's buddies, where would one be? Much love and appreciation to the other two M's on the shelf—Karen E. Quinones Miller, author of *Satin Doll*, forever giving, forever sharing, and forever dreaming; and Mary B. Morrison, author of *Soul Mates Dissipate*, who warmly sings my praises to all she meets while encouraging me to reach for the brass ring. Mary, you are special indeed. Ladies, I am honored to call you both sister friend.

And one should never forget friends who have always been there: Curtis Richard, Debbie Buie, Muslimah Toliver, Khadijah Bandele, and Maryann Whelan, thank you for believing.

A special thank you to my editor, Melody Guy, for trusting the voices of her writers. You are much appreciated.

Last but definitely not least, my best friend and partner in life, Arnold Mallette, thank you for telling me to "get a real job or do something about those five manuscripts in your office. Go for it. Self-publish." Arnold, thank you for the mighty shove.

When in the arms of death a loved one departs,
the flood of tears that are mournfully shed
will never wash the pain from our hearts.
The precious memories that remain in our heads
are ours until the day from this life we all part.

PROMISES TO KEEP

ONE

LORD, how she hated cold weather. Just looking at a snowy winter scene or a frigid rainy day on television chilled her to the bone and made her want to go back to bed and snuggle under her fluffy down comforter. That's why, when summer ended a month ago, Nola sank to the depths of doldrums. She was one woman who had looked forward to menopause because of the notorious hot flashes she had heard so much about. As luck would have it, it hardly affected her at all. She was just as cold if not colder. If she could make it through the next five years, she was going to retire at fifty-eight and wing her way to Florida on the fastest thing flying. If Ron wasn't ready to leave New York, he was going to be left behind—there weren't but so many more winters her bones could take. Already through her kitchen window she could see the russet-colored leaves of autumn falling from the trees, and the only flowers left in her garden from the hot days of summer were marigolds of yellow and orange. In anticipation of a cold, snowy winter, Nola hugged herself and shivered; for some reason she was really cold this morning.

"Nola, you know it's all in your mind."

Turning around, she gave Ron her "leave me alone" look as he sat down at the kitchen table. Even after thirty-three years of marriage, he still didn't believe that she was really cold. That's because Ron was one of those weird people who didn't get cold, therefore he couldn't begin to understand how she felt when the temperature dropped below fifty degrees. He wore neither scarf, gloves, nor hat in the dead of winter unless there was a blizzard and he didn't want to get wet. Without her cashmere-lined leather gloves, Nola's fingers would freeze and ache to the bone, and without her cozy wool tams, her head ached and an awful chill radiated down her spine. When that happened, she just wanted to take to her bed. How two people could be so different and stay married she didn't know, especially when setting the thermostat was cause for a summit every other day throughout the winter months. She always won because she gave Ron no rest from her tongue. For the sake of peace, he wore cotton shorts and T-shirts around the house like summer never ended for him.

"Your blood is probably made out of ice water," he said, taking a strip of bacon off the plate sitting on the table.

"Seem to me this ice water went a long way in warming you up last night. In fact, brought you to the boiling point."

"Sho'nuff did, but baby, look at you. A big ol' ugly flannel nightgown under that ugly, bulky mohair sweater you've had since high school, and wool socks that Bigfoot could wear."

She looked down at her feet. "So, I'm cold."

"Nola, I keep telling you, you got poor circulation. You need to do some aerobics to get your blood up."

Nola cut her eyes at Ron. His barbs about her drab sleepwear and her refusal to exercise, beyond yoga, were older than their marriage. He didn't think yoga was anything but a lazy person's excuse for exercise, but was that the kettle calling the pot black? Ron's idea of exercise was playing golf, and in her opinion, that was a lazy man's way of playing ball. That's why she was still wearing her flannels and still practicing yoga— she was warm, she was limber, and she was in shape.

"You know something, Ron? You—" The devilish glint in his eyes and the mischievous smile on his lips stopped Nola from saying another word. He almost had her.

Grinning, he winked at her.

Slowly rolling her eyes and turning her back to him, Nola reached over and turned on the burner under the frying pan; she had waited for him to come down before scrambling the eggs.

"Not biting, huh?"

"Nope," she replied, not looking at him. "In fact, I don't know why you'd want to get me started so early in the morning. Can't you get it up without a war of words with me?"

He chuckled. "Come over here and see if—"

"Good morning, Poppie," Meika said sweetly, scampering gaily into the kitchen.

Ron clamped his mouth shut and immediately started rubbing his chin. "Mornin', baby."

Nola chuckled softly to herself when Meika went over and, tiptoeing, kissed Ron on the cheek. He looked really embarrassed, but she didn't think that Meika heard anything, and even if she did, she doubted whether Meika had a clue as to what they were talking about. Every now and then they slipped up and forgot that Meika was living with them; they had grown accustomed to having the house to themselves since Troy had moved out and gotten married six years ago, and Vann hadn't come back home when he graduated from college. He liked Atlanta and felt he had just as good a chance as any in New York and decided to start his career in finance there.

Meika turned away from Ron and went over to Nola, her arms up, ready for the hug she knew she'd get. "Good morning, Mama. Kissy face."

Picking Meika up and bear-hugging her, Nola kissed her all over her face. "Good morning, baby. Mmm, you smell good," she said, putting her back down on the floor.

"Daddy let me put on some of his perfume."

"My, you must be special," she said, pushing Meika's frizzy hair back off her heart-shaped face. She'd comb it after breakfast. "You meeting your boyfriend today?"

"Mama, I'm too little to have a boyfriend."

"Yes, you are," Ron said. "I don't want none of those knuckleheaded little boys in your class calling here asking if you can come out to play."

Nola patted Meika on the behind. "Go sit at the table."

Meika skipped over and climbed up onto the chair next to Ron. "Poppie," she said in a very serious tone, "I don't like the boys in my class."

"Oh no? Why?"

"Because they're bad. They pick on me and Francine. They throw paper balls at us."

Ron smiled. He was remembering how much fun it was to throw paper balls at the girls he liked. "Who's *they*?" he asked.

"Larry and Shane."

"They're picking on you because you're pretty."

"But, Poppie, I don't want them to throw paper at me. I don't like them."

"That's just it, Meika. They like you," Nola said, turning back to the stove. She dropped a pat of butter in the frying pan. "Little boys always pick on little girls they like."

"I don't think so, Mama. If they liked us, they would be nice to us."

Thinking that it must be wonderful to be so young and innocent, Nola poured the already beaten eggs into the hot frying pan. "Honey, boys, and grown men, too," she added, glancing at Ron, who had picked up his newspaper and was reading the headlines, "are afraid to be nice to the girls they like because they're afraid their friends might think they're sissies."

Ron lowered his paper. "Don't tell her that."

"Why not?" she asked, scrambling the eggs. "It's the truth."

"It is not."

Looking directly into Ron's eyes, Meika nodded in agreement with Nola.

"Look what you've done," he said, looking at Meika. "You got the child thinking like you. Don't be filling her head with that liberated woman stuff. Let the girl grow up unbiased."

"Oh, so you want her to grow up ignorant in the ways of men."

"You were ignorant once upon a time, weren't you?"

Nola raised her brow. "I'll have you know, I was born wise."

"I bet you were, but let Meika experience her own life, not yours."

Letting them go on talking about her, Meika reached out toward the plate with the bacon on it but it was out of her reach. She got up on her knees and, leaning on the table, reached out and took a strip of bacon.

"Oh please. Look who's talking," Nola said, hastily scrambling the eggs to keep them from sticking. She turned down the fire under the pan. "I can't count the times I overheard you telling Troy and Vann about what it meant to be a man and what you thought women were about. The irony of it all is, you didn't know then and you don't know now what a woman is about."

Munching on her bacon, Meika, still up on her knees in her chair, looked from Nola to Ron.

"I must know something," Ron said, "I'm still married to you."

Troy came into the kitchen. "Morning, folks. It's never too early for you two to debate, is it?"

"Your mother is trying to turn your daughter against men."

Meika sighed impatiently.

"I'm doing no such thing," Nola defended, portioning out the scrambled eggs onto three plates.

"To be fair, Dad," Troy said, going past the table to Nola, "you advised me and Vann about girls as far back as I can remember; I don't think I was even out of diapers yet."

"See," Nola said.

Ron huffed. "Traitor."

"No, Dad. I'm just telling it like it was. Some of what you said I used, some I didn't. Either way, I was glad you told me. Let Ma school Meika. I want her to be prepared for those smooth talkers out there when she's ready to start dating. Besides, I want her to be a strong woman like her grandmother."

"Oh man," Ron said. "That's all your mother needs to hear."

Beaming proudly, Nola kissed Troy on the cheek. "That's my baby. He's not threatened by a strong woman," she said, handing him two of the three plates.

Ron shook his head. "Your baby is big and rusty. He's got a baby of his own now."

"Mama, knock-knock," Meika said suddenly.

Ron chuckled.

Troy looked at Meika. His eyes twinkled. "Who's there?" he asked. He set the plate with the hefty helping of eggs in front of Ron and the plate with the smaller portion in front of Meika. Then he reached back and took his own plate.

"Not you," Nola said, lightly slapping Troy on the arm. "That's my knock-knock joke. Who's there?"

Smiling, Meika said, "Baby."

"Dad, look at this," Troy said. "I'm the one who taught her knock-knock jokes in the first place and she throws me aside and plays it with Ma."

"That's what I'm trying to tell you. She's becoming a clone of her grandma."

"Don't be jealous, boys," Nola said, smiling at Meika. "Baby who?"

"Baby daddy," Meika replied, throwing back her head and laughing.

Troy laughed just as hard, while Ron simply chuckled and shook his head. He didn't get it. Nola couldn't help but laugh herself. The joke wasn't funny, but Meika's laugh was contagious. Pleased with herself, Meika went back to nibbling on her strip of bacon.

"Dad, I remember Grandma calling you her baby till the day she died," Troy said, setting his plate down on the table.

Ron picked up his fork. "Well, that was my mother."

Nola and Troy exchanged knowing looks. They both smiled.

Seeing them, Ron waved his hand at them. "Nola, you finally got the little girl you always wanted. Mark my word, Meika's gonna be a little Nola in pigtails in no time."

"So what's wrong with that?" Nola asked, putting her hands on her hips. "It can't be all that bad, you married me."

"Under duress."

"I never—"

Troy waved Nola into silence. "Ma, relax. He's just trying to get you going. That's not what he told me and Vann. In fact, he told us to find nice girls like you to settle down with."

"Go ahead, son. Betray me. Tell your mother about our private father-son conversations. Vann'll be home for Thanksgiving. He'll stand up for me."

Meika looked at Troy. "Daddy."

Troy sat down across from Ron. "Yeah, well, I'm ready for both of you."

"So you think you can handle me and your brother?"

"Damn right."

Nola shot Troy a warning look. "Watch your mouth."

He looked at Meika. "Sorry, baby."

"That's all right, Daddy. I know that word, damn."

"Meika!" Nola said. "I don't want you using that word."

"It's a bad word, right?"

"Yes." Nola went back to getting breakfast ready, but she intended to have a talk with Troy about what he said in front of Meika.

"Dad, you and Vann used to gang up on me all the time out back playing basketball. And look who turned out to be the better player."

"Me," Ron said, shaking salt onto his eggs.

Nola watched Ron's heavy hand with the salt.

Meika tapped on the table. "S'cuse me. Daddy."

"I don't think so, Dad. I started taking you to the hoop when I was fourteen."

Ron salted his eggs again. "Naw."

"Ron," Nola said, "you know what the doctor said about salt."

"The doctor said a lot of things, but he didn't say I had to stop enjoying my food," he said, taking four strips of bacon. "And don't think I don't know that this is that phony bacon."

"Daddy."

"Okay, smarty," Nola said, carrying the pot of grits to the table. "It's turkey bacon. It tastes about the same, maybe better."

"Not to me," Ron said, tasting his eggs.

Thumping on the table with her fork, Meika exhaled loudly. "Daddy!"

"Yes, Meika. I'm right here. What is it?"

"We still going to the movie?"

Nola plopped a spoonful of buttery grits on Ron's plate. "What are you going to see?"

"I'm taking her to see *The Lion King*," Troy answered, taking a slice of toast and lightly buttering it. He handed it to Meika. "I didn't forget."

"Goody." Meika picked up another piece of crispy bacon.

"I hear that's a good movie," Nola said. "What time are you going, Troy?"

"We're going to the matinee after I get back from Manhattan. I have to take care of some business. You mind watching Meika till I get back?"

"Of course not, but I have a dental appointment at two."

"I should be back before one."

Ron gulped down a forkful of eggs and grits. "You didn't have to bother asking your mother to watch Meika, you're lucky she lets you have any time with your child at all."

Nola flipped her hand at Ron. "You're just jealous I'm not babying you."

Ron ignored her. "Son, you going anywhere near the West Village?"

"What do you need?"

"That guava tonic from that health food store over there on Sixth Avenue."

"I was planning on taking the FDR Drive uptown. I gotta meet someone at the Metropolitan Museum at Eighty-second, but I'll detour if you want me to."

"Naw, I can wait. I'll be over there on Monday."

Smiling, Nola looked at Meika nibbling on a strip of bacon. Ron was right, Meika was the little girl she always wanted. After she had Troy, she couldn't have any more children, and since Ron didn't want to adopt, her dreams of having a baby girl were dashed forever. The nine dolls she'd saved from her own childhood stayed wrapped in plastic bags inside cardboard boxes in the attic, gathering dust and cobwebs. That is, until Meika came to stay. Now Meika played with four of the dolls and claimed all of them as her own. She had more videotapes of Meika playing with the dolls than of anything or anyone else. Still, she wouldn't trade her boys, Vann or Troy, for anything—they were her life's breath. They had brought her such joy. Though, admittedly, she used to wish secretly that one of them had been a girl. There was so much she wanted to share with a girl; so much she wanted to contribute to a girl blossoming into a woman that her own mother had not shared with her. Like her period—she had learned about it from her girlfriends in the sixth grade on the playground; and her first real crush, which was on a boy named Patrick she was crazy about in her eleventh-grade class. No one told her that her first crush didn't necessarily have to feel the same about her or that all he might be after was her virginity. Her girlfriends didn't know enough to warn her, while her mother must have surely known, but didn't take the time to pull her coattail. Nola found out on her own the old-fashioned way—the old one-night-stand way. After she lost her virginity, she lost what she never really had, Patrick. She didn't want that heartache for Meika. Meika was going to be a very knowledgeable teenager.

From the day Meika was born, Nola doted on Meika as much as her mother, Cordelia, would allow, which was quite frequently. Cordelia was always eager for Nola to baby-sit so that she could run the streets. That's why, after Cordelia and Troy divorced, Nola was ecstatic that he had gotten custody of Meika and had asked to move back home until he could get his own place. She was more than happy to give up her sewing room to Meika—she wasn't sewing much anymore anyway. So far, she had been able to discourage Troy from moving out by saying that she could help him raise Meika until he either found the right woman or was ready to go it alone. Not necessarily in that order, but he was in no hurry either way. Troy had the freedom to come and go as he pleased. He had a live-in baby-sitter and cook. But she never felt like he took advantage of her. He had his own phone, and he paid rent just like an adult was supposed to. She figured if she didn't cramp his style and let him be an adult, he'd forget about leaving altogether. Two years had passed, they were all getting along just fine, and more important, she had her baby girl.

"Mama," Meika said, "you and Poppie gonna come to the movie with us?"

"I can't," Ron said quickly. "I gotta meet some friends."

"Golf?" Troy asked.

"Yep."

"Next Saturday, Dad, I'm going out there on the green with you old men."

"Us *old* men are ready for you. We'll show you that eighteen holes aren't for wimps."

"We'll see. You might get your feelings hurt."

"Bring your wallet, son."

"You're on, Dad. Next Saturday, do or die."

"Bet," Ron said, satisfied. He and Troy never bet above fifty dollars, but the money wasn't the incentive. He enjoyed hanging out with his son. He had taught Troy the game of golf over a year ago and Troy had begun giving him some serious competition.

Sitting down at the table, Nola took a slice of toast and two strips of bacon. "Meika, Mama can't go either," she said, carefully biting into a piece of dry toast. "I have to get my teeth fixed today. But I want to hear all about *The Lion King* when you get home."

"Okay," she said, daintily picking up a piece of egg with her fingers. "I'll bring you some chocolate candy, okay?"

"Thank you, sweetheart," she said, smiling again. Meika knew her weakness for chocolate, but no candy was as sweet as she was.

TWO

D
ADDY," Meika whispered, her eyes fixed on the screen, "can you hold Mama's candy? I wanna eat my popcorn."

"Sure," Troy said, taking the large chocolate bar and putting it in his jacket pocket. "You keep taking your grandma chocolate every time you go to the movies, she's gonna get fat."

Stretching her eyes wide as the lion cub was running frantically, trying not to be trampled by a stampeding pack of hyenas, Meika gasped, "Daddy, they'll hurt little Simba."

Troy put his arm around Meika's little shoulders, and leaning down to her, whispered, "He'll be fine, he's the star. He has to live all the way till the end of the movie."

Looking at him, she inhaled sharply. "Then he's gonna die?"

"No, baby. The star never dies."

"You sure?" she asked in a frightened little voice.

"I'm sure. Now look at the movie, you're missing it," he said, looking back at the screen himself. "See, he's okay, his daddy saved him." Troy breathed a sigh of relief when Meika looked back at the screen. He didn't like it when she was frightened.

Then, softly, "Daddy."

"Yes," Troy answered, pulling his eyes away from the screen. He was really enjoying the movie, although he had thought that he wouldn't.

"You'd save me just like Simba's daddy saved him if somebody was trying to run over me, right?"

He saw that Meika was worried by what she saw. Maybe the

movie wasn't such a good idea after all. Maybe it was too violent. "Baby, no one's going to hurt my baby. I won't let them."

"Good," she said, again looking back at the movie and stuffing her mouth full of popcorn.

Troy didn't think he was any good at explaining life to a five-year-old. His mother was better at it. This movie was supposed to be a cartoon, yet it was just as bad as an adult movie rated R because of the violence—animals were getting killed left and right. Maybe exposing Meika to death so soon wasn't ideal. He wanted her to have a great childhood like he had; lots of fun and free of worry and abuse. That's why he sought custody and won her away from Cordelia. Cordelia was never any good with Meika—no patience at all when it came to potty training or teaching her to read; always too willing to drop her off with anyone who'd take her. Since he had to do everything for her anyway, it made sense to have custody.

Beeep . . . beeep . . . beeep . . .

Quickly digging down inside his jacket pocket, Troy pulled out his car key ring with the remote alarm beeper on it signaling him that, possibly, someone was breaking into his car. "Damn," he said, starting to stand up. "C'mon, Meika."

Meika stared unblinkingly at the screen.

Troy shook her. "Meika."

"Mister, sit down, my kid can't see through you."

Sitting down again, Troy whispered in Meika's ear. "We have to go and check on my car."

"No, Daddy, I wanna see the movie."

"Shh!" came a voice from in front of them.

Beeep . . . beeep . . . beeep . . .

"Hey! Shut off that damn thing!"

"Yeah, man!"

"I didn't pay my money to hear that damn noise."

Troy had no choice. He had to go check on his car. "Look," he said, taking Meika's face in his hand and pulling her attention away from the screen. Her eyes strained to look back at

the movie. "Listen to me. You stay right here. Don't you go anywhere. I'll be right back. Don't move. You hear me?"

She did not look at him, but she said softly, "Yes, Daddy."

"Okay," he said, letting go of her face and rushing up the
aisle toward the red neon Exit sign at the back of the theater.
At the door, he turned once to see if he could see where Meika
was sitting, but at that distance he couldn't differentiate her
from any other child in the darkness. Out in the lobby before
going outside, he showed the manager his ticket and his beep-
ing beeper. "My car alarm went off. I have to check my car. I'll
be right back, my daughter's inside."

"No problem."

"Thanks." Troy rushed outside and, turning left, raced
toward the sound of his screaming car alarm.

"YEAH!" MEIKA cheered, applauding along with the rest of the
children as Simba regained his kingdom and stood majestically
atop the mountain. Her daddy had been right, the star didn't
die. When the lights came up and the people sitting next to
her eased past her and everyone else started parading slowly
out of the theater, Meika looked around for her daddy. Not
seeing him, she settled back in her seat and started eating
what was left of her popcorn. She watched as the theater emptied out. She ate until the last popcorn was gone and the last
person had walked up the aisle.

Looking around the dimly lit theater, then up at the high
ceiling, Meika suddenly felt scared, and very small. She set the
empty popcorn container down on the seat next to her.
She turned in her seat, got up on her knees, and looked
back at the door. It opened. She started to smile but saw right
away that it wasn't her daddy who came through the door; it
was a man with a big black plastic trash bag in his hand. He
moved slowly down the aisle, row after row, pulling the
garbage bag behind him, picking up empty popcorn buckets,

paper cups, and candy wrappers. Silently, she watched him come closer.

When the man caught sight of Meika, he jumped. "Hey! You scared me."

She said nothing. Nor did she smile.

The man looked around. "You by yourself?"

Meika started to nod but changed her mind and shook her head instead.

"Where's your mommy?"

"I don't know."

The man let the bag slip to the floor. "Who did you come here with?"

"My daddy."

"Where is he?" he asked, sitting down on the arm of the aisle seat.

"He left."

"Is he in the bathroom?"

She shook her head.

"Where did he go?"

She shrugged her shoulders. "I don't know, but he's coming back."

"You sure?"

"Uh-huh."

"Well, everybody's gone and the next show is gonna start in fifteen minutes. Why don't we go outside and talk to the manager," he said, standing.

She shook her head. "No, my daddy said to stay here."

"You can wait with the manager."

Again, she shook her head.

The man looked down at her for a minute. He wasn't about to touch her. "I'll be back." He left the garbage bag and rushed up the aisle to the door.

Meika watched the man leave. Left alone, she slowly looked around the big, dimly lit, empty theater. She began to take tiny little gulps of air, building herself up to cry.

THREE

THERE was something to be said about pretty, even, white teeth, and Nola's teeth were pretty. The dentist had done a good job with her bridgework. Drawing back her lips, she studied her front teeth in the hall mirror from every possible angle. No one would ever guess that they weren't the real thing. If her old dentist, with his foul breath self, had told her thirty years ago about dental floss, she might still have all of her own teeth today. But that's okay—if his breath was any indication, he probably keeps his teeth in a glass on his night table while he sleeps. Wouldn't that be ironic? She ran her tongue across her teeth one last time. They felt good. Then rubbing at the tiny white specks around her mouth, she turned away from the mirror.

She had noticed Ron's golf bag in the entryway when she came in. The soulful sounds of James Brown singing "Papa's Got a Brand New Bag" coming from his den meant he had scored well. Thank goodness. If he hadn't, she'd have to contend with his crankiness and the repeated playing of "(Sittin' on) the Dock of the Bay" until she'd want to push him off that dock. Depending on how long he'd been home, she might hear only a few more James Brown songs, but at least they'd be different songs.

When Nola drove up, she saw that all the lights on the first floor were on, yet once inside she saw no sign of Meika. If she had been home, she would have met her at the door with her chocolate bar, talking nonstop about what she'd seen. Nola checked her watch—seven-fifteen. Troy must have gone elsewhere after the movie—he often did. Oh well. She figured she'd go and find out how Ron's golf game went. By the music playing, Nola knew what she'd see. She went and stood in the doorway of the den. Ron didn't even see her there. He was hearing the music and doing his out-of-step imitation of the hustle while popping his fingers and bobbing his head like a sick pigeon. All with his eyes closed. Giggling softly behind her hand, Nola wished that the video camera wasn't in the chest by the window. She had to remember, for moments like this, to put the camera where she could get her hands on it. The record ended, and Ron started for the turntable.

She clapped.

Spinning around, Ron smiled broadly. "Hey."

"Hey, yourself. Had a good outing, I see?"

"The best. Eighteen holes. Two under par," he said proudly, hitting his chest once with his fist.

"Congratulations," she said, stepping inside the den and sitting in one of the overstuffed chairs in the center of the room. Crossing her legs, Nola didn't let on that she still didn't know a thing about golf and wouldn't know if two under par was a good score or not—she figured the pros didn't have anything to worry about. However, as long as Ron was happy, she was tickled.

" 'Preciate it," he said, turning back to the turntable. He gingerly lifted the 45 off the spindle with his fingertips on the record's edge.

Nola watched Ron slip the old record inside the faded paper jacket and then into a plastic zip-seal storage bag. As many times as she had seen this ritual, she still marveled at how meticulous Ron was. He treated his original soul record collection as if it were a precious gem, and she guessed to him it was. Those records didn't even have a scratch on them. With everything else, however, he couldn't care less. She had long ago lost count of how many glasses and plates he'd broken over the years.

"I got two hundred dollars each out of Ali and Joe and two rounds of drinks."

"Good for you. It's about time you got some of your money back."

"Look," Ron said, huffily, "I can't win every hole every time I get out on the green."

"I didn't say you did, Ron. It's just been awhile, that's all. Don't be so sensitive. I'm glad you won."

"Yeah," he said, dejectedly, turning back to his records.

Nola picked up a history magazine from the side table and scanned the listing of cover stories. That was close; her big mouth almost got her in trouble. She knew darn well how sensitive Ron was about his golf game. After eleven years, he was not as good as he wanted to be, but he was better than he used to be. He worked hard at it. He was doggedly persistent. No one could ever say that he wasn't. Yet he came home most times sullen and irritable because his buddy, Ali Howell, won most holes. Ron and Ali, both, started playing on a whim when their arthritic knees and agile, younger men forced them off the basketball court. She was glad that Ron took to golf. It gave him something to do with his Saturdays while she ran her errands. He was an annoyance when he went shopping with her, wanting to go but rushing her all the way through. Browsing and window-shopping wasn't his thing unless he was in a record store or in a sporting goods store. He never came out of either empty-handed.

"So, everything go all right at the dentist?" Ron asked.

Grinning like a Cheshire cat, Nola showed him her teeth.

"You satisfied?"

"Quite."

Ron clicked off the stereo. "Good. What we got to eat?"

Running her tongue across her smooth, clean teeth, Nola flipped open the magazine and busied herself reading an article. She hated when he asked her, *What we got to eat?* If Ron had his way, he'd have her not only cook the food, but spoon-feed him, too.

"We're not eating tonight?" he asked, sitting down behind his desk. The leather seat seemed to sigh when he sat down on it.

Nola dropped the magazine back on to the table. "Ron, I just got in. After my appointment, I went out to the mall in Green Acres and picked up some things for Meika and those sweaters you said you wanted. I didn't give a thought about dinner. It's Saturday, why don't you order a pizza?"

He frowned. "Pizza's fine for Meika. She loves it. Any veal stew left over?"

"Ron, tell me something. Why didn't you go and look to see if there was any stew in there? Why did you have to wait for me to get home?"

"Because I didn't know what you wanted to have for dinner."

She just shook her head. This discussion was as old as their marriage. So many times she wanted to tell Ron to go eat a mix of salt and pepper, and did one time. They argued for hours after that. She wasn't in the mood this night.

"There's just enough stew for you," she said.

"Good. Troy should be home soon. Why don't you order a pizza. I'll run out and pick it up while you're warming up the stew."

"Fine," she said, getting up and reaching for the cordless telephone on his desk. Since Meika came, she dialed the number at least once a week and knew it by heart, but she hesitated dialing. "You hear from Troy?"

"Nope."

"The movie ended hours ago. I wonder if he fed Meika."

Riiing.

The telephone rang in Nola's hand. Backing up to the chair, she sat.

Riiing.

"Hello?"

"Mrs. Nola Kirkwood?"

The strong unfamiliar male voice, sounding very business-like, made Nola apprehensive. "Yes."

"This is Detective Richard Lopez of the Eighty-fourth Precinct, downtown Brooklyn. Do you have a grandchild by the name of Meika Kirkwood?"

Gripping the telephone, Nola bolted straight up out of her chair. "Meika?" she asked, alarmed.

Ron looked at Nola questioningly. "Is that Meika?"

"No, it's the police."

"Why are they calling about Meika?"

"Mrs. Kirkwood, we have your granddaughter here at the precinct."

"What? Why?"

Ron got up and started around the desk. "What's he saying?"

"Your granddaughter was left at the movie theater in Brooklyn Heights."

Nola could feel her heart thumping in her chest. "What do you mean, left? Where is my son?"

Ron got close up on Nola. "Did something happen to Troy?"

"Oh, God," she said. She laid her hand on Ron's chest for support.

"What is he saying?" Ron asked.

"Mrs. Kirkwood? Your son left his daughter unattended in the movie theater."

"No. He would have never done that."

"What did Troy do?" Ron asked.

"I don't know, Ron. I don't know what he's saying."

"Mrs. Kirkwood?"

22

Ron snatched the telephone out of Nola's hand. "Who is this?"

"Is this Mr. Kirkwood?"

"Yes. And who are you?"

Nola could feel her knees weakening under her. Troy would never leave Meika alone anywhere unless . . . She clung to Ron.

"I'm Detective Richard Lopez of the Eighty-fourth Precinct. The manager of the Cinema called us about a five-year-old girl left there by her father."

"That can't be."

The startled look in Ron's eyes chilled Nola. Although she feared the worst, she needed to know what was being said. She pushed the intercom button on the telephone base before snatching the handset back from Ron and pushing the talk button off.

"Sir," Detective Lopez was saying, his voice suddenly filling the room, "the little girl's name is Meika Kirkwood. She gave me your wife's name and this phone number. Is she your granddaughter?"

"Yes," Nola quickly replied. She leaned down closer to the telephone base so she could speak directly into the intercom. "Is she all right?"

"Yes, ma'am."

"Where is my son?" Ron asked loudly.

"Well, sir, the manager of the theater said your son went out to check on his car because the alarm had gone off. He said he was coming right back, but he never did."

Nola and Ron gasped in unison. Confused, they stared at each other. Nola clutched Ron's arm tighter.

"Sir? Ma'am? Are you there?"

"We're here," Ron answered. "How long ago was this?"

"According to the manager, your son left the theater around three-thirty this afternoon."

23

They both glanced at the wall clock. It was seven-fifty-five. "Oh no," Nola said, beginning to feel cold.

"My son has been missing all afternoon?" Ron asked, incredulously.

"That's the way it appears."

"That can't be," Ron said.

"Oh, my God," Nola said fearfully. "How is my granddaughter?"

"She's fine."

Ron bent closer to the intercom. "Did you check my son's car?"

"Sir, would you come down to the precinct? We're on Gold Street."

Nola shook Ron. "Yes. We'll be right there."

"Ask at the desk for me, Detective Richard Lopez. I'll keep your granddaughter with me."

"Wait a minute," Ron said. "What is your name again?"

"Detective Richard Lopez."

"We'll be right there," Ron said, jabbing the intercom button to end the call, and at the same time, reaching over and switching on the answering machine. He started to bolt out of the room, but Nola was still holding on to him. Her legs had frozen and she couldn't move. Ron turned back to her.

Tears leaped instantly into her eyes. "I'm scared," she said. "Troy would never, never walk away from Meika. Why hasn't he called us?"

Ron wrapped Nola up in his arms. For a quiet, frightened moment, they held on to each other, afraid to say what they were both thinking—something bad had to have happened to Troy.

Pulling out of his embrace, Nola looked into Ron's eyes for that optimistic glint that always managed to be there when life threw stumbling blocks in their path. "Troy is all right, isn't he?"

"Troy is fine," he said, taking Nola's trembling hands into his own. "It might not be what we're thinking. Troy might be at the precinct by the time we get there."

Nola fought hard against crying. What she was seeing in Ron's eyes belied what he was saying. She could see that he didn't believe his own words.

"Come on," he said, starting to walk again but, this time, helping Nola along.

To Nola, it suddenly felt like winter. She began to shiver. They stopped in the hallway long enough for them to grab their jackets and Ron's car keys. They had stepped outside the house when Nola remembered her pocketbook. She rushed back inside and snatched it off the hall table, and at the same time knocked the book Troy had left there earlier in the day onto the floor. She raced out of the house, leaving it there.

While she kept asking, "Where is he?" Ron kept his eyes steadily on the road ahead, squinting only when oncoming high beams momentarily blinded him. Every now and then he'd say, "There are some ugly people in this city."

Whether he realized it or not, his words only frightened her more. She began to pray.

FOUR

THE minute Nola laid eyes on Meika she could see that she had been crying. Her eyes were red, her lower lip hung like it did when she was pouting and didn't get her way.

Meika quickly slid down out of her chair and ran straight into Nola's arms. Crying, she clung to Nola's neck.

Seeing that Meika was safe with Nola, Ron turned to Detective Lopez. "What happened to my son?"

Detective Lopez pulled two chairs out from the table. "Sir, would you and Mrs. Kirkwood please sit down? I know you're concerned, as well you should be, but we need to take this one step at a time."

Ron refused to sit. "I want to know what happened to my son. Where is he?"

"Sir, please."

Nola and Ron glanced anxiously at each other.

Detective Lopez waited with his hand on the back of one of the chairs. He looked at Meika. "If you like, there is an officer who could look after your granddaughter while we talk."

"No, Mama," Meika said, holding on to Nola even tighter.

"It's okay, baby. You're not going anywhere." Nola rubbed Meika gently on the back.

"Please, sit down."

Seeing that they weren't getting anywhere and still carrying Meika, Nola sat in the chair closest to Detective Lopez. She sat Meika on her lap.

Ron, reluctantly, sat down. "Do you know what happened to my son?"

"No, sir, we don't."

Meika pressed her face into Nola's breast and began to whimper. "Is Daddy dead?"

Hugging Meika tighter, Nola began to rock her. "No, baby, no. Your daddy is not dead." At least she prayed to God that he wasn't.

Meika pulled back slightly. Her eyes filled with tears. "Mufasa died."

"Who's Mufasa?"

"Simba's daddy. He was the lion king before Simba. And Simba was the star of the movie and the star never dies. But daddies die. Simba's daddy died, you know."

Stunned, Nola looked at Ron. She could feel goose bumps pop up on her arms. Ron was just as stunned. He looked as if someone had walked on his grave.

Detective Lopez cleared his throat. "Are you sure we can't take your granddaughter for a soda or something?"

That was not what Meika wanted. She nestled deeper in Nola's arms and laid the side of her face against her breast.

Nola cradled Meika, and although this discussion about what might have happened to Troy really was something she did not want Meika to hear, neither did she want Meika taken from her arms. Again, she rocked her.

Taking a piece of bubble gum from his jacket pocket, Detective Lopez sat down on the edge of the table across from Nola. While unwrapping the gum, he continued to look at Ron. "What we know, Mr. Kirkwood, is that your son left the theater to respond to his car alarm around three-thirty P.M. He said he'd be back, and that his daughter was inside. The manager said that when your son left the theater, he ran north toward Cranberry Street."

"And he didn't come back?" Ron asked, finding that hard to believe.

"No, sir." Detective Lopez popped the gum into his mouth. As an afterthought, he held a piece out to Meika. She shook her head no, and hid her face in Nola's bosom.

Knowing that gum was something that Meika never turned down, Nola kissed Meika on top of her head.

"Did you check his car?" Ron asked.

"We don't know his car. We immediately canvassed the area for car alarms that had gone off and no one remembered hearing one. If we knew exactly what block the car was parked on and the make and model, we might've found someone who saw something."

"My son drives a 1994 Nissan Maxima—four-door, black," Ron said.

Detective Lopez wrote that down on the small notepad he took from his shirt pocket. "Does he have any outstanding tickets that you know of?"

"I don't think so."

"Has he ever been towed by traffic enforcement?"

"Hell no!"

"Sir, I'm just checking all the bases. It's tight in the Heights. If your son's car was parked illegally, it could have been towed, which would have explained why the car alarm went off."

"Well, my son was no scofflaw and he would not park in an illegal spot and go to a movie. And if his car was towed, he wouldn't still be trying to get it back at this hour. He would have called home."

"Detective," Nola said, "if Troy's car was towed, he would not have left Meika to go chasing after it."

"Ma'am, this is an unusual situation. Why don't we check for the car? I'll need the license plate number so that we can start a trace."

"I can get that for you as soon as I get home," Ron said, "but if Troy's car is near the movie house, I can find it."

"You're free to go look for the car as soon as we're finished here."

Ron folded his arms high up on his chest. "I don't need your permission to do that."

Taken aback, Detective Lopez raised his eyebrows. "Sir—"

"Mama, Daddy ain't lost, is he?"

"No, baby," Nola answered, continuing to rock Meika. "Detective, what took you so long to call us? I know Meika told you my name and number right away. I drilled it into her, she knew it by heart."

Detective Lopez checked his notepad. "Well, ma'am, the manager didn't call us right away. The precinct received the call at approximately seven-fifteen this evening. The manager said that he was giving your son the benefit of the doubt that he'd come back, like he said. He kept your granddaughter in the theater through a second showing."

Meika lifted her head. "I saw *The Lion King* two times."

"I know, baby," Nola said. "You have a good time?"

Meika nodded twice. "But Daddy didn't come back."

"We know," Ron said, rubbing Meika's arm. "Did Daddy tell you where he was going?"

She shook her head.

"Sir, your granddaughter told the manager and an usher that your son said that he'd be back, like he told the manager himself."

"Why the hell did the manager wait so long to call the police?"

"Again, sir, the manager said that he had no reason to believe that your son wasn't coming back. In fact, he said he heard the remote beeper himself. At the time, he didn't think your son was abandoning his child."

Bang! Ron hit the table with his fist.

Meika jumped.

Ron stood. "Wait a damn minute!"

Nola stroked Meika's head. "Ron," she said, giving him the eye and then glancing down at Meika. They didn't curse or fight around Meika and scaring her now with Troy missing was much too much for her to deal with at once.

Ron got the message. He lowered his voice. "My son didn't abandon—"

"No way did Troy abandon this child!" Nola adamantly chimed in.

Meika started to whimper.

Rocking her gently, Nola whispered into her ear, "Shhh. Daddy's all right, baby."

"My son is a man of high principles and morals," Ron said through clenched teeth. "He fought to get custody of his daughter. He wouldn't take her to a movie to abandon her. And if he thought she or himself was in danger, he would never have left her. How dare you insinuate that he did."

Detective Lopez's face reddened. He stopped chewing. "Sir, ma'am, no one is saying that your son abandoned his daughter. However, every possibility must be investigated. Why don't I take some preliminary data just in case—"

"Just in case of what?" Ron asked, guardedly.

Glancing down at Meika wrapped in Nola's arms, Detective Lopez slowly rolled his eyes back to Ron, who was glaring at him.

Nola reached over and laid her hand on Ron's arm, hoping to calm him. On the way to the precinct, they had both been afraid and were even more so now. The moment the detective said that Ron could go look for Troy's car himself, Ron had become agitated, but when he intimated that Troy had abandoned Meika, Ron had begun smoldering. And when he was like that, he was ready to fight.

"I'm fine," he said, not blinking or looking Nola's way. He was fixed on Detective Lopez, who was beginning to write in his notepad.

"How old is your son, Troy Kirkwood?"

"Ronald Troy Kirkwood Junior," Nola answered. "He's twenty-nine years old."

"We need a description of him."

"Oh God," she said, beginning to feel sick. She rocked Meika faster.

Ron didn't sit down again. He walked away from the table. "He's six-one, about one-eighty, about my complexion, maybe a shade—"

"He looks like his father," Nola interjected. "Wait a minute, I have a picture." Digging inside her pocketbook, she pulled out her wallet and flipped through the plastic dividers until she found a college graduation picture of Troy and behind that, the latest picture that had been taken Labor Day in the backyard; he was holding Meika in his arms. His laughing eyes twinkled; his smile lit up his face. Meika had that same smile. It had been a wonderful family barbecue. No one could have told Nola that three months later she'd be giving that picture to the police to identify Troy. Her eyes filled with tears as she handed the pictures to Detective Lopez. "I have others at home."

"Mama, you said that's your favorite picture of me and Daddy."

"It is, baby," she said, hugging her tighter.

Walking to the door, Ron reached for the doorknob. "Detective, may I speak to you out in the hall?"

"Sure," Detective Lopez replied, taking his notepad with him.

Clearly, it was because of Meika that Ron was taking the discussion out into the hallway, and as much as Nola wanted to hear every word that was about to be said, she didn't move.

Out in the hall, Detective Lopez was pulling the door up behind him when Ron took hold of his arm and pulled him away from the door.

"Hey!" Detective Lopez exclaimed. He yanked his arm free.

The two men eyeballed each other. Detective Lopez's hand was on his holstered gun at his side. "Mr. Kirkwood, I think you had better calm down."

Ron took stock of what he had just done. He stepped back. "Okay. I'm calm. I want to file a missing persons report."

"Sir, your son is a twenty-nine-year-old adult who is—"

"I don't care how old he is. He is missing. It is out of character for him. I want him found. If I said his car was stolen and had the license plate number, you'd begin a trace immediately, am I right?"

"Technically."

"Well, technically, his car is missing, but I believe my son's life is far more important than a lost or stolen car. I want an immediate trace on him."

Detective Lopez sighed audibly. "Sir, I understand that you're upset, but—"

"You have no idea how upset I am," Ron said, slowly folding his arms high up across his chest.

"Oh, I have an idea, sir. But we have to follow procedures. Your son has to be missing twenty-four hours before we can legally investigate. He may show up this evening with an explanation for—"

"Hold up! You know damn well my son is not going to show up this evening with an explanation like he's a kid who stayed out past his curfew. His daughter means everything to him . . . and he wouldn't put me or his mother through this hell. He—"

"Then why did he leave his daughter alone in the theater? She's only five years old. No caring parent in his right mind leaves a five-year-old in a theater and runs off, no matter what the reason."

"What are you insinuating? My son has always been responsible. Believe me, if he left his child behind, he had a damn good reason for doing so. He'd give up his life for her."

Detective Lopez turned and walked a few paces away, when he stopped; he paused before turning back. He slipped his notepad in his jacket pocket and took the gum out of his mouth, holding it in his hand. "Mr. Kirkwood, I mean you no disrespect. You know your son, I don't. But the fact that he left his daughter to check on his car does not look good. It looks irresponsible."

This time, Ron, gritting his teeth, walked away.

"I'm quite sure," Detective Lopez continued, "that your son is as good a father as you say. But look at it this way. Mothers who go to answer the telephone while they're bathing their babies don't think that their children could drown in two minutes; or parents who turn their backs in the store, or leave their kids in the car while they dash into a store, never thought their kids could be snatched. You're lucky nothing happened to your granddaughter, and count your blessings that Children's Protective Services wasn't called into this."

Ron whirled around. "You're talking apples and goddamn oranges!" he bellowed. "No, no one snatched Meika. Thank God for that. But my son, a grown man, is missing. Did you ever think that somebody could have snatched him?"

"Sir—"

"And as for Children's Protective Services, they don't have a goddamn thing to do with my granddaughter. She has grandparents that will move heaven and earth to keep her safe."

"Mr. Kirkwood—"

"No, Detective," Ron said, oblivious to the police officers who had come up behind him, "you listen to me, and let me make this perfectly clear so that there is no misunderstanding. My son is not a child who wandered off or drowned in a bathtub. He is missing! And every minute you waste trying to convince me that he's been irresponsible, despite what I've told you about him, you could be out in the street looking for him. Now, I *will* file a missing persons report, and I *demand* that you or anybody with a badge, I don't care if it's a goddamn meter maid, but it better not be, go with me into the Heights to look for my son's car."

Detective Lopez drew himself up tall. He glared eye-to-eye with Ron. They were both breathing deeply.

Squaring his shoulders, Ron drew himself up even taller. "Mister, I've worked and paid taxes in this damn city all of my adult life, and I've been law-abiding since I stopped sucking my thumb and pissing in my pants, and this is one time I am asking . . . no, *demanding* that my tax dollars work for me. Get your ass out there and find my son. Do I make myself clear?"

Detective Lopez's gaze narrowed. "Look, man, you had better—" Detective Lopez sensed that he and Ron were not alone. He looked at the army of uniformed officers and plain-clothes detectives standing around them. They looked as uncertain as he felt and were no help in helping him decide what to do.

Ron had seen all of the officers come up and had said nothing about their presence.

"Detective Lopez, go pick up the missing persons form," a woman's voice ordered behind Ron. He turned and was surprised at the number of officers staring at him, but they were all men.

"Detective," the woman said again.

Detective Lopez responded with a salute. "Yes, ma'am." He pivoted and quickly walked off down the hall.

Ron looked past the officers behind him to the office behind them on the opposite wall. Standing in the doorway was a tall white woman with captain's bars on her shoulders. A stark narrow streak of white hair swept back off the center of her forehead to the crown of her short haircut.

"Return to your posts," the captain said to the officers. They all saluted her and left immediately. "Sir, we'll do our best to help locate your son. Have you called any of the local hospitals or any of his acquaintances, as yet?"

"Well . . . no," Ron replied, trying to calm himself. "We only just found out that he was missing."

"Under the circumstances, we'll proceed with the filing of the missing persons report. Detective Lopez will go with you to the site you believe your son's car was last known to be, and as soon as you get home, you should call the emergency rooms and admitting offices of the local hospitals, just in case your son was injured while he was checking on his car. Again, we'll do our best to locate him. I'm sorry for this unfortunate incident."

"Thank you, Captain," Ron said, feeling better knowing that something was about to be done. "That boy of yours needs a heart."

"He's a good detective."

At that moment, Detective Lopez returned with the report. He handed it to Ron, who could see clearly the sour look on Lopez's face. It was obvious that Lopez wasn't too happy with him or the captain. Lopez did not glance in the captain's direction, nor did he look Ron in the eye.

"Mr. Kirkwood, I'm Captain Aniston. If I can be of further assistance, feel free to call my office."

"Thank you, ma'am."

She nodded. "Detective Lopez will assist you with the report in a minute. If you will go on back to your wife and granddaughter, he'll be with you in a minute."

"Thank you, ma'am," Ron said again as he turned and went back into the interrogation room. As he closed the door, he heard the captain say, "In my office." The door down the hall slammed hard.

Rocking a now sleeping Meika, Nola looked up. "The captain doesn't play, huh?"

"You heard all that?"

"The door isn't soundproof," she replied, looking with dread at the form in his hands. "I guess we should start filling that out."

Ron took his reading glasses from his shirt pocket. Putting them on, he sat and began studying the papers.

Sighing softly, Nola shook her head sadly. "The last time we sat down to fill out papers on Troy, he was in his senior year of college."

Ron nodded in agreement. "Back then we were planning his future, now we're possibly—"

"Shhhh!" she said, shaking her head. "Don't."

FIVE

THIS was one time Nola appreciated Ron's doggedly tenacious nature. While Meika slept in the backseat of the car after eating a slice and a half of pizza and drinking an orange soda, they drove slowly through the quiet, narrow, one-way streets of the Heights, peering at every black car along the way. They sought to speak with the manager of the theater but he had gone home at eight, and the night manager knew nothing about Troy. Ron wanted to ring doorbells and ask questions, but Detective Lopez squashed that idea.

"That's police business," he said. "Someone will be assigned that task. Meanwhile, I suggest, strongly, that you go home, wait by the telephone, and let us do our job."

Nola had taken Ron's hand and pulled him away from Detective Lopez to keep him from responding to what he perceived as sarcasm. Truth to tell, she didn't much like Detective Lopez's coldness any more than Ron did, but they needed his help. Of course, she didn't expect Detective Lopez to be very pleasant or empathize with them after Ron was the cause of his being called on the carpet. When he came back into the room, he was chastened and humbly helped them fill out the report like a dedicated tutor. As long as he did his job, she couldn't care less about his attitude, but at the same time, if they had to request that he be taken off the case, she wouldn't hesitate to demand it. Of course, the ideal scenario would be that there was no case.

Even after Detective Lopez and the two uniformed officers left them in front of the theater, Ron drove from block to block, from Cadman Plaza West to the Promenade along the East River, and from Henry Street down into Old Fulton Street at the foot of the Brooklyn Bridge into Furman Street, though they knew the unlikelihood of Troy's parking his car that far away. They drove the long desolate stretch of Furman Street under the Brooklyn-Queens Expressway along dark closed-up piers, feeling uneasy and vulnerable with no other soul on foot or in cars. There was not one car parked along the way. She and Ron double-checked the locks and the windows as they both glanced at the gas gauge—this was no time to run dry. Ron had a habit of gassing up only when the tank was less than a quarter full. After all these years, it still drove her crazy to see Ron pass up one gas station after another because he felt that he had enough gas in reserve, below the empty mark, to get them where they were going. To show her, he'd get them where they were going, then have to gas up on the way home, usually well after dark. Sometimes they got home on fumes and a prayer, and nothing she said ever convinced Ron that his refusal to keep his tank at least half full was not only unsafe but stupid. That was a part of his tenaciousness she hated. One day, he'll learn the hard way—when he stalls out on the Verrazano Bridge in midspan. Just as long as it is not this night on Furman Street.

Ron sped through and at the end of Furman Street took the only left turn that took them up to Atlantic Avenue where the bright lights, traffic, and people were a welcome sight. Making their way home in silence, Nola prayed that Troy would be at home waiting for them with some wild unbelievable story about being taken by aliens and awakening to find himself on the roof or something. She was open for any excuse he had, no matter how crazy. Even a call from a doctor saying that Troy was hit by a car and lay unconscious in some hospital bed with a broken arm or leg would suffice over news of his death. God, how she prayed that his death wasn't a reality she'd have to deal with. If Troy was home when they got there, what-ever the reason was for his leaving Meika would definitely be discussed—that is, after she hugged him senseless.

Finding the house ghostly quiet and the answering machine light unblinking dashed Nola's hopes instantly. Ron looked as bad as she felt—his face, his eyes, his mouth drooped like soft taffy strung between the fingers of a child. Together, they put Meika to bed, careful to not wake her for fear of seeing the disappointment in her eyes that her daddy was not home.

Between the two of them, Nola and Ron called several hos-pitals in Brooklyn and Manhattan, to no avail. Their fear in-tensified. Troy could not have fallen off the face of the earth without someone seeing him. Then, disregarding the lateness of the hour, they called the people listed in his telephone book. The only person that Nola did not want to personally call was Valerie Lewis, and that was because that was the last place she wanted Troy to be. Troy had ended the relationship with Va-lerie more than two months ago, and as far as Nola knew, Troy hadn't had much contact with Valerie since.

The day their relationship ended had been a blessed day for Nola and Meika—they both hated Valerie, and there was no doubt that the feeling was mutual on Valerie's part. To Nola, Valerie was just as bad as if not worse than Cordelia. At first Valerie pretended to like Meika, bringing her cheap plastic toys that fell apart hours after they were taken out of their boxes. Valerie wanted Meika around her and Troy less than she wanted a swarm of bloodthirsty mosquitoes at a backyard bar-becue. Valerie went along on outings with Meika and Troy but it was obvious she would rather have had Troy all to herself, and after a while when she thought that she had Troy wrapped around her little finger, tipped with a long false nail that looked more like a grizzly's claw than a human nail, Valerie dropped the pretense and found ways to get Troy to leave Meika at home. Most times, they went to clubs or R-rated movies that were inappropriate to take a child to. Valerie was quick to ask Nola in front of Meika if she wouldn't mind watching her while they went out for the evening. Although that irked Nola, she kept her mouth shut while almost bursting a vessel in her head from wanting to give Valerie a piece of her mind.

In the end, Nola was glad that she had not meddled, and had had the foresight to not offer her unsolicited opinion, because eight months after Troy and Valerie started going together and just after Valerie suggested they move in together, Troy broke off the relationship. That was good news, but Nola wanted to know why.

"Ma, let's just say that Valerie isn't right for me and I'm not right for her."

"So, if she's not right for you, why did you go out with her in the first place?"

Troy had shrugged his shoulders and said, with a straight face, "It had been a while, okay. She looked good, and a man got needs. Need I say more?"

No, he did not have to say more. Admittedly, it had been a while since Troy had dated, but he could have made a better choice than Valerie Lewis.

Ron called Valerie's number twice but got no answer. It did not surprise Nola one bit that Valerie was out—it was Saturday night, and she was probably with some man she had met at a bus stop or standing near a hydrant. No, she would not speak to Valerie. She would leave it to Ron to talk to her—he was more tolerant of her, which also irked her.

"Who else can we call?" Ron asked, staring at the telephone.

"I don't know."

"I think we oughta call Vann. He should know that his brother is missing."

"Not yet. We don't need to worry him needlessly. It'll be for naught when Troy shows up."

Ron looked worriedly at Nola.

She knew what he was thinking, but she could not let herself think the same. She had to keep hoping.

They crawled into bed well after three Sunday morning, exhausted, frustrated, and scared. Ron dropped off and began snoring right away, while Nola was not so lucky. She prayed that she could black out and give her aching head a rest from worry. When she got tired of staring up at the black ceiling and could not stand another deep, throaty goose honk erupting from Ron's mouth, she slipped out of bed and went into Meika's room and crawled into bed with her. Poor baby didn't even stir as Nola snuggled up close to Meika in the single bed. The light fragrance of the coconut-scented grease she'd used in Meika's hair earlier brought back the memory of the breakfast they'd all shared. Troy had been in such a good mood, which was not so unusual in itself, he had always been so even-tempered.

It seemed Meika had also inherited his disposition. She was rarely cranky and such a pleasure to be around. There was no doubt that she would raise her if, God forbid, something had happened to Troy. In fact, that's what he wanted. He had put her name on all of his insurance policies and bank accounts as beneficiary. This was Troy's way of providing for Meika. He did not want her and Ron financially burdened if it came down to them raising his baby. And that was just it, Meika was Troy's baby, and he was hers. Not knowing where he was or whether or not he was okay tore at her heart. She felt empty. It reminded her of how she felt twenty-five years ago when her belly had been big with her third child, a girl, who never cried when her bottom was smacked. She was stillborn. Her heart had ached then, like it was aching now because her arms were empty after waiting for her baby to come into the world.

Dear Lord, she began to pray in her heart, *please let my baby be all right. Please let Troy find his way home sound of mind and sound of body.*

As Nola drifted off to sleep, she felt no better.

SIX

DESPITE what Detective Lopez said, and in spite of the fact that no one remembered seeing Troy outside the theater, all day Sunday, Ron, Ali, and Roosevelt prowled the streets of the Heights looking for Troy's car and knocking on doors asking questions. At home, Nola anxiously manned the telephone, too afraid to leave the house in case Troy called. But it was never his voice that answered her hellos; mostly it was Troy's friends calling to see if they'd heard from him. With each call Nola's blood pressure shot up a notch, and if it weren't for her dear cousin Beatrice, Nola would have completely fallen apart.

Beatrice stood over Nola like a mother hen. "Nola, I made a meat loaf, some nice mashed potatoes, and some string beans—your favorite meal."

"Thanks, but I'm not hungry."

"You have to eat something. If you don't want meat loaf, I also brought you some smothered pork chops, some yellow rice, some carrots, some fried chicken, and some peach cobbler." Beatrice reached for the telephone Nola held in her hand.

Nola pulled the phone back out of Beatrice's reach. Ten times it had rung, unanswered, in her ear, but she did not want to give up. She covered the mouthpiece with her free hand.

"You have got to eat something," Beatrice said.

Nola's stomach growled, yet her desire to eat was dulled by worry. She shook her head.

"Nola, you have got to eat something."

"Just make sure Meika eats."

"She's eating now. You're the one I'm concerned about. If you let yourself get run down, you won't be much help to Troy when he comes home. He'll have to turn around and worry about you."

Nola gave up on the ringing, unanswered telephone. She ended the call with a press of the talk button. "Troy will be coming home, won't he?"

"Of course he will," Beatrice said, resting her hand on top of Nola's. "Why don't you leave this telephone in here and if it rings, you can answer the one in the kitchen. I know you're hungry, I heard your stomach growl."

For a minute Nola thought about it. She hadn't eaten all day and the smell of Beatrice's meat loaf was tantalizing. The woman did not play in the kitchen. In fact, Nola's mother used to say that Beatrice put her foot in her cooking. Everyone, including Troy, Vann, and Ron, always wanted to eat Thanksgiving and Christmas meals at Beatrice's because they knew they were in for some serious eating. Her food put a hurting on everyone, including Beatrice herself. Beatrice had a time of it trying not to pack any more poundage on her already hefty body. Of course, Beatrice didn't mind being fat, and for that matter, after twenty-six years of marriage, obviously Roosevelt didn't mind it either. Besides, he couldn't bother Beatrice about her weight when he had his own well-fed belly to contend with. He and Beatrice were a match made in heaven. His sentiments were the same as hers. A long time ago Beatrice said, "I like to cook, I like to eat, and as long as I'm healthy, I'm gonna enjoy every single crumb I put in my mouth." And she meant it. There wasn't a soul who sat down at her table who didn't feel the same way. Whenever Nola knew that she was going to sit at Beatrice's table, she would not eat all day, leaving her stomach empty and ready, and she planned in advance what she would wear—something with an elastic waistband.

And, stupidly, because Nola wanted her boys and Ron to gobble up what she cooked at home, for years she tried to compete with Beatrice in the kitchen. By the time she was in her early thirties, she had to call it quits—it was a waste of time trying to outdo a master in her own element. Interestingly, that's when she and Beatrice became the best of friends. They had always been close, but for the longest time, perhaps because she was always competing with Beatrice, they were only cousins. Now they were closer than some sisters.

Nola let Beatrice convince her to eat something. As was to be expected, the mashed potatoes melted in her mouth and the meat loaf was delicious. Still, Nola was able to eat only half of what was on her plate. Her thoughts were on Valerie and how nasty she was on the telephone when she finally returned Ron's call.

"I ain't seen Troy in more than two months. I thought you knew that."

"Well, I—"

"Mr. Kirkwood, why are you calling me? Where is Troy?"

Ron quickly put his hand over the mouthpiece. "She wants to know where Troy is."

"Don't tell her a thing," Nola whispered.

"Ah . . . Valerie . . ."

Beep! The call-waiting signal beeped in Ron's ear.

"Hold on a minute, I have another call." Ron pressed the flash button. "Hello?" he asked anxiously. He listened, there was silence on the other end. "Hello?"

Nola wished that they were on the speakerphone in the den instead of on the cordless extension in the kitchen. "Who is it?"

"Damned if I know. They just hung up," Ron said, disgust-edly looking at the telephone in his hand.

"They didn't say anything?"

"Not a damn thing. Dead quiet. Then they hung up," he said, starting to put the telephone down.

Nola grabbed his hand. "Ron! Valerie's still on the other line."

"Oh damn!" he said, quickly pressing the flash button. "Valerie? Hello?"

"I have things to do, you know."

"I'm sorry. I—"

"Mr. Kirkwood, what do you want?"

"Did you speak to Troy this past weekend?"

"Why would I speak to Troy? There is nothing left to be said between us. As you probably know, Troy broke off with me."

"If you do hear from him—"

"I doubt it. Isn't he seeing someone? Forget it, I gotta go." Click.

Frowning, Ron looked at the telephone. "Sorry to have bothered you," he said, placing the telephone back on the base.

"She hung up on you?"

"Yep."

"Bitch," Nola spat. She didn't dislike Valerie for nothing. "What did she say?"

"Said she hasn't seen or heard from Troy in two months."

As good as that news was, it left Nola even more frightened. Somebody had to have heard from Troy. Even if it had been Valerie, it would have eased their fears and concern for Troy and Meika. For Meika, the wait was just as worrisome and draining. She seemed to hold her breath each time the telephone rang, letting it out only when she realized it wasn't her daddy. Between videos, coloring books, toys, and games, Nola tried her best to keep Meika occupied. But it was clear that Meika wasn't herself. She played with her toys, but there was sadness in her eyes and silence from her lips when she normally would have been chatting and laughing. Meika didn't have to be told that something was drastically wrong. It was like Nola's own mother used to say, "Children today are born older than in my day." Meika was born old. By the time Nola gave Meika her bath and put her down for the night, she realized how right she was.

"Mama."

"Yes, baby," Nola said, snugly tucking the covers around Meika.

"I feel sad about my daddy."

"Oh, baby, I know," she said, sitting down on the side of the bed. She kissed Meika on the forehead and reclined alongside her. "I'm sad, too."

"If Daddy died like Simba's daddy, he won't be coming home, will he?"

Nola was speechless. There was a sudden stinging in her nose. Briefly, she pressed her finger just under her nostrils. As old as she was, Troy's death was a thought she herself didn't want to dwell on. When she was Meika's age, she knew nothing of death. In fact, she didn't experience the loss of a relative until she was twenty-seven, and that was when her grandmother died.

"Somebody bad took Daddy, right?"

"Well . . ." she began, feeling uncomfortable about trying to explain the evil in the world to a five-year-old. She had told Troy and Vann about the bogeyman but she had also told them that she and Ron would protect them. How could she tell Meika that the bogeyman might have taken her daddy and that she and Ron had not been able to protect their son after all? "Honey, didn't we just pray and ask God to take care of your daddy?"

Looking as if she would cry, Meika nodded. She then drew Bobo, her time-worn, matted, brown-haired teddy bear, closer.

"Honey, God will take care of your daddy, no matter where he is."

"Even if it's in heaven?"

Meika was not letting Nola off easy. "Of course, baby. That's where God lives. Remember the story I told you about God loving all his children?"

Nodding slowly, the corners of her mouth turned down, Meika could not have looked sadder. Nola pulled the blanket up around Meika's shoulders and held her.

"What else did I tell you?"

"You said God loves mommies and daddies just like he loves little children."

"That's right. And you know what else?"

"What?"

"Sometimes, God takes mommies and daddies and little children home to live with him in heaven," she said, fighting her own fear that Troy may have been called home to Glory. At this point, her job was to allay Meika's fears.

"That's where Simba's daddy is, right?"

"Yes, but that does not mean that your daddy went to live in heaven, he just hasn't been able to get to a telephone yet. When he comes home, he's going to tell you all about what he was doing and how much fun he had." If only, she thought, pulling on Meika's braid.

Meika didn't stir, and for a moment she appeared to be thinking. "Mama?"

"Yes."

"When I die, will I see Daddy in heaven?"

Nola's breath caught in her throat for the coldest moment. It didn't seem to matter what she said; to Meika, Troy was already gone. "What makes you think your daddy is in heaven?"

" 'Cause he told me so," she said in the tiniest little voice.

Her heart sank. "When did he tell you that?"

"Last night."

Oh Lord. "Meika, your daddy wasn't home last night."

"I saw him when I was sleeping."

"Oh, honey," Nola said, shifting her body so that she could look down into Meika's eyes. It was like looking into the eyes of an old soul who'd done a lot of living and seen a lot of sadness, which Meika hadn't, except of course when Cordelia first started missing her visits. "Meika, your daddy is not in heaven. You just dreamed that he was. He's—"

A pool of tears welled up in Meika's eyes. "Yes, he is."

Meika was so sure Troy was dead, it frightened Nola. "Baby, you were just dreaming."

"No, Mama. Daddy was real."

Nola fell silent. Nothing she could say could change Meika's mind. Whether she was dreaming or not, Meika knew that Troy never went a day away from her without calling at least twice to say hi. Holding Meika tighter and stilling her own self against crying, she wiped gently at the tears that rolled down Meika's cheeks.

"Meika, until we know for sure where your daddy is, we'll just pray that he's okay. And, baby, if he is in heaven . . ."

Sniffling, Meika wiped at her nose.

". . . you know he can love you from there, too."

Lord Almighty, this was so hard. Swallowing to wet her suddenly dry throat, Nola pressed her lips together and, looking up at the ceiling, closed her eyes. *Lord, please don't let this baby suffer, please bring Troy home.* Like she used to do when Meika was a baby, Nola gently stroked Meika's cheeks with the back of her hand, hoping that she would be lulled into the blessed arms of sleep. "Close your eyes for Mama and go on to sleep, okay?"

"Okay."

"Sweet dreams."

Meika didn't say her usual "Sweet dreams" back. Her eyes were wide open, not even looking like she was about to fall off to sleep.

"Mama, you gonna die one day, too?"

Nola almost couldn't see for the tears that suddenly blinded her and muted her voice.

"Mama?"

Holding Meika close, a little cough gave Nola back her voice. "Meika, you'll be an old lady by the time I die," she said, kissing her repeatedly all over her face until she began to giggle. "Now go to sleep."

Meika turned on her side facing Nola.

It took all she had to not weaken and cry as she rubbed Meika's back until her eyes began to slowly open and close, and finally stay closed. Stealing over to the door, Nola flicked off the light switch, leaving the room bathed in a soft warm night-light. For a minute she stood looking across at Meika to make sure that her eyes stayed closed. They did. Meika had drifted off into the arms of the angels. Nola prayed that Troy was not one of the angels cradling his child.

She slipped out of the room, pulling the door up behind her but leaving it slightly ajar. Rushing into her own bedroom and pushing the door closed, with a deep sigh came a flood of tears. Her heart was filled with a blistering agonizing pain. She tried to clutch her heart, she tried to still the pain, but her pain would not be soothed.

SEVEN

NEITHER Nola nor Ron had any intention of going to work Monday morning, though they could not have made it if they wanted to—they were too worn out. Monday was no different from Sunday, except Ron struggled to muster the courage to call Troy's job and inform them that he would not be in. They both agreed that it was too soon to say anything else when they did not know in fact what the final word would be. That done, Ron scoured the Heights alone and camped out at the precinct while she stayed in her curtain-drawn home walking from room to room with Troy's cordless telephone tucked away in her housedress pocket. If Meika could have fit in the other pocket, she would have carried her there, because Meika followed behind her like a small shadow, as if she were afraid to lose sight of her. And that was all right—Nola didn't want to lose sight of her either. The fact that the police still had no answers, unfortunately, meant that she had no answers for Meika. It hurt her to her heart to see that the sadness in Meika's eyes was more of mourning than worry.

By Tuesday morning Nola decided to go back to her job as a bank officer at Chase bank. Staying home with her hands tied was making her overly anxious and edgy, while Meika needed to be around laughing, playing children who could, hopefully, lift her spirits. As it was, the cloistered walls of the house seemed to close in, stifling them. Opening the curtains did not help. The only noises that permeated their silence were the sounds of the television that no one was watching and the ringing telephone that brought no news of Troy. On her way to work Nola dropped Meika off at her kindergarten class with instructions to her teacher to call her immediately if Meika appeared to be having a hard day.

Ron, too, went back to work, but he and Nola agreed that, between the two of them, they'd call the precinct every hour on the hour. Detective Lopez had been officially assigned to the case and it was apparent by the way he fell silent whenever he heard their voices that they were getting on his nerves, but he kept his cool. Whatever Captain Aniston said to Detective Lopez put him in check; he held his opinion and tongue, but what little he did report, they did not want to hear. No one in the Heights remembered hearing a car alarm, which meant they still did not know what block Troy had parked on; and no one, besides the manager, remembered seeing Troy on the street outside the theater. It was like he had been invisible that day, like he had passed mysteriously into another dimension that no one else saw. Strangest of all, it seemed to Nola that unless they made a fuss, no one else would have cared that he was missing.

But she missed her child like she missed air while swimming underwater holding her breath; and like she missed food when she fasted for a week for Lent every year. What Ron was feeling, he was not saying. He spent every spare moment he could driving around looking for Troy's car. At home he was quiet and withdrawn, staying in his den, not eating much, and not talking much about anything, but knowing him, he was probably angry with himself because he had not found Troy or his car. He had always been proud that Vann and Troy, as young men growing up, looked to him to help solve a lot of their problems, from jock itch to career choices, and now he could not solve the most important problem in Troy's life. Nola understood his brooding and left him to himself.

As for herself, from sheer worry alone, she was not sleeping more than two to three hours a night, which made her useless at the bank. Tuesday was hard, but Wednesday was unbearable. All that was on her mind was Troy and where he could possibly be. She fought against her mind telling her that he might be dead. That she could not and would not accept. She found herself continually asking customers to repeat their questions because she was not paying attention. They looked at her like she was crazy, and she did feel like she was indeed slipping into a world of fantasy wherein Troy came home, smiling, saying that he had bumped his head and had just come to remember who he was. More than she would admit to Ron, Nola imagined that she had seen Troy several times—in stores; in passing cars that she could never seem to catch up to; and even at tellers' windows. She saw him everywhere. Leaving work Tuesday afternoon, she almost got run over by a bus because she stopped in the crosswalk and stared at a man walking on the other side of the street. And actually, he looked nothing like Troy; it was the way he swaggered that caught her eye.

Ever since Troy was sixteen and a guard on his high school basketball team, he'd had a proud, animalistic swagger. The kind that girls swoon over and other boys either imitate or are jealous of. Humph, humph, humph, how the young girls loved that swagger. Troy had no problems getting dates, sometimes juggling two girls on the same night. When she found out, from the influx of telephone calls, that Troy and Vann—who didn't have the swagger but had the same body and the same rugged good looks—were both stringing along a bevy of hormone-throbbing Lolitas, she lectured them about disrespecting women, sexually transmitted diseases, and fatherhood before manhood. Of course, Ron, being a proud daddy, told them both, behind Nola's back, that they were only young once, to get as much as they could. He even supplied the condoms. And being healthy virile young men who got erections when the wind blew, whether a girl was on their minds or in their line of vision, nothing Nola said meant a damn thing until they both met the girls they did not want any other man touching. Cordelia opened up Troy's nose and left her scent burning in his nostrils, while Michelle drove a Mack truck through Vann's.

"Miss? Excuse me. Are you working?"

"Oh. Pardon me," Nola said, beginning to shuffle the papers on her desk.

"Sir," Mr. Fanon, the bank branch manager, said, rushing up, "why don't you sit over here? Mr. Lewin will assist you."

Relieved, Nola looked down at her desk as the man walked away and sat at another bank officer's desk.

Mr. Fanon sat down in the chair alongside Nola's desk. "Nola, is there something wrong?"

She started to deny that there was, but she had been thinking about requesting time off. She blurted, "My son is missing."

"My goodness," Mr. Fanon said, concerned. "For how long?"

"Almost four days now."

"My goodness," he said again, touching her arm. "Nola, you should have told us. You should not have come to work."

"I thought it best that I keep myself busy, but I see I can't concentrate."

"Do you have any idea where he might be?"

"No," she answered, fighting the urge to cry. "We have no leads."

"Are the police involved?"

Nola nodded. She'd been a bank officer for twelve years, under several bank managers at the same branch, yet Mr. Fanon was by far the nicest.

"Why don't you take some time off?"

"Is it possible on such short notice?"

"Under the circumstance, we have to overlook the rules of adequate notice."

"Thank you," she said, relieved. "I know it's only two-forty-five, do you mind if I—"

"No problem. I'll contact Personnel and inform them," Mr. Fanon said, standing. "You let me know if we can be of any assistance to you and your family."

"Thank you."

She left work with no idea as to when she'd return—it all depended on Troy. On the way home, she stopped off at Miss Minnie's to pick up Meika. Same as yesterday, Meika was waiting at the window, her little forehead pressed up against the pane, her once big bright eyes dull, no longer sparkling. She had on her coat. Before Nola could put her foot on the first step, Meika opened the door and ran into her arms.

"You're early," Miss Minnie said, coming to the door.

"Yes, I left work early. I didn't feel too well."

"A cup of hot senna tea will cure most anything that ails you."

"I don't think it'll cure what ails me, Miss Minnie."

"Listen to me, child. I been around a long time. When your colon is clogged, your whole body is thrown off. I think Meika could use a little sip, too, she hasn't been her talkative little self."

"Miss Minnie, we're—"

"I took her temperature, she seems to be okay."

"Miss Minnie—"

"I got some tea right here in the house. Let me get you some."

"No thank you!" Nola said, the tense tone of her voice stopping Miss Minnie before she could turn away. The hurt look in her eyes, which were as clear as those of a woman half her seventy-two years, did not surprise Nola. Miss Minnie was a kind, giving heart who'd give a stranger the shoes off her feet and did not take well to being turned down. She had hoped that she would not have to tell Miss Minnie about Troy because she'd worry herself to death over him. Putting Meika down on the stoop, Nola adjusted Meika's coat before taking her hand.

"Meika's fine. She's a little worried about her daddy. We haven't heard from him since Saturday."

Miss Minnie brought her hand to her bosom. "My word. I hope he's okay."

"I hope so, too," she said, starting to turn away.

"Can I do something to help?"

"There's nothing anyone can do right now. The police, I guess, are doing their best. We can only wait."

Meika laid her head against Nola's side. Nola began stroking Meika's hair.

"Poor baby," Miss Minnie said, looking down at Meika. "You call me if you need me."

"Thank you, I will," she said. "Oh, by the way. I won't be going to work the rest of the week. I'll keep Meika home with me."

A slight breeze stirred Miss Minnie's thin hair. A wisp of gray hair fell over her forehead. She pushed it back and held it back with her hand. "Nola, that's best. You let me know if I can be of any help. I'll take Meika any time of the day or night."

"Thank you," Nola said again, starting to open her pocketbook. "I'd like to pay you for yesterday and today."

"Oh, child," Miss Minnie said, waving her hand. "I can wait on that. You go on and see about your boy. I'll put him in my prayers."

"Thank you," she said, starting off down the walkway. Silently, hand in hand, she and Meika started walking the half block home. Meika's soft little hand reminded Nola so much of the many days she held Troy's hand when he was a little boy, but when he was five, he'd only let her hold his hand when they crossed the street. The minute his feet hit the sidewalk, he would pull free and take off running—most of the time trying to keep up with Vann, other times because he thought he was too big to hold his mother's hand.

"You're not grown yet, little boy," she once said to him.

Troy came right back with, "Vann said I was a baby 'cause you had to hold my hand all the time. I'm not a baby. I'm a big boy."

What could she say to that? She couldn't tell him that he wasn't a big boy, and she didn't want to wag her finger at Vann because, more than likely, he'd bully Troy more than he already did, so she ended up not saying a thing. She let him run off to catch up with Vann. However, it amazed her how early that macho thing got started in boys. Vann was only seven at the time and maybe she didn't need to hold his hand crossing every street, but he was far from being old enough to cross wide main streets without her on his heels. As it was, he was a handful because of his mouth. He was quick to speak his mind. Even at age seven she had to get on Vann for telling the little girl down the street that she was the weaker sex because she didn't have a peter. She didn't know where he got that from. The child's mother didn't like it one bit and let her know it in a bombastic squall. Nola made Vann apologize and after she tried to straighten him out, she sent him to his room without his must-have chocolate chip cookies. Of course, she blamed Ron for creating in him that machismo attitude that innocent girls were going to be forced to deal with on the playground and in the classrooms.

Ron didn't see what all the fuss was about and defended Vann and himself. "I'm a man. It's my job to teach my sons to be men."

She smirked at him. "Then it's my job to teach my sons to be sensitive and loving men—something they shouldn't be ashamed of."

Ron had looked at her like she had said she was going to teach his boys to be devil worshipers. "Don't you dare raise my boys to be punks," he had ordered. "I ain't having it."

For a long time, Ron argued that she was raising sissies and she argued that he was raising chauvinists. They didn't speak for two weeks, and in the end, she let Ron have his way only because she knew how important it was for boys to have a father who spent time with them, who was genuinely interested in them, and who talked to them, but she worked all the harder to give them some balance. She couldn't complain about how they turned out, both Troy and Vann were fine young men. They never gave her a day of serious trouble, and although Troy's marriage didn't work out, and Vann never did marry the mother of his two children, he and Michelle were still together. All in all, Troy and Vann were no worse than any other young men who learned early that the world was theirs.

"Mama," Meika said, shaking Nola's hand. "Do Poppie got a new car?"

Nola had also noticed the champagne-colored car parked in the driveway behind Ron's car, but she recognized immediately that it was the unmarked police car that Detective Lopez had driven on Saturday night.

"No, baby. That's not Poppie's car."

The fact that Detective Lopez's car was there at all and that Ron was home early unnerved her. Fearing the news that awaited her, Nola felt a nervous flipping sensation in her stomach.

EIGHT

R ON rushed from his den at the sound of Nola's key turning the tumbler. He met her at the door.

Fear gripped her. Nola could see the pain etched in every
feature of Ron's face. His eyes were sunken far back in his
head, his brows were tightly knitted, his skin was taut across
his cheeks, and his lips were thin and trembled.

"Nola," Ron said, his voice shaky.

She began shaking her head.

"Detective Lopez . . . Detective Callahan . . . he . . . they
found—"

She didn't want to hear it. Her head was still shaking.

A tear slipped from Ron's eye.

Nola glanced down at Meika. Meika was staring up at Ron.
There was no hope in her eyes, only sadness.

Ron, too, looked down at Meika. Tears raced down his
cheeks. He quickly looked away.

Laying her hand tenderly on Meika's back, Nola felt the
slightest tremble. She wasn't sure if it was Meika trembling or
if it was her own hand, but she did know that her heart was
quivering.

"Meika, let's go upstairs," Nola said, quietly.

She took Meika by the hand past Ron as he lost his fight
against crying. Meika glanced back at him, but together she
and Nola went slowly up the stairs to Meika's room. With her

hands shaking, Nola turned on the television. "I'll be right back, okay?"

Meika watched Nola leave. She didn't look at the television. She climbed up on her bed and picked up Bobo. Cradling him, she began to cuddle him like a baby. "Don't be sad, Bobo. Daddy's in heaven." Meika lay down and drew him close to her body as she curled herself up into a tight little ball.

GRIPPING THE handrail, the wobbly feeling in Nola's legs kept her from moving any faster down the stairs than she was. But then, what was the use in rushing headlong into an abyss of horror that she had hoped and prayed she would never have to confront. The baby who had come to life in her womb and whose birth had renewed her life; the boy whose sweet smile melted her heart, whose laughing eyes were a joy to behold; the man-child whose blooming manhood and cracking voice left her in wonder; the man who now had his own child and who was supposed to outlive her was gone and she hadn't even said good-bye. The pain of his birth was nil compared to the intense, raw pain that filled her heart and soul.

Outside the den door Nola closed her eyes and took deep gulps of air, readying herself for the inevitable words that had only to be said aloud. Her hands shook uncontrollably. She clasped them together, trying to steady them, but then realizing that she would never be ready for the news of Troy's death, she pushed open the door and stepped inside.

Detective Lopez was saying, ". . . there is no way of telling what happened until Forensics do their job."

Nola's legs felt like jelly and seemed about to buckle under her. She reached back for the doorknob. She held on to it. "Forensics?" she asked, finding it hard to catch her breath.

Detective Lopez and Detective Callahan both stood and looked back at Nola.

Ron turned away from the window and rushed to her side.

She searched his bloodshot watery eyes. They told her everything. She grabbed on to a double fistful of his shirt.

He slipped his arms around her.

"Oh, God," she cried.

"Come, sit down," he said, beginning to pull her toward a chair.

She moved along with him, though she felt like she was struggling to stay afloat in a vicious current that was determined to pull her under. "Why, Ron? Why?"

An odd-sounding croak escaped from Ron. His face contorted into a mask of pain. "Our boy was murdered, Nola."

She moaned.

Detective Lopez continued standing near his chair. He shoved his hands down in his pocket and pulled them out again. Detective Callahan stepped closer to Nola and Ron.

"Oh God," Nola cried. "Why Troy? He was such a good person. Who would kill our child, Ron?"

"I . . . don't . . . know," Ron answered, trying not to cry but failing.

"Oh, God, oh, God," she cried, sinking, letting the current take her, leaving her too weak to hold on to Ron. Hearing the words didn't make it any easier. Her heart ached worse, her tears were more bitter, and her world was darker.

Ron caught Nola as her knees gave way, closing her up in his arms although he was weakened by that same anguish.

"Let me help you," Detective Callahan offered. He helped Ron ease Nola down into the chair beneath her.

Detective Callahan went back to stand with his partner. He and Detective Lopez then remained standing and remained respectfully quiet while the parents of the victim gave in to their anguish, their loss. It was something they were used to doing.

It was Ron who pulled himself together first. He pulled a wrinkled white handkerchief from his front pants pocket, using it first to dry his eyes and then to blow his nose on. He lifted Nola's chin. He took a dry corner of the handkerchief and began to dry her face. "Do you want to go lay down?"

Nola raised her head and opened her eyes. She wailed no more, though her tears continued to flow.

"Mrs. Kirkwood," Detective Lopez began, "I'm sorry to have brought you such bad news. I had hoped that—"

"You had hoped what, Detective?" she snapped, glaring at him through teary eyes. "If you hadn't wasted such precious time talking about procedures, my son might not be dead."

Detective Lopez's face flushed ruddily. He shifted from one foot to the other.

"If you hadn't been so condescending and listened to us in the first place, my son would be alive. You—"

"Nola," Ron said, gently massaging her shoulder, "we can't blame Detective Lopez, it's—"

"Why not, Ron? If he had done his job without putting us through the third degree, Troy would be standing in this room talking to us, not him!" She pointed an accusatory finger at him.

Looking down, Detective Lopez shoved his right hand inside his pocket and quickly pulled it out again. "I'm sorry for your loss."

"You're not sorry!"

"Nola, listen to me."

"No, Ron! You listen to me." She tugged on his sleeve. "You know it's his fault. He wouldn't listen to us."

Kneeling in front of Nola, Ron cupped her face in his hand. He blocked her view of Detective Lopez. "Nola, listen to me."

Straining, she tried as she might to look around Ron at Detective Lopez. "You should be the one that's dead."

Ron shook her. "Nola, Nola. Listen. There might not have been anything Detective Lopez could have done to save Troy. He didn't know where he was. I couldn't find Troy either, remember?" Ron's voice cracked.

Nola heard Ron's anguish. She looked at him. His cheeks were wet. Deep thick lines etched his forehead, while the laugh lines on either side of his mouth belied the torment in his eyes. Troy had begun to show those same character lines, making him look more and more like Ron. But Troy's character lines would never get deeper because he would never grow older. Covering her face with her hands, Nola laid her head against Ron's shoulder and cried.

Holding on to Nola, Ron's own tears came.

"Sir," Detective Lopez began, "if you and Mrs. Kirkwood would like to be alone for a while, we can wait outside."

Ron was unable to answer.

"We'll just wait outside," Detective Callahan said, starting out of the room.

Nola suddenly pulled out of Ron's embrace. "No!"

Detective Callahan stepped back against his chair.

Ron stood. He quickly dried his face.

"Nola, maybe we should take a minute and—"

"No. I don't need a minute," she said, wiping her face and nose with both hands. "I want to know where my son is."

"Nola, Troy is in the city morgue," Ron answered. "I've already identified his body."

"Oh, God. I want him out of there."

"Mrs. Kirkwood, that's not pos—"

"I do not want my son exposed on a piece of cold slab while strangers paw all over him. I want him respectfully laid to rest, and then I want to know how he died and who's responsible for his death. I want that animal—"

"Mrs. Kirkwood," Detective Lopez said, "we found your son only six hours ago. A preliminary examination shows that he was shot, but . . ."

"My God!"

". . . an autopsy has to be performed to determine the exact cause of death."

"You just said he was shot. What else do you need to know?"

"There might be other—"

"Detective, did you hear what I said?" Nola asked, suddenly standing. "I do not want my son's body mauled by heartless people who don't care about who he was in life. Troy was my baby. I know what's best for him."

Ron took her hand. "Nola, an autopsy has to be done."

"It's the law, ma'am," Detective Callahan said.

"I don't care about the law. I do not want anyone cutting up my baby."

"Ma'am, we understand that," Detective Lopez said, "but, the only way we're gonna find out how your son died, and possibly who killed him, is to do an autopsy. We know it's hard on families to understand this at a time like this."

"Nola, we'll never rest if we don't find out everything about how Troy died," Ron said. "He would want us to do everything to get at the truth. You know how inquisitive Troy was about life and death. Remember when he cut up his first frog in school? He badgered that teacher until she could halfway explain if the frog's brain died first or his heart, because Troy said the heart was still pumping in his hand and the frog's legs were still twitching. Remember how upset that teacher was to be put on the spot like that? She wanted Troy suspended from school for disrupting the class. Remember that?"

With her hand pressed against her lips to still the cry that wanted to burst from her, Nola nodded. She remembered.

"Troy would want us to know how he died."

Sadly, she nodded in agreement.

"And, Nola, we have to call Vann. We've put off calling him long enough."

NINE

VANN came. He brought his children, Sharice and Kareem, but their mother, Michelle, did not come. Vann did not say why. In his struggle to come to grips with losing Troy, Vann was uncharacteristically quiet but strong in his take-charge way as he and Ron made the arrangements for a closed-casket funeral. The two of them insisted that Nola not look upon her baby one last time as she wanted to. She went along with them because she did not have the strength to say otherwise. It was on a bitterly cold, gray, rainy day at the start of Thanksgiving week that Troy was laid to rest deep in the wet muddy ground. The decision not to view him should have been hers alone, because on good days, she was glad that she hadn't looked at him; on bad days, she wished she had.

Unable to sleep, on the dawning of Thanksgiving Eve, Nola found herself downstairs sitting in the den, going through unopened mail that belonged to Troy. Ron had been paying off Troy's few bills as they came in. Much of what was left was junk, including the thick American Express envelope that caught Nola's eye. It was suspicious in that it was much too thick to be a bill, yet it was a bill envelope. Perhaps it was full of merchandise advertisement. Using Ron's silver letter opener, Nola slit the envelope open. She didn't expect the bill to be very high as Troy used it only in emergencies. She pulled from the envelope pages of expenditures. She was astounded.

The total amount due was shocking—seventy-five hundred dollars.

"What in the world?" She quickly scanned the pages upon pages of charges—televisions, CD players, VCRs, jewelry, clothes—everything that was part of a fantasy shopping spree was listed. Yet none of those things were in the house. Then she looked at the dates: October 29, 30, 31, November 1, 2, 3, 4, 5, 6, 7. Troy's murderer had gone hog-wild with his credit card from the first day he disappeared. Ron had canceled the account less than a week after Troy's body was found, yet, amazingly, charges were made without a problem, which was very ironic since Troy worked for American Express. American Express knew that Troy was dead yet they allowed the charges anyway. Nola did not worry for a minute that she would have to pay the bill, but she wondered if the police or American Express could use the bill to trace the murderer.

Alarmed and angry, Ron wasted no time rushing off to the post office and overnight-expressing a copy of Troy's death certificate to Customer Services at American Express, along with a letter explaining the theft of the card.

Still Vann remained quiet. He sat as if in a daze, saying nothing at all about Troy. His silence made it all the more difficult for Nola even to consider celebrating Thanksgiving Day. They did not have their usual gathering of family and friends at Beatrice's, though Beatrice came over bringing food aplenty that neither she nor Ron had the stomach for. A dark, heavy cloud hung over a day that she used to always look forward to. In fact, the whole holiday season was ruined. Christmas slipped feebly by with gifts only for Meika, Sharice, and Kareem. No beautiful colorful lights adorned the windows or roof, and no festive garland hung at the door. A small Christmas tree for the kids, picked up at the last minute by Vann, was the only symbol of the holiday. What little time had passed did nothing to begin the healing of Nola's broken heart. She could only pray that Meika was young enough to leave the pain of her loss behind. If not, Nola made a promise to Troy that she'd spend the rest of her life trying to make his baby's life as good as he would have wanted it to be.

For the first two weeks after Troy died, Meika slept with Nola while Ron slept in his den on the pull-out sofa. When Meika went back to her own bed, she shared it with Sharice. Nola was grateful that Vann brought Sharice and Kareem with him, they both kept Meika busy enough that she didn't have a chance to mope. Thank God for that.

All in all, Meika seemed to be coping better than all of them. Troy would have been proud. His baby was already on her way to becoming the strong woman he wished for her to be.

Vann, too, noticed how composed Meika was. "We should all be so brave," he said, sipping from his mug of tea.

"If only," Nola agreed. She watched Vann set his mug down on the table. As he began to tap lightly on the side of the handle with his finger, she noticed for the first time that he had grown a mustache. He looked very little like the lanky kid who left home thirteen years ago.

"You look good with a mustache."

He was surprised that she noticed. "I've been wearing it awhile now," he said, reading the headlines.

"You're welcome," she said, for lack of anything else to say. Since Vann had been home, the two of them had not had a minute alone together and now that they were alone, she did not know what to say to him. True, she had never been at a loss for words with Troy and she and Vann had always had a comfortable mother-son relationship, though nothing like him and Ron. This was all the more reason why Troy would always be missed. She was closer to him. Slowly stirring her orange spice herb tea, Nola sighed.

Vann opened the newspaper.

"Would you like a muffin? They're blueberry."

"Not right now, thanks," he said, closing the newspaper. He folded it and lay it on the table.

Again, Nola stirred her tea. "Is your tea cold? I can make some fresh if you like."

Wrapping his big hands around his hot mug, Vann looked straight into Nola's eyes. "My tea is fine, Ma, but we're not."

"No, I guess we're not. We'll never get over losing Troy."

"Perhaps not, but we have to start talking again."

"What do you mean? We're talking."

"Not about Troy, we're not. Ma, we need to start talking, specifically, about Troy."

Quickly picking up her teacup, Nola pushed her chair back from the table and, getting up, took the cup over to the sink.

"Ma, I know I've been closed, but we can't go on not talking about what happened."

Nola set the cup down hard in the sink. "Did Kareem like flying back to Atlanta by himself?"

He knew what she was doing. "It was an adventure for him. Now Kareem wants to be a pilot when he grows up."

She began to run water in her cup. "That's good. Michelle must have been glad to have him back home. The holiday must have been lonely for her with all of you up here. You know, I thanked her for letting Sharice stay longer, Meika loves having her here. Michelle said there wasn't much to miss in the first grade and that she'd help Sharice catch up as soon as she got back. Too bad she couldn't come with you, I would have liked to have seen her. I was thinking about taking the kids—"

Bang! Vann brought his fist down on the table. The glass salt and pepper shakers rattled, making Nola turn back around to face Vann.

"Ma, you know damn well you couldn't care less if Michelle had come up here or not. You can't stand her. Now please, come back over here and sit down. We have got to talk about Troy."

She did not want to talk about Troy. "Why would you say that? I like Michelle."

"Ma, I am not getting into all that. Michelle's not your problem anyway, Troy is. I don't know all the details of how he died and none of us know why he died. You and Dad think that because you don't talk about what happened, it'll all go away. It won't."

"Well, Vann, you haven't said a whole lot since you've been here, either."

"No, I haven't. I had to deal with Troy's death in my own way. But you and Dad, you're going about this all wrong."

Reaching behind her, Nola turned off the faucet. "Of course you'd see it that way. It's okay for you to mourn the way you want to, but the way your father and I mourn is all wrong. Vann, where is your heart? Can't you respect the way we mourn our loss?"

"If this is how you plan to mourn me, don't. You're both like zombies around here."

Closing her eyes, Nola tried to quiet the anger she felt building up inside her. It was just like Vann to rush her, to irritate her, to accuse her of not handling Troy's death in the way he wanted her to. She wasn't ready to talk about what happened to Troy. At first, she and Ron, both, wanted to know why Troy was killed, but dealing with the reality of his death overwhelmed them and neither knew where to go for answers and, perhaps, they were afraid to know more.

"Ma, I don't want you to be like this over me. We have to talk."

"Not right now, Vann. I don't—"

"*Now*, Ma. *Now!*" he shouted, jabbing his finger into the table.

Nola froze. Vann had never yelled at her like that. She wanted to cry.

He could see that he had hurt her. "Ma," he said, his voice lower, "I want to talk about Troy, now. You need to talk about Troy, now. If you had seen your face when I first slept in Troy's room, you'd know that you need to talk now, not tomorrow. And don't think I don't know that you sit up in that room sometimes for hours on end when I'm not here."

Nola covered her ears. She closed her eyes. "Stop it!"

Vann stood quickly and grabbed Nola's arms and pulled them down.

Her eyes popped open. "Vann!"

"You can't close out what's going on. Troy is gone, Ma. We buried him. Don't you want to know what caused him to lose his life?"

She snatched her arms free. "Stop it! I don't have the strength." She went to the refrigerator. She opened the door but closed it back right away.

"Well, I do."

"Vann. I'm not ready to talk about Troy. It's too soon. It hurts too much. Don't you understand that?"

"I understand, Ma, but unless we find out why Troy was killed, it's going to always hurt. Haven't you noticed that Dad has started to drink more than his two cans of beer on a Saturday night? He's been drinking a six-pack every day since we buried Troy."

"That's temporary."

"Do you really think so?"

Now that she thought about it, she didn't know.

"Ma, I've been watching you both for two months. You don't talk to each other anymore. Y'all pass like ships in the night and Dad sleeps in the den. Why do you think that is, Ma? Is it because he can't handle the hurt in your eyes and you can't handle his? The way I see it, you're both drowning in your own individual sorrow. But you guys are going to have to work together to get through this."

Nola tried hard to force her anger at Vann way down in her gut. She knew that he meant well but he was only making her feel more miserable. No one was more aware than she that Ron was having a hard time dealing with the way Troy died— so was she. They just hadn't found a way to deal with it together, and it wasn't that she hadn't noticed Ron's drinking, she had, but chose to ignore it. As she saw it, there was nothing she could do to make him stop drinking or come back to their bed. She had her own problems.

Vann sat. "Ma, I'm really worried about Dad."

"Your father will be fine. He just needs some time to get over Troy's death."

"As simple as that, huh? He'll wake up one morning and he'll be fine, right?" He pushed his mug away. "Ma, I know you know better. I think you both need counseling."

"Counseling?"

"Why not? You just lived through a devastating tragedy. Instead of Dad hiding in his beer and you hiding behind Meika, don't you think you need to talk about it with a professional, or with other people who've had the same experience?"

Nola went back to the sink. She picked up the sponge and began wiping around the inside of the sink. "I am not hiding behind Meika. She needs me. I'm taking care of her, raising her like I promised Troy I would."

"Ma, I heard you tell Cousin Beatrice that you might never go back to work because Meika needed you. That's just an excuse. You always worked when me and Troy were growing up."

"But I . . . I . . . that was another time," she said, knowing full well before she said it that it was easier to manage her home life and her job with Meika than it was with Troy and Vann both underfoot.

"Ma, you've made Meika your reason for living. That's a lot of pressure to put on her. Do you know that the few times you haven't been home, Meika has been very independent? Yet the minute you come home, she becomes a baby. You cradle her like she's an infant and she lets you."

She tossed the sponge onto the counter. "I do not treat Meika like a baby."

"Denying it don't make it so. Think about it, Ma. Haven't you noticed that Meika's not happy . . ."

"Well, her—"

". . . and it's not all about Troy? Meika is sad because of you and Dad. You both buried yourselves with Troy."

"That's not true."

"It is," Vann said. "Look, Ma, I have to catch a flight back to Atlanta on Thursday. I do not have time for you and Dad to snap out of your self-imposed emotional exile on your own."

Beginning to tear, Nola felt like crawling up into a hole. Vann was accusing her of doing more harm to Meika than Troy's death had done. That wasn't so. "Vann, you can go on back to Atlanta. We'll be as all right as we've always been."

"You won't be all right, and if I go back home and leave you and Dad all messed up like this, I won't be all right either. Ma, please. You have to fight to get your life back. You're not doing Meika any good like this."

Falling back against the sink, Nola felt like a dam had burst inside her. It was the first time she cried since burying Troy.

Vann sprang up from his chair and rushed to Nola. He embraced her. "I'm sorry, Ma. I didn't mean to make you cry, but I can't leave you like this. C'mon, sit down with me."

Together they went back to the table. He helped Nola into her chair. "I'll make you some fresh tea."

While Vann busied himself getting her tea, Nola sat dreading talking about the how and why of Troy's death. She had wanted to forget all the ugly, sordid details. Admittedly, she hadn't seen how her and Ron's silence was affecting Meika. And it was no surprise that Vann would be the one to open her eyes. As much as she hated to admit it, he was right. She sat up straight and wiped her tears away. If she wasn't doing right by Meika, then she wasn't keeping her promise to Troy. Resting her elbows on the table, she ran her hands through her hair. She was exhausted—emotionally and physically. She hadn't returned to work yet and with all the rest she'd been getting, especially since Ron's snoring was not keeping her awake, she should have more energy. If Vann knew how little she missed sleeping with his father, he'd probably be pushing her to see a sex therapist, which would be a waste of money. Sex had never been her and Ron's problem, though it might be now.

"Here's your tea."

"Thank you," she said. She wistfully dunked the tea bag several times before pressing her spoon against it on the inside edge of the cup to drain it. Then she laid the tea bag on the corner of her saucer.

Vann topped off his tea with some boiling hot water. Sitting again, he opened the jar of honey. He scooped out a heaping spoonful and held it over Nola's cup. They both watched as the thick golden honey slowly oozed from the spoon into the hot tea. Vann did it twice more into his own mug. Pensively, they both stirred their tea.

Vann tasted his tea. It was just right. "Now, I know that Troy was shot in the chest and in the face."

Dropping her spoon in the cup, Nola sat back. "I can't do this."

"Yes you can. You have to."

"No, I don't! I don't have to relive this ugliness."

"Yes you do."

"Why? What for?"

"Ma, because you didn't look at Troy, you've been able to convince yourself that the way he died wasn't real. Well, I saw him. It was ugly, and it was very real."

"I didn't know you could be so cruel."

Vann pushed his mug away. "This is not about me trying to hurt you. I love you, and I love Troy. Ma, what you don't know about Troy's death is what's eating at you. Trust me, you won't have any peace until you know."

"Vann, I do not want to think about this right now." Feeling afraid, feeling like a child who wished that she could climb onto her mother's lap and feel safe, Nola wept.

"Ma, please."

The kitchen door suddenly swung open.

Vann looked away from Nola into his father's stern face.

Seeing Nola's face, Ron asked, "Why is your mother crying?"

Nola stopped crying and, like Vann, she looked at Ron. She knew for sure that she couldn't talk about Troy now; Ron became angry whenever Troy's name came up.

Vann stood. "I'm glad you're home, Dad. We're talking about Troy." He stepped away from the table, closer to Ron.

Ron's eyes went cold. He clenched his jaw.

Seeing the muscles in Ron's neck pop out, Nola reached out to Vann, her fingertips just touching the sleeve of his sweater. "Vann, don't—"

"No, Ma. We have to talk about this."

Ron slammed his newspaper down on the counter. "I will not—"

"Dad! This is your house and you've always been the boss. I respect that. But I am telling you, if you and Ma don't face Troy's death head-on, you're going to destroy this family. Do you think for one minute this is what Troy would want?"

"You're right. This is my goddamn house and I am the boss," Ron snapped. "If you don't like what's going on here, take your ass back to Atlanta, 'cause, boy, your ass is outta bounds."

"Boy?"

Nola saw the angry glint in Vann's eyes. "Ron, Vann, why are we fighting amongst ourselves?"

Neither one answered her. Ron's and Vann's eyes were

locked in an ugly glare. Nola looked down at the thick veins running just under the skin of Ron's clenched fist and at his big angular knuckles looking like they were as hard as rocks. Although he had not laid a hand on Vann since he was sixteen years old, she feared that he might now. He had never been as angry as he had been since Troy was killed.

"Vann," she said, tapping Vann on the arm, "maybe we shouldn't talk about this."

Vann only saw Ron. He only heard Ron. "Boy, huh? Dad, I haven't been a boy since I was eighteen and left this house."

Ron bristled.

"You know something? You can throw me out of your house, but that won't change the fact that you've been drowning your sorrows in gallons of beer and pulling further away from your wife."

"Boy, what I do is none of your business."

"Okay. I see we're not connecting. So, Dad, I am going to let that *boy* remark slide, but let me tell you something about how Troy and I felt about you. In our eyes, growing up, you were the man. Do you think you're that man now?"

"Vann!" Nola exclaimed, leaping up out of her chair and quickly pulling on Vann's arm. She tried to pull him back, farther away from Ron, but she couldn't budge him. The muscles in Vann's arm were rigid. "Vann, what's gotten into you? What are you doing?"

Grimacing, Ron snarled in Vann's face. He started to slowly raise his fist.

"Ron! My God! What are you doing?"

Ron's fist stopped at his chest. Sweat popped out on his upper lip.

"Ron," Nola said again.

Ron dropped his fist and, suddenly turning, started to stalk off.

"Don't you walk away from me!" Vann ordered.

"Vann!" Nola shrieked, again trying to pull him back. She

Gloria Mallette

couldn't understand why he was pushing Ron so hard, and worse still, she was afraid of what could happen.

Stopping abruptly, Ron whirled back around. "Boy, don't you know I'll kill you for talking to me like that?"

"Ron, please go," she pleaded, trying to get in between them. "Vann, don't do this."

Holding Ron's gaze, Vann pulled Nola from in between them and effortlessly pushed her aside. "Didn't you just lose one son, old man?"

Ron began to work his jaw, grinding his teeth hard.

Nola couldn't take it. "Vann! Dear God. Let your father go! I don't want you two fighting. I can't handle this. I can't!"

Still ignoring Nola, Vann pushed harder. "Man, don't you see your house falling down around you? Am I supposed to sit on my hands and close my eyes to what I see happening to you and Ma? I don't think so. Not as long as I draw breath will I sit still for this. And yes, I said don't walk away from me, and I meant it. I am the man you raised, deal with it."

Nola saw in Ron's face a rage that she had never seen. With his fists clenched, he charged at Vann like a bull.

Vann didn't back down. He stood his ground. He barely winced when Ron rammed into him and, grabbing up a fistful of his sweater at the throat in his left hand, angrily raised his right fist, poised, ready to strike. Reacting instinctively, Vann latched on to Ron's raised wrist and also gripped the wrist of the hand clutching his sweater.

Up in each other's faces, their eyes didn't waver. Ron was breathing hard, his face contorted in an ugly sneer. Yet Vann didn't blink. He looked as calm as if he were watching television.

Nola inhaled sharply. Never had she known Vann to blatantly challenge Ron, and never had she seen Ron so crazed. His eyes were glaringly black. He worked his jaw repeatedly. Nola felt like she was about to throw up. She tried harder to push Vann away—it was like pushing on a wall.

74

"Boy," Ron said, his lips trembling, his voice cracking, "you better stand down."

"Vann, please," Nola begged. "Ron, please don't hit him."

"If I don't, Dad, what are you going to do? Hit me?" Vann asked, letting go of Ron's wrists. He let his arms drop down to his sides. "I can take it. Can you?"

Sucking in her breath, Nola searched Ron's face to see if he was going to answer that question with his fist. He had never been a violent man and had left much of the disciplining to her, unless the boys' deeds called for a heavier hand. Like the time Vann got caught stealing a beer from the corner store. He had the money but he was underage. Ron had taken him down to the basement. In his stubbornness, Vann didn't cry out, but the sound of the belt striking his body tore at her, hurting her just as much. Vann couldn't easily sit for a week and, as far as she knew, he never stole a thing after that. But Vann was no longer that sixteen-year-old. A whopping wasn't the answer here.

Ron's hand began to shake. He and Vann glared eye-to-eye, though Vann stood a good four inches taller and seemed to be made out of granite. Until Nola saw Ron release Vann's sweater with a thrust, and his fist drop to his side, and his eyes lose their fire, she thought she'd never breathe again. Ron's shoulders began to heave. He dropped his head as he was turning away, but his sobs suddenly exploded from him in deep gulps. Quickly reaching out, Vann caught Ron by the arm and yanked him back around. He pulled his father into his powerful arms. Ron's head dropped onto Vann's shoulder. They both cried, breaking Nola's heart. When Ron raised his arms and hugged Vann back, she plopped down in Vann's chair and cried also. But then, suddenly, her crying caught in her throat. A calmness shrouded her. Her heart felt lighter. She felt like she was gathered up in a strong warm embrace. She could almost feel Troy's presence. She no longer wanted to cry. She knew, somehow, that they were going to be all right.

TEN

ONCE again, Nola had to remind herself to thank Beatrice for being there for her. Meika and Sharice were at her house—out of harm's way—most likely eating enough delectable desserts to give them sugar. If they had been home, she wondered if Vann would have been as brutally forthright as he had been. She was still reeling from his ambush of Ron, who, because he didn't see it coming, was looking a little shell-shocked. With Vann's help, Ron sat down in his chair at the head of the table. He kept folding and unfolding his shaking hands. He kept biting down hard on his lip, trying hard to stop crying. Vann dragged his chair up close to Ron and sat with his left hand on his arm and his other on his shoulder, talking softly as if he were comforting his child. She let them be, it was their moment.

"Dad, don't think I don't miss Troy. He was my little brother. We talked on the phone just three days before he came up missing. He said he was bringing Meika down this summer. We were gonna hang out, me and my little brother," Vann said, sniffling, pushing the tears away from his mouth with his finger. "I miss talking to him, and in my gut, I know I won't rest until I know who killed him and see his ass in hell. Dad, we have to pull ourselves together for Meika, for Troy. It would hurt him to know that we fell apart and gave in without a fight."

That made Ron cry all the harder.

"I'm sorry," Vann said, rubbing Ron's shoulder. "I didn't mean to make you hurt more. I wish to God we could just close our eyes and wish it all away, but we can't." He turned to Nola. "Ma, are you okay?"

She nodded slightly.

He nodded back at her. "Dad, it'll be all right, I promise. We'll get through this together."

Taking a deep breath, Ron reached across to the napkin holder in the center of the table and, after being unable to separate them to take one, he took three. He pressed them against his eyes before wiping his face dry.

Like Vann, Nola waited.

"I should have been there for him," Ron said, hoarsely. He tightly balled up the damp napkins in his hand.

"Dad, you can't blame yourself."

"I do. Meika asked me," Ron said, hitting his chest with his fist, "me, to go to the movies with them. I told her I had a golf game, a stupid golf game!"

"Ron, she asked me, too," Nola volunteered, "but I went to the dentist. If I had been there, I could—"

"You could have what?" Vann asked.

"Well . . . I—"

"You could have done nothing, Ma. If you had been there, you would have stayed inside the theater with Meika while Troy went outside. The only thing that would have been different, the police would have been notified sooner."

Nola hit the table with the palms of both her hands. "Yes, but Troy would be alive today."

"I hate to tell you this, Ma, but not necessarily. If Troy was killed right away, you would not have known for a while because you'd figure that he was taking care of his car."

Nola pressed her fingers to her left temple. "Maybe, but—"

"Ma, we can't go on maybes. If—"

"You weren't here, Vann. If you had been, you'd be thinking the same way we are."

"No, I wasn't, but—"

"Vann," Ron began, "that's the whole point of this. You weren't here, we were. There was nothing you could have done, but I could've been there with Troy. I could have gone with him to check on his car. He would not have been alone."

"No, Dad. You don't know if you could have made a difference either. If there was more than one man, or even just one man with the gun, you could have been killed, too."

"Or I could have been killed instead of Troy. It would have been better. Everybody wouldn't be hurting like this."

"Ron!" Nola said, laying her hand on top of his. "Pain is pain, sorrow is sorrow. Neither has a name."

"That's right, Dad. We wouldn't be hurting any less if it were you or anybody at this table. Your being there may not have changed a thing. In fact, if Troy had taken Meika with him, she might have been killed, too."

"You don't know that for sure, son. Nobody knows that for sure."

"That's my point exactly. Nobody knows for sure, but lately, murderers have not been leaving witnesses behind who might finger them. Hell, they've killed two-year-old babies."

"Lord," Nola said, prayerfully.

"You both would have been killed."

Fresh tears slipped from Ron's eyes. He used the balled-up damp napkins to drag them away. "I still think there was a chance I could have saved him."

"Dad, we can *could* ourselves to death and nothing would change. Troy's death is not on your hands. He was a big boy and you could not go around holding his hand, fighting his battles, taking his punches for him. You know how he was. When he was a kid, he didn't even like me, his own brother, taking up for him. He wanted me to be there to watch his back, but he took care of his own fights."

Ron let his hand drop to the table. "He was a fighter, wasn't he?"

Nola and Vann both nodded.

"I taught you both how to box, didn't I?"

"Yes, you did."

A little smile touched Ron's lips. "Troy was planning on playing golf with me. Did I tell you that?"

"No."

"I didn't? Well, Troy thought golf was an old man's game, but he promised me he'd play the next Saturday. We had a bet. But he didn't live to see—"

Nola wiped at her wet, tired eyes.

"Troy just might've beat you, Dad."

"I probably would have let him."

"Yeah, right," Vann said, smiling sadly. "You know there wasn't much he couldn't do."

"He was smart," Nola said.

"Yeah," Vann agreed.

Ron smiled again. "He was smart like you. Made me proud he thought a lot of his old man to bring his friends to me to talk to. He got that from you, didn't he?"

Vann nodded.

"That boy followed behind you like a puppy dog when he was little."

The memory made Vann smile again.

"Nola, you remember when Vann started school how Troy damn near cried all day?"

"Yeah. He wanted his bro-bro," she said, dabbing at her eyes.

Vann closed his eyes and shook off the threat of tears.

"For a long time," Ron said, "I thought Troy was going to be a follower because he was always following behind you. Then somewhere along the line, he started thinking for himself. And he did all right for himself, too. He had a good job, a beautiful little girl, he got a bundle saved, a nice car. . . . We have got to get his car. He loved that car."

"Don't worry about the car, Dad. I'll take care of it."

"They didn't release his car because he was shot in it."

"I think they're still checking it for evidence, but it'll be released eventually. Hopefully, there's something there to give us some answers."

Nola sucked her teeth. "The police don't willingly give answers."

"We can make them," Vann said, taking his hands off Ron and sitting back. "We can use politicians, we can use media if we have to, and, we can become nasty warts on the police's tailbone. Every time they scratch, we'll be there to make them itch again."

Ron looked at Vann quizzically. "We? You said you were going home in a few days."

"I am, but I'm coming back."

That surprised Nola. "When?"

"I figure—"

"Vann, how are you going to do that?" Nola asked. "You have a family. You have to make a living."

"Ma, I have liquid assets, a decent portfolio, and Michelle is working. Her and the kids won't starve and the mortgage is manageable."

"But Michelle might not—"

"Of course I'll have to talk to her first, but I don't think she'll have a problem with it. I figure I can take a six-month leave of absence if need be, without hurting too much."

Nola and Ron's faces both squinched up at the same time. Her tears emptied right away, while Ron's welled up and flooded his eyes.

"You'd do that?" Ron asked.

"In a heartbeat."

Ron was amazed. "Won't you lose your job?"

"Dad, I've been taking care of business since I've been here."

"You mean with that laptop you brought with you?" Nola asked.

"It's like I'm right in Atlanta. I haven't missed a transaction."

"If you're sure," Ron said, "I wouldn't mind having you around."

"I'm very sure."

"But we'll help you out anyway," Nola said, again dabbing at her cheeks. "I have savings. I can send money to Michelle every few weeks."

"No, Ma. That's your nest egg. Besides, if you're not going back to work for a while, you'll need to hold on to your money."

"We're not going to discuss this," Ron said, sounding stronger. "You have a family. Your mother and I will help you out. We're all in this together. Our money has been ours for years and our mortgage is paid off."

"That's why we can help you," she said.

Vann shook his head.

"Just listen a minute," she insisted. "Troy has savings and he took out policies. They were meant to be put in trust for raising Meika. If need be, you'll use some of that."

"Ma, there won't be a need."

She looked at Ron. The sadness was still there, but the anger was gone. "Ron, talk to him."

"Let the boy . . . man alone. He knows we're here if he needs us."

From Ron, Nola looked at Vann. He looked every bit the man his father raised. She would have given anything to also be able to be looking at Troy sitting at his place at the table.

Ron sat with his eyes lowered, resting on the balled-up napkins he repeatedly fingered. "Do you think Troy knew that I loved him?" He asked no one in particular.

"Of course—" Nola started to answer but Vann raised his finger, signaling to her that he would answer that question.

"Dad, I know that you love me, and we've had our battles. I have no doubt that Troy knew that you loved him."

That, Nola agreed with wholeheartedly. The one time Vann said that he hated his father was in his senior year of high school, when Ron kept him from playing basketball for two weeks because he stayed out with the car well past midnight, after a game, with a carload of rowdy boys playing loud music. He got pulled over by the police because of it. Fortunately, no one was drunk or high off drugs. They were just young and stupid, celebrating a win. Vann was bitterly angry about having to miss games and would not speak to Ron or her for weeks because she didn't override Ron. His team won games without him, making him more sullen, and only after he and Troy talked and Troy told him that he had been wrong did Vann apologize for being irresponsible. He didn't tell Ron that he was sorry for saying that he hated him, but at the end of the punishment, he bought Ron an ornate sterling silver cigarette lighter. No more cold shoulder, no more pouting. Ron had since given up smoking, but he kept the cigarette lighter on his desk in his den as a paperweight. Proof of his son's love ever present.

Buzzzz!

"I'll get it," Vann said, getting up from the table. "Maybe it's a lost pizza delivery boy."

"You hungry?" Nola asked.

"Starving," he replied, pushing the swinging kitchen door open with the palm of his hand. He left the kitchen.

"We have plenty of food already cooked," she said, getting up from the table. She rubbed Ron's arm as she passed him. "I'll warm up dinner."

Buzzzz!

"I'm coming!" Vann called, quickly unlocking the door. He pulled it open. A blast of cold air hit him in the face. He batted his eyes once. "Yes?" he asked the woman.

The woman wore a short black skirt, a short, waist-length

bright red fur jacket, and a black Russian fur hat pulled low on her forehead, hiding much of her eyes, but not her full red lips. Under her arm she carried a large gold and red gift-wrapped box.

"How you doing, Vann? Visiting?"

Vann didn't need to see her eyes to know who she was, her voice told him that.

Pushing the hat back off from her eyes, she smiled.

Frowning, he pulled the door up behind him. "Cordelia, what the hell are you doing here?"

She stepped back. "My, don't hurt yourself trying to hide how glad you are to see me. Happy holiday to you, too."

Looming above her, Vann looked down his nose at her. Her red jacket contrasted boldly with her black hat. "Aren't you afraid Jack Frost is going to nip at your ass in that short jacket?"

She posed, sticking one black-opaqued leg out to the side, her free hand on her hip. "Hey, you know me, Vann. I'd rather be cute than warm any day."

"Haven't changed a bit, have you, Cordelia?"

"Can't change perfection."

"I see you're still tripping on yourself," he said, annoyed by the ugly smirk on her lips.

"I love myself, honey," she said, kissing the fingertips of her red gloved hand and then touching them to her cheek.

Vann frowned. "Cordelia, you know damn well you're not welcome here. Why the hell would you show up here without calling?"

She sucked her teeth. "Maybe I don't know the number."

"That's a lie."

"I don't have time for this," she said, suddenly lunging into the narrow space between Vann and the doorjamb, pushing her way past him into the entryway. " 'Scuse me. I'm here to see my daughter, not you."

Too late he tried to block her with his body. "Damnit!"

"Vann!" Nola called from the kitchen. "Do you want ham or turkey, or both?"

Vann gripped the doorknob tighter and stared out at the sprinkle of snowflakes beginning to fall. His parents had enough to deal with without the added stress of Cordelia's presence.

"Vann, close the door," Nola said, opening the kitchen door. "You're letting the heat out. Who's at—"

Cordelia turned around.

Nola stopped dead in her tracks. Her heart skipped a beat. The headache that had only minutes ago begun to fade returned with a vengeance.

"Hi, Nola. Merry Christmas."

ELEVEN

IT was no surprise to Nola that a blast of such bitter, cold air would blow in someone as bitter and callous-hearted as Cordelia. The sheer hell Cordelia put Troy through with her crack addiction—stealing his money, stealing the bonds that Ron bought for Meika, pawning Troy's jewelry and any jewelry he bought for her, selling things right out of his house for pennies, and selling herself right in their bed just to get a fix, devastated Troy and ended their marriage. The court declared Cordelia an unfit mother and as God was her witness, Nola wasn't about to let Cordelia slither her way back into Meika's life or any of their lives.

Nola was beginning to feel that old intense anger well up in her gut that seeped from her very core every time she saw Cordelia. Although she could not remember the last time she let Cordelia cross her threshold, she could remember the last time she saw her in Family Court two years ago. It was the day Troy got full custody of Meika and Cordelia was ordered to stay away from the house because of her threats against her and Troy.

"Thank you, *both,* so much for your warm Christmas hospitality," Cordelia snipped, rolling her eyes from Nola to Vann. "For your information, I'm not here to see either one of you. Where's my daughter?"

Vann slammed the door. "My niece is not here, and if you had called, you could have saved yourself the trip."

"I want her out of my house," Nola said.

The kitchen door suddenly swung open. "What's going on out here?"

Cordelia glanced past Nola toward Ron. She then set the gift-wrapped box on the floor against the wall. "Hey, Mr. Kirkwood," she said, her tone friendlier. She started peeling off her red leather gloves, one finger at a time.

In her mind's eye, Nola could see herself slapping Cordelia across the face. "Don't even take a piece of lint off of your body. You're not staying."

Cordelia's gloves stayed on. "I have a right to see my daughter."

"No, you don't," Nola said. "You were told by the judge to make an appointment no less than two weeks in advance, and it looks to me, like always, you do whatever the hell you feel like doing. You have no respect for anything or anyone."

"I lost your number. What was I supposed to do, let Meika think that I forgot about her? It's Christmas."

"As far as you're concerned, it means nothing. It's no different than any other day. What has it been? A year? A year and a half? You didn't seem to lose the address, you're standing here. You could've written a letter."

Ron stood alongside Nola.

Likewise, Vann went and stood on the other side of Nola. He folded his arms across his chest. "Like I said, Cordelia, you haven't changed."

"Look, I didn't have time to write. I just got back in town and I had a lot to take care of. I know y'all always hated me, but—"

"No, Cordelia, you always hated yourself," Ron said, stepping forward. "I suggest you leave now, we got your message. Leave us a number where we can get in touch with you, and we'll make arrangements for you to see Meika. And please, make it somewhere decent."

"Yeah," Vann agreed. "You'll get your two hours, I'll bring her to you myself."

"Humph," Cordelia said, putting her hand on her hip and smirking at Vann. "Protecting the baby of the family, as usual, huh? What's wrong, Vann? You scared to let Troy bring Meika himself? Are you scared I'll seduce him?"

All eyes were riveted on Cordelia. Ron sneered.

Vann glowered. "You turn my stomach."

Nola was livid. "Bitch," she said, moving closer to Cordelia.

"Oh no! You didn't call me a bitch!"

"I certainly did," Nola said, putting her hands on her hips. "You don't like it?"

"Hell, no I don't, you old-ass bitch. You—"

"Hey!" Ron shouted, staring at Cordelia.

"Hold up!" Vann said, stepping threateningly closer to Cordelia. "You don't call my mother a bitch."

Cordelia backed up. "She called me a bitch first, but you didn't hear her, did you?"

"You get your junkie ass out of my house, right now!" Nola shouted. "And mark my word. As long as I got breath in my body, it'll be a cold day in hell before I ever let you get your hands on Meika."

Cordelia glared bitterly at Nola.

Vann rushed to the door and grabbed the doorknob. "I think you should leave, Cordelia," he said, opening the door.

Cordelia's hand on her hip dropped to her side. Smirking, she looked Nola up and down. She then spread her gloved hands out in front of her. "Look at me. I'm clean. Can't you tell I'm clean?"

Ron was unimpressed. "What are we supposed to tell from looking at leather?"

"My hands are steady. Look at my face, look at my eyes. Clean."

"What, a day? A month?" Vann asked. "What do you want, a medal?"

"For your information, I've been clean a whole year, and the judge said, as long as I stay clean, I got a right to see my daughter."

Nola again shook her head. "No, you'd have to go through me first," Nola said.

"I ain't afraid of you, Nola. In fact, I ain't afraid of none of you," she said, narrowing her eyes at Nola. "You can't stop me from seeing Meika. What am I talking to you for anyhow? You're not the one I got to deal with. Where's Troy? I wanna talk to him."

Vann and Ron exchanged furtive glances, which didn't escape Cordelia. Suspicious, she looked from one to the other.

Nola tried to hold strong with her glare, but thinking about where Troy was weakened her. She averted her eyes and looked toward the large picture of Troy that had sat on his coffin and was now hanging on the wall in the living room above the mantel.

Cordelia looked at the picture of Troy. "Where is he?"

"Cordelia," Ron said, getting right close up on her. "This is not a good time to come into this house and mess with us. You've been nothing but trouble ever since you chose crack over my son and my granddaughter. You say you're clean? Personally, I don't give a good goddamn if you are, because coming here like this, knowing damn well that you'd stir up trouble and piss us off, proves that clean or not, you're still nothing but trouble. If you had been any good, Troy's life could've been a whole lot better, but since you made his life miserable, you lost the right to play mother to his child. We'll see to it that Meika—"

"Wait a minute," Cordelia said, turning away from them to look searchingly into the living room. "Wait a damn minute."

Vann took her arm. "Your time is up. Let's go."

"Not so damn fast," Cordelia said, yanking her arm back from Vann. Again, she looked around the living room. "What's going on?"

The three of them watched her. They exchanged worried glances.

"Troy isn't here, is he?" she asked, her eyes lingering on his picture a minute before dropping down to the brass praying hands, the white candles on either side of them, and the white Bible, all beneath it. When she turned around, her eyes were wide and her mouth was open.

Not that Nola expected to see anything else, but what she saw in Cordelia's eyes, a glimmer of a twinkle, turned her stomach. "Get out!"

"Is Troy dead?"

"Get her out of here!"

Pulling the door open wider, Vann took hold of Cordelia's upper arm and started pulling her backward, yet firmly, toward the door.

She jerked her arm free. "Where's Troy?" she asked, her eyes darting from Nola's face to Ron's. "Is he dead?"

Turning her back on Cordelia, Nola stomped off toward the kitchen.

With a simple sideways nod of his head, Ron told Vann to put Cordelia out just as he followed quietly behind Nola.

"Tell me! Is Troy dead?" she asked again, starting to go behind Ron.

Vann quickly grabbed Cordelia's arm, but this time, his hold was a grip. "Let's go," he said, pulling her to the door.

She spun around. "He is dead, isn't he?"

"Just go."

"Oh my God. What happened?"

"Cordelia," Vann said, slowly but firmly pushing her across the threshold out onto the stoop, into the frigid snowy night, "don't come back." He closed the door in her face and double-bolted it. With his back up against the door, Vann puffed up his cheeks and let the air ooze out between his lips. He hoped that that was the last they'd ever see of her—she was no good for Meika or his parents. They'd never deal with her now that Troy was gone.

On the other side of the door, Cordelia raised her fist to bang on the door, but changed her mind. Her hand stopped only inches away. Instead, she squinted at the door as if she could see right through the thick mahogany wood. She suddenly about-faced. Grasping the sides of her hat, she pulled it back down over her forehead, and then gripping the handrail, stepped gingerly down the stairs to the walkway. She glanced back and glimpsed Vann looking at her from behind the drapes. Sneering at him, she shouted, "You can't keep her from me!"

Cordelia stalked off, leaving her tracks in the fresh snow and her words hanging in the frigid air.

TWELVE

HE snow let up enough for Vann to catch his flight back to Atlanta to spend New Year's Eve with Michelle and his children.

Nola and Ron knew that Vann had left them better off than when he came and, more important, left them eager for his return. It wasn't easy for Ron to admit that he needed Vann to lean on—it wasn't the manly thing to do. What he did say was "I'm not quite myself yet." And that Nola knew to be true — neither of them was. The new year was upon them and they hadn't even bothered to make New Year's resolutions. Their hearts weren't in it. They used to make a game of it, and throughout the year, the one who kept most of his or her resolutions was taken out to dinner. This year Nola had no reason to celebrate New Year's Eve or to prepare for the year to come as she had done in the past. As far back as she could remember, she had done what her mother and her mother's mother had done in the hope of having luck and prosperity in the new year—she washed up all the dirty clothes, put clean sheets on all the beds, baked a ham, made corn bread, cooked up a mess of collard greens, a pot of black-eyed peas, a pan of macaroni and cheese, a slew of pigs' feet, and a little pot of chitterlings to satisfy Ron; he was the only one who liked them. She had long ago forgotten what each dish or chore was supposed to symbolize, but she concluded that none of those things kept

Troy from getting killed, proving that they were nothing more than old wives' tales. If she had a resolution at all, it was to never believe in old wives' tales again.

Only because of Meika did Nola make an effort to do anything at all. Together, out in the front yard, they made a snowman. Meika called him Mister Bobo.

Ron wasn't much fun, which didn't surprise her. He came out to shovel the stoop, the walkway, and the front sidewalk, but ended up with lower-back pain before he made it out to the sidewalk. After Ron crept back into the house in search of the heating pad, Nola picked up the shovel and pushed the snow from the sidewalk into the gutter. She had never had to help shovel snow before, not with two boys and a husband in the house. When Troy moved back home, he had done all the shoveling. Shoveling snow was the least of missing Troy. Seeing Ron sitting alone watching football without Troy for the first time in years was another reminder that he was truly gone.

Vann took a few weeks to straighten out his business and was back by the end of the third week in January, time enough to help Ron shovel the mounds of snow piled up in the driveway. The day he got back he was rived up about getting on with finding Troy's murderer, but they hadn't taken into consideration the bad weather. There was a great possibility that nothing of any significance would be learned about Troy's death with people off the streets, hibernating inside their warm homes. As crowded and as well-worn the sidewalks, the streets, and the stoops of Brooklyn are in the summer, they were as barren and deserted in the winter. It was one thing to ask questions of people when they were out and about, but another when they were cozily tucked away in their homes after they had pushed against the stinging wind, or trudged through the snow thinking only of getting in out of the cold. Most people might not want to be bothered by questions, and as badly as they wanted answers, in good conscience, they couldn't bring themselves to bother anyone, especially in the preten-tiously upscale neighborhood of Brooklyn Heights.

"We might have to wait till spring," Nola said.

Vann wasn't the least bit dissuaded by the weather. "I'll make up flyers and pass them around," he said, easily remedy-ing their apprehension about intruding by using Troy's com-puter to make up a flyer:

> *Did you see Ronald Troy Kirkwood, Jr., on Saturday, Octo-ber 29, 1994?*
>
> *He was last seen at 3:30 P.M. on Henry Street between Orange and Cranberry.*
>
> *Did you hear a car alarm on any surrounding streets on October 29?*
>
> *Did you see his car? A black, 4-door, Nissan Maxima, New York license plate #CBA 434?*
>
> *Did you see the person or persons who may have shut off the alarm or driven the Nissan Maxima?*
>
> *Please call Vann Kirkwood, (718) 555-1234.*
>
> *All calls are confidential.*

The top half of the flyer had a picture of Troy, smiling, looking so full of life.

Vann spent hours in the Heights, mostly by himself, some-times with Ron, and sometimes with his boyhood friend, James, slipping flyers in mailboxes, mail slots, under doors, under windshield wipers; and with store owners' or superin-tendents' permission, on storefront windows or in stacks in lobbies. The telephone number on the flyer was Troy's and since Vann slept in his room, it was convenient for him to take the calls. However, no calls came, and the few messages left on the answering machine, every now and then, were from friends who didn't know that Troy had passed. But Vann wasn't letting the fact that no one was responding to his flyers stop him. He requested a meeting with Detective Lopez for himself and Ron.

"Detective, I need to clarify some points of confusion my family and I have," he said, opening up his own notebook of facts about Troy's killing and flipping the pages until he found what he was looking for. "First off, we know that my brother disappeared on the twenty-ninth of October, a Saturday, and was found on November first, a Tuesday."

"Correct."

"The coroner put the time of death at Monday evening—"

"Yes, between the hours of eight and midnight."

Ron glanced down at Vann's notes as he put a check mark next to the time.

"The autopsy showed that my brother was shot in the face and in the chest, but it was the shot in the chest that actually killed him—the bullet tore through his heart."

Detective Lopez eyed Vann suspiciously. "That's right," he confirmed, his hand resting on top of the case file.

"Okay," Vann said, skimming his notes. Looking up, he glanced at Ron, then looked steadily at Detective Lopez. "Detective, we thought that Troy was killed in his car because he was shot in the face in the backseat, which was evidenced by the splatter of brain tissue and bone fragments on the backseat where he was found, but . . ."

Clearing his throat, Ron lowered his eyes.

". . . but because there was very little blood from the wound, it was determined that he was shot in the chest somewhere else, and then put back in the car. How did they come to that conclusion?"

Again, eyeing Vann suspiciously, Detective Lopez flipped open his case file. Taking his time, he studied some of the pages.

Vann glanced once more at Ron and saw that he was looking down at his tightly clasped hands. Vann laid his hand lightly, but briefly, on Ron's forearm to assure him that everything was all right.

Detective Lopez used his tongue to move the gum in his mouth against his right cheek. "The victim—"

"Troy," Vann corrected.

Looking up from his file, Detective Lopez moved his wad of gum to the other side of his mouth. He gave Vann an irksome look before looking down again. "For the record," he began, "it was determined that Troy Kirkwood died elsewhere because of the small amount of blood found in the car. There was no blood flow from the chest wound on the seat or on the floor of the car, and no blood on the blanket thrown across his body, despite the fact that his sweater was soaked with dried blood, which means he could not have been shot in the chest in the car. We know that he was shot in the face in the car at close range because of the soot on his face, and because of the brain tissue and bone fragments on the seat, and because of the bullet dug out of the seat cushion. From that wound, there was no coagulation of blood, and the amount of blood was minute."

Sick to his stomach, Vann pushed on. "What size gun was used?"

"Thirty-eight."

"Damn," Vann said, writing that down in his notes.

Ron pressed his fingertips hard into the backs of his hands. "If Troy was already dead after being shot in the chest, why did they have to shoot him in the face and blow out his brains?"

"Maliciousness, plain and simple," Vann answered.

"Sir, why a killer goes that extra mile has often baffled us. We can only guess that the person who killed your son either wanted to make sure he was dead or was attempting to disfigure him perhaps to throw a wrench in identifying him."

"Like I said, malicious."

"But why disfigure him?" Ron asked. "His fingerprints told who he was."

"Yes, perhaps it was a delay tactic. That's why the perp took the time to remove the license plate and scratch off the registration sticker and the vehicle identification number. Remember, all personal identification was missing."

"I hate that they took his ring," Ron said.

Vann took note of that. "You talkin' 'bout that gold eagle Troy designed and had specially made?"

Detective Lopez began writing.

"Yeah," Ron said. "He talked about getting one made up for your birthday this year."

Vann's nose suddenly stung. That was just like Troy to do something like that. Troy often did that with things he especially liked, which is why the two of them had matching money clips, watches, cuff links, and tiepins.

"Was there anything distinctive about the ring?" Detective Lopez asked.

"I never saw another one like it," Vann answered. "The wings were delicately cut—"

"Diamond cut," Ron added.

"Yes, diamond cut. The wings spread around the finger from the top, forming the band that came together on the inside of the finger," Vann explained, showing how the wings swept around the finger on his own ringless finger. "The face of the eagle sat on top of the finger and had these half-karat matching diamonds for eyes. His birthstone was an aquamarine or a bloodstone but he didn't like the colors of either one, so he chose the diamond. Remember that, Dad?"

"Yeah, he said they weren't strong enough colors for the eyes of an eagle."

"He was crazy about that ring."

Detective Lopez continued to write. "What size?"

"It fit my finger," Vann said. "It must have been about an eleven. Oh, and it was wide, it covered about half of a joint."

"We'll keep our eyes open for it. We'll check the pawn

shops," Detective Lopez said. "By the way, did you cancel his credit cards and report his registration and license plate as stolen through the Department of Motor Vehicles?"

"We canceled everything that was in his name," Ron said, "and we changed the locks on our house. But there is a problem. There was seventy-five hundred dollars' worth of merchandise charged to my son's credit card after it was canceled."

"Your wife called that info in. You didn't have to pay it, did you?"

"No."

"Good. At this point, until we find the killer, we can't begin to guess his reasons or motives."

"What about other fingerprints?" Vann asked.

"Other than your brother's fingerprints inside the car on the dashboard, the ones outside the car belonged to a meter maid who ticketed the car. There was no trace evidence left by the killer, the car was wiped clean."

Jotting quickly, Vann wrote down everything Detective Lopez said. "According to my notes, you told my father that Troy's car was found down on Furman Street along the East River."

"That's right, about two hundred feet from the corner of Old Fulton Street. His car was parked on the west side of the street next to a fire hydrant."

"See, now, that makes no sense to me," Ron said. "I drove down in that area the same Saturday night Troy was first missing, and I must've drove around down there at least two more times, Sunday and Monday, with Roosevelt before Troy was found. He wasn't down there."

"If you'll recall, sir, it was determined that the victim . . ."

Vann frowned.

". . . uh . . . your son was not killed in his car, not on that night. At this point, we can only guess that he was killed somewhere else and driven back to that site. Besides, if he was down there before Tuesday, he would have been discovered immediately. That's not a legal place to park, the car would have stood out."

"I want to go down and look at Furman Street," Vann said, jotting quickly. "What's down there, factories, shipyards?"

"Not much else, but we've already canvassed the area. No one was around after seven P.M. that night or any night other than a security guard for a building at the start of Furman Street."

"Did you question him?" Vann asked, tapping his finger with the pen.

"He saw nothing. The car was reported by an alert officer. No one else paid any particular attention to the car—there are no witnesses."

Vann pointed his pen at Detective Lopez. "I bet that guard saw something that night, he just didn't know what it was."

Detective Lopez's annoyance with Vann grew. He stood. "Like I said a minute ago, the guard saw nothing. The car was parked fifty feet away from the glass door he sat in front of. Unless he had a periscope attached to his glasses, he didn't see a damn thing beyond that door. Don't go down there bothering him. And as for those piers, they're locked up tight after seven—no one walks down there, it's off the beaten path. It's possibly one of the most isolated stretches of Brooklyn at night."

"Look, Detective," Vann said, not satisfied. "For three days, Troy was held somewhere. He disappeared in the Heights, his body was found in the Heights, so he was probably held in the Heights. Someone—"

"That may not necessarily be the case, Mr. Kirkwood. However, when we find out the where, hopefully we'll find out the who."

"Can't your forensic pathologist determine from fibers on

Troy's clothes or under his shoes where he might have been held?"

Detective Lopez chuckled. "I see all those cop shows are making armchair detectives of civilians."

"Hey. I'm just trying to find my brother's killer."

"Mr. Kirkwood, a forensics expert is working on this case. We're doing all we can to find your bother's killer, but without a witness and no evidence, unless someone comes forward, we may not find a killer. That is a real possibility. For now, the question is whether this was a random killing or a hit. Although your brother's wallet was stolen, we've ruled out robbery as a primary motive."

"Why?"

"The car was left behind."

"Well, it wasn't like it was a Mercedes or Jag," Vann remarked.

"Nowadays, it could have been a Volkswagen Beetle and it would have been taken. Did your brother have enemies?"

"Not that we know of, except maybe his ex-wife."

"What's her name?"

"Cordelia Kirkwood."

Detective Lopez jotted down Cordelia's name on the outer cover of the case file. "Where can we find her?"

"Who knows. Anyway, it might be a waste of time talking to her, she says that she just got back in town."

"We'll see. What did your brother do for a living?"

"He was Assistant Director of Customer Service at American Express."

"Legit job. Was he involved in anything illegal on the side?"

Glaring at him, Vann retorted, "Are you?"

Though he stopped writing, Detective Lopez didn't look up. He chomped down on his gum and stabbed the case file once with the point of the pen. "Mr. Kirkwood, when we know where your bother was killed, who killed him, and why he was killed, you will know. Until then, I suggest you let us do our job."

"Hey, if you're not getting anywhere, then—"

Ron leaned toward Vann and whispered, "Let up." Then to Detective Lopez he said, "My son has never been dirty. He was as legit as they come. I hope you understand that we're trying to make sure that his case does not get pushed to the bottom of the pile."

Detective Lopez looked up. "Believe me, sir, you can trust that every effort is being made to—"

"No, Detective," Vann said. "I cannot trust that every effort is being made. In this precinct alone, this case is just one of maybe, what . . . maybe hundreds?"

"All cases are thoroughly investigated, but to be honest, we may not be able to solve this case."

"Why not?" Ron demanded.

"Sir, there are no witnesses once Troy Kirkwood left the theater. There is no motive, no suspects, no trace evidence. In other words, no leads."

Vann frowned. "How many murder cases do you have, Detective?"

"Like I said, all cases are thoroughly investigated."

"I'm not doubting that, but this is the only case that is important to me. I have a vested interest in doing my own investigation, Troy was my brother."

"And my son," Ron added.

"I understand that, but neither of you are authorized to conduct your own investigation."

"Who can stop us? Is there a law against it?"

Detective Lopez shoved his chair back with the back of his leg, almost knocking it over. "What is it with this family?" he asked, looking at Ron. "First you jumped on my back, then your wife, now your son. Why can't you people be like other families?"

"And how's that?" Ron asked, standing.

"Mourn. Go back to your life. Let us do our job. Believe it or not, Mr. Kirkwood, we have been known to apprehend a murderer or two without the help of family members who don't know their ass from their elbow. I mean, what is it with you people?"

Vann closed his notebook and sat back. "For the record, Detective, *us people* do know our ass from our elbow. In fact, we even know when to wipe our ass. If you have a problem with me questioning you, then you need to get your ass off of this case."

"Hold up," Ron said, touching Vann's shoulder.

"Mr. Kirkwood, I don't know who you people think you are, but there are rules and procedures that—"

"Detective," Ron said coolly, "you and I have been down that road before. Those rules and procedures don't mean a damn thing if they don't result in answers, and so far, three months have gone by and we know nothing more today than we were told the day you found my son's body."

"Mr. Kirkwood, it takes time to investigate a murder."

"If there is no suspect, I'm sure it does, and I've heard the longer there is no suspect, the less likely one will ever be found. Maybe if my son had been a celebrity or a white man—"

"I was trying not to say that, Dad, but—"

"Just a damn minute!" Detective Lopez said. "Are you implying that we're sitting on this case? That we don't consider this case just as important as any other?"

"Implying?" Vann asked.

Detective Lopez started toward the door, but suddenly turned back. He went back to the table. It was Vann he addressed. "Maybe you need to take a good look at me, partner. I don't come from a rich family. I had to fight my way out of Brownsville. My knuckles were raw and bloody from having to protect myself day in and day out. Nobody did me any favors. I had to put myself through two years of college. I walked those same mean streets of Brownsville as a rookie and arrested old friends and enemies alike. On the force, white cops treated me no differently from many of the perps they arrested. I had it tough, coming and going. I'm not impressed by celebrity or the color of a man's skin. I work just as hard on a homeless person's case as I do on a rich man's. When they're both murdered, they're both going six feet under, whether it's Potter's Field or Heavenly Acres, they're both covered in dirt. In my book, dead is dead, and for your information, your brother's file has been on top of my desk since day one. Before either of you judge me, know what you're talking about."

Vann looked at Ron and saw that Ron looked a mite contrite, but he wasn't in the least. "Detective, everyone has a sad tale to fall back on. Maybe if you had kept us informed of what you were doing, we wouldn't be up in your face, my brother."

"What my son is saying, Detective, is that in our eagerness to find out why Troy was murdered, we might be a little overbearing, but we will solve this case."

Detective Lopez snorted. "Did you say a little overbearing?"

Vann couldn't help but smile. He wouldn't want to be the detective on this case with someone like him and his father looking over his shoulder. He had no qualms about making mincemeat of Lopez, that is, if he wasn't taking care of business. Lopez was on notice that if he didn't actively look for Troy's killer, he would ride him like a tailgater until the deed was done.

"Well, Detective," Ron said, "you should understand that my son was and *is* important enough to us for us to not sit back and wait for scraps of information. We're going after the whole enchilada ourselves and if we find out something you don't know, we'll pass it on, like we hope you'll do in turn. We don't plan on working against you, but if we have to work alone, we will."

Vann nodded his approval. It felt good to have his father back.

Detective Lopez fixed his gaze on Vann. "If you don't mind my asking, Mr. Kirkwood, what do you do for a living?"

"Me? CPA and financial adviser."

"That explains it."

"*It*, meaning?"

"*It*, explains why you keep your own notes and question me like I'm a rookie, like you know my job better than me."

"Maybe I do."

Ron put his hand down heavily on Vann's shoulder.

Throwing up his hands, Vann chuckled.

"Mr. Kirkwood, maybe you should stick with assets and liabilities, the streets don't play with amateurs. You could get hurt."

"Maybe you need to learn more about assets and liabilities, Detective," Vann said, reopening his notebook. "They're not for amateurs either. A man could lose his shirt and maybe even his life if he's not careful."

Ron agreed with a slight nod.

"That's not the same thing."

"Don't bet on it, but let me tell you something about numbers. No matter what's done with numbers, there's always a result, unlike what's happening in this case."

"If you people would—"

"*We* people are not about to leave this case to chance, and since it would be better if we worked together, do you mind telling us what we should be looking for?"

Dropping his head forward, Detective Lopez closed his eyes, and exhaled loudly.

Ron and Vann glanced at each other and then back at Detective Lopez as he began raising his head.

Slowly chewing his gum, he eyeballed Vann. "You're a hard brother."

THIRTEEN

Vann's methodically aggressive inquisition of Detective Lopez didn't surprise Nola a bit. It would have surprised her if he hadn't been aggressive. As it was, he had been one of those "why" kids who drove her up a wall mostly because she couldn't answer some of his questions. Who in the world knows why birds were given wings so that they could fly and people and dogs weren't? She had tried to tell Vann that people and dogs were too big to fly, but he came back with "Worms and mice aren't." Sometimes he made her want to pull her hair out. That's how she and Ron came to buy him and Troy their first set of encyclopedias. Whenever Vann had a question after that, he searched through a volume or two on his own. His methodical nature apparently came from his affection for numbers, which he developed way back when he was ten and realized that as heavy as the gallon bottle of pennies he'd saved was, once rolled up into fifty-cent rolls, it didn't add up to the twenty dollars he needed to buy the Converse All Stars sneakers he wanted. From that day on, he saved only quarters or dollar bills and kept a ledger of every quarter or dollar bill he dropped in his bottle. He was born to be an accountant. When the $100,000 insurance benefit from Troy's job came, Vann was all business. He immediately invested $50,000 in stocks, $25,000 in mutual funds, and $25,000 he split between a money market account and a savings account so that Nola could have ready access for Meika's needs. The monthly $600 Social Security stipend that came in for Meika he put in a separate checking account for daily use. Every account was in Nola's name, but every penny was for Meika's upbringing and education. Although she could have set up the accounts herself, she let Vann handle it because he was good at setting his emotions apart from the task at hand. Surely she would have cried somewhere along the way.

The fact that Vann was so analytical and always had such a cool head was all the more reason she was glad he came back to help them find out why Troy was killed. He would leave no stone unturned and he would stay on the case and not be overwhelmed by the emotional loss as she and Ron were.

Odd that for so long she used to think Vann insensitive, maybe even a little callous, but now, seeing the sacrifice he was willingly making for Troy, she realized that he was just not one to carry his emotions on his sleeve. And funny how life is, she used to complain about Vann's take-charge nature. In fact, secretly, she called him bossy and a know-it-all. It was Ron who defended Vann and boasted about how swift he was. As well he should, he was boasting about his own creation. Like Vann said, "I am the man you raised."

Because Vann was there, Ron was able to go off to work every morning confident that Vann would follow up on Detective Lopez's suggestion that they figure out what Troy did every minute of the day he disappeared. Time and again Nola and Ron could remember only that they all had breakfast together, that she had gone off to the dentist, and that Ron had gone off to play golf while Troy took Meika to the movies.

But Vann repeatedly questioned that. "Are you sure Troy stayed home after breakfast until he was ready to go to the movies?"

"I think so," she said, though there was something nagging at her that never would make itself known.

"Ma, are you sure? Could he have gone out after you left?"

"I don't remember."

In the kitchen Meika scooped up the last of her chicken noodle soup. She ran her tongue along her lips, sucking in the last of the broth. Then leaving her bowl on the table, she carried her spoon with her into the living room. "Mama, can I have some ice cream?"

"What do you say when you ask for something?"

Meika put the spoon in her mouth and, still with her mouth wide open, she smiled.

"You know what to say," Nola coached.

Meika's eyes suddenly lit up. She took the spoon out of her mouth. "Please!"

"Good girl," she said, smiling. "Meika, you're the only little girl in the world that eats ice cream behind chicken noodle soup."

"You always say that."

"That's because—" she caught herself. She stared at Meika. They'd had the very same conversation that fateful day while she was waiting for Troy to come back from his errand. She gave Meika chicken noodle soup for lunch, and afterward, Meika asked for ice cream. How could she have forgotten?

Vann noticed the pensive gaze in Nola's eyes. "Ma, you remember something?"

Putting the spoon back in her mouth, Meika returned Nola's stare.

"Ma?"

Nola had gone back to that Saturday morning breakfast when Troy was talking about his plans for the day.

"Ma?"

Snapping out of her daze, Nola looked at Vann. "Let me get Meika some ice cream first," she said, pushing herself up off the sofa. "Vanilla or chocolate?"

"Both!" Meika exclaimed, pivoting and skipping ahead of Nola back into the kitchen.

Pensively, Nola washed out the same bowl the soup had been in. Troy had gone uptown to Eighty-second Street and Fifth Avenue to meet someone. Who could it have been?

"Mama," Meika said, turning in her chair.

"Huh?"

"Knock-knock."

"Who's there?"

"Bugs."

"Bugs who?"

"Bugs Bunny Rabbit," Meika replied, covering her mouth and giggling.

Nola laughed on cue. That one she had heard at least twenty times. "You got me that time," she said.

It was heartwarming to see that Meika was still able to tell jokes and laugh, and until she laughed, Nola had almost forgotten how good laughter felt.

"I get you all the time," Meika said, smiling broadly.

"Yes you do, and that was such a good one, I'm going to give you a big scoop of vanilla and a big scoop of chocolate."

"Yeah!" Meika said, clapping her hands.

"Yeah, and?"

"And . . . thank you."

"You're welcome."

An equal scoop of vanilla and chocolate ice cream each is what Meika got—no bigger, no smaller than her usual serving, and for a minute Nola stayed and watched how Meika scooped a smidgen of vanilla ice cream onto the tip of her spoon before dipping the spoon into the chocolate ice cream and taking the same amount onto the spoon. Only then did she slowly glide the spoon into her mouth and roll the cool ice cream around on her tongue before swallowing, all the while alternately swinging her legs back and forth under the table, just like Troy used to do when he was a child. Through Meika, Troy still lived. Smiling to herself, Nola couldn't help but marvel at the little things that made Meika happy; and who knows, the gift Cordelia brought for her in the red and gold box might have made her just as happy, but she'd never know. It was dumped in the garbage long before Meika came home, and she saw no need to tell her that Cordelia had even been there.

"When you finish, put your bowl in the sink, okay?"

"Okay."

"Your daddy used to eat his ice cream like that when he was a little boy, too."

"I know. He told me that," Meika said, sadly. "Mama, I still miss Daddy."

"I know, baby," she said, reaching over and gently stroking Meika's left cheek. "I miss him, too, but remember, I told you that your daddy is always going to be with you. Like right now, every time you eat your ice cream, he smiles and enjoys it just as much as you do."

Meika smiled as she slowly eased her spoon up the side of the chocolate ice cream. "Then I'm gonna eat real slow so he can smile for a long time."

Nola teared. She quickly left the kitchen so that Meika would not see her. She went back to the grim task that awaited her in the living room. Vann was watching the evening news; he muted the sound when she sat down.

"I feel so beat," she said, rubbing the back of her neck.

"When this is all over, Ma, you and Dad should get away for a few weeks. Michelle and I can take Meika whenever you like."

"Maybe," she said, looking at the television.

Taking his notebook off the coffee table, Vann crossed his leg, held his pen at the ready, and said nothing, not wanting to rush her.

Nola collected her thoughts. "During breakfast that morning, Troy said that he had to run an errand. I don't know how I forgot that."

"Stress. Did he say what that errand was?"

"No, he didn't, but he said he had to meet someone at the Met."

Vann raised his brow. "The opera? Is it open on Saturday mornings?"

"It wasn't the opera, it was the museum."

"Oh. I was wondering, because Troy was tone deaf. He was the only brother in school that couldn't pop his fingers in sync with the music."

Nola chuckled. "Yes, I remember he came home one day upset because somebody said he must have had some white genes tucked away somewhere. He asked me if we had any white people in our family."

Though Nola chuckled, Vann thought it was the saddest chuckle he'd ever heard.

"When I told him not to my knowledge, he got even more upset. He said, 'Boy, I don't even got an excuse!' " She remembered how much having no ear for music bothered Troy. He couldn't sing along with the popular tunes and, worse, he couldn't dance a lick. He used to say the only good thing about being tone deaf was that he didn't waste his money on albums. Of course she knew it was a ploy to cover up how bad he really felt because he used to watch Ron dance to his soul music, and Vann his rock music, with a look of yearning in his eyes.

Nola glanced at the news anchor's lips moving. He looked so austere when, according to the picture insert over his right shoulder, he was talking about a cat stuck up a tree and rescued by the local fire department. The anchor had the same look on his face when he reported that Troy had been found dead in his car. Then, that look was justified.

"Ma, do you know who Troy met at the museum?"

She looked away from the television. "No, he didn't say who he was meeting or why. Do you think there's a connection?"

"I don't know, but if there is, we need to know who he met with."

"How in the world can we find that out?"

Slowly shaking his head, Vann replied, "I don't know."

Neither one said anything as they pondered the problem. Vann shook his foot, Nola slowly twirled a strand of hair above her ear around her finger. She suddenly stopped. "Vann, the last time I was at the museum, I didn't sign in at the door, but I had to sign in when I went to a specific gallery."

Popping his fingers, Vann snapped to attention. "That's it! I remember having to sign in myself a few times. What I could do is go there and, hopefully, find out if Troy visited any area that required a signature."

"Will they let you have access to their sign-in books?"

"Maybe not me, but they'll give it to the police. I'll call Detective Lopez," he said, springing up off the sofa and going to the telephone in Ron's den.

Alone, Nola prayed that Troy had signed in and so had the person he went there to meet. She looked up as Vann came back into the room. "What did he say?"

"He wasn't there. I left a message."

"Now we wait," she said, again massaging the back of her neck. "I wonder if the animal that killed Troy ever thinks about him."

"I would think that a person who kills, kills to satisfy some sick need or kills to solve a problem. In other words, Troy's killer doesn't think about him. He satisfied his need and he solved his problem."

"Oh, Vann, is it as cut and dry as that?"

"I think it is. See, I know there are evil men in this world, I just wonder why God lets them live so that they can kill, maim, rape, and do just about anything they want without repercussion for so long, if ever."

"I don't know if it's so much that God lets men do evil, as it is that he sometimes has a hands-off approach. What we keep forgetting, Vann, is that God gave Lucifer dominion over earth when he kicked him out of heaven."

"I remember something about that from when you used to

send me and Troy to Bible study. Lucifer used to be an angel, right?"

"According to the Bible, he was the most beautiful, the most intelligent, the most perfect, and the most powerful angel in heaven, and was second only to God. But that wasn't good enough, he wanted to be equal to God himself."

"So, like man, a little power went to his head. He started tripping. That's a sin, right?"

"Seems so. God didn't like it. Lucifer caused an insurrection amongst the angels. He got some angels to side with him and went up against God's rule of heaven."

Vann turned his whole body toward Nola. "If God was all-powerful, why did he let the rebellion happen? Why didn't he stop it?"

"I guess he could have, if he wanted to," Nola conceded. She remembered that Vann had asked her that same question when he first heard the story. "Maybe God wanted to see how far Lucifer would go, or maybe He wanted to show the other angels what the end result of vanity and sin would be."

"Sooo, that's when Lucifer was kicked out of heaven."

"That's when there was war in heaven and Lucifer and the angels that sided with him were cast out onto the earth. That's when Lucifer became known as Satan and took evil as his god. His only purpose is to get revenge against God by wreaking evil on man and causing man to sin and turn his back on God."

"So God knows that. So how is it that Satan can do what he wants at will?"

"Because he has dominion over earth; and because he has the same power, intelligence, and beguiling ways he had in heaven; and as you know, he's good at what he does. It doesn't hurt that he has plenty of human henchmen at his command."

"In other words, we don't really have a chance?"

"Well, if we keep God in our hearts, we do. But remember, He gave us free will. The person that killed Troy didn't have to do the evil that Satan tempted him with. He had a choice."

"So we're back where we started, Ma. Why didn't God intervene and save Troy? All the time there are reports of people who should have died and didn't. And people say, 'It was a miracle, the hand of God saved him,' or 'There was divine intervention.' Why not divine intervention for Troy?"

Nola shrugged her shoulders. Again, a question she couldn't answer. As much as she knew about the Lord, she didn't know how He decided who was worthy of being saved. What she did know, was that to question God was to leave oneself open for Satan to slither in. She had to keep the faith for her own salvation, yet, like Vann, she had questioned, why Troy? "Vann, I can only tell you like my mother told me; God calls us home when it's time, and only He knows when that time is."

Riiiing!

"I'll get it," Vann said, quickly standing. "But I don't believe that, Ma. I believe Satan blindsides God sometimes when He's busy elsewhere and snatches lives for the fun of it."

Riiiing!

Vann rushed off into the den.

Nola had never looked at it like that before; Satan was sneaky, but wasn't God on top of everything? If it was Troy's time, she prayed that in that time between life and death, he didn't suffer, that his death was swift, that God held his hand. If He didn't, why didn't He? Oh, Lord, if she didn't stop, she'd drive herself insane trying to figure out the forces of good and evil, something that was best left to the church.

"Hey," Ron said, stamping his feet on the mat in the entryway.

"I didn't hear you come in. How was your day?"

Ron didn't bother to take off his coat or his boots. He crossed to the chair opposite the sofa and sat down heavily.

Seeing the droop of his mouth and how angry his eyes were, Nola started to worry. "What's wrong? What happened?"

Ron raised the folded paper in his hand. "I was just given this outside. It's a summons."

"For what?"

"Cordelia is taking us to Family Court for—"

"No!" Nola bolted up off the sofa. "She can't have Meika! I won't let her!"

"Mama, who can't have me?"

Nola whirled around and faced Meika. She certainly wasn't going to tell Meika that Cordelia was back, not when it had hurt her when Cordelia left her in a drug den alone the last time she had her for a court-ordered visit. Nola fought to calm herself. She concentrated on her breathing. When she thought that she could speak calmly, she said, "The bogeyman."

Right away she could see that, unintentionally, she had frightened Meika. Meika's eyes grew wide and she immediately went over to Ron and began to climb up onto his lap. With one hand he helped her up. Still wide-eyed and looking at Nola, Meika rested her head back against Ron's chest. His arms encircled her. Since Troy died, Meika turned to Ron for that masculine strength she sorely missed.

Going over to Meika and bending down to her, Nola kissed her on the cheek. "I'm sorry. I didn't mean to scare you."

Ron gave Meika a little squeeze. "You know me and Mama wouldn't let the bogeyman get our baby."

Meika turned her head slightly and looked up at Ron. "You'll beat him up?"

"I sure will. Then the police will come and put him in jail for a long, long time."

"Good," Meika said, softly, seeming to relax. "My daddy say the bogeyman is bad and he's gonna beat him up if he bother me, but he's not here no more."

Ron and Nola looked at each other. It hadn't crossed either of their minds that Meika might be feeling vulnerable, unprotected, since Troy died. Nola was more determined than ever to keep not just the bogeyman away from Meika, but the bogeywoman, too.

FOURTEEN

VANN was beginning to think that maybe he had missed his true calling. Maybe he should have gone on the police force after college so that he could have become a detective; maybe by now he would be a captain or a commissioner. Then again, *maybe* had always connoted indecisiveness, and indecisive he was not. He had decided on accounting as a career and, at this point, he wouldn't give it up for anything in the world. Yet it was odd that he was investigating Troy's death with such ease, almost like it was second nature to him. Lopez certainly would not agree with him on that. He probably thought he was the biggest wart he'd ever had on his ass. At the end of their last meeting two weeks ago, Lopez was highly annoyed with him and ordered him to stay away from the museum until he obtained a warrant and looked into the possibility of Troy having signed in that day. Only because his father told him to, he'd sit back for half a minute and let Lopez do the job he said was his. However, if Lopez took too long to do his job, he'd find a way to get a look at the museum's sign-in books on his own—there was always a way.

With so much time on his hands, for a second time Vann tore Troy's room apart looking for clues. He had hoped that Troy had written down appointments he kept outside of his office, especially for that fateful Saturday—he hadn't. Not even a slip of paper was found with a note about whom he was meeting. When Troy was found, his pockets were empty of everything, except a chocolate bar. His mother would never know that.

With nothing to go on, the flyers were their only hope. Meanwhile, Vann's days were spent in front of his computer doing work for his clients—adjusting trial balances, checking stock quotes and options, reconciling bank accounts, closing the books for the past year; and talking alternately with his office and with Michelle. As the weeks passed, he sensed her irritability with him.

"The kids miss you."

"I miss them, too," he said, wondering about her. "Do you miss me?"

Michelle said nothing.

"That's a hard question, huh?"

She sucked her teeth. "Don't start, Vann, I'm at work."

With the cordless telephone in his hand, Vann sprang up off the bed. He rushed to the bedroom door and pushed it closed, softly, making sure that the lock clicked. "Michelle, I wouldn't have to start if you acted like my being gone meant more to you than being free of one of your migraines."

"Goddamnit," she whispered, harshly, "Vann, you made the decision to go back to New York. You didn't care what the hell I thought, and not for one minute did you care whether I needed you at home or not. So don't badger me about whether or not I miss you, worry about what you're doing."

"I asked you if you minded if I—"

"No, you told me you were going back. Telling and asking are not the same, Vann."

Vann began to pace. "I know the difference, and I know I asked you."

"Forget it. It doesn't matter. Besides, you'd do anything to please your mother, and now that Troy is gone you got her all to yourself."

That stung. "Michelle, did you sit up all night trying to figure out how to get back at me? How to make my life miserable? You're the one that seems to be pissed because you and my mother don't have a relationship."

"I don't care."

"Oh, you care. But if she were to ever hear you say crap like that, you can forget about her liking you."

"Hey, I don't need your mother. You're the one that seems to still need her milk."

"Keep it up, Michelle. You're doing a good job pissing me off," he snarled.

In Vann's ear, Michelle's breathing sounded like a steam engine. He didn't know who was breathing harder, he or she. He waited for her to say something, anything, because he was afraid of what he might say.

"You know something, Vann? Personally, I think you're using Troy's death as an excuse to get away from the problems we're having."

Pressing his lips together, he again rushed to the door. This time, he eased it open and, sticking his head out, peeked up and down the hall. Seeing no one, he again closed it, softly, and went over to the window.

"Vann. Vann, are you there?"

"Tell me, Michelle. Other than my mother, what are our problems?"

"Play dumb all you want, but for one thing, you keeping secrets that I feel compromise our relationship is a problem, a big one."

"I am not going to talk about this stupidness."

"Well, I am," Michelle said. "If what you're keeping to yourself potentially affects me, I should know about it."

"Damnit, Michelle. I tell you everything you need to know."

"Really? Then I need to know why you have a safe-deposit box that I can't have a key to."

Vann hit the side of the window frame. "If it concerned you, Michelle, you'd have a key. I have clients that I must maintain a high level of privacy for that has nothing to do with you."

"Think again, smarty. Some of those clients call the house, making it my business to know their business. If you don't want me to know, tell them not to call my house."

He was so tired of this argument, he wanted to put his fist through the window. The telephone calls and his stupid mistake of leaving the keys on the bed once while he took a shower left him with one argument after another with Michelle. First she accused him of seeing another woman, then she accused him of keeping secrets. The first accusation she couldn't prove and was unfounded, the second was none of her business. No matter what his explanation, she was never going to be satisfied.

"Look," he said, switching gears, "aren't the kids out of school Monday for Presidents' Day?"

"Like every year."

Ignoring the sarcasm, Vann plunged ahead. "Why don't you bring them up? I'll pay for the airline tickets from this end."

"Oh, you want me to come, too?"

"Michelle! Damnit! If you had come with me like I asked you to, we could have been together all along."

"Why should I disrupt my life and the lives of my children just because you say so? What I don't understand is why you're so willing to disrupt your life as well as ours."

"For your information, it's called family. Instead of sitting there bitching at me, maybe you should figure out what the hell that means."

"Screw you, Vann! Me and my kids are supposed to be your family, too, although you haven't bothered to give me your last name."

"That's the real problem, isn't it?"

"Don't flatter yourself, though I should be grateful that you let me put Kirkwood on my children's birth certificates."

Vann wanted to put his fist through the wall. He could feel the veins pulsate in his neck. "Michelle, let it go."

"Don't tell me what to do. You don't have the right. And since I'm not your wife, Vann, why should I give up my job and my life here to follow behind you while you try and track down your brother's killer?"

Nola began climbing the stairs to the second floor.

"Michelle, you're wrong and you know it. I'd be doing the same thing for you if it had been your sister."

"Don't do me any favors," she snapped. "I wouldn't want you out there playing Sherlock Holmes for me, any more than I want you out there now."

"I'm not playing Sherlock Holmes, I—"

"Yes you are, Vann. Wake up!"

"Goddamnit, Michelle! You don't ever support anything I do."

Stunned, Nola stopped herself from knocking on the bedroom door. She tilted her head toward the door and listened.

"Why the hell do you always have to bitch about things I need to do? I'm doing what any man would do if a member of his family was killed."

"Not any man, Vann. You. You got this superman complex that you have to put your two cents in and show everybody how smart you are."

"So that's what you think about me?"

"No, that's what you think about yourself. Believe it or not, Vann, there are people who can do what you're trying to do, even better. In case you don't know who they are, they're called cops. Let them look for Troy's killer, that's what they're paid for. Why don't you come home and try taking care of your children?"

"Get off my goddamn back! You take care of the children."

Alarmed, Nola placed her hand over her heart.

"Don't yell at me! I don't have to keep taking this shit from you. Me and my kids can do fine without you, you're not here anyway."

Vann yanked the receiver from his ear. Clenching his teeth and working his jaw hard, he squeezed the receiver, trying to strangle it. He didn't need this shit. His relationship with Michelle was getting worse. Maybe they were better off apart. He brought the receiver back to his ear.

". . . and I don't think you ever did. I don't think you're capable of love."

"Thanks for your usual confidence in me, Michelle. I can always count on you to make me feel like a man."

Nola shook her head sadly. It pained her to know that Vann's relationship with Michelle was in such shambles.

"Vann, don't give me that male castration crap. This is all your fault. Accept it. I'm tired of trying to make you understand my needs. I have work to do. I gotta go."

Vann didn't know which of them hung up first. He took the receiver from his ear and clicked off the talk button. He threw the telephone contemptuously onto the bed. It bounced onto the carpeted floor. After so many years together, their relationship was in no way getting easier. They were arguing more, avoiding each other more, and disliking each other more than they should. Michelle found fault with everything he did and wasted no time criticizing him for it. And, perhaps, he was guilty of that as well, that's why he couldn't marry her. He turned a deaf ear to any urging from her that it was about time they made it legal, but making their union legal might put him in his grave.

Tap . . . tap . . . tap. "Vann?"

He turned away from the window. "Yeah."

Nola opened the door and stuck her head in. "Is everything all right?"

He had hoped that she hadn't heard him talking on the telephone. "Sure," he replied, taking note of the menu in her hand. "What's for dinner?"

She handed him the menu she brought with her. "Chinese. I'm going to call in the order and have Ron pick it up on his way in," she said, trying to not show her own discomfort about the things she overheard. He was hurting and he was trying hard to put on that stone face of his that said he didn't care. She knew better. "Honey, why don't you go home for a few weeks and be with your family?"

"I can't. I don't want to lose any time on this case," he said, studying the menu. Actually, he wasn't sure he had a home to go back to.

"You can pick up where you left off when you get back. Your father will stay on top of things here."

"No, Ma. I will stay on top of this myself. Besides, Lopez might miss me."

Rolling her eyes comically, she said, "I'm sure he will, but if you don't go home, make sure you call Michelle every day."

"I will. I wouldn't want Sharice and Kareem to forget about me."

"What about Michelle?"

He sighed heavily. "Why don't I go pick up the food? What do you, Dad, and Meika want?"

"I have a list right here," she said, handing it to him. It wasn't the first time Vann avoided talking about Michelle. "Vann, if you need to talk, I'm right here."

"I'm fine, Ma," he said, starting for the door. "I'll be back in a little while."

He rushed out of the room before she could press him into talking about his relationship with Michelle. It was just as well, he was feeling bad enough without being reminded that he had been too young to make a commitment to a family. He hadn't waited as she had asked him to and he had lived to regret it. Whether he and Michelle decided to go their separate ways or not, it was going to be his decision alone.

FIFTEEN

THAT flicker of a glint she had seen in Cordelia's eyes when she surmised that Troy was dead should have warned Nola of the trouble Cordelia would cause. If it were at all possible, Troy would claw his way out of his grave if he knew that she had resurfaced and was trying to make a claim on Meika. He had vowed never to let Cordelia get her hands on his child again. Neither Ron nor Vann thought Cordelia had an iota of a chance of getting custody, not with her drug abuse and negligence history, but Nola was worried. Her mother used to say, "There is nothing for certain in life but death," which didn't make much sense to her until she graduated from high school and didn't get the new car her father promised her and that she dreamed of, but rather the ugly, dull, dented used car he could afford. That's why she wasn't counting on nothing going wrong. The fact that a summons was issued at all meant that the court was willing to entertain Cordelia's custody suit and that alone was cause for worry. It wasn't until after they consulted a lawyer that they learned that Troy's custody of Meika, without a will, was no longer valid upon his death, clearing the way for Cordelia to file suit for custody. Second only to news of Troy's death, that was the worst possible news Nola could have gotten.

She had thought that protecting Meika from the ugliness of Troy's death was the toughest thing she'd have to do, but it was nothing compared to protecting her from the ugliness of

Cordelia—the woman was ugly to the bone. Her pretty face and curvaceous body camouflaged a black soul. Troy had been fooled and for a hot minute, so had Ron—but Nola had never been. Not from the moment Cordelia had looked at her like she had scored a coup when she and Troy were caught having sex in his bed two days after they met. If Cordelia had shown some modicum of shame or embarrassment or humility, she might have risen a notch or two in her eyes, but she didn't. She continued sitting astride Troy, keeping him from getting up by holding him down with her hands pushing against his chest, while continuing to slowly move her body like a belly dancer in heat, her gaze steadily on her, and a smirk on her red lips. The scent of her perfume and the muskiness of their sex hung heavy in the room. At that moment Nola not only saw the evil in Cordelia's eyes, she felt it in her soul. Under her feet it felt like the carpeted floor quaked, sending a tremor up her legs. She barely had the strength to whisper, "Get dressed," before she turned on her heels and walked out of the room. Later, though he was harshly scolded, Troy apologized fervently for having sex in her house, but not for having sex with Cordelia.

To her dismay, it didn't much matter to Troy that he was grounded for a month and forbidden to see Cordelia again because, like the alley cat that Cordelia was, she had sprayed Troy and he was hers. Nothing said against Cordelia was ever persuasive enough to keep Troy from wanting her or marrying her. The deed was done.

THE COURT officer turned to the open court and read from the sheet of paper in his hand. "Case number 50643/95—*Kirkwood versus Kirkwood.*"

Mr. Lipscomb stood immediately. "Kirkwood Senior, Respondent, present," he said, indicating with his hand that she and Ron should stand also.

Ron stood up instantly.

As Nola began to stand, Beatrice touched her arm. "I'm praying."

"We'll need it," she said, looking at the judge, who was pouring water from a glass pitcher.

Vann stood to let them pass. "It'll be over before you know it."

"I hope so," Nola said, following behind Mr. Lipscomb and Ron to the front of the courtroom, to the table to the left of the bench. They sat.

"I'll do all the talking," Mr. Lipscomb whispered to them. "Keep in mind, if whatever is said or decided today is not in your favor, it is not the final decision. We can keep fighting as long as there are adequate grounds."

Nola prayed silently, "Lord, please see us through." Leaning back slightly, she saw Cordelia as she sat down with her attorney at the table across from them. She hadn't seen her the whole hour and a half they had been waiting their turn to be called. Cordelia didn't look like herself. She was immaculately dressed in a tailored navy blue suit. A far cry from the short skirts that left nothing to the imagination and tight jeans that strained at the seams. A strand of pearls, probably fake, lay demurely around her neck. A pair of single pearl studs sat delicately on her earlobes. No one would guess that she ever lay down in a garbage-strewn crack house or sold her body to get a fix.

Judge Fiske tapped her gavel. "Mrs. Schulman, state your case."

"Your Honor," Mrs. Schulman began, standing, "my client, Mrs. Cordelia Kirkwood, is seeking to regain full custody of minor child, Meika Kirkwood, age five, who is presently residing in the home of her paternal grandparents, Nola and Ronald T. Kirkwood Senior. Full custody was granted to Ronald T. Kirkwood Junior in 1992 in this court. However, as of October 29, 1994, Mr. Kirkwood Junior is deceased. His death thereby vacates his custody order."

Nola leaned toward Mr. Lipscomb. "How does she know the date Troy died?"

"A death certificate can be obtained by anyone as long as they know the name, approximate date of death, and place of death."

Is nothing held private, Nola wondered.

"Your Honor, we are petitioning the Court for the immediate return of Meika Kirkwood to the custody of Mrs. Cordelia Kirkwood, the biological mother."

The thought of that happening nauseated Nola.

"My client is also concerned that Respondents are nearing the age of retirement and are, therefore, too old—"

"Too old?" Nola asked aloud, insulted by the inference that she and Ron were decrepit.

"Respondents are well past their prime, and—"

"Your Honor!" Mr. Lipscomb interrupted, standing.

"If I may finish."

Judge Fiske tapped her gavel once—then twice. "Order!"

Mr. Lipscomb pushed on. "Mr. and Mrs. Kirkwood are—"

"Too old to properly supervise and raise the minor child, who is only five years old," Mrs. Schulman stated.

"By today's standards, Counselor, age—"

Bang! the sound bounced off the walls. "I said, order! Mr. Lipscomb, sit down!"

He did so immediately.

"Mrs. Schulman, you know better than that. This Court will not tolerate bias in any way in arguing a custody suit. Sit down!"

Mrs. Schulman eased down in her chair and crossed her legs.

Seeing the self-satisfied smirk on Cordelia's face, Nola fixed an angry glare on her. Ron nudged her to get her to stop.

Judge Fiske studied her file. "I have reviewed the original custody order. At the time custody was granted to Mr. Kirkwood Junior, Mrs. Kirkwood was declared an unfit mother because of her drug addiction. Counselor, what is Petitioner's present condition?"

"Mrs. Kirkwood has been drug-free for one year. She has recently returned from a drug rehabilitation center in Kentucky.

I have affidavits from the director, medical personnel, and a counselor of the Whitney Drug Rehab Center in Louisville, Kentucky, attesting to her voluntary participation in the program and to her being drug-free for the past year."

"Do you have a copy for the Court?"

"Yes, Your Honor," Mrs. Schulman replied, handing a set of papers to the court officer. "As you'll see, Your Honor, qualified, licensed counselors certify that Mrs. Kirkwood is stable and exhibits no threat to herself or her child."

Nola glanced over at Cordelia. She was sitting tall. She held her back straighter than the chair she sat in. Every time Cordelia was referred to as Mrs. Kirkwood, she cringed inside. She hated that she still carried their name. Never had she seen trash whitewashed to look so much like a Girl Scout, but no one was fooled, Girl Scouts don't have to go through drug rehabilitation.

The judge accepted the affidavits, perused them briefly, and looked up. "Is Petitioner presently employed?"

"She is, Your Honor," Mrs. Schulman answered, consulting her file. "She works as a secretary at National Bedding Incorporated in Manhattan. Her net biweekly income is seven hundred thirty-seven dollars."

Writing down the information, the judge asked, "Do you have a paycheck stub in your possession at this time?"

"We do," Mrs. Schulman replied, flipping through her papers momentarily before pulling out the original of two pay check stubs, and a copy. She handed them both to the court officer.

Judge Fiske studied the original and the copies before handing the originals back to the court officer. "How long has Petitioner worked for this company?"

Taking the check stubs and slipping them back into her folder, Mrs. Schulman answered, "One month, Your Honor. She just returned to New York two months ago."

"Where is Mrs. Kirkwood's legal residence?"

"Here in Brooklyn. She rents a one-bedroom apartment in a private home in Crown Heights. Her address is listed on the check stubs and on the petition. However, Your Honor—"

"That'll be all," the judge said, continuing to write.

Mrs. Schulman sat down and, patting Cordelia's hand, whispered, "It looks good."

Nola took a deep breath. Now she was nervous. Why hadn't the judge questioned the kind of mother Cordelia had been?

"Mr. Lipscomb, does the Respondent have any arguments against this petition?"

Standing, Mr. Lipscomb picked up his pen and began rolling it between his fingers. "Your Honor, for a little more than two years, Meika Kirkwood has resided in the home of Mr. and Mrs. Ronald Kirkwood, her paternal grandparents, along with her late father, Ronald Kirkwood Junior. There are only six sporadic visits on record by Petitioner, Cordelia Kirkwood, in the first eight months, and not one visit in the past sixteen months. Clearly, that is abandonment."

Cordelia shook her head adamantly.

"Petitioner's original weekend visitation rights were rescinded when she took minor child to a dangerous, rat-infested drug den, where she procured drugs and eventually left the child there while she went off to some unknown location. If it were not for a drug intervention counselor, who took the child to the police, we can only guess what might have happened. That incident, and others too innumerable to recite, which are on file with the original custody petition filed by Ronald Kirkwood Junior, not only attest to child endangerment but to Petitioner's inability to properly parent her child. It has been proven, unequivocally, that Petitioner is incapable of providing a safe, secure, moral, stable environment for the proper rearing of minor child, Meika Kirkwood, which has, for the past two years, been afforded her by her paternal grandparents. Therefore, Ronald and Nola Kirkwood are petitioning the Court for full custody of Meika Kirkwood."

Ron took Nola's hand under the table and squeezed it. She glanced at him in agreement. No way was Cordelia going to win.

"Is that all, Counselor?"

"Tell her about what Troy wanted," Ron whispered.

Judge Fiske, perched high upon her bench peered down at Ron. "Mr. Lipscomb, remind your clients that only your voice will be heard in this Court on their behalf, unless they are dismissing you."

This time Nola squeezed Ron's hand. She sensed from the expression on his face that he, too, was uneasy about the way things were going.

Mr. Lipscomb placed his hand on Ron's shoulder. Ron and Nola both looked up at him. They understood the warning in his eyes. "Sorry, Your Honor," he said, removing his hand. "It won't happen again."

"See that it doesn't. Was there anything else?"

"Your Honor," he said, starting to roll his pen between his fingers again, "there is no question that Ronald Kirkwood Junior's death was untimely and, as such, he had not made out a will to direct this Court in the placement of Meika Kirkwood. However, he did make his wishes known to his parents. It was his expressed desire that Meika Kirkwood remain in the home of his parents. As custodial parent, Ronald Kirkwood Junior's wish should be honored in death as it was in life."

"So noted. You may be seated," Judge Fiske said, folding her hands on top of the file. She waited while Mr. Lipscomb did so.

Nola crossed her fingers under the table.

"The Court has taken into account the arguments presented by both sides. The first order of business is to appoint an attorney to represent the rights of minor child, Meika Kirkwood, and a child psychologist to make sure none of these proceedings or the death of her father cause any harm to her well-being. By the next session, I want a report from both parties as to their findings after meeting with the child."

Anxiously squeezing Ron's hand, Nola leaned toward him. "Psychologist?"

"This is crazy," he whispered back.

Mr. Lipscomb put his hand out in front of Nola.

She sat back.

"Meanwhile, the minor child, Meika Kirkwood, will remain in the home of the Respondents, Ronald and Nola Kirkwood. The Petitioner, Cordelia Kirkwood, is granted visitation."

"No!" Nola said aloud.

"Damnit!" Ron spat.

Vann gripped the back of the bench in front of him. "This isn't right!"

Judge Fiske fixed her gaze on Ron and Nola.

Covering her mouth with her free hand, Nola tried hard not to cry out again. Tears slipped hurriedly down her cheeks.

"Visitation will begin this Saturday, February 25, 1995, at ten o'clock A.M. and end the same Saturday afternoon at four o'clock. Petitioner will pick up minor child at the home of Ronald and Nola Kirkwood exactly at the ten o'clock hour and drop off the minor child exactly at the four o'clock hour. Is that understood?"

Nola looked at Judge Fiske and shook her head.

Ron lowered his eyes.

Mr. Lipscomb stood. "If the Court please."

"Go ahead, Counselor. Make it brief."

"Your Honor, it was stated, emphatically, at the last court session, two years ago, that Petitioner's visitation was limited to supervised visits of two hours, once weekly. Additionally, the Court ordered Petitioner to not come within two hundred feet of Ronald and Nola Kirkwood or their home because of the threats she made against them."

"Let me say this, Counselor. I trust that everyone involved in this case grew up in the last two years and will conduct themselves as adults."

Ron winced at the insult. Nola's chest heaved as she fought hard to keep from screaming, "You condescending bitch!"

"Therefore," Judge Fiske continued, "I see no need at this time to censure Petitioner for her childishly destructive acts of two years ago and thereby rescind stipulations set forth at that time."

Cordelia started to clap her hands but Mrs. Schulman placed her hand on top of hers, stopping her. Smiling broadly instead, she clasped them together in her shaking lap.

Nola felt sick. Was this a bad joke? Was it April Fool's Day? Had the judge lost her ever-loving mind?

"Petitioner has evidenced to the Court that she has been working hard to clean herself up and start her life over. I see no reason why she should not be granted once-weekly visitation with her child, unsupervised."

Ron's shoulders slumped.

Nola felt like she was going to throw up.

"We'll see how the visits go and the Court will evaluate and go on from there."

Sitting down again, Mr. Lipscomb sat rigidly in his chair. He did not turn to look at Nola or Ron.

Cordelia's smile became a toothy grin.

"I will, however, admonish Petitioner that if she should, in any way, exhibit signs of her past life on the smallest scale, all visitation rights will be rescinded posthaste and full custody will be awarded to the Kirkwoods. Is that understood?"

"Yes, ma'am," Cordelia quickly replied.

"Counselors, see the clerk for the date of your next court appearance to further consider the question of custody. The court-appointed attorney and psychologist will be in touch with the Kirkwoods within a two-week period." That said, Judge Fiske picked up her gavel and, banging it once, ended the hearing.

"Next case."

SIXTEEN

NOLA had a headache—a throbbing, pounding, blinding headache that had Cordelia's name written all over it. The painkiller she had taken the minute she got home was not working, but maybe that was because she could not get out of her mind the highbrow, self-satisfied smirk Cordelia had given her as they passed each other leaving the courtroom. What she would not have given to see that smirk slapped off her face. Ron had seen her, too, and had said, loud enough for Cordelia to hear, "Winning little battles don't count if you don't win the war." Looking across the table at him nursing the can of beer he had taken a half hour ago, she wondered if he still felt that way. As far as she was concerned, this battle counted.

BEFORE MR. Lipscomb left them outside the Family Court building, he said, "It looks like the judge is willing to give your daughter-in-law a chance."

"Ex-daughter-in-law," she said, correcting him.

"Thank God," Ron said.

"She may be your ex-daughter-in-law, Mrs. Kirkwood, but she is forever your granddaughter's biological mother. In a custody suit, the court is in the habit of first recognizing the rights of a biological parent over all others, sometimes, unfortunately, to the detriment of the child. What anyone else wants, if anything, is secondary."

"But Troy won against Cordelia," Beatrice offered.

"Yes, he was the better biological parent. However, he is no longer here and as I told you before, grandparents have practically no rights in this country." Mr. Lipscomb lifted his arm and checked his watch. "If your granddaughter was twelve years old or older, the judge would have spoken to her to determine her preference. Until she is older, the court will decide who gets custody."

"Meika is a very articulate child," Beatrice said, "she knows what she wants. Are you saying that the judge won't talk to her now because of her age?"

"Under the law, she's too young to make a responsible decision," Mr. Lipscomb explained, again checking his watch. "For instance, if a child under the age of twelve runs blindly into the street and gets hit, the driver is liable, even though the child was in the wrong. The law says that that child wasn't old enough to make a responsible decision."

"We don't have a chance, do we?" Nola asked.

"Mrs. Kirkwood, it is not hopeless. Why don't you contact my secretary and set up an appointment so that we can discuss this further? We can argue other issues about the drugs, Mrs. Kirkwood's lifestyle, her acquaintances, and the probability of her being unable to provide adequate housing or after-school care for the child."

TO NOLA it did feel hopeless. All of that information was already in the file. As she saw it, all Cordelia needed to win was a bunch of letters, which were most likely lies, a new suit, and a new job to convince the judge that she was no longer the woman of two years ago.

"If I hadn't been sitting there," Beatrice said, taking a dainty sip of tea from her cup, "I would not have believed it. It was as if the judge didn't hear a word your lawyer said."

"Seemed that way to me, too," Vann agreed. "It's simply incredible. We can't let this happen."

"Let?" Ron asked, getting up from the table. "Doesn't look to me like we have any control over the situation. That judge trounced us!"

"That she did," Beatrice agreed. "If I didn't know better, I'd think it was personal."

Holding her cup of tea with both hands, Nola tried to warm her hands. "We need to turn up the heat," she said to no one in particular.

Ron began pouring what was left of his beer down the drain. "Anyone sitting in that courtroom would've thought we did something wrong. Cordelia is the one who did something wrong, she's the junkie," he said, crushing the beer can up in his hand like it was a piece of paper. He tossed it into the recycling container under the sink. "And I don't believe for one damn minute that she isn't still a junkie."

"You know, Dad, if we can get something on her or catch her using drugs, we can use that in court."

Nola suddenly got up from the table and started out of the room. "I'm going to turn up the heat."

"How can we find out?" Beatrice asked, looking from Vann to Ron.

"I can probably find out," Vann said. "I used to know some of the people she knew. If she's using, they'll know."

Leaning back against the sink, Ron folded his arms high up on his chest. "If I could go back to the day Troy married that junkie, I'd wring his neck."

"You don't mean that," Nola said, coming back into the kitchen.

He realized the import of his words. "No, I guess I don't."

Sitting again, Nola glanced up at the wall clock over the refrigerator. "Meika is the only good thing to come out of Troy's marriage. Vann, do you mind picking her up from Miss Minnie's?"

"No problem," he said, getting up to leave. "Dad, wanna take a walk?"

Ron didn't answer yes or no. He dropped his arms to his sides and started out of the kitchen, passing by Vann.

"Ma, you need anything from the store?"

"I can't think of anything."

"We'll be right back," he said, bending and kissing her on the cheek. "It'll be all right."

"From your mouth to God's ears," she said, finding it hard to believe that nothing had gone right since Troy died. This certainly was her winter of discontent.

Beatrice saw the worried look on Vann's face. "She'll be fine," she said. "Where's my kiss?"

He kissed Beatrice on the cheek also.

"Thank you, baby. Now go on."

As soon as Vann left, Nola began rubbing her ashy hands together, trying to warm them with the friction. They didn't get any warmer, but they did get ashier. "I need some lotion."

"I have some right here," Beatrice said, lifting her large black pocketbook off the floor onto the table. She rummaged through it until she found what she was looking for. She handed the small pink tube to Nola.

Nola squeezed out a dab of white cream into her left hand and began to slowly rub it into her skin. She inhaled the fresh lavender scent as the ash started to vanish and her hands started to look better—softer. Squeezing out a second dab, she screwed the top back on and handed it back. This time she concentrated on the inside of her hands and in between her fingers.

Looking at Nola, Beatrice snapped her pocketbook shut and

placed it back on the floor next to her chair. "I didn't think it would go this badly."

"Neither did I."

"I wonder if you can ask for another judge?"

"I don't know, but I plan on asking Mr. Lipscomb. This just doesn't look good."

"What if the judge gives Meika back to Cordelia?"

It was only a question but Nola's heart thumped in her chest hard enough for her to feel it. This morning she would not have thought it remotely possible. If it happened, it would devastate her and in the end, it might kill Meika, if Cordelia's life was anything like it used to be.

"Bea, did you see that story on the news last week about the little girl that was beaten to death by her drug-crazed mother?"

Beatrice shook her head sadly. "It was sickening."

"That could happen to Meika," she said, feeling herself welling up.

"We won't let that happen to Meika, Nola. We'll all fight for her. If we can get another judge, maybe there's a chance that we'll win."

Nola wiped at her eyes. "Bea, we're depending on a lot of ifs, and maybes, and chances. We won't win that way. We have to do something definitive that's guaranteed."

"Like what?"

"I don't have a clue," she replied, resting her head in her hand. "God, how I wish Troy were here."

"If only."

"Bea, I don't think I'll ever stop thinking about him."

"You won't, and neither will I. In time, maybe a little less, but never altogether."

"Never," she said, sadly. "This morning when I woke up, I thought about the day he was born."

Beatrice smiled. "Child, that was a happy day for all of us. You carried that boy so big and high up, Roosevelt swore you swallowed a beach ball. He used to tell Ron to prick you with a pin to see if you'd burst."

"You tell Roosevelt I ought to prick him with a pin. His stomach is bigger than mine was when I was nine months pregnant."

For a minute they both laughed in an easy, lazy kind of a way.

"Anyway," Nola said, sighing, "I was thinking about how Troy looked when he was born."

Beatrice frowned. "He was ugly."

Smiling, Nola nodded. "He was the ugliest thing I ever saw. Looked nothing like Vann did. Troy's face was all lumpy and scrunched up."

"You said he looked like an alien."

"He did. He scared me. But, Bea, when he opened that ugly little mouth and cried, I cried, too. He was my baby, my precious little boy." The memory overwhelmed her; she hid her face in her hands and cried.

Beatrice hoisted her body out of her chair and went and stood behind Nola and, gently massaging her shoulders, waited out the tears, unmindful of her own tears.

SEVENTEEN

SQUEEZING her small body up into the corner against the armrest of the sofa while hugging Bobo tightly in her arms, Meika still wore her coat. Her eyes were brimming as she followed Cordelia's every move around the room.

"Why don't you take a sip of your soda," Cordelia suggested, impatiently, referring to the can of orange soda sitting on the folded paper towel on the coffee table. "It's hot in here. Don't you wanna take off your coat?"

Meika just stared at her, wide-eyed, pulling Bobo even closer up to her neck.

"Keep the damn coat on, I don't care. I'm not the one burning up." Cordelia plopped down on the other end of the sofa. Crossing her legs, she took a cigarette from the pack on the end table and lit it. She took a deep drag and blew the smoke out the side of her mouth toward Meika. "You don't talk much, do you?"

The smoke engulfed Meika. She batted her eyes and tried to hold her breath.

"We been here an hour and a half already. You don't wanna eat, you don't wanna take off your coat, you don't wanna watch television, you don't wanna do nothing but stare at me. What's up with you? Living with that woman make you retarded?"

Meika stared straight ahead.

Sucking her teeth and rolling her eyes, Cordelia recrossed her legs. "Well, do you have to go to the bathroom?"

Her stare remained unchanged.

"You better not pee on my sofa, you spoiled little brat."

Meika's lower lip slid out into a sulky pout.

"Look, kid, how about giving me a damn break? You act like you don't know me, goddamnit. It's not my fault your father took you from me."

The tiniest little whimper came out of Meika, but she still didn't blink.

Cordelia took another drag on her cigarette. "Don't go getting yourself all worked up. I haven't done a damn thing to you. All of a sudden you act like you can't talk, but I know you can 'cause I heard you tell those people you didn't wanna come with me—crying and acting like a big baby. I bet they spoil you rotten, don't they?"

Taking a deep breath, Meika changed her arm positions; she put her right arm on top of her left around Bobo's neck, choking him.

"That's an ugly, old mangy bear. He looks like he's been in a fight with a grizzly. I bet your grandmother gave you that ugly thing, didn't she?"

"Bobo ain't ugly. My daddy give me Bobo."

"We're talking, are we? Well, I bought you a new bear. You can throw that ugly one away," Cordelia said, looking at the cream-colored bear with the big red bow around its neck sitting on the chair across from them. "Isn't he pretty?"

"No."

Cordelia flicked her ashes into the ashtray on the table. "Figures. No taste. Just like your father."

Meika frowned and stuck out her bottom lip even farther.

"Damn. Don't go getting mad at me. I didn't say anything bad about your daddy."

Meika's face didn't change.

Cordelia took a deep drag on her cigarette. "I see this is gonna be loads of fun." She blew the smoke straight out ahead of her before turning again to look at Meika. "Do you like the doll I brought you for Christmas? She's almost as big as you were when you were two years old. And you know what else? You had a pretty red dress with white lace at the collar, just like your doll."

Although Meika's lip came in, her brows were furrowed.

"Do you know what doll I'm talking about?"

"You ain't never brought me no doll."

Cordelia jammed out her cigarette in the ashtray. "I should've known that witch wasn't gonna give you that doll. Your grandmother is a vicious witch!"

"My mama ain't no witch! You a witch!"

Cordelia turned her whole body toward Meika and leaned in as close to her as possible from where she was sitting.

Frightened, Meika tried to pull back farther, but couldn't.

"She is a witch if I say so, Miss Smart Mouth, and you get this straight right now. That damn woman is not your mama! That witch is your goddamn old-ass grandmammy, not your mama. I'm your goddamn mama!"

Meika's bottom lip shot out again. She took a deep breath and held it.

"Get used to calling her Grandmammy, honey, 'cause I'm the only mama you'll ever have." Cordelia suddenly scooted across the sofa to Meika and grabbed one of the buttons of Meika's coat. "Now open up this goddamn coat and take it off before I rip it off!"

A piercing scream exploded from Meika. Digging her heels into the cushion, she clutched Bobo even tighter, while trying to hold on to her coat.

"Shut up!"

Tears poured, her screams grew louder.

Cordelia bolted up off the sofa. "Goddamnit, Meika! People are gonna think I'm killing your ass up in here. Shut up! Shut up!" she screamed, raising her hand to hit Meika but stopped in midair. "Oh, hell no. That's all they need to know, that I hit you, on the first visit, too. Oh, hell no!"

Continuing to cry, Meika pressed her face into the top of Bobo's head.

Cordelia began shaking her hands out in front of her to release her tension. She took a deep breath. "Okay . . . okay." She sat next to Meika. She took hold of her and tried to pull her onto her lap.

Arching her back, trying to pull away, Meika's screams grew loud again, but Cordelia wasn't letting go of her. She pulled with all her might and yanked Meika up onto her lap anyway and clamped down on her, holding her prisoner inside her unyielding embrace.

"I'm sorry, okay? I didn't mean to yell at you. Please stop crying. I didn't mean it."

Though she stopped screaming, Meika, still trying to pull away, barely able to catch her breath, cried, "I . . . want . . . my . . . mama. I . . . wanna . . . go home to my . . . mama."

"Okay! Okay! Soon, goddamnit!" she growled through her teeth. Then softening her voice, "Meika, you gotta stop crying. Your mama'll be upset if she thought you cried the whole time you were here. You don't want her to see your eyes all red and puffy, do you? She'll cry if she see you crying. You don't want your mama to cry, do you?"

Meika suddenly stopped struggling. A pitiful whimpering replaced the crying. She held her body tense. She would not let her head rest against Cordelia's breast.

"I'll make a deal with you. If you stop crying, I'll let you play with my charm bracelet," she said, holding her wrist up in front of Meika's face and shaking it so the charms dangled and the gold sparkled.

Meika stopped whimpering altogether. Staring at the bracelet, she licked at the snot that oozed down onto her upper lip.

"If you like it, you can have it."

Reaching out, Meika touched the dog charm with the tip of her finger.

Taking that as a good sign, Cordelia opened the lobster claw clasp and, slipping the bracelet off, handed it to Meika.

It dangled, it sparkled. Meika was mesmerized. Her tears stopped. She reached around Bobo with her other hand to take the other end of the bracelet.

"Let me put it on for you," Cordelia offered, taking the bracelet and wrapping it with ease twice around Meika's tiny wrist before latching it. It was snug enough to not slip off over her hand. "My, that looks pretty. You like it?"

Slowly twisting her wrist side to side, suddenly starting to hiccup, Meika stared at the bracelet.

Cordelia could feel Meika's body relax in her arms. Relieved, she reached down and took the can of soda off the paper towel and held the can to Meika's mouth.

"*Hiccup!*"

"Take a sip before you hiccup yourself to death."

Meika didn't reject the offer of the soda, and she didn't sip, she drank until she had to stop and catch her breath. When she pulled back from the can, a string of shimmering snot linked her to the can, which nauseated Cordelia. She made a face and looked away. Meika hiccuped and then licked again at the snot above her lip.

"Ugh! That's nasty," Cordelia said, setting the can back on the table. She took the paper towel and wiped Meika's face dry before using it to also wipe away the stream of snot above her upper lip. "I tell you what. If you promise to not tell your mama about your pretty bracelet, you can take it home with you."

Meika looked up at her. "How come I can't tell my mama? She like pretty bracelets."

"Because your mama doesn't like me and she doesn't want me to give you anything. If she found out that I gave this to you, she'll take it from you and throw it in the garbage. You don't want her to throw your pretty bracelet away, do you?"

Meika shook her head.

"Do you have a secret place to hide your bracelet that nobody else knows about?"

"Under my pillow."

"Your pillow?"

"I hide my teeth under my pillow. My daddy said hide them under my pillow for the Tooth Fairy. And you know what happened? Every time the Tooth Fairy took my teeth, she left me a quarter."

Cordelia glanced sideways at the door. "Oh, brother," she mouthed to herself. "I mean a real secret place that no one else knows about, not even the Tooth Fairy. You have a shoe box?"

"My mama bought me new boots. I still got the box."

"Good. Why don't you put your bracelet in that box and put it way back in your closet, in the corner. That way, only you'll know it's there."

"Can I play with it?"

"You can, only when no one else is in the room. Afterwards, you have to make sure you put it back, okay?"

"Okay."

"It'll be our special secret."

"Okay," Meika said, shaking her wrist, charmed by the charms.

"And don't let your mama unpack your bag, she might find it and you know what'll happen."

"She'll throw it in the garbage."

"That's right. Tell your mama you're a big girl and can unpack your own bag."

"I am a big girl. My daddy said so."

"Well, he was right. When you come next time, I'll have something else for you, something prettier than this."

Meika's eyes sparkled. "What?"

"You'll have to wait till next time, but you can't cry when I pick you up."

"I won't."

"Good, you are a big girl." Cordelia kissed Meika on the cheek.

While Meika played with her bracelet, Cordelia took Bobo out of her arms and sat it alongside her on the sofa. Then, taking her time, she unbuttoned her coat and eased her arms out, one by one. She slipped the long gold necklace from around her own neck and hung it around Meika's neck. Meika didn't seem to notice that Bobo was no longer in her arms.

EIGHTEEN

I T might have been easier to push a mule up a hill than to get Lopez to show Vann the page with the names of the people on it who had signed in at the Research Library at the Met. In fact, in the forty-five minutes they argued, Lopez wore out three pieces of fresh bubble gum talking a bunch of malarkey about the privacy of the other people on the list. Their privacy meant nothing to Vann, not if it kept him from finding Troy's murderer. When Lopez begrudgingly relented, it dawned on Vann that Lopez meant to give him the information all along, which is why Lopez called him in the first place.

Vann's patience was wearing thin. "Man, stop playing games with me."

"This is no game, Kirkwood. I need your word that you're not gonna contact any of these people," Lopez said, holding on to one end of the paper, unwilling to release it completely. "It could mean my job."

"You got my word," he lied. Lopez's job wasn't Vann's problem and he didn't believe him anyway. If he was that concerned, he would have blacked out the other names.

Lopez let go of the paper and Vann sat back to study it.

"We're concerned only with the two names before your brother's and the two names after. If he had a scheduled meeting, chances are whomever he was meeting came in before or just after him. Do you recognize any of those four?"

"James Wilson, Hubert Kloss, Jane Edelstein, Andrew Lipp-setti. Let me think a minute," he said, although he knew for certain that he didn't recognize any of the names. He pretended to be thinking by looking up at a spot on the wall behind Lopez every now and then and squinting his eyes like he was really concentrating, but he was really checking out the rest of the names on the list whenever he looked down again.

"It's possible you might not have known everyone your brother knew. You did say you've been living in Atlanta."

"True. Have you spoken to any of these people?"

"Some," Lopez said, pulling a piece of bubble gum from his front pants pocket. Unwrapping it, he used the wrapper to take the stale wad out before plopping the fresh pink square into his mouth. He sucked on its sweetness before beginning to chew as he took his time wrapping up the spent gum.

Vann had watched Lopez's curious little routine several times now and noticed that Lopez changed chewing gum more frequently when he seemed to want to make him wait—it was an annoying stalling tactic. "Got a serious sweet tooth, huh?" he asked, to keep from saying "Cut the crap" or anything else that might make Lopez clam up altogether.

"It's the lesser of two evils—cigarettes or sugar; lung cancer or rotten teeth. The teeth I can fix."

"I hear dentures are better than the real things these days," Vann quipped. "Do you know if one of these people met with Troy?"

Lopez stuck his finger inside his left ear and rapidly shook it like a dog scratching himself with his hind leg. His itch satisfied, he leaned back in his swivel chair, chewing his gum, looking at Vann, noncommittal.

Shifting his position in his chair, Vann stared coldly at Lopez chewing his gum like a cow chewing her cud.

In his own good time, Lopez answered, "We showed your

brother's picture to everyone we managed to track down on the list. Nothing."

"In other words, I'm not privy to anything you found out."

"Let's just say that there was a guy that remembered seeing your brother, and don't ask me who."

"Did he see who Troy was with?"

"Said he was by himself," Lopez replied, rolling the wad of gum folded up inside the wrapper between his fingers until it had taken on a perfectly round shape. He then flicked it with his thumb up against the side of the beat-up old gray metal cabinet, where it slid down toward the wastepaper basket, hit the rim and bounced down onto the floor along with the others that had missed the basket.

"This was definitely Troy this guy saw?"

"Said he remembered your brother because he had a coughing fit, like something went down the wrong pipe or something."

"Then other people should have noticed him, too."

"We haven't located anyone else. However, did I mention that this guy was sitting at the same table?"

"And?"

"Nothing."

"He didn't see anyone sit down next to Troy?"

"Nope."

"Troy spoke to no one?"

"Not that this guy recalls."

"Well, how long was he there?"

"The guy?"

"Yes."

"An hour, he said. Seems your brother sat at the table reading a book."

"That's it?"

"That's it."

"Damn," Vann said, looking down the whole list. Several

names down from Troy's, the name Cookie caught his eye. "What about this 'Cookie' person, is it a she or a he?"

Lopez shrugged his shoulders. "Don't know, couldn't track him or her down. Could be some kid. Who knows?"

"Could be a nickname," he said, writing the name down in his notebook.

"We thought about that, but without a real name or an address, it could be just about anybody."

"Suppose the person came in much later?"

"Your mother said your brother was back home by one. There's no need to look any further than that page. The way it looks, it's possible the person he was supposed to meet didn't show."

"Maybe the person just didn't sign in."

Lopez shrugged. "Maybe not, but we'll keep looking for others," he said, standing and reaching across his desk for the page.

Standing also, Vann handed the list back. "Where do we go from here?"

"We're not ruling out the probability that someone will remember hearing your brother's car alarm. We'll stay on it," Lopez said, picking a pamphlet up off his desk.

"My family would appreciate that," Vann said, closing his notebook. He started out of the office.

"Kirkwood," Lopez said, stopping Vann at the door. "You're slipping. You didn't ask me what book your brother was reading."

He had not thought to ask because he did not see how what Troy was reading mattered. "I know you can't wait to tell me."

"*Stolen Credit.*"

That was surprising. "He got that from the Met?"

"No, he brought it in with him. I checked with American Express. He wasn't stealing from them. How were his personal finances?"

"Better than most."

"Then it probably means nothing."

Vann took a second to make a notation—*Stolen Credit*—in his notebook. He continued on out of the office. He didn't know if there was any significance in Troy reading that particular book, but he'd check it out. As to the name Cookie, he had a strong feeling that he'd heard Troy talk about a Cookie something or other. When or in what context, he couldn't remember, but he was sure that it had been a woman he was talking about.

Vann left the precinct no closer to solving Troy's murder. If something didn't point him in the right direction soon, he didn't know what he'd do. Admitting defeat to his parents after getting their hopes up wasn't going to be easy; neither was admitting his failure to Michelle. She would never let him live it down, not when she had told him from the start to stay out of it. Things between them had been sour for a long time and while he jumped at the chance to get away, even using Troy's death as an excuse, for the past year Michelle had been trying to get him to talk about their future together. He had run out of excuses as to why he couldn't marry her and avoiding the topic had pushed them farther apart. How was he supposed to tell her that he didn't feel for her what he felt a man should feel for a woman in order to marry her until death do them part?

Sure, Michelle was a good mother, a good cook, a good lover, and, mostly, she was a good woman. Two of those things alone should have been enough to make him want to marry her way back before they had Kareem or Sharice, but they weren't. Every time Michelle harangued him about marrying her or threatened to leave, he tried to talk himself into going through with it—he never could. Four times at bat over the years and he had failed to follow through at the last minute, forcing Michelle to pack up her and the kids' clothes in anger, but the farthest she ever got was to the front door, and after pouting for a couple of weeks, she'd let it go until the next time she felt the need to make them legal. He knew how much he was hurting her, but he couldn't give her what she wanted most, his name. To her that piece of paper meant the world, and to him, it was just that, paper. He gave her more than most husbands gave their wives—a house, a car, she kept her own paycheck, and he paid all the household bills, including all of Sharice's and Kareem's expenses. What more did she have to have? His blood?

Vann had asked himself time and again why he couldn't follow through and marry the mother of his children, and the only answer he could come up with was that maybe he didn't love her enough, but what did that say about him? Was he incapable of love or was there more to love that he just didn't know about or understand? Whatever the reason, he had to make a decision: live with Michelle on her terms—marriage—or without her on his terms.

NINETEEN

So much of Troy's room was still so much his. His clothes still hung in his closet; his cologne still sat on his armoire; his plaqued college degree still hung above it; and his canvas bedroom slippers still sat under the chair near the window; yet his aura wasn't as strong anymore, Vann's own had slowly overpowered it. He wore Troy's clothes, slept in his bed, and sometimes used his cologne, making Troy's scent his. But still Nola liked to go into his room to sit a spell and cradle the navy blue sweatshirt Troy last jogged in in her arms; it still smelled of his muskiness. Bringing it to her nose, she inhaled and tears filled her eyes as visions of Troy filled her mind.

"Ma."

Nola quickly lowered the shirt and hastily dried her eyes.

Sitting down on the bed next to her, Vann put his arm around her. "Why do you do this to yourself?"

She stroked the sweatshirt. "I miss him so much."

Vann looked down at the sweatshirt. "I know I do, too, but Ma, you come in here whenever you're feeling low. What happened?"

"Nothing really. That other insurance check came in today."

"Was it for two hundred and fifty thousand?"

"Yes."

"I'll take care of it Monday morning."

"Are you sure no one can touch this money but me and Ron?"

"Yes. Troy was divorced from Cordelia. You and Dad were named sole beneficiaries. No one else is entitled."

"Good, then Meika is set. You're listed as beneficiary on everything we have. We don't want Cordelia to get her hands on a penny, if she, God forbid, should get custody of Meika."

"You should also revise your wills."

"We plan to," she said. A lone tear eased down Nola's left cheek. She sucked in her breath and quickly blew it out to stop more tears from flowing.

"Ma, it's not gonna get any easier anytime soon."

This she knew, but knowing it didn't make it any easier.

"How did it go with that psychologist today?"

"I don't know. He talked to Meika alone. Can you believe that? She's only five years old. He told me the judge will tell me anything she wants me to know at the next session March fifteenth."

Vann took his arm from around her shoulders. "He didn't tell you anything because he's appointed by the court, he's their boy. I wouldn't worry about it. He probably talked to Meika about you, Dad, Cordelia, and even Troy in an effort to gauge how she feels about everyone."

"But she's only five, Vann. How in the world can she tell him anything about how she feels?"

"Ma, you always say yourself how articulate Meika is. Believe me, she knows how to express her feelings."

"That's true, but what's really bothering me is that she's been to see Cordelia four times and the last three times she's gone with her like she couldn't wait to be with her. I asked Meika what they do together and she said they've gone ice-skating, they've gone to the Children's Museum, and they've gone to the movies. I don't understand it. Cordelia never had much time for Meika before. Now, all of a sudden, she's mother of the year. She buys her clothes and toys, and God knows what else she does, to make Meika like her, and it's all a lie, Vann. If, God forbid, Cordelia gets custody, will she be able to keep that up?"

"She can't, it's not in her."

"That's what's so sad. Cordelia is setting her own child up to be hurt." Nola refolded Troy's sweatshirt. "I told Mr. Lipscomb that and he said in the court's eyes there's nothing wrong in what Cordelia's doing. In fact, the judge wouldn't expect anything less. He said that we should trust the wisdom of the judge to see through it all."

"He's probably right, Ma," Vann said, wanting to take the sweatshirt from her, it only made her cry.

"I don't think so," she said. She slipped the sweatshirt back inside the large clear plastic bag she kept it in, and then sealed it shut by wrapping the excess plastic around the shirt twice. "I don't trust that judge, she has a nasty attitude. If Troy were here, Cordelia wouldn't be getting away with this."

"Ma, a lot of things would be different if Troy were here," he said, noticing for the first time that the red light on the answering machine was blinking. Getting up, he started around the bed toward the nightstand on the other side. "For one, you and Dad would be bantering with each other playing your game of one-upmanship."

"We don't do that," she defended, turning and watching Vann reach for the answering machine.

He pushed the rewind button. "Yes, y'all do. You and Dad have been doing that as far back as I can remember. The first time I heard you say, 'Oh yeah, that's what you think,' I must've been in diapers. Those were fighting words because once you said it, you and Dad would argue. But it wasn't until I was in high school that I really understood what you guys were doing."

"And what do you perceive that we were doing?"

Tilting his head and giving her the eye, he said, "You know . . . foreplay."

The answering machine clicked.

"Vann!"

"Well, that's what it was."

"How can you say something like that to your own mother?"

"C'mon, Ma. Y'all played games all the time, day and night. You'd put on your boxing gloves and Dad would get his back up, but all the while he'd have this devilish grin on his face and you'd act like you were all mad. Your mouth would be saying one thing, and your eyes would be saying another. Shameless flirting. That's all it was."

Smiling, she flushed. "I wasn't flirting. I was really angry with your father."

"Yeah, right. That's why at night you guys would keep it up for a minute and then it would get real quiet and then the bed would start squeaking."

"Vann!"

"Don't deny it, Ma. It's real. You and Dad are sexual beings."

Quite embarrassed, Nola was scandalized. "Vann, if you were over here, I'd slap you. You were supposed to be sleeping."

He laughed. "It was more fun listening to you and Dad. Troy and I used to bet a dollar on who'd score with the biggest zinger and how long it would take for you to start giggling. I usually won the dollar."

Nola covered her eyes in shame.

"Ah, Ma. Don't be embarrassed. Troy and I learned a lot from you and Dad. Believe me, that was better than the birds-and-the-bees talk Dad gave us."

She uncovered her eyes. "I tell you. Young ears are worse than having a spy in the house."

Vann pushed the play button.

"Mr. Kirkwood, my name is Bernie Stein. I'm calling about a flyer I found in with my mail."

Inhaling sharply, Nola bolted up and rushed around the bed and latched onto Vann's arm.

He held his breath.

"I just returned to New York. I've been in Europe since late October. If you have not as yet solved the question of what happened to Troy Kirkwood, I think I might be of assistance. My number is 555-4111."

Beep.

"Oh my God," Nola said.

Vann picked up the telephone. "I had given up on those flyers," he said, punching in the number. "I didn't think anyone would ever respond."

"I didn't think so either."

They both held their breath as Vann listened to the ringing in his ear—five . . . six . . . seven . . . "I don't think anyone's—"

"Hello?"

"Hello! Mr. Stein?"

"Yes."

Nola questioningly squeezed Vann's arm.

He nodded. "Mr. Stein, my name is Vann Kirkwood. You called me about the flyer I left about my brother, Troy Kirkwood."

"Oh yes. I've been in Europe since October."

"Yes, you mentioned that. I hope your trip was pleasant."

"Thank you, it was. We have a home in Brussels, and we"—Vann rolled his eyes up to the ceiling—"stay there for six months out of the year. My wife would stay there all year round if she could. She was born there."

"Flemish or French ancestry?"

"French. I've learned to speak the language myself since we married thirty-five years ago."

Nola shook Vann's arm. He silently shushed her.

"That's wonderful, but isn't Brussels just as cold in the winter as it is here?"

"Of course, but my wife would rather be there than here. She says old snow makes New York look and feel dirty."

"I agree. However, my brother, Troy, used to love the snow."
The line was suddenly silent.

"Mr. Stein?"

"You said 'used to.' Was your brother never found?"

"Not alive."

"I am so sorry."

"Thank you. Did you see him back in October?" Vann asked, crossing his fingers.

Nola gripped Vann's arm tighter as she stared into his face.

"I studied the picture in the flyer, I believe I did."

Vann wanted to cry. He almost did.

Seeing Vann's expression, Nola teared.

"Your brother's car was parked in front of my house on Cranberry Street."

He asked, "Are you sure?" but he was saying, *Thank you, Lord,* in his mind.

"Yes. It was a Saturday afternoon. My family and I were waiting for the limousine to arrive to carry us to the airport when a car alarm went off."

"Oh, God," Vann said in a hushed voice.

Nola's heart leaped frightfully in her chest. She held tightly on to Vann's arm to keep from fainting. Finally, they were getting answers and it was still just as scary.

"I remember that the alarm was so unpleasantly loud that it was annoying. The car was parked right under the front window. After several minutes, I looked out and saw this young man, a black man, running down the middle of the roadway from Henry Street. He must have had one of those remote beepers because he shut the alarm off before he actually got to the car. I would not have thought any more about the incident, you know us New Yorkers, we're used to alarms going off, but what was interesting here was, whilst the young man was circling the car, inspecting it, two men, who got out of a dark blue car parked across the street, came up and started arguing with him."

Vann bit down on his lower lip. Nola shook him, he did not

respond to her. "Did they have a gun on him? Did they force him into his car?"

Nola shuddered.

"I did not see a gun or a struggle, and your brother did not get into his car. I did think it odd, at the time, that the men were arguing with your brother. In fact, the argument did get rather heated. I quickly surmised that perhaps your brother knew these men because he started across the street with them to their car."

Vann began to feel sick. "He went voluntarily?"

"Well, I can't say that for sure. One man may have been holding on to your brother's arm."

Nola felt Vann's arm stiffen, making her tense up even more.

"Mr. Stein, do you remember what the men looked like?"

"What men?" Nola asked, anxiously.

"Wait!" Vann whispered to Nola.

"I'm sorry," Mr. Stein was saying. "I didn't really concentrate on what their features looked like if that's your question, and I pretty much forgot anything particular to them individually other than that one man was black and the other Caucasian."

Disappointed, Vann looked down into Nola's eyes. He saw and felt her anxiety. "Did my brother get into the car with both men?"

"Yes . . . uh . . . no. If I recall correctly, one man, I don't remember which one it was, got into the backseat with your brother. You know, Mr. Kirkwood, now that I'm talking about it, both men had your brother by the arm when they walked across the street. I should have realized that something was amiss since your brother didn't appear to need assistance to walk."

"Mr. Stein, you could not have known that Troy was in trouble," Vann lied. It angered him that Mr. Stein hadn't seen that something was desperately wrong. All the clues were there. Why would two men have to assist a strong, healthy-looking young man, and why would Troy get in the backseat of another car with any one of those men when his own car was across the street and Meika was inside the theater? Troy was a fighter. Only a gun would have made him think twice about resisting. They had to have had the gun even then, and if they had to help him across the street, he could have already been shot. However, he would not say anything to alienate Mr. Stein—he was the only person who had come forward.

"Mr. Stein, did the other man drive the car off?"

Nola's eyes widened with alarm. If Vann didn't tell her something soon, she was going to scream.

"Actually," Mr. Stein began, "I don't know. That's when my limousine arrived and my family and I got caught up in the madness of rushing off to catch our flight. I'm sorry that I was not more observant and cognizant of the apparent danger."

Vann shook his head. "Sir, so much happens on the streets in this city that look bad but are perfectly innocent."

"Mr. Kirkwood, my wife would say just the opposite."

"Most women would," Vann said. "Mr. Stein, did the car my brother was in pull off at that time?"

"I'm sorry, I didn't notice. By that time, we were rushing back and forth collecting our luggage."

"Of course. I would guess that they didn't, no one was in the driver's seat."

"Actually there was."

Three men against Troy alone angered Vann even more. "There was a third man?"

"No, a woman."

"A woman? Are you sure?"

Nola began shaking Vann. "What woman?"

"Yes, I—"

"Mr. Stein, would you hold on just a sec, please?" Vann asked. He immediately put his hand over the mouthpiece. "Please, Ma. I'll tell you everything, but let me talk to the man."

Feeling hurt and frustrated, Nola started to back away but

Vann pulled her back to him and held her. She laid her head against his chest. Not knowing was driving her mad.

"I'm sorry, Mr. Stein, you were saying."

"I didn't see the woman's face, but I saw her hands on the steering wheel."

"How could you tell it was a woman?"

"She wore red gloves. I don't know any men who wear red gloves."

"Neither do I," Vann said pensively.

"I'm sorry that I didn't see more."

"Mr. Stein, you have been of more help than you realize. You're the only person to come forward from the hundreds of flyers I passed out. My family and I are most grateful."

"I wish I had done something that day."

"Yes, but you're doing a lot for us now. May I impose and ask a favor of you?"

"Why . . . yes."

"I'd like your permission to give your name and telephone number to the detective assigned to my brother's case. He may have questions to ask, but I assure you that he will not harass you or your family."

"Of course you may."

"Mr. Stein, thank you. The police think my brother just got into his car and drove off on his own. You've settled that argument for us. Thank you. You have a good day."

"Good day."

Letting go of Nola, Vann hung up the telephone.

"Did he see who killed Troy?" she asked, immediately.

"No, he didn't see that much. However, he did see the men who forced Troy into another car."

"Oh my God," she said, covering her mouth with her hands. Tears began to stream down her cheeks.

Vann put his arm around her again. "Dad should be home any minute now. Let's go downstairs. I wanna tell you both, together, what Mr. Stein saw."

TWENTY

How does one cope with the ugliness of the details leading up to a child's death? They had all been biting at the bit to get some information and finally hearing something concrete made Nola ill. She and Ron were both stunned. While they were satisfied that they had been right all along that Troy would never go willingly anywhere and leave Meika without calling home, they were incensed that he had been snatched off the street, in broad daylight, so easily. No doubt the men had guns. Why else would Troy not have struggled?

Ron was restless in his anger. He paced the living room endlessly. "If I could get my hands on those bastards, I'd kill them," he said, repeatedly punching his left palm with his fist.

"Is it possible that Troy knew them?" Nola asked.

Vann looked at her. He had been wondering the very same thing and he was beginning to believe that it was possible. "Dad, I think you had better sit down."

"Why? Can it get any worse?"

"Maybe. Something Mr. Stein said bothers me."

"What is it?" Nola asked.

Vann began rubbing his hands together. "Mr. Stein said that the person behind the wheel was wearing red gloves."

"Who was it?" Ron asked.

"He didn't see the face, only the hands on the steering wheel."

Ron sat down in the armchair. His forehead was deeply creased in rows of thick worry lines. "What can he tell from looking at somebody's hands in gloves?"

"It's not so much what he could tell, but what we know."

"What do we know?" Ron asked irritably.

Nola knew immediately. "It was Cordelia! She was wearing red gloves the first day she showed up here. She was driving the car, wasn't she?"

"That's what I'm thinking," Vann said.

Ron put up his hands. "Wait a minute! You're not saying that Cordelia had something to do with killing Troy?"

"Ron, she hated Troy!"

"Yeah, but she'd been out of town."

"You always liked her, didn't you?" she asked accusedly.

"Nola, don't start with me. I'm just saying that, according to those letters from those people at the clinic, Cordelia didn't come back to New York until the end of December."

"Lies."

"If that's true, Dad," Vann said, "Cordelia couldn't have been here in October, but who's to say that she didn't fly into town on October twenty-ninth and fly out that night or the next morning? It can be done."

"It's done every day," Nola said. "We all know that Cordelia is vindictive enough to have killed Troy. Remember, Ron, Troy said that Cordelia attacked him when he first took Melka and left her. In fact, she tried to stab him before he took the knife away from her."

Ron remembered. "He was real upset about that. He should have had her arrested then."

"Well," Vann began, "as much as I hate to have to deal with Lopez, I have to pass this info on to him, along with Mr. Stein's name. Maybe Lopez can check flight manifests to and from Kentucky on the twenty-ninth. If Cordelia's name pops up, we got her."

"Meanwhile," Nola said, "we have got to keep her away from Meika."

"I don't know if we can do that, not with the court order."

Ron slammed his fist down on the arm of the chair. "The hell with that court order! If that bitch killed Troy or had anything whatsoever to do with killing him, she'll never see Meika again because she's gonna be in her grave sucking on dirt."

"Shh!" Nola said, looking toward the hallway. "Meika might hear you."

"Hell, Nola. She oughta know the truth about that woman."

"Not this way, Ron. Not when we're angry."

"I'll always be angry. We shouldn't let Cordelia take Meika tomorrow."

"Dad, until we know for sure that Cordelia's guilty, we can't keep her from seeing Meika. The judge might take her from us for disobeying her order."

Nola stood. "This is wrong."

"It may be, Ma, but if we say anything to Cordelia before we have proof, we'll tip our hand and she'll try and cover her tracks or snatch Meika or tell the judge we're harassing her."

"Damn," Ron said, getting up.

"We have to wait, Dad," Vann said, calmly.

Nola felt helpless. "I hate this. I know Cordelia is guilty."

"As much as I hate to admit it," Ron said, "Vann is right. We have to wait."

"Obviously, you'd agree."

"Goddamnit, Nola! Do you think I wanna sit on this? Hell no! If Cordelia killed Troy, I want her ass just as much as you do."

"You don't act like it."

"How could you say that to me?"

"Dad, we're all too emotional. We have got to calm down."

"Did you hear what your mother said? What's she trying to say?"

"I'm saying—"

"Ma! Hold up. You and Dad want the same thing. You can't accuse him—"

"Why are you attacking me?"

"Ma, I'm not attacking you."

"Nola, you were always like a bull in a china shop."

"You were always mule-headed."

"You're a hard-nosed, stubborn woman."

"Okay! Okay!" Vann said, putting up his hands. "Both of you stop it."

"Your father—"

"Not another word, Ma!"

Nola shut up, but she glared at Ron.

"Ma, Dad, we can't be fighting amongst ourselves."

"I'm not fighting," Nola defended.

"No, she's having her way like she always does."

"Dad! Enough!" Vann ordered, giving Ron a warning look. "I've heard enough out of both of you. Now stop it."

Duly chastened, Ron angrily turned away.

Nola folded her arms and stared at Vann. She didn't like the way he was speaking to her.

"Ma, this is ridiculous. We're at each other's throats."

"Well, he—"

"Stop it! No more recriminations from either of you. If we fall apart, we get nothing done. Aren't we supposed to be holding strong? Holding tight? Let's stop this."

Nola, too, turned her back on Vann.

"Look, we'll find out soon enough whether Cordelia is guilty. It takes time."

Ron turned back. "That's all I was trying to tell her."

Not wanting to acknowledge Ron, Nola didn't look at him.

"Ma, when Cordelia picks up Meika tomorrow, you do like you always do, *stay* inside. I'll take Meika out."

Nola sat heavily in her chair. "Since when do you tell me what to do?"

"Since you and Dad started losing control and acting like children."

She sucked her teeth. She then mumbled, "I didn't lose control. He did."

"Me?"

Vann threw his pen across the room. It hit the wall.

Nola shot Vann a surprised glare.

"That's it," Vann said. "If you two don't cut it out, I am packing up and going home."

That certainly wasn't what Nola wanted. She looked at Ron but she did not say anything. She sat back.

Ron sat and began to immediately drum his fingers on the arm of the chair, but he, too, was silent.

Vann waited until he was sure that neither would speak. "That's better. Ma, where's Meika? I haven't seen her since I got home."

"Up in her room."

"All this time?"

Ron glanced at Nola and looked away.

"I gave her a snack when we got in. She went right up to her room afterwards, said she wanted to play. She's been doing that a lot lately, even closing herself up in her room. Plays in there all alone and doesn't come out until I call her."

"Is that good, Ma?"

"I guess. I spoke to that doctor about it today and he said it was perfectly normal for a five-year-old to play alone. I told him she was going to be six in May and he said it was perfectly normal for a six-year-old, too."

"Typical," Vann said. "Psychologists see things as either normal or abnormal. No behavior falls in between."

"In this case," Nola said, "they might be right. Since visiting Cordelia, Meika has gone from a normal little girl to an abnormal child. She isn't acting anything like herself. She's eerily quiet now. That giddy way she had of telling jokes is gone; she's not as talkative as she used to be; and she seems to be pulling away from me. Of course, I can thank Cordelia for that."

"Meika is probably confused, Ma. Does she say anything about Cordelia? Does she like her?"

A pang of jealousy went through Nola. Her own feelings were hurt that Meika liked going with Cordelia and, in fact, went eagerly. On Saturday mornings, Meika got herself up early long before anyone else was up and about.

Vann could see that Nola was upset. "I'm sure Cordelia is working overtime to make Meika like her. Kids don't know when they're being scammed."

"She'll slip up," Ron said. "You can count on that."

Nola stood. "I'm going upstairs to check on Meika."

Ron waited for Nola to get out of earshot. "Vann, when you and Troy got grown, I thought we were through with raising children. Nobody could have told me that we'd have to start over again with Meika."

"Dad, if you can't raise Meika, I'll do it. It's not fair that you have to start all over again."

"Your mother wouldn't hear of it. Actually, I don't have a problem with raising Meika, I just don't want to have to deal with Cordelia for the next fifteen years."

"I know that's right."

"By the way, how did it go with Lopez today?"

"Besides him acting his usual pain-in-the-ass self, he did say that a man saw Troy in the Met's Research Library."

"That's good news," Ron said, excitedly.

"Yes and no. The guy didn't see with whom Troy met. I saw the list of people that signed in. I didn't recognize any of their names. However, the only odd thing that stood out about Troy to the man, besides his coughing, was that he was reading a book that wasn't from the Research Library."

"Did he say what the book was?"

"*Stolen Credit.* Lopez wanted to know if Troy had financial problems because of that title."

Ron flipped his hand. "No way."

"That's what I told him. I think I'll try to get my hands on a copy tomorrow, maybe—"

Ron put up his hand. He held it up while he appeared to be thinking.

Vann waited.

"You don't have to, I have Troy's copy in the den."

Taken aback, Vann gaped at Ron. "For real? How did you get it?"

"Troy must have left it on the hall table when he came home to pick up Meika. I found it on the floor the night Troy was missing. It's in my den."

Vann jumped up and raced into the den. Ron wasted no time following behind him. He went straight to the bookshelf over the stereo and plucked the book from between the two large ones it was sandwiched between. He handed it to Vann, who almost snatched it. Quickly flipping through the pages, he stopped cold when he got a third of the way through and saw the piece of paper stuck in between the pages. He stared dumbly at what was written there.

"What is it?" Ron asked, looking over Vann's shoulder.

The note was in Troy's handwriting—*Cookie. 11:00, the Met Research Library. Question: How do they get credit cards???*

"I be damn," Vann said.

"Cookie. You said that name was on the list."

"Did Troy ever mention that name before?"

"Not that I can recall. Maybe he talked to your mother."

"I'll ask her. Did he ever call Cordelia Cookie?"

Ron thought about it. "I never heard him call her Cookie, though no telling what he called her behind closed doors."

"Probably bitch," Vann said, closing the book. He clutched it to his chest. "Whoever this Cookie is, he, if it's a he, might know what happened. I don't think those people that confronted Troy on Cranberry Street just happened to be there. I think they knew he was going to the movie in the Heights. They may have followed him there or were waiting in the area for him. They're the ones that set off his alarm to bring him out. This Cookie person might've been the one who set him up. But why? And what do stolen credit cards have to do with it? If anything."

Holding on to his desk, Ron slowly lowered himself into the chair. "I saw a report on stolen credit cards awhile back on one of those newsmagazine shows. There are people who steal other people's cards, charge them to the max, take the goods and disappear, and then some innocent people are left with huge bills that they have to pay unless they can prove that they weren't responsible. This is a big conspiracy."

"Conspiracies get people killed, Dad."

Ron nodded sadly.

"Troy worked for a credit card company. He must have known something he wasn't supposed to know."

Suddenly raising both hands to his head, Ron's eyes bugged. "Those charges on Troy's credit card!"

"What about them?"

Ron dropped his hands hard down onto his desk.

"The same people who charged that seventy-five hundred dollars on his card are probably the same people who killed him. Bastards," Ron said, staring at the book in Vann's hand. "Suppose they opened up other accounts in Troy's name?"

"Everything was closed out. No one can reactivate his accounts or Social Security number."

Ron got up and went around to the front of his desk. He sat on the edge in front of Vann. "Vann, that's not true. It's been done before, and remember, new accounts were opened up after Troy was dead."

"Yes, but they were opened up before his death was reported

to the Social Security Administration and before his old accounts were closed out."

"But it probably took a month before information was updated. Hell, it takes a company longer to process address changes than it does to open up a new account. And they're offering instant credit all over this country."

"This is true."

"Vann, these people are unscrupulous. They wouldn't be intimidated by the fact that a stop has been put on one credit card. They probably didn't try to make another purchase on that American Express card after Troy's body was found. If they're true to the profile that reporter outlined, they can use Troy's personal information to open up other accounts."

"If they did, we should have received bills by now."

Ron shook his head. "Not if the fools were smart. They probably used another address, or maybe even a P.O. box number."

Vann looked down at the title of the book. "Man. Are you telling me that greed got Troy killed?"

"Son, money is the root of all evil. We need to get a copy of Troy's credit reports." Ron checked his watch. "It's too late to call the credit bureaus, and they won't give information out over the phone anyway."

"Damn. That's true. I'll type up request letters and get them out first thing in the morning."

"Send them to all three bureaus and don't forget, send copies of the death certificate."

"I got it covered," Vann said, beginning to feel that the who and why of Troy's death was not as far out of his reach as it had seemed earlier in the day. If Cordelia did somehow figure in the equation, he couldn't swear that he wouldn't put his hands around her neck himself.

"I think we should call Lopez," Ron said.

TWENTY-ONE

MEIKA sat on the floor outside of her closet with her legs tucked under her, playing with the trinkets she took out of her secret box. She couldn't wrap the gold charm bracelet around her wrist as Cordelia had done and it kept slipping off. The gold chain around her neck lay flat against her chest and hung almost to her lap. Even the ring she wore on her thumb that Cordelia told her was a diamond, not that she knew what that meant, kept slipping off, too. On each of her teddy bears sitting in front of her, red ribbons were tied in big bows around their necks. Every so often she picked up one of the two pretty weighty boxes wrapped in gold paper that she was told not to open until her birthday. She really wanted to open them, but she knew that if she did, Cordelia said she'd know and she'd never give her anything pretty ever again. Meika liked pretty things so she'd keep her promise not to open the gold boxes.

"Meika," Nola called from outside the bedroom door. "Can I come in?"

Startled, Meika quickly yanked the chain over her head and threw it into the shoe box. Her breathing accelerated as she threw the ring and the bracelet in on top of the gold boxes.

Tap . . . tap. "Meika."

Hurriedly, she thrust the top onto the box and sat it far back in the corner of the closet. The top popped off. Meika crawled quickly into the closet on top of her shoes and tried to put the top back, but it was caught and wouldn't fall in place.

Nola opened the door. "Meika, where are you?" she asked, looking around the room, and then, hearing a noise coming from the closet, turned and, seeing the door open, looked down on the floor. All she saw was Meika's feet and her rear end. Nola laughed. "Meika, what are you doing in there?"

Grunting, Meika struggled to get the top to fall in place.

"Meika, come out of there."

The top fell in place.

Nola took hold of Meika's ankles and pulled her out of the closet—shoes and all. "Child, look at you. You look like a little rabbit trying to burrow into the ground. What are you looking for in there?"

"Nothing," Meika said. She turned over onto her back.

"Yes, you were doing something. Let me see what's back there."

"No, Mama!"

Meika's frantic tone stopped Nola cold. She stared at her.

Quickly springing up off the floor, Meika pushed the closet door up, catching a shoe in the door. She didn't bother to remove the shoe. She picked up her two teddy bears and carried them over to her rocking chair and sat down. Bobo she sat on the floor at her feet; the cream-colored bear Cordelia gave her she held in her lap. She began to rock.

Nola watched her for a minute. "Honey, do you talk to me like that?"

Lowering her eyes, Meika said softly, "I'm sorry."

"My goodness," Nola said, somewhat amazed. She went and stood over Meika. She felt her forehead—it was cool. "You don't feel hot. Are you upset about something?"

"No."

"Are you sure?" she asked, sitting down on the floral pink bedspread. "Did Dr. Lee upset you?"

"No."

"No? Are you sure? You seem upset. You don't wanna tell Mama what's bothering you?"

Meika shook her head. She continued to rock.

Meika hadn't been this sullen even when Troy died and it worried Nola. She would blame Dr. Lee if Meika had acted this way only today, but the finger could be pointed solely at Cordelia. Since the first visit with Cordelia, Nola had seen subtle changes in Meika's temperament—she was a little moody and definitely standoffish. She had thought it was because she had been made to go with Cordelia, so she had tried to explain as best she could about why the judge made that decision. It seemed Meika's subsequent eagerness to go meant that she had accepted Cordelia and was having fun, but apparently, something was wrong or else why would she be pouting and rocking like she was angry?

"Sweetie, are you upset because you have to go see Cordelia tomorrow?"

The rocking stopped. "I like seeing my mommy."

Surprised, Nola stared at Meika. She hadn't heard Meika call Cordelia Mommy in well over two years. In fact, she hadn't been calling Cordelia anything. "Did Cordelia tell you to call her Mommy?"

"Uh-huh," she said, starting to rock again.

"You like calling her Mommy?"

"Uh-huh. She's my real mommy. She said you just my grand-mammy."

"Grandmammy?" She could not have been more insulted or hurt if she had been slapped. The pain could not have been any less. She got up and went over to the window and looked out. It hadn't snowed in two weeks. Yet all afternoon a cold, still grayness filled the sky; not even a breeze shook a naked branch. And now a dark, ominous, steely gray filled Nola's eyes and was matched only by the heavy foreboding in her heart. If she didn't know better, she'd think the summer sun was never going to come out and warm her up again. Rubbing away the goose bumps that popped up on her arms, Nola wished that she could just as easily massage her heart. Troy's death had triggered an avalanche of trouble that weighed her down, but she was hoping that soon there would be an end to Cordelia, as well as an end to winter.

Behind her, Nola could hear Meika rocking. She turned back to her and wasn't surprised to see Meika looking at her. The wide-eyed innocence in her eyes was masked by the confusion that was obvious in the way she clutched the bear that she brought with her from Cordelia's on the first visit, while Bobo had fallen flat on his face on the floor. It was Cordelia's bear that Meika now carried around the house, that she whispered to, that she held to her heart. If Nola thought that she could get away with it, she would have taken the bear while Meika slept and burned it until it was less than a memory, but she couldn't do it. It would be another loss for Meika. Never mind that the attachment Meika bestowed on the bear had been stolen from her, Ron, and Bobo. Nola could not hurt her grandbaby like that.

"Mama," Meika said, softly, "you mad at me?"

"Oh no, baby," she said, going back to sit down on the bed in front of Meika. She held her arms out to her.

Immediately sitting the bear down on top of Bobo's back, Meika climbed up onto Nola's lap.

Nola hugged and squeezed Meika like she never wanted to let her go.

"Kissy face, Mama."

Gladly obliging, she kissed Meika all over her face in quick little pecks that tickled her. Meika giggled until she was out of breath. When she finished kissing her, Nola hugged her tighter. Nothing ever felt as good to her as a child's warm body against her bosom.

"I love you," she whispered in Meika's ear.

"I love you more."

"No, I love you more. Sweetie, do you feel better?"

"Uh-huh."

"Good. I feel better too."

"Mama, I don't feel so good when I think about my daddy."

She knew that feeling well. "Next time you think about your daddy, think about all the times he made you laugh."

"Huh?"

"Well, didn't he make you laugh when he played horsey with you?"

"Uh-huh."

"And didn't he make you laugh when he carried you high up on his shoulder, and when he tickled you under your feet, and when he played knock-knock with you?"

"Daddy was funny," she said, smiling.

"See, he just made you smile, didn't he?"

"Uh-huh."

"So whenever you think about your daddy, think about the things he did to make you laugh, okay?"

"Okay."

Nola needed to take her own advice. She needed to remember Troy's brilliant smile, his jokes, his silly antics with her and Meika, and, most of all, his dazzling charm.

"Mama, how come you don't like my mommy?"

She thought for a moment before answering. Meika was too young to understand fully the kind of conniving witch Cordelia was. As much as she hated Cordelia, she didn't want to scare Meika with the depth of her hatred, but she wasn't about to lie either. "Sweetie, sometimes, Cordelia isn't a very nice person," she said, finally.

"She's nice to me."

"Well, honey, mommies are supposed to be nice to their own children, but sometimes some mommies aren't nice to other people's children or other people's mommies."

Meika thought about it. "You're Daddy's mommy, right?"

"Yes, I am," she answered, realizing that being a mother lived on past death.

"My mommy don't like my daddy's mommy?"

"No, she doesn't."

"Oh," she said, slowly twirling the bottom of her T-shirt around her finger. "How come?"

"Well …" she said, unsure as to how to begin. How does one tell a child that her mother was lower than a snake's belly, that she was a drug addict, a whore? Nola couldn't bring herself to say those things, to be that forthright. "Meika, do you remember last year when the little girl down the street had a birthday party and didn't invite your little friend next door?"

"You talking about Sharon, Mama?"

"That's right. Sharon invited you to her party, right?"

"I don't like Sharon. She's mean to Lynette."

"How is she mean?"

"Sharon broke Lynette's doll's head off 'cause she wouldn't give it to her."

"What did she do with the head?"

"She threw it down the hole in the street."

"That's right, down the sewer. Sharon never did anything like that to you, did she?"

"No."

"That's because she likes you. She was always nice to you, right?"

"Uh-huh."

"Even though she was nice to you, you still saw that she was mean to Lynette, right?"

"Uh-huh."

"And you don't like her because she's mean to Lynette, right?"

"Uh-huh."

"That's how Cordelia is. She's nice to you, but she's mean to other people."

Meika's brows knitted tightly into a little crease above her nose.

"Do you understand?"

"Was she mean to you, Mama?"

"Yes, she was, but she was meaner to your daddy and that made me not like her. She made your daddy very sad. That's why he took you from her and brought you here to me."

"Did she make Daddy cry?"

"Yes, she did. She hurt him real bad and made him cry a lot."

Meika's eyes welled up. Her face became a sorrowful frown. "I don't like my mommy no more," she said, looking at Cordelia's teddy bear on top of Bobo.

"That's all right," Nola said, gently rocking Meika, though she could hear someone running up the stairs.

"Ma," Vann said, suddenly bursting into the room. "You have got to hear this!"

Quickly shaking her head, she said, "I'll be down in a minute."

"Oh," Vann mouthed, looking at Meika. "Okay. As soon as you can."

"Ten minutes."

"Five," he said, backing out of the room.

Meika suddenly slipped out of Nola's arms. She went over to Cordelia's bear, picked it up by the leg, and carried it to Nola. "I don't want this no more."

Nola took the bear. "Honey, you like this bear," she said, though secretly pleased. "Don't you want to keep him?"

"I don't like him no more."

"Do you want me to save him for you?"

"No," she replied, moving back away from the bear. "Throw him away."

"Are you sure? We could put him in the closet for a little while."

"No. Throw him away. I don't want nothing she gave me no

more," Meika said, backing up to her rocking chair and sitting down. Picking up Bobo, she hugged him.

"Okay, if you're sure." Nola got up off the bed. "I'll be right back." She went straight to the garbage can out in front of the house and shoved the soft, cream-colored bear facedown into the rancid-smelling food and household debris. A mild, although brief, twinge of guilt touched her conscience for taking pleasure in doing what she was doing, but it was only a mild twinge and she got over it real quick. In no way did she want anything of Cordelia's in her house. If she could take that genetic part of her that was in Meika and throw it away, she would. Being that it was impossible, she'd have to pray that none of Cordelia's ways ever reared their ugly heads in Meika.

TWENTY-TWO

Y OU bitch! You turned her against me!" Cordelia screamed.

Smug though silent, Nola stood in the doorway holding on to Meika's hand while Vann, gingerly but firmly, pushed Cordelia down the walkway to the sidewalk. As much as she hated to see Meika so upset and throwing a tantrum in the front yard when Cordelia tried to take her away, Nola felt selfishly smug.

Crying, Meika hid behind Nola.

Ron, standing guard at the foot of the stoop, looked back up at Nola. "Take Meika to her room."

Gladly, Nola stepped back into the house, closing the door to the ugliness that was upsetting Meika.

"Cordelia," Vann said, "get used to it. Meika does not want to be with you."

"That's because that bitch—"

Grabbing her arm, he squeezed it. "What did I tell you about calling my mother names?"

"Ouch!"

"Don't make me hurt you, Cordelia."

"Get your goddamn hands off of me!" she shouted, trying hard to peel Vann's fingers off her arm. "I'm gonna call the cops on your dumb ass!"

"Hey! Go ahead."

"I will, and they'll make you give me my child."

"Cordelia, you're stupid. No cop is going to let you take a screaming, kicking kid anywhere."

"I have my court order."

"Meika's welfare comes before that damn court order or you. Why don't you try putting what's best for your child before your own selfish wants and leave her alone."

"I'm Meika's mother. I want her with me."

"What you want doesn't count. My mother is the only mother Meika wants and needs."

Cordelia yanked her arm free and stepped back from Vann. "Fuck you and your mother!"

Vann lunged at Cordelia. She jumped back out of his reach.

"You're a lame ass like your stupid brother!"

Incensed, Vann charged at her.

Quickly backing away, Cordelia about-faced and started running.

Vann thought about running after her but after the first few steps, pulled up. What was the use? Short of grabbing Cordelia, there was nothing he could do to her.

"Just let her go," Ron said. "She's nothing but trouble."

"I hate that bitch!" he said, looking at Cordelia race toward the corner. "When they put her ass in jail for killing Troy, I'm going to petition the court to fry her ass."

"Vann, we have to prove first that she killed Troy."

"Trust me, I'll prove it," he said, starting up the walkway. Together he and Ron went back into the house. Vann double-bolted the door. No sooner had they sat down in the living room when the doorbell rang.

"I'll get it," Ron said.

"It better not be her," Vann said, going to the door also.

Ron peered through the peephole. "It's the police," he said, opening the door to two police officers. One officer stood a few steps down from the officer who rang the bell.

"Mr. Vann Kirkwood?"

"That's me," Vann answered, stepping up alongside Ron. "What's up?"

"The lady in the patrol car," the first officer said, nodding backward once in the direction of the cruiser sitting at the curb, "says that you twisted her arm and that you kept her from picking up her daughter."

Vann glanced over the officer's shoulder at Cordelia sitting in the backseat of the cruiser. "You have that liar just where she oughta be."

"Did you assault the lady?"

"I did not, but I should have."

"Sir—"

"Officer, I did not twist her arm. If I had, I would've broken it. Cordelia was pulling and tugging on my niece, who did not want to go with her."

"The lady has a court order for visitation, and—"

"Officer, I don't care what she has. If Meika does not want to go with her, Cordelia cannot drag her like a dog and make her go."

"Sir, if the court order says that she goes, then she goes."

"No."

The second officer climbed up a step.

"Sir, if you interfere with the order, I'll have to arrest you," the first officer threatened.

Ron stuck his arm out and pushed Vann back. "Officer, we're trying to do what's best for my granddaughter. We did not try to stop that woman from taking Meika. Meika did not want to go and we are not going to make her go."

Vann stepped forward again. "Would you make your child go somewhere with someone she was afraid of?"

"Sir, there is no court order between me and my kids. If you have a problem with the order you have, take it up with the judge. For now," he said, putting his hand on his gun, "I have to enforce it. Get the kid."

"No, the hell I won't."

The second officer stepped up.

"Vann!" Ron called. "Go into the living room."

"Dad, there is no way I'm—"

"Stand down!" Ron said, sternly.

Vann closed his mouth immediately.

The officers laid their hands on the butts of their guns while their eyes were trained on Vann.

Vann cut his eyes away from Ron to the officers. They had a threatening look in their eyes to go along with their threat to draw their guns. He was no fool, he knew that if they drew on him, they would have to arrest him; and jail was a place he had never been and had no intention of ever going. Besides complicating his own life, it would be one more hassle for his parents to deal with. With that in mind, he heeded his father's order to stand down. He turned abruptly and went off into the living room. He flopped down in the chair that faced the entryway. He snatched the throw pillow he'd sat on from under his butt and tossed it across to the sofa, where it bounced off the back and landed on the floor.

"Officer, I'll get my granddaughter," Ron said, starting to close the door.

The officer stuck out his hand and kept the door from closing. "Leave the door open."

"No problem," Ron said, opening it up wide. He went to the foot of the stairs. "Nola!"

She rushed to the top of the stairs. "What is it?"

"The police are here. Bring Meika down."

"I put her to bed. She's too upset to go anywhere."

"Nola, Cordelia called the police. They have to enforce the order. Bring Meika down."

"Ron, she just stopped crying. I am not making her go with that woman."

Both officers stepped into the house. The first officer had his hand on his gun still.

"Nola, do like I say. Bring Meika down."

"I will not."

"Nola, bring her down. It'll be all right," Ron said, winking secretly at Nola.

From where she stood at the top of the stairs, Nola could see the legs of one of the officers. She didn't understand Ron's wink but she understood instantly that the police would take Meika, forcefully, if they had to. That would traumatize her even more. About to turn away, cold air sailed up the stairs, stopping her. "I'll get Meika, but somebody had better close my damn door unless somebody intends to pay to fill up the oil tank." She turned on her heels to go back to Meika's bedroom.

Ron turned back to the officers. "Do you mind pushing the door up?"

The second officer closed the door behind him. Like two soldiers, they stood at the ready, their hands on their guns still, ready to do what was necessary to enforce the court order.

Nola looked down at Meika sleeping soundly. She hated to wake her but she had to. Except for Meika's shoes, she hadn't undressed her and while she slept, took a minute to put her shoes back on. She then picked Meika up and held her to her bosom, cherishing her warmth and softness.

Meika groggily lifted her head. "Mama, where we goin'?"

"You have to go with Cordelia."

Meika woke completely. "I don't wanna."

"Honey, you'll be back home this afternoon. If you go to sleep when you get there, it'll be time to come back home when you wake up."

"I wanna sleep in my bed," Meika whined.

Nola's heart couldn't take it. Damn Judge Fiske! She needed to see what her ruling was doing to Meika, to her—it was tearing them apart inside. Nola put Meika down on the floor. "When you come home, I'll have your favorite ice cream and pizza waiting for you."

"I don't want no ice cream and no pizza. I wanna stay home with you," Meika said, pouting, her eyes filling with tears.

Nola took Meika's hand. "I want you to stay home too, but, honey, this is something we have to do. I'll make it up to you when you come home, I promise," she said, leading Meika out of the bedroom. She half expected Meika to pull back. She didn't. Together they started down the stairs. Halfway down, Meika caught sight of the officers and started screaming, pulling back to keep from going any farther.

Vann leaped up out of his chair.

"Bring her down," the first officer said.

"Nooooo!" Meika screamed.

Meika's shrill screams pierced Nola's soul. She picked Meika up and wrapped her protectively in her arms.

"Don't you see you're scaring her?" Vann asked, rushing into the foyer.

"Sir, step back," the second officer said, moving slowly toward Vann with his left arm extended and his right hand on his gun.

Keeping his eyes on the second officer while sidling closer to Vann, Ron called to Nola, "Do like the man said, Nola. Bring Meika down."

Meika cried, "No, Mama! Noooo!"

"Ron! I can't—"

"Nola! Please."

Thinking that Ron had taken leave of his senses, Nola glared at him as she continued carrying Meika, crying and clinging to her neck, down the rest of the way.

The first officer put his hands around Meika's waist and was about to take her out of Nola's arms. Meika raised her head to see who had her. Seeing the white face of the officer, she began screaming and kicking frantically, wildly lashing out with her arms to ward off the officer.

Vann took a step forward. Ron pulled him back as the second officer lay in wait to restrain him if need be.

Looking to Ron to help her hold on to Meika, Nola was stunned to see him calmly watching as the officer pulled Meika out of her arms. "Ron!"

The officer struggled to hold on to Meika. He tried holding on to her legs with one arm and her upper body with his other.

Meika, flailing and kicking all the harder, hauled off and punched the officer in the nose.

"Damnit!" the officer shouted. He released Meika's upper body so that he could cup his nose, but he still held Meika around her upper legs.

Meika lay halfway out of the officer's arms. She threw her head back and arched her back, her upper body and head angling for the floor.

"Don't drop her!" Nola screamed, reaching out to catch Meika.

Neither Ron nor Vann made a move to catch Meika.

Nola caught Meika under her arms, but Meika suddenly brought her right leg up and kicked the officer in the chin, slamming his teeth together and shutting his mouth with a snap!

"Aagh!" he growled. He let go of his hold on one of Meika's legs.

Nola snatched Meika from the officer's weak hold on her.

Groaning, the officer bent forward with both hands cupped around his mouth.

Vann chuckled.

Smiling, Ron rubbed his chin.

"What's wrong with this girl?" the second officer asked, going over to his partner.

"Well, Officer," Ron said, coolly, "other than you and that woman out in your car, there's nothing wrong with Meika. We told you that she didn't want to go with that woman."

Crying, loudly, Meika threw her arms around Nola's neck. Her breathless sobs sent Meika into a fit of coughing and convulsed her body.

"Honey, it's all right," Nola soothingly whispered in Meika's ear, while gently patting her on the back.

"You see what you guys have done? How can you do that to a kid?" Vann demanded.

"Vann, don't incite," Ron said, looking at the officers. "Officer, this is how she was earlier. This is why we couldn't let her go."

The second officer put his hand on the first officer's shoulder. "Louis, you all right?"

"Hell no! My teeth hurt, I got blood in my mouth, and my nose is bleeding."

"Louis, there's nothing we can do here. Let them settle this in court."

Louis straightened up. "But the woman has an order. She—"

"Yeah, but it'll be child abuse if we let this kid go out of here like this," the first officer said. "Let the court settle it."

Lowering his hands, Louis looked down at them. They were bloody. "Damn," he said, digging down into his pocket and pulling out a Burger King napkin.

The second officer started for the door. Opening it, he waited for Louis.

Holding his head back with the napkin jammed up his nose, Louis, without another word to anyone, toddled out past his partner.

"Take care of this in court," the officer said.

"We intend to," Ron said.

The officer left hurriedly, leaving the door open.

"It's all right now, Meika. They're gone," Nola said, continuing to rub Meika's back.

Vann rushed to the door and looked out. Cordelia was standing on the sidewalk talking to the officers.

She shouted, "You can't leave her! I'm supposed to have her today!"

Louis, his head back, holding on to his mouth and nose, said nothing as he eased himself down into the passenger seat.

"Miss, go home," the first officer said, sliding into the car behind the wheel. "Nothing can be done about this today."

"You're supposed to make them follow the court order."

"Not if it means hurting that kid. Do yourself a favor, miss. Go on home. Talk to the judge about it."

The officers pulled off, leaving Cordelia with her hands planted on her hips, cursing after them. She turned abruptly and, seeing Vann, started up the walkway.

"You're not gonna get away with this!"

"And you're not getting away with killing Troy!"

"What?"

"You heard me. We know you had something to do with killing Troy."

"Are you crazy? I didn't kill Troy!"

"Don't bother denying it. Someone saw you."

"That's a goddamn lie! Ain't nobody seen me nowhere near Troy. You're out of your goddamn mind! I—" she said, suddenly shutting up. She touched her temple once. "Damn! I knew it. I knew it was you who sent the police to my house to question me about Troy. Well, y'all can go to hell 'cause y'all ain't putting his murder on me."

"You put it on yourself," Vann said, stepping back into the house and slamming the door.

Cordelia raced up the steps. She began banging on the door. "Open this goddamn door!"

Meika jumped. Frightened, she looked at the door.

Nola gently laid Meika's head back down on her shoulder.

"I didn't kill Troy! I didn't have nothing to do with his death!"

Vann could hear the fear in Cordelia's shaky voice. "Go away, Cordelia, before I call the police on you!"

Banging again, Cordelia screamed. "Give me my daughter!"

"Bang on that door one more time, you'll regret it!"

"Fuck you!" she shouted, banging again.

Vann started to unlock the door.

"Ignore her," Ron said. "Her hands will give in long before the door will."

"Fuck all of y'all! Y'all ain't gonna get away with this!" Cordelia banged on the door one final time. Turning with a hard jerk of her shoulders, she trotted quickly down the steps. She caught sight of the next-door neighbors, Derrick and Pam, standing in their yard looking at her. "What the fuck y'all looking at!"

Pam looked at her husband, Derrick, who continued staring at Cordelia.

Cordelia flipped them the finger and stomped off up the street. "They don't know who they're fucking with! I'll show them!"

NOLA SAT on the stairs holding Meika on her lap while Ron, leaning against the banister, rubbed Meika's back. "When the judge finds that Cordelia is suspected of killing Troy, and learns how upset Meika was today, she'll have to cancel Cordelia's visitation rights."

"But is she officially a suspect?" Nola asked.

"She isn't at this very moment," Vann answered, "but that's because we haven't told Lopez what we know. If we can prove that Cordelia is Cookie and—"

"I don't know if I've ever heard Troy call Cordelia Cookie."

"Ma, we don't know what he called her behind closed doors."

"True."

"As I was saying, if we can find a witness that saw Cordelia in New York on the day Troy died, she is fried."

"Suppose we can't get a witness?" Nola asked, checking to see if Meika had fallen asleep—she was so quiet. She had.

"Ma, let's not dwell on can't."

"Fine. But I was thinking. Troy told me that Cordelia sold off all of her clothes and jewelry to get drugs. Have you noticed the clothes she's been wearing? Kind of ritzy, don't you think, for someone who just got out of rehab and who has only been working for a few months?"

"I haven't paid her much mind," Ron said.

"I've noticed," Vann said, "and I've wondered."

"How can she afford a private attorney and all those things?" Nola asked. "Clothes tell a lot, and so does jewelry. I thought those pearls she was wearing in court were fake, but now I don't know."

Vann popped his fingers. "Weren't there clothes and jewelry charged on Troy's credit card?"

"I believe so."

"There sure was," Ron said. "The stores are listed on the billing statement. Maybe we can get a list of what was bought and compare it against what Cordelia's been wearing."

Vann patted Ron on the back. "That's a good idea. Where's the statement?"

Looking from one to the other, Nola gently rubbed Meika's back in a light, circular motion.

"In my den," Ron replied, putting his arm around Vann's shoulders. Together they started for the den. "You were kind of aggressive with those cops, boy."

"I don't think so."

"You were."

Vann paused.

"Control, son. Control your temper, control the situation."

"Yeah, well, it wasn't me they had to worry about," Vann said, chuckling. "Meika got that cop good, didn't she? He left here meek as a bloody lamb."

"That isn't funny," Nola chided. "Meika is going to get sick from all this craziness and Cordelia doesn't seem to give a damn."

"Did she ever?" Ron asked. "Nola, why don't you take Meika upstairs? Vann and I have some work to do in the den."

TWENTY-THREE

IN her sleep Nola began turning over. Instinctively, she reached out to make sure that she did not roll on top of Meika. With her eyes closed she felt for her. Her hand touched nothing but the cool flatness of the sheet. She opened her eyes. Meika was gone. Sitting halfway up, she looked around the dimly lit room. The shadowy corners and the open closet door exposing the blackness within unnerved her.

"Meika."

Stark silence answered her. Throwing the covers back, she bolted up off the bed and dashed out of Meika's room into the hallway.

"Meika."

Again only silence. She started for her own bedroom when, behind her, she heard the front door downstairs close. Turning back, she ran to the top of the stairs and flicked on the light switch, flooding the stairs with light. She was taken aback. She expected to see Ron or Vann, but it was Meika at the foot of the stairs looking as calm as if it were high noon and bright, and not the darkness of the early-morning hour that she had been out in. She looked so small. In her hands she carried a white shoe box.

"Meika. Where have you been?"

"Nowhere," she said softly, starting up the stairs.

"Were you outside?"

"Uh-huh."

"What for?"

Meika stopped climbing the stairs. "Nothing."

"Nothing? Nowhere? What in the world is going on, Meika? You never go outside during the day by yourself, why were you out at this hour—in the dark?"

"I don't know."

"Meika, you're a smart little girl. You do know. Isn't it dark out there?"

"Yes."

"What were you doing out there?"

"Nothing."

"Nothing? Child, get up here."

Holding on to the banister, Meika began slowly climbing the stairs.

Nola waited patiently for her to reach the top. "What's in the box?"

"Nothing," she answered, dropping her eyes.

"Little lady, do not tell me *nothing* again," Nola said, taking the box from Meika's hands. It felt empty. She pulled the top off. It was empty. "Why did you take this shoe box outside?"

"I went to the garbage can."

"What for?"

"I don't know."

"Meika, did you throw away your shoes?"

"No."

Nola did not understand this at all. "Meika, you know better, don't you?"

She nodded meekly.

"What did you do outside?"

"Nothing. I just wanted to go outside."

She didn't know what to think. "Okay, Meika. Do not ever do this again. Do you understand me?"

"Yes."

She took her hand. "Did you lock the door back?"

"Yes."

"We'll talk about this in the morning. It's back to bed for you, young lady."

She was completely stumped. Could Meika have been sleepwalking? That was something she had never done before. Was this something that had come out of all the chaos? The next time she took Meika to see Dr. Lee, she'd ask him.

TWENTY-FOUR

Y OUR Honor, because of Respondents' unethical manipulation of Meika Kirkwood's emotions, my client was horribly humiliated in public by her daughter's crying tantrum. In addition, my client's character was maliciously maligned by Respondents; and she was physically threatened by their son, Vann Kirkwood. More importantly, she was devastated by Respondents' refusal to let her take her daughter for her weekly visit, a visit that she had been so eagerly anticipating."

Cordelia sniffled and dabbed at her nose. Judge Fiske glanced at her.

Looking at Cordelia, Nola sucked her teeth contemptuously. She knew the tears were all an act. She didn't feel the least bit guilty about telling Meika that Cordelia had been mean to Troy as she had no doubt that Cordelia was planning to make up ugly things to tell Meika about Troy.

She nudged Ron. "She's downright evil," she whispered.

He nodded.

Mr. Lipscomb stood. "Your Honor, my clients in no way manipulated the emotions of Meika Kirkwood. Nor did they refuse to let Petitioner take Meika Kirkwood. Meika Kirkwood, on her own, refused to go with Petitioner. That is why she threw a tantrum. Mr. and Mrs. Kirkwood, by holding on to their granddaughter, did what any parent or guardian would do to protect a child. It hurt them just as much to see Meika Kirkwood so upset. What would you have had them do, turn their backs on her?"

Judge Fiske rested her chin in her hand. She looked blankly at Mr. Lipscomb.

"No, Counselor, that is not the case," Mrs. Schulman said firmly. "How do you explain the fact that on three prior visits, Meika Kirkwood went without a fight to Petitioner's home? Until that last visit, or should I say, last attempt at visitation, the child got along quite well with my client. Why did her feelings about visiting her mother change from one Saturday to the next?"

Judge Fiske banged her gavel once. "Counselor, I will ask the questions. You may be seated."

Mrs. Schulman sat at once. She whispered to Cordelia. "Don't worry, I know this judge. She doesn't like people who use children to win custody."

"Mr. Lipscomb," Judge Fiske began, "it sounds to me like your clients have been playing dirty."

Ron gasped in disbelief.

Mrs. Schulman reached under the table and touched Cordelia on the thigh.

Cordelia smiled behind her hand.

"Your Honor," Mr. Lipscomb began, "my clients have gotten Meika Kirkwood ready each and every Saturday morning and have willingly handed her over to Petitioner."

Nola and Ron, both, nodded repeatedly.

"Have your clients told the child anything to make her afraid of Petitioner?"

Ron shook his head no while Nola continued to look at Judge Fiske.

"Your Honor, my clients have been a major part of Meika Kirkwood's life for the last two and a half years."

"So I've heard."

"In that time, Petitioner had all the time in the world to get to know her daughter but chose not to."

"I beg to differ, Your Honor," Mrs. Schulman interjected

though still seated. "Petitioner's visitation was limited to two supervised hours a week. In the last full year, she was in a rehabilitation center trying to get her life together so that she could take on the responsibility of parenting her own child."

"I disagree," Mr. Lipscomb said, looking directly at Mrs. Schulman. "Petitioner was strung out on drugs the first full year and did not keep up her visits. The last full year, no one knew the whereabouts of Petitioner. There was no contact. That is abandonment under the law. My clients, since the death of their son, have committed their lives to making sure that Meika Kirkwood is secure in their home; that she get the proper schooling; that she is loved unconditionally; and that she grows up to be a moral, principled young lady. Therefore, in no way would they, intentionally, do harm to her in any way, through word or deed, that would upset her as badly as was described."

"Nice speech, Counselor, but it's rhetoric. Sit down."

Confused, Nola looked at Ron—he looked just as perplexed. They both looked questioningly at Mr. Lipscomb when he sat down. Looking quite indignant, his face flushed, Mr. Lipscomb put his hand up, just in case, to stop Nola and Ron from speaking. He stared at Judge Fiske. Taking Mr. Lipscomb's lead, Nola and Ron both looked up at Judge Fiske.

The judge pulled a document out of her case file. "We can go back and forth for hours on this matter arguing who did what, and place blame on everyone's shoulders. I have here in front of me Dr. Lee's report, which states that Meika Kirkwood is a well-adjusted child of above-average intelligence. The report states clearly that Meika Kirkwood suffers some lingering distress from the passing of her father, which is understandable. Mr. and Mrs. Kirkwood have done very well in nurturing Meika Kirkwood and she cares a great deal for them and is quite close to them. However, there is an expressed interest on the child's part to be with her mother. The report states Meika Kirkwood likes her mother and enjoys being with her."

Feeling as if the oxygen was slowly being sucked out of the room, Nola inhaled deeply.

Judge Fiske slipped the document back into the file and clasped her hands on top of it.

Cordelia sat up even taller. She bit down on her lip.

Nola dropped her throbbing head. She looked down at the table. This was a nightmare come to light.

Ron stared angrily at Judge Fiske.

"In that the child, Meika Kirkwood, visited with Dr. Lee the day before she was to visit Petitioner, this Court believes that something was indeed said to the child that upset her. Mr. Lipscomb, I advise you to warn your clients against such defamatory behavior in the future."

"Yes, Your Honor."

Unable to sit quietly any longer, Ron raised his hand. "Your Honor, we have done nothing to—"

"Mr. Kirkwood, you are out of order."

"But you're saying—"

Bang! "Mr. Kirkwood!"

Nola took Ron's hand.

"Please, Mr. Kirkwood," Mr. Lipscomb said, leaning across Nola to speak to Ron. "You can do more damage to your case than your daughter-in-law. If you don't be quiet, the judge will sanction you in a heartbeat. You will lose your granddaughter forever."

Ron clamped his mouth shut. He glared at Judge Fiske.

Wanting to cry out, Nola covered her mouth with her other hand. In telling Meika that Cordelia had been mean to Troy, she had spoken the truth. Was she supposed to lie when Meika asked her why she didn't like Cordelia? That she wasn't going to do, not when Troy told her so much of the ugliness he endured with Cordelia, not when she had witnessed some of that ugliness herself.

"This Court has an obligation to protect the rights of the children whose cases come before it," Judge Fiske said, again adjusting her glasses. "Therefore, this Court would be remiss in its duties if it did not do what was best for any child caught in an emotional tug-of-war. Petitioner has shown that she has made great strides in turning her life around and she is to be commended."

Nola groaned. Ron closed his eyes.

Cordelia smiled defiantly.

"This Court has received numerous written accolades from Petitioner's employer and co-workers, in addition to the minister of her church. She has evidenced a great deal of interest in wanting to make up for invaluable lost time with her daughter, and it should be understood by Respondents, who are no doubt loving and caring grandparents, that, because of the love they have for their late son and for his child, they are obligated to give the child the opportunity to get to know the only biological parent she has remaining."

Hurtful tears emptied from Nola's eyes.

Ron continued to hold his eyes closed.

"It is the order of this Court, that Respondents, for a period of five months, hand over—"

"No! I will not!" Nola screamed.

Ron's eyes popped open.

Cordelia covered her mouth with both hands and began to rock excitedly.

"Oh yes, Mrs. Kirkwood, you will," Judge Fiske stated, emphatically.

"But Your Honor—"

"Be silent!"

Nola trembled in her outrage. She balled up her fists. Ron put his arm around her shoulders.

Judge Fiske shook her head and frowned at Mr. Lipscomb.

Mr. Lipscomb held Judge Fiske's gaze while he whispered to Nola, "This is not a final ruling. Try to hold on for a few minutes more."

Nola lay her head in the crook of Ron's arm and wept.

"If I may, Your Honor," Mrs. Schulman began, standing quickly.

"You have one minute and no more."

"Thank you. My client will need financial assistance and is, therefore, requesting that any Social Security payments received on behalf of Meika Kirkwood be forwarded to her and that any insurance or bank accounts left by the late Ronald T. Kirkwood Junior be made available to her for her daughter during that period."

"Money is all she really wants," Ron whispered.

"Mr. Lipscomb, have your clients comply with the Social Security payments during the five-month period, and if there are other monies left to Meika Kirkwood, Mrs. Schulman, have your client seek adjudication in Surrogate Court."

"She will, Your Honor."

"Let's end this. Respondents, Mr. and Mrs. Kirkwood, will hand physical custody, temporarily, of Meika Kirkwood, over to Cordelia Kirkwood on Friday, March 24, 1995, at six o'clock P.M."

"Oh, God," Nola whimpered.

"That's a little more than a week," Ron whispered in disbelief.

"That's Troy's birthday," Nola said sadly.

Judge Fiske glanced at Nola and Ron but chose to disregard them. "This temporary custody order will run until six o'clock P.M. August 31, 1995. Throughout this period, Dr. Lee will see Meika Kirkwood on a monthly basis, and a social worker will visit the home of Petitioner on a biweekly basis. Mr. and Mrs. Kirkwood are granted liberal weekend visitation with Meika Kirkwood that will begin at six o'clock Friday evenings and end Sunday mornings at noon. The first court-ordered visit will be Friday, March 31, 1995. Each party will be responsible for picking up the child from the other. The

Court will trust that everyone," she said, peering down at Ron and Nola, "will abide by this order and put the welfare of the child first. Both Respondents and Petitioner are admonished not to speak ill of the other to Meika Kirkwood or in her presence. The Court will not tolerate such behavior and the guilty party will be sanctioned. Next case."

Before the gavel hit the wooden block, Cordelia leaped up out of her chair and hugged her attorney. "Thank you, thank you, thank you," she said gleefully.

"You're welcome," Mrs. Schulman said, hurriedly picking up her file and briefcase. "Let's get out of here."

"I hear you," Cordelia said, grabbing her coat and rushing out ahead of Mrs. Schulman. She didn't bother to look at Nola or Ron.

"Houston versus Houston!" the bailiff announced.

The banging of the gavel didn't make Nola stir. Drained and feeling no stronger than a limp, overcooked asparagus shoot, she continued to sit.

Mr. Lipscomb tucked his briefcase under his arm. "We have to free up the table for the next case," he said. "If you would like to meet with me later this evening in my office, we can discuss what just happened and how we can turn it around."

"We'll be there," Ron said, taking hold of Nola's elbow.

Feeling Ron's usually steady hand on her elbow shake, Nola looked up at him. His eyes were glassy, his face was tight, his lips quivered. She could see that he was as devastated as she was. She sucked in her breath and pushed herself up out of her chair. Looking into each other's watery eyes, they pulled from within the strength that had carried them through Troy's funeral, and through so many other troubles they had faced in their long years of marriage. Ron pulled his shoulders back and held his arm out to Nola. She slipped her arm through his and together, with their heads up, they walked out past all the pitying eyes.

TWENTY-FIVE

NOLA was all cried out. She was numb. She was tired, too tired to go out again, later that evening, to see Mr. Lipscomb. It was a waste of time. Nothing he could say, nothing he planned to do would sway Judge Fiske. She seemed to be of one mind, and that was to put Meika back with Cordelia regardless of what she'd done in her past; regardless of what it might do to Meika; regardless of how much it would hurt her and Ron. The bottom line was, they were going to lose Troy's baby.

Ron had not stopped pacing since they got home. "Vann, did Detective Lopez check the manifest for flights in and out of Kentucky on October twenty-ninth?"

"He checked up to a week before and after. He found nothing, and he couldn't track down that Cookie person who met Troy at the Met."

"Then as I see it, there's only one thing left for us to do," Ron said, looking at the picture of Troy on the mantel. "We're going to have to take Meika and go away."

"Dad, you can't do that."

"We have no choice," Nola said, speaking up.

Vann looked at Ron. It was him he had to reason with. He got up out of his chair. "Dad, don't do this. The thought of you and Ma on the run, hiding in cheap hotels, wearing wigs and floppy hats, would give me nightmares."

"Wherever we go, we won't have to disguise ourselves."

"Where's that? Mars?"

Ron shot Vann an annoyed look.

"Vann, wherever your father and I go, Cordelia and that damn judge will never find us."

"I don't believe I'm hearing this. Dad, there isn't a corner of this world that computers don't reach that someone, somewhere can't get on-line and respond to a missing persons report or kidnapping alert, and that's what it would be, kidnapping."

"Then that's what it will be."

"Dad, you don't mean this."

"Vann," Nola said, impatiently, "if it were that easy to track someone down, then why is it that all those kids they profile on talk shows and on the sides of milk cartons are still missing? Why haven't they been found yet?"

"Because they—"

"Because they just can't find them," Ron said. "We could move to Alaska. I always wanted to go there."

That alone told Vann that they were grasping at straws. "Are you serious? Ma wouldn't last ten minutes in Alaska. She gets cold if I blow my breath on her. See Dad, you're letting your emotions speak for you, you're not using your head."

"So sue me, goddamnit!" Ron blurted. "I need a beer." He stomped off through the dining room into the kitchen, almost taking the door off its hinges when it slammed into the wall.

Vann started to follow behind Ron.

"Leave your father alone!"

Vann stopped and turned back to Nola. "We're losing it, Ma. We really are falling apart. You and Dad can't take Meika and run."

"Why did you speak to your father like that?"

"What? What did I say?"

"You said he wasn't using his head."

"I wasn't implying that he was stupid or anything."

"Well, that's the way it came out, Vann," she said. "For your information, I would live inside a walrus's belly inside a glacier igloo, if it would keep Cordelia from getting her hands on Meika."

"That's insane, Ma. It doesn't make sense."

"With no other choice, it does to us. Vann," she said, suddenly sliding to the edge of the seat cushion, "how would you feel if someone sat in judgment over you and ordered you to relinquish Sharice or Kareem to a person you know to be the Devil incarnate?"

"I'd fight the system with every ounce of—"

"Shut up!" she ordered.

He was stunned. "Ma?"

"Don't say another word, Vann."

Vann drew back his head and peered down at Nola. She hadn't talked to him like that since he was a teenager and it didn't feel any better now than it did then.

The sound of a glass breaking made them both look toward the kitchen. Vann again started for the door.

"Didn't I tell you to leave your father alone?"

"Wait a min—"

"Sit down, Vann."

"Ma, I'm a grown man. What's up? Why are you talking to me like this?"

"A grown man, huh?" Nola stood. She was a good foot shorter than her son, but she felt a foot taller. "Is that supposed to mean that I'm no longer your mother and you don't have to listen to anything I say?"

He wanted to say that it meant that she could not tell him what to do anymore, or even speak to him like that. But that unflinching warning look that she used to give him when he was a child acting out stopped him. Just as he did when he was a child, he shoved his hands deep inside his pockets and, shuffling over to the armchair, sat down heavily and fixed his eyes on the long brass floor lamp in the corner across the room.

Nola studied her grown son. He was pouting. He was mad at her for checkmating him. "Vann," she said, sitting, "you have always voiced your opinion, never mind what anyone else thought. And I'm not saying that it's bad, son, because more times than not, you've been right. I'm saying that everything isn't black or white, up or down, or round or square. Honey, where is your heart? I don't understand how you got to be so cold. Your father was thinking. He was thinking about what was best for Meika. Going away might be our only way out of this mess. What you said to your father was rude and hurtful. You hurt him."

Vann continued staring at the floor lamp. Grinding his teeth, he worked his jaw.

"Vann, your dad and I are very proud of you. I don't want you to ever think that we're not. After Troy was killed, you gave us the strength to go on. In a way, you took us by the hand and took us along with you, and we're grateful, but you're doing it with all the finesse of a commandant."

He pulled his hands out of his pocket and looked sideways at her. "Your being proud of me is news to me."

"Really? And why is that?"

Slowly turning his head he looked at her, eye-to-eye. "If Troy were here, he'd be the one you'd be saying that you were proud of, not me."

"How could you say something like that? You and Troy have always been equal in my eyes."

"Maybe your eyes have been crossed, Ma, because Troy was the one you doted on, not me."

"What?"

"As far as I'm concerned, nothing was ever equal."

Nola never had a clue that Vann felt that way, that he was jealous of his brother. Sitting back, she stared at him, speechless.

Vann suddenly stood. "Forget it. I'm outta here."

"If I have to tell you to sit down again," she warned, "you'll be sorry."

Taken aback, he gaped at her. "Ma, look at me. I am a grown man."

"And you're not so big and rusty that I won't hit you upside your head."

He chuckled. "This isn't happening."

"It is. Sit your ass down," she said, giving him the "I'm not playing" look she perfected from the time he started crawling.

"I don't believe this," he mumbled, flopping down into the chair again. "I'm getting out of here."

"Vann, you don't throw an open can of worms out at me and walk away. I doted on you and Troy equally."

Brooding, he trained his eyes on the floor lamp. He followed the brass pole from the base up to the white shade and down again.

"Maybe I babied Troy more. Maybe—"

"Maybe?"

"That's right, *maybe*. Maybe I had to hold his hand longer, but he needed me to."

"Oh please, Ma. Troy was just as independent as me."

"Not until he was in his late teens. You keep forgetting, Vann, Troy was two years younger than you, he was the baby. By the time you were six, you were so far ahead of him, in every way, he didn't begin to catch up to you until he was fourteen years old. He wasn't as strong as you, he wasn't as fast as you, he wasn't as smart as you. Even you treated him like a baby until he could hang out with you, learn from you, and go the distance in basketball with you. It wasn't until then that he began to stand on his own."

"That's bunk."

"Not from where I stand. I watched you and Troy through adult eyes, a mother's eyes; you watched Troy and me through a child's eyes, a son's eyes, a brother's eyes. Our eyes don't see the same things."

He thought about it. It made sense. Could he have been so wrong? In his gut, he knew that he could not have been. "That could be true, but I don't think you ever loved me as much as you loved Troy. He was your favorite."

"Did you say you were a grown man? You sound childish. You and Troy are both my favorite."

"Are? Ma, Troy's dead."

"Not in my heart and he shouldn't be in yours."

"He's not," he said, meaning it and feeling bad for having said it. Every day, passing Troy's picture on the mantel, he said, "Hey, Troy," and some nights he sat up late talking to him, letting him know that he was still trying to find his killer. He would always love Troy but that old feeling of jealousy was surfacing. He'd never talked about it before with anyone other than Cousin Beatrice and Michelle. Maybe it was time.

"Vann, Troy's death has been very difficult on all of us. The way you feel surprises me."

"What surprises me, Ma, is that you didn't know that I've been angry with you for a very long time."

His words cut through her like a dull knife. Batting back her tears, Nola could not believe that he had been harboring such feelings about her.

"Life is full of ugly surprises, isn't it, Ma?"

Vann's words hurt her, but those same words did very little to hide his own hurt. She pulled herself together and slid across the sofa, closer to him. "Vann, I couldn't love either you or Troy more than the other, you were both my babies. If I didn't love you the way you wanted me to, I'm sorry. But, I'm grateful to God that you never took your disappointment with me out on Troy; I loved that you and he were so close."

Now that Troy was gone, Vann was glad, too. He would hate himself if he had mistreated Troy or pushed him away. When they were coming up, Troy never played the brat or snitched on him the hundreds of times he jacked him up on the sly. He could almost see Troy tagging along to the playground, to the basketball court, to the corner store, always copying his every move. Feeling a stinging in his nose, Vann squeezed it between his thumb and forefinger. He missed Troy, but the truth was, something else was bothering him.

"Ma, Troy was missing for days before he was found and neither you nor Dad called me. Why was that?"

"I told your father to wait. I didn't want to worry you needlessly."

He let his head drop back against the chair. For a few seconds he stared up at the ceiling. "Needlessly, huh? Could it be you didn't want me around to distract you?"

She could hear the little boy in him whining. "Vann, what's wrong with you?"

"Not a thing."

"Don't you get it? I'm your mother. I was thinking of you, both of you. Troy was missing and I was frantic. If I had called you right away and it turned out that he was all right, I would have disrupted your life for nothing. I didn't want you to worry."

"Wasn't that my decision to make? Ma, you should have told me what was going on right from the start."

She threw up her hands. "Fine, I was wrong."

"Yes, you were. Didn't you think that I'd be just as worried about Troy? I loved him just as much as you, except you were always hugging on him, never on me."

She was stunned. "That's because you wouldn't let me hug you."

"I was a child. That doesn't make sense."

"Oh, no? Vann, you were your father's child from the start. You literally had no use for me once you started to crawl."

"Ma, that doesn't—"

"Make sense? Nothing ever makes sense to you, Vann, un-less you give it your seal of approval. If you don't understand it, then it doesn't make sense."

"That's not fair. You're attacking me like I'm the reason everything has gone bad."

"Well, you're not the reason, and I am not attacking you. I'm trying to get you to see that everything in life is not laid out like a foot chart on the dance floor. Everything doesn't happen as we expect it to. Case in point, when you were a baby, you never let me baby you. You were not like most babies. You never liked me holding on to you, carrying you all over the place. You—"

"Maybe you didn't like babying me, Ma."

"Don't get smart, mister," she warned, speaking between her teeth.

He shifted in his seat.

"Vann, you were always very independent and very impa-tient. Did I ever tell you that you popped out of me like a cork from a champagne bottle?"

"Great imagery, but no."

"Well, you did. You came into the world kicking, ready to take off. Troy was nothing like that. He had to be dragged out of me, it was like he didn't even want to be born. He was . . . ," she said, looking for the right words, ". . . he was laid back, mellow. He loved being hugged and kissed and held for hours. And I liked kissing him, and hugging him, and holding him. Like I said before, even as a baby, you wouldn't let me do that to you. You had to be asleep for me to coddle you. Awake, you'd wiggle out of my arms. You had to be on the go. You didn't like to be pinned down. I never held it against you that you didn't want to be in my arms. I didn't feel that you didn't like me because you didn't want me holding on to you. I loved you just as much. I just figured you were born to be independent and didn't like me smothering you. Would you have wanted me to force my affection on you?"

"Maybe you should have."

She sighed and shook her head. "I showed you in other ways how much I loved you. If I failed, I'm sorry. I didn't know that you felt cheated."

"That I did, and now that Troy's gone, you have his daughter to give the love you had for him to. Even she comes before me."

She felt like he had slapped her face. "Vann, I know you don't mean what you just said. I know you don't feel threatened by Meika."

"I am not proud of it, but maybe I do," he said, his voice cracking. "Think about it, Ma. You're willing to take Meika and go underground forever. You'd—"

"It wouldn't be forever. Just long enough for Meika to grow up and make her own decisions without the court intervening."

"Twelve years is a long time. I'd be twelve years older. Don't you think I need you, you and Dad both? And what about my children? They'd be twelve years older, too. Don't you think they need their grandparents?" Vann again squeezed his nose.

Nola brought her hand to her mouth. She hadn't given a thought to Vann or to Sharice and Kareem. His children would grow up in the time she and Ron were in hiding. Was Vann right? Was she blinded by her love for Meika?

"See? You forgot about me again, but that's all right. That I do understand."

"My God. Vann, you're right. Your father and I were caught up in the heat of desperation," she said, feeling herself welling up. "But you have to know, that if it had been you who had died, and—"

"That would have been better, wouldn't it?" he asked, getting set to stand.

She gasped.

He stood. "Let me go, Ma, before I say something more

that I'll regret. I never intended to say these things to you—ever."

At this moment Nola, too, was afraid of what else Vann might say. Yet she could not let him leave.

"Please, Vann, sit down."

He couldn't. He didn't want to. He shook his head.

"Please," she said, softly, almost pleadingly.

Though he was hesitant, he slowly sank into the chair.

Nola rubbed her hands. They were cold, but that wasn't unusual. "Vann, if it had been you, and Michelle was unfit to raise Sharice and Kareem, I would do for your children what I am doing for Meika. If it meant running, I would have left Troy and Meika behind."

Squeezing on his nose didn't work anymore, tears brimmed and rolled down his cheeks. He cleared his throat. He tried wiping his tears away with his sleeve but they kept coming, so he hid his face behind his hand.

Nola saw that he was crying and it relieved her to know that he was letting go of a lot of his anger with her. Getting up, she went to him. She knelt down on the floor to the right of his legs. "Vann, would you let me hold you?"

A trickle of tears slipped from his eyes. Nola opened her arms. Vann bent over toward her. She took him into her arms and held him like she had held Troy so many times.

Vann let himself be held. It felt good. He couldn't fathom why in the world he would have wiggled out of his mother's arms so early in life. If her arms felt as good then as they did now, he had missed out on a thousand hugs. He cried. He felt like he was indeed her baby.

Nola cried because Vann was letting her love him.

He almost didn't want to end their embrace but he pulled away gently. He helped her up off the floor. He wiped his face dry with his sleeve. "Ma, I know this is stupid, but it's something that I've always wondered about. How is it that Troy got to be junior even though I was the firstborn?"

She raised her hand. "Guilty. It was me. I was positive that you were going to be a girl and I was determined to name my little girl Vannah."

"You must have been disappointed."

"Vann! Of course I wasn't disappointed. I was blessed to have had a healthy, beautiful baby boy. When you popped out, you filled my heart completely. You were worth waiting for. The only thing was the name. I was stuck on it. I refused to back down. I called you Vann. Do you hate your name?"

He felt stupid. "No, Ma."

"Good. I will say this in your father's defense. He wanted to name you after him, but I wouldn't let him. I cried. He gave in. That's all there was to it. No ulterior motive, except love."

He bowed his head. "Oh, man."

"I love you, Vann, and I am very proud of you. In your heart you know this, don't you?"

"I guess I do," he said, softly.

"Which is why I worry about you."

He looked up. "I'm fine."

"Yes, you're doing very well in your career. It's your home life I worry about."

"Don't worry about—"

"Vann, why have you never married Michelle?"

He simply looked at her. "I didn't think you'd dance at my wedding."

"In other words, you didn't think I approved of Michelle."

"Something like that."

"Vann, listen and understand what I'm about to tell you. I am a mother. Your mother. Like most mothers, I don't think any woman is good enough for my son. If it were up to me, only the Virgin Mary or an angel from heaven would qualify. Fathers feel the same way about their daughters. Just wait until Sharice meets the man she wants to marry. I guarantee you, you'll give him a hard time even if he's the cream of the crop."

He smiled. "I wish you had explained this to me years ago."

She chuckled drily. "In truth, I don't know if I knew this years ago. I was still young and so were you. I'll tell you what your grandfather told me. He said, 'Understanding, wisdom, and knowledge come with age, experience, and time.' Hopefully, you'll benefit from what you and I have just talked about. It's now part of your experience, and you are at an age where you understand, but you have a lot of wisdom and knowledge yet to gain."

He kissed Nola on the cheek. "I love you, Ma."

"I love you more," she said, kissing him back. "I have a call to make. Why don't you go talk to your father. I think you're ready."

THE broken glass lay in the sink. Two empty beer cans sat on the kitchen table in front of Ron. In his hand he held a third as he racked his brain for what to do. Not one sane solid solution came to mind. Vann had been right. He wasn't thinking and everything was falling apart around him. He had no control over what was about to happen to Meika. How could he face Vann or Nola when he didn't know what to do?

Behind Ron, the door opened. He lowered his head.

"Dad."

He did not respond.

"I'm sorry."

Ron turned his beer can up to his mouth and gulped.

Vann waited until Ron lowered his can. Then, standing alongside him, he rested his hand on his shoulder.

Ron still wouldn't look at Vann.

Vann moved slowly around the table until he was standing across from Ron. "Dad."

Finally, raising his eyes, Ron was surprised to see the tears in Vann's eyes.

"Dad, I'm sorry. I didn't mean what I said. I was thinking about myself and not Meika. I didn't want you and Ma to leave me behind," he said, feeling like a son and not the commandant he had been accused of being. "It seems at heart I'm still a needy child myself. I'm sorry if I hurt you."

Taken aback by the revelation, Ron choked up. He set the beer can down on the table and pushed it away. "That's all right, son. I've had time to think. You were right. We can't run. It would be hard on Meika, your mother, and on you. If we were caught, we'd be put in jail and lose Meika anyway."

Pulling a chair out, Vann sat. "We have to come up with something else."

"Son, I don't know what can be done to stop Cordelia, but what I do know is, it's gonna kill your mother the day Meika leaves this house."

Vann clasped his hand tightly in front of him on the table. "Short of killing Cordelia, I don't really know what to do myself. While you were in Family Court, I went to Troy's job and picked up a list of addresses for all the stores on that last American Express bill. Lopez and I went, first, to Macy's on Thirty-fourth Street. We were able to get a description of the jewelry, the clothes, and the entertainment units that were bought there. The women's clothes were all in size eight. Cordelia is a size twelve if she's anything, maybe even a size fourteen."

"How do you know that?"

"Michelle is a ten and Cordelia is certainly bigger than her."

"Damn."

"My sentiments exactly," Vann said, starting to pop his knuckles.

"What about the VCRs, the televisions, the CD players? Where were they delivered?"

"They were picked up in shipping and carried out by whoever bought them."

Ron hit the table with his fist. "Goddamnit! When are we gonna get a break? Troy didn't deserve to be cut down like that."

"No he didn't."

"I can't believe we're no closer to finding the person who killed him than we were five months ago."

Vann looked down at his knuckles. He had popped them so much over the years, they looked like rocks.

"It came!" Nola said excitedly, rushing into the kitchen.

Ron quickly turned around. "What came?"

"The reports from the credit bureaus!"

Ron's heart thumped. "How many?"

"Three!" she exclaimed, handing the weighty large white envelopes to Ron.

"I hope they tell us something," Ron said, taking the envelopes. Slowly, he turned back to face the table. He looked warily at Vann. They looked steadily into each other's eyes, almost afraid to look at the envelopes.

Nola clapped her hands. "Snap out of it! We are not going to know what's in them unless we open them."

Vann took one of the envelopes out of Ron's hand. Nola snatched one back herself. Her pulse raced. The three of them looked at each other with restrained anticipation as if they were waiting for a go-ahead whistle to blow. Then, as if they heard it, they all began tearing open the envelopes. Vann got his open first. He snapped the pages open, there were ten in all. His eyes moved across and down the pages with the speed of a man who was used to scanning pages of numbers. His eyes grew wider from page to page.

Ron ripped a corner of the pages he pulled out of his mangled envelope. Quickly unfolding the eleven pages, he realized right away that he didn't have his glasses but he didn't want to waste any time looking for them. Squinting, he held the pages a full arm's length away.

Using her finger like a letter opener to open her envelope, Nola didn't flinch from the burning sting of the paper cut she got. Reading the report she sucked on her finger. She knew well what every numerical and alphabetical code meant. Already there were five *x*'s on each new account indicating that no payments had been made in the five months since the accounts had been opened.

Vann looked up from his report. "I don't understand how just anyone could get credit cards in someone else's name, and not one credit card company caught on. I don't get it. It boggles my mind."

"Not mine," Ron said, scanning his third page. "It all comes down to corporate greed."

"In other words, the almighty dollar," Nola concluded, sitting. "If you notice, most of the accounts were opened by the end of November, just in time for Christmas shopping."

"The almighty dollar," Ron said.

Vann spread the report out in front of him. "There is almost fifty thousand dollars' worth of charges here. How in the world did they get this much credit on Troy's line?"

"Easy," Nola said, pushing her hair back off her face. "Troy was a good credit risk. He had a good job, he had only one major credit card and two department store cards and he paid his bills on time. Any creditor would have given him as many credit cards as he wanted."

"Which they did, posthumously," Ron said. "What do we do about this?"

"Nothing," she advised. "At least not yet."

"Why not?"

"Dad, we can straighten out Troy's credit report later. I don't think we'll have problems proving fraud. He's dead. However, if we close out the accounts too fast, we'll lose track of the killers."

Looking again at his report, Ron asked, "Where do we start?"

"With the address," Nola said. "Look at the top of the report. West Eighty-eighth Street in Manhattan."

Ron turned back to his first page. "That's why we didn't know anything about the charges."

Vann quickly turned back. "Didn't Troy go uptown that last day?"

"He went to the Met," Ron replied. "That's up at Fifth and Eighty-second."

"That's more than a coincidence. That Cookie person might live at that address."

Nola's throat suddenly went dry. "Do you suppose Troy was killed there?"

"Ma, I think it's more than a supposition. I think the person Troy met had to know that he was going to the movies down in Brooklyn Heights. He may have told this person because he may not have felt that his life was in danger."

"Which means he trusted this person," Ron concluded. "It couldn't be Cordelia."

"Maybe, maybe not."

Closing her eyes, Nola quietly massaged her temples. She hadn't been to a doctor, but she knew that her blood pressure had to be up. She was getting too many headaches.

"Are you all right?" Ron asked.

"Not really," she said, opening her eyes.

"Ma, Troy might not have been killed at that address. He could have been killed anywhere."

"Maybe, but I wouldn't rule that address out," Ron said. "If Troy was killed uptown, why would the killers bring his body and his car all the way back into Brooklyn?"

"That is a long way to carry a body," Vann said.

Annoyed, Nola asked, "Will you two stop referring to Troy as a body?"

"I'm sorry," Ron said quickly. "Anyway, someone's getting their mail at that address in Troy's name. Whether that person lives there or not, I don't know. It might just be a mail drop."

Vann suddenly pushed his chair back and stood. "What are we sitting here for? Let's go check this address out."

"No way," Nola said. "If the person who killed Troy is at this address, we need to call Detective Lopez and stay away from there ourselves. That person could kill us as soon as look at us."

Although he sat back down, Vann wasn't convinced that he shouldn't at least go uptown and get a look-see. "Ma, Lopez will take too long. Suppose this person decides to relocate. We might not get another chance to grab him."

"Or her," she added.

"I don't think they're going anywhere," Ron said. "As long as he or she thinks we don't know about them, they'll stay put."

"You hope. Look, Dad, it won't hurt to go take a look at the house. At least get the lay of the land."

"Ron, I don't think that's a good idea."

"Well, I do. We could take a look uptown, then stop off at the precinct as soon as we get back into Brooklyn."

"Let's go," Vann said eagerly.

Nola wasn't as enthused. "Why don't you call Detective Lopez first. I don't think we should go uptown without him knowing about it."

Knowing that she was afraid, and knowing, too, that she wouldn't be satisfied until he called Lopez, Vann went to the wall phone. "Ma, I'll call Lopez, but I'm telling you, a herd of wild horses won't keep me from checking out that address."

"I'm with you, son," Ron said, gathering up his copy of the credit report and getting up from the table. "Nola, you don't have to come with us. We can drop you off at Beatrice's. We'll pick you and Meika up on our way back."

"Detective Richard Lopez," Vann said into the telephone.

"Not on your life," Nola said, refolding her copy of the credit report. "If you and Vann are going, I'm going. Beatrice wants Meika to spend the night anyway, which is just as well. I don't know how I'm going to act when I see her."

Vann hung up the telephone. "Lopez is out of the precinct. He's expected back after six. Gives us plenty of time to get uptown and see what we're dealing with. Let's do it."

"Did you leave a message?" Nola asked, standing.

"No. He probably won't return the call once he hears that it's me anyway."

"You should have left a message, Vann. He might surprise you."

"Ma, the only way Lopez can surprise me is if he woke up one morning and became a real detective."

"Don't forget your report," Ron said, heading for the kitchen door. "Let's go. I wanna get through rush-hour traffic."

"Dad, you got a minute?"

Ron and Nola stopped and looked back at Vann.

She sensed from the way he was looking at her that he wanted to speak to Ron alone. "I need to run upstairs for a minute," she said, leaving the kitchen.

Vann busied himself folding his copy of the report. He had to find the right words.

Ron waited.

Vann stuck the report back inside the envelope. He looked at his father. He humbly extended his hand. "Dad, that was a great idea you had about sending for the credit reports. We will find Troy's killer."

Extending his own hand, Ron and Vann firmly shook, each feeling a surge of warmth and admiration for the other. Ron smiled. "Let's go, son."

TWENTY-SEVEN

WHAT they were doing felt so clandestine, so scary, Nola dreaded every minute that ticked by. The streetlights had come on, though they didn't do much to lighten up anything other than the space around the light pole by several feet. It didn't help that it wasn't a calm day. Every so often the wind whipped up a stray piece of paper or plastic bag that sailed past the car. Large newly budding tree limbs and branches above them cast an ever-changing road map of shadows across houses, stoops, the street, cars, and, thankfully, Ron and Vann's faces, offering them some margin of cover, sparse though it was. Listening to Ron and Vann talking up front like they were detectives, one would think they were only minutes away from nabbing Troy's killers. The only problem was, those minutes had turned into an hour and thirty-five minutes. Nola's back was hurting from slumping down in the backseat for so long, and she was freezing—it was raw out. Very few people walked past them and none seemed to notice them sitting in the car, though no telling who, from behind their blinds and curtains, had seen them park and were wondering why they were still sitting out there. No one had come or gone from number 112 so they had no idea what any of the residents looked like, nor did they have any idea of what to do if they did see anyone. Ron had to grab Vann to keep him from bolting from the car to confront the first man he saw stop in front of the house to light up a cigarette. Afterward, the man walked on out of the block without a backward glance.

Vann had never been very patient, though he had never been excitable or jittery either, which he was from the moment they parked across the street from the four-story brownstone with the tall black double doors. He kept tapping on the steering wheel with his thumb and asking, "When are these people coming home?" It was worse than hearing him ask, "Are we there yet?" time and again when they used to go on long car trips. At least then he was a child.

When Ron could not take Vann's tapping a minute longer, he put his hand on Vann's hand to stop him. They exchanged a brief look before returning to their vigil of watching the house. Neither was ready to give up.

Nola was ready to go. "I'm freezing."

Vann sighed heavily. "See, Ma. That's why you should've stayed home. We can't keep turning the car on and off. There is nothing more obvious than an idling car loaded with people."

"Then let's go. We've seen the house."

"But we haven't seen anyone yet."

"Vann, you said you wanted to see the house. You didn't say anything about wanting to see anyone."

"Surprise, Ma, I do."

"I knew I should not've trusted you on this. First you said we'd wait for just a few minutes, then it was a half hour, now you wanna wait all night. I don't wanna stay here, it's too dangerous."

"Oh man," he said, looking hopelessly at Ron.

"Okay, look," Ron said, turning sideways in his seat to look back at Nola. "Nola, it's not that late. This is the first real break we've had since Troy died. We can't leave yet."

Pushing her glove back from her watch, Nola held up her arm and, moving it around, tried to catch a sliver of light.

When she finally did, she peered at her watch. "I'm just as ecstatic as you are that we have a solid lead, but it's six-fifteen. Don't you think we should get down to the precinct before Detective Lopez leaves for the day?"

"He works evenings."

"Well . . . then . . . we should try and catch him before he goes out on a case."

"Damn, Nola. Next time, don't come with us."

"I won't."

"Damn," Ron said, facing forward again.

"Please, Ma, just a few minutes more. People are just starting to get in from work about now."

That's exactly what she was afraid of.

"When we finish downtown," Vann said, "I'll take you to dinner at a restaurant of your choice."

"Don't try to appease me. I'm not in the mood. You two have fifteen minutes and not one minute more beyond six-thirty."

"Thank you," he said, looking back at the house, wishing that he had not forgotten his cell phone. He would have called a cab and put her in it.

By the minute Nola grew more uneasy. They really could get killed. "I'm freezing. I want to leave now."

"Aw, shit!" Vann said, angrily, striking the steering wheel with the ball of his hand.

"Watch your mouth!"

"Nola!" Ron exploded. "I knew you didn't have the heart for this. You're too damn chickenhearted. I remember that one and only time you went on the Cyclone. You screamed until you almost had a heart attack. You embarrassed me in front of my friends and everybody in the damn park."

"Fine. I'm chickenhearted and I'm damn proud of it. It's dark out here. I want to go home."

"Ma!"

"Vann, there are no lights on the outside of that house. We

cannot see anyone or anything clearly. The murderers could already be inside for all we know. Suppose they've been looking back at us all this time? Maybe they were waiting for it to get dark so that they could shoot us."

Ron punched himself in the thigh. "Take her home!"

"Aw, Dad! If we leave, we might miss something important," Vann said, totally pissed off. He glanced back at Nola. "Ma, nobody's gonna shoot us. They don't know who we are. Calm down."

"Oh no? They shot Troy, didn't they? Look, I'm scared. You two are sitting up there without a clue as to what to do if you did see someone go into that house. Don't you know that these people are psychotic, cold-blooded murderers? They won't hesitate to shoot us. You kids wanna play cops and robbers, then get some backup like real policemen. I am not going to another funeral. Take me back to Brooklyn, *now!*"

Grumbling, Ron stared straight ahead and shook his head.

Wishing they had left her bound and gagged at home, Vann let his head fall sideways against the window with a thump.

"Start it up!" Ron ordered, reaching back for his seat belt.

Vann didn't move a muscle.

Nola rolled her eyes at Ron and then scowled at the back of Vann's head until he lifted his head away from the window. She could hear them both breathing like mad bulls but she didn't care how mad they got with her. At least they wouldn't get themselves killed. Finally starting the car, Vann took his time turning on the headlights. The darkness would not let Nola see Vann's eyes through the rearview mirror, but she knew he was smothering in his anger with her. She didn't care because when he got tired of waiting, he would throw all caution to the wind, go up to the door, ring the bell, and demand to know who killed Troy. No, she was not sitting still for that, not without the police knowing about it.

She sat back as Vann started pulling out of their parking space.

Ron suddenly lurched forward. "Wait a minute!"

Vann slammed the brake to the floor. "What's wrong?"

"Look."

The dark figures of a woman and two small children suddenly appeared in front of the house. They turned into the yard. Shadows of the children went ahead of the woman up the stairs, while the woman went farther into the yard to the side of the stairs, where they couldn't differentiate her form from the opaque blackness that engulfed her.

From the backseat Nola peeked out of the rear side window. Her heart sank to the pit of her stomach. It was not Cordelia. Oh, how she had prayed that it would be.

Vann turned off the headlights. He put the car in reverse and eased it neatly back into the parking space. He shut off the engine.

Restrained by his seat belt, Ron leaned toward Vann, trying his best to see the woman move. "I can't see her. Where did she go?"

Peering hard into the blackness, his forehead and nose pressed into the glass, Vann tried to make out where the woman was. "The kids are still at the door. They're waiting for her, she's probably getting the mail. There was no mail slot in the door at the top of the stairs, there's probably a mailbox on the side."

"I wonder who she is?" Nola asked.

"One thing for sure, it's certainly not Cordelia," he said, feeling disappointed.

The form of the woman suddenly came out of the darkness and she climbed the stairs. It took a minute before she unlocked the door and opened it. She turned on the light. The entryway was illuminated. A second door with lace curtains stood only a few feet away. With her back to the street, neither Vann nor Nola could see the woman's face as she let her children go ahead of her. The woman pushed the door up behind her, locking out the plane of blackness on the outside. In a short time, the lights on the second floor came on, illuminating the closed white mini-blinds.

There was a collective release of breath as Nola, Vann, and Ron settled back. Without being prompted, Vann started the car again. He turned on the headlights and quickly pulled out. The car's beams bounced off the parked cars on the other side of the street, lighting a path out of the dark block.

Nola didn't know what to think. Could the woman, a mother, be involved in killing Troy? "I doubt that she lives in that big house by herself with those two children," she said, holding on to a shred of hope that Cordelia might be somewhere in the picture after all.

"She doesn't," Ron said. "There were three doorbells at the top of the stairs."

"At least it wasn't a total waste of time, huh, Ma?"

"I hope not."

"The question is," Ron said, "do the killers live there?"

TWENTY-EIGHT

LOPEZ was not thrilled to see them. Too late he started to about-face and go back the way he came, but Vann had already called his name. Looking at the sick expression on his face and at his moving lips, Nola could only imagine what Lopez was saying to himself about them.

"We have something solid," Vann blurted, rushing at Lopez, forcing him to take a step back.

"I'm busy on another case," Lopez said, showing Vann the folder in his hand. "We're making progress on your brother's case, however, I can't talk to you right now. Why don't you give me a call tomorrow evening."

"Just a damn minute," Vann said. "Are you brushing us off?"

This is the very reason she told Vann to call first. Other detectives, uniformed police officers, and civilians were watching them. "Ron, Vann," Nola said, "maybe we should make an appointment."

"I can't work with this man," Vann said, starting to turn away.

Nola quickly slipped her arm around Vann's waist and kept him from walking off.

"This makes no damn sense," he said, glaring at Lopez. "We have answers, and he has no time."

"I got this, Vann. Let me handle this," Ron said. "Detective, I'm sure you're very busy but this can't wait."

"Mr. Kirkwood, this is an important case I'm working on and—"

"And my son's case isn't?" Ron boomed.

Slapping the folder in his hand against his right side, Lopez huffed and walked away.

"That's it!" Vann said. "I'm not putting up with this jerk anymore."

"You're right, son," Ron said, raising his voice. "I want another detective on this case. It makes no damn sense that every time we try to talk to this man, we have to put up with his shit."

Glancing back, Lopez cut his eyes at Ron.

"I'm writing the commissioner," Vann threatened. "I'll have your damn badge."

Nola could not believe what was happening.

Lopez went over to the desk sergeant. "Sarge, I can't talk to these people."

"If you were an intelligent man," Vann said, "you could talk to us people."

Nola took hold of Vann's arm. "That's enough. Ron, we should just leave."

"We should have stayed uptown and taken care of this ourselves," Vann said.

"Sir," the desk sergeant said, addressing Ron respectfully, "if you'll give Detective Lopez a minute, he'll be right with you."

"I would like to see Captain Aniston," Ron demanded.

"Captain Aniston is off the premises. If you'll sit—"

"Never mind," he said. "I know who to talk to. Let's go."

Nola looked at Ron and Vann. They wore the same bookend faces of anger as they stalked toward the door. She followed behind them out of the precinct.

* * *

THE DESK sergeant and two plainclothes detectives started talking to Lopez at the same time.

"Who the hell are they?"

"Richard, maybe you should talk to them. Maybe they got something."

"DAD. WE should have asked for another detective way back in January."

"Vann, if I've learned anything since Troy died, I've learned that hindsight only makes regretful people sorry and we don't have time to be sorry about what we should've done. We have to act on what we have to do now."

"I'm with you on that."

Rushing to catch up to them, Nola slipped her arm through Ron's. "Where are we going?" she asked, hunching her shoulders up to her ears to protect her neck from the cold air.

"Home. But first thing tomorrow morning, I'm calling our alderman."

"Mr. Kirkwood!"

Neither Ron nor Vann stopped.

Nola looked back. Detective Lopez was running to catch up with them. "Ron, maybe we should listen to what he has to say."

With Vann matching his stride, Ron picked up his pace, pulling Nola along.

Lopez kept running. He caught up to them as Vann was unlocking the passenger side car door. "Mr. Kirkwood," he said, addressing Ron, "can I talk to you a minute?" Lopez tried to catch his breath. He exhaled clouds of white breath into Ron's face.

"A minute ago you didn't have a minute," Vann said, pulling open the door. He pulled the front seat forward for Nola to climb into the back. She made no move to get in.

"You people barge in on me any old time you want," Lopez argued, "like I ain't got nothing to do but sit around on my hands, waiting for y'all to show up and make my day. I got other cases, other families to deal with that think their cases are just as important as yours. You people gotta cut me some slack."

"Cut you some slack?" Ron snapped. "My son doesn't have any slack down in his coffin. You're no closer to arresting his killer than you were five months ago."

"Sir, some cases go years unsolved."

"This case won't. I guarantee you, my son's killer will be caught. You, on the other hand, Lopez, are of no help to us. You are a hindrance. If you can't handle this case, step aside."

"Mr. Kirkwood, I'm doing my best."

"Detective, it isn't good enough."

Lopez was exasperated. He put his hands on his hips and glanced vexedly back at the precinct. "Mr. Kirkwood, me and my partner plan to follow up on a lead we got—"

"What lead?" Vann asked, letting go of the back of the seat. "You haven't told us about a lead."

"I can't apprise you of our every move. Things don't always pan out."

"We don't care if every lead you have don't pan out," Ron said. "Telling us about the little things, the little leads, lets us know that you're at least on the case, that you haven't shoved it under a rug somewhere."

"I wouldn't do that."

"Man," Vann said, irritably, "we don't know that. You don't apprise us of anything, and when we bring you information, you get a shit attitude with us."

Lopez shook his head. "You people aren't hearing me."

"Oh, we hear you, Detective," Ron confirmed. "That's why I'm requesting a new detective tomorrow morning."

Lopez threw up his arms. "Look, I can't do no more than I've been doing."

"Ron, let's be fair," Nola said. "We did barge in on Detective Lopez tonight."

Lopez nodded his appreciation to Nola.

"Nola—"

"Just a minute," she said, putting her hand on Ron's arm. "We have been disrespectful of Detective Lopez by disregarding his time and the importance of the other cases that he's working on."

"No, Ma. It's not like that. He—"

"Vann, you've said yourself that he can't possibly work all the cases he has, right?"

"Yeah, but that doesn't mean he's excused from working Troy's case."

"I haven't stopped working the case."

"See, he's still working the case," she said. "Detective, would it help if we gave you notice when we need to see you?"

"How much notice?" Ron asked. "A month? A year? Our leads could go cold by then."

"No, sir, a few hours tops. Call me. If I'm not in, leave a message. I swear I'll call you back, I'll even come to you. But when you barge in like you did tonight, I can't always be at your disposal."

"That's fine. Isn't it, Ron?"

"I don't know," he mumbled, looking off up Flatbush Avenue.

"Vann, is it all right with you?" Nola asked.

Vann, too, was looking off up Flatbush Avenue at the triple lane of red taillights in the stop-and-go traffic of drivers heading home from Manhattan. More and more he wished that they had left his mother at home, despite the fact that if it were not for her, he might be locked up by now for assault on a police officer. He was tired of battling Lopez, and if he had to, he'd find the killer himself.

"Vann?" Nola asked again.

He slowly turned his head and looked at her. "I just wanna find Troy's killer."

"So do we," Lopez said.

"Finally," she said, "we do agree on something."

"Let's go," Ron said, again taking Nola's arm.

Vann started around the front of the car.

"Not just yet," she said, patting Ron's hand on her arm. "Detective, we have some very important information you should know about."

Ron tugged at her arm.

"Ma!" Vann exclaimed over the roof of the car.

She went on. "My husband and son asked for and received copies of Troy's credit reports. If you recall, he was killed at the end of October."

"Yes."

"Well, several new accounts were opened up in his name in the month of November, and someone is still charging on those accounts."

Lopez's eyes widened. "A trail!"

"Better than that," she said, "we have an address."

"Are you serious?"

Vann smirked. "That's what we came here to tell you."

"Can you come back inside so that we can talk?"

"Humph!" Ron said, looking away.

"We wouldn't want to barge in on you," Vann quipped.

"Vann, please," Nola said, cutting her eyes at him.

"Hey, I thought he didn't have time for us. Am I right, Dad?"

"That's the impression I got."

Nola looked at Ron standing as straight and as tall as a giant oak in an unbending, unwavering stance that said he wasn't about to be obliging. She knew what she had to do. "Detective, why don't you give us a minute. We'll be right in."

Lopez glanced at Ron and Vann. "Yes, ma'am." He started back toward the precinct.

Nola turned on Ron and Vann. "You two stubborn, egotistical, bullheaded mules ought to be ashamed of yourselves. We're the ones that are wrong for not making an appointment or, Vann, leaving a message."

"Ma, we don't need him."

"Yes we do. Both of you need to drop the attitude and get over yourselves. We have Meika to think about."

Vann slapped the roof of the car. "Damn. Fine. If that's what you want."

Nola held Ron's gaze. She felt his anger.

"Vann, lock up the car," Ron ordered, glaring down at Nola.

"Ron, I know—"

"Nola. Don't ever talk for me or make me look like an idiot in front of another man again."

"I was just try—"

"Shut up!" he snarled.

"Dad!"

"Excuse me?" she asked, appalled that Ron dared to speak to her like that. "I know that we're all upset, but—"

Ron snatched hold of Nola's upper arm, he dug his fingers into her.

"Ron!"

"Nola, as long as we've been together, you know damn well I can speak for myself, and so can Vann. Don't ever put yourself between us and another man again. We can handle ourselves."

"Take your damn fingers out of my arm before I break them."

Ron did not let up on his hold.

Vann rushed around the car. "Hold up! Ma, Dad. Come on. Don't you guys go getting into a fight out here," he said, pulling on his father's arm to get him to loosen his viselike grip on his mother.

With his left elbow, Ron shoved Vann aside. "Son, this is between me and my wife."

"Your wife, Dad, but my mother. You're hurting her."

Ron cut his eyes at Vann.

Vann challenged Ron's gaze.

Nola could feel the tension between Ron and Vann. Lord knows she'd die if they got into it again. "Vann, don't worry about me. I can handle your father. If he does not let go of me, he'll wish he had."

Ron stood firm though he loosened his grip.

She felt it.

Vann knew that his mother didn't play, but neither did his father. He remembered the one occasion he had seen them physically fight. At the time, he was more worried about his father than his mother. There wasn't a thing that wasn't nailed down that she didn't pick up to throw at him, including a chair, the iron, and the ironing board; that's how angry she had gotten. The only thing that stopped her was when his father quickly grabbed her from behind and held on to her with her arms pinned down to her sides. With a lot of fight in her still, she struggled until, from sheer exhaustion, her anger subsided and she ended up in tears. And what had made her lose it then? His father was trying to tell her what to do and had slapped her when she refused. That was the last time, that he was aware of, that his father ever touched her. It was a scary day for him and Troy.

"What are you going to do, Nola? Throw a fit?"

"All over you if I have to."

Vann could not believe what he was hearing, standing out there on the sidewalk a stone's throw from the precinct with policemen passing all around them. "Hey!" he whispered harshly. "Are y'all crazy, acting like this? Dad, what you doing, man?"

Though she could feel Ron's grip weaken, Nola did not pull herself free of him. He was going to have to let go of her on his own.

Finally, he did let go. He went back to the car and, leaning on the roof of it, dropped his head onto his folded arms.

Nola turned away from him.

Vann followed her. "Ma, you all right?"

"Give me the keys to the car."

"I'll take you home."

"You wanna do something for me? Go inside that precinct and talk to Detective Lopez about the credit reports and that house. If you don't do it, I will."

"I'll do it."

"Fine. Give me the keys," she said, holding out her hand. "You and your father can make your own way."

Vann placed the keys in the palm of Nola's gloved hand.

Going around the car to the driver's side, she unlocked the car and got in.

"Dad, step back from the car."

She didn't care if Ron was on the car or not when she put the key in the ignition, started it up, and pulled out. How they'd get home, she didn't really care either, because when they got there, she wasn't going to be there.

TWENTY-NINE

BEATRICE certainly didn't keep her house as warm as Nola's, nor were her blankets as cozy as her comforters, which is why Nola was still curled up in a tight ball under the covers with only the top of her head exposed, hugging herself, putting off the inevitable of having to get up and look into Meika's eyes. True to her "I'm not taking your side just because you're my cousin" self, Beatrice said she would have done the same thing to Ron and Vann if it meant catching Troy's killers. Yet she claimed that she could see why Ron got mad, male ego and all. As far as Nola was concerned, Ron's ego was his problem; his putting his hand on her was hers. Regrets, she had none, except for maybe running away from home like a spoiled child out to get even with her parent. What she should have done was stay home and kick Ron out of the bedroom, then she could have slept in her own warm bed. If kicking him out of the bed didn't satisfy her need to get back at him, she could have hidden his watch or his car keys and sat back smugly while he frantically searched every nook and cranny. She had been doing vindictive things like that to get even with him for years, yet he never caught on. He thought he was just prone to misplacing things. When she was satisfied that he had suffered enough, she'd offer to help him search for what he was looking for, and then, magnanimously, she'd point him in the right direction. No fuss, no muss, no more arguments, her need for revenge sated.

There was no such feeling this morning and, worse yet, she

had no idea of how things had gone with Detective Lopez. Last night she had been too angry to talk to Vann or Ron when they called.

"Mama!"

Nola pulled the covers down just enough to peek out at Meika. "Good morning."

Meika jumped up onto the bed. "Good morning. You getting up now?"

Seeing the twinkle in Meika's eyes warmed her more than the blankets she was under. "Do I have to?"

"Uh-huh. Cousin Bea said come downstairs and eat breakfast."

"Tell her I don't want breakfast."

"Okay," she said, sliding down off the bed and skipping toward the door.

"Wait a minute. Where's my kiss?"

"Oh, I forgot," Meika said, skipping back to the bed. Their kiss was a loud *smack!*

"Thank you."

"You're welcome," Meika replied, skipping off again, leaving the door open in her wake.

Nola drew the covers around her even tighter.

Buzzz!

The sound of the bell ringing reminded Nola that the rest of the world was up and about. Sighing, she turned away from the door, covered her head up altogether, and sank deeper into the bed. This was one of those days that getting up just wasn't worth the effort. She began to drift off to sleep.

The covers were suddenly snatched off her!

"Hey!" she shouted, sitting bolt upright and grabbing for the covers.

Beatrice stood on the far side of the bed, smiling mischievously, holding on to one end of the two blankets. "I'm just making sure you're alive under there in that ugly old granny gown. It's a wonder Ron still gets it up for you."

"It's not the gown, smarty, it's what's under it."

"I don't wanna know about that."

"Bea, you better cover me back up before I burn all of your wigs."

Beatrice threw the covers back over Nola. "You're so ugly this morning."

"That's because I'm cold," she said, lying down again. She nestled snugly under the covers.

"Woman, please. I turned up the heat. Don't you see me sweating? It feels like the tropics in here."

"Beatrice, you sweat when you light a match."

"So, you freeze when you touch an ice cube."

Slanting their eyes and glaring playfully at each other, they burst out laughing.

"Bea, you're so crazy."

"So are you," Beatrice said, dragging the heavy wooden armchair from the wall up to the bed. Holding on to the arms of the chair, she lowered herself with a grunt. "Ron and Vann are downstairs."

Nola groaned.

"Nola, what did you expect for them to do? Wait around for you to give them permission to talk to you?"

"They could have given me time to breathe."

"You mean time to sulk."

"Sulk, breathe, either way, Ron owes me an apology."

"And if he doesn't?"

"Then I'm not talking to him."

"Nola, you're sulking worse than a teenager. Get over it."

"Get over it? In case you haven't noticed, my life has been pure hell since Troy was killed."

"I know that."

"Well, then I shouldn't have to put up with abuse from Ron, of all people."

"From what you told me, he just had hold of your arm."

"He was hurting me—that's abuse."

"Nola, you know good and well that Ron would never hurt you. Both of you are probably just stressed out."

"That's no excuse."

"No it isn't, but you're this close," Beatrice said, measuring off an inch space with her thumb and forefinger, "to catching Troy's killers. Ron says there's going to be a stakeout at that house you went to last night. They want to tell you about it."

"Well, at least they did that right. What else did he say?"

"He said he'll talk more about it when you come downstairs."

Nola stared up at the ceiling. "What kind of mood is he in?"

"He seems himself. He's not upset or anything. I'm sure he's sorry about last night."

"Humph. If he was sorry, he'd be up here instead of you."

"Why should he come up here with you acting all crabby?"

"Thanks a lot," she said, drawing the covers back over her head.

Beatrice pulled the covers down again. "Nola, you don't have time to bury your head in this bed."

"I know that," she said, sitting up and pulling the covers up to her chin. "Bea, I need a break from this madness. We all need a break. Like you said, we're stressed out. We're snapping at each other; getting overly sensitive; and to make matters worse, that damn Cordelia is taking Meika from us. I feel like I'm caught in a tornado and I haven't been spun off yet. Troy's death turned our lives upside-down and we haven't been able to recover."

"I know, but you can't let his death tear you and Ron apart."

"I don't think it's tearing us apart, I just think it's testing us, seeing if we're worthy of being a family."

"Of course you are."

"Bea, you don't understand. Before Troy died, we had only to deal with who we were to our own individual selves. Now we have to deal with who we are and what we mean to each other."

"What does that mean? Don't we know who we are and what we mean to each other?"

"I used to think we knew, but it seems to me, in our hearts, we're harboring a lot of pain, a lot of anger against each other."

"But a lot of families hold their pain in."

"Yes, and that's how they're destroyed."

"So what's your point? Who's harboring in our family? Ron?"

"No. Vann. He's angry with me."

"Why?"

"It's something he's been holding against me for years."

"Oh?"

"Yesterday he told me that he didn't think I loved him. Bea, can you imagine my son, growing up in my house, thinking that I didn't love him?"

Beatrice dropped her eyes for a brief but noticeable second. Nola felt betrayed. "Bea, you knew?"

"Nola, well, in truth, I never thought that Vann felt unloved. I knew that he thought that Troy was your favorite."

She drew back. "You knew. Why didn't you tell me?"

"Nola, who am I?" Beatrice asked, bringing her hand to her chest. "Vann and Troy were the children I never had. They lived with you, but they also shared their lives with me. And most of what they told me when they were troubled, they asked me not to tell you."

"But you kept secrets from me about how my sons felt about me."

"But they trusted me. Wasn't it better that they talked their troubles out with me, rather than trying to find answers out in the street with people who might've given them bad advice or led them into drugs or crime?"

"Yes, but—"

"Nola, Vann knew that you loved him, he just thought that you cared a little more for Troy."

"That's not true."

"I told him that Troy probably felt the same way he did when Ron doted more on him."

"Apparently, that wasn't a good enough explanation, Bea. Yesterday, that wasn't a little boy who was griping about feeling unloved, it was a grown man."

"Did you straighten him out?"

"I hope I did," she said, feeling unsure. "I pray that I did. He cried, we hugged, but I wish I had known how he felt years ago."

"Maybe I should've told you, but, at the time, Vann was adamant that I not tell you. I didn't want to break his trust."

"In hindsight, we wish we could have done so many things differently," Nola said, reaching behind her back and lifting her pillow up against the headboard. She leaned back against it. "I wish that I had gone to the movies with Troy and Meika that day."

"I don't think it would have made a difference."

"I know I might not have made a difference, but I would have had a little more time with Troy."

"That's why we have to make every moment we have with each other count, Nola."

Nola began to tear. "Bea, do you think I was a good mother to Troy?"

"Nola, you were a wonderful mother to Troy and Vann, both."

"I tried my best."

"You did more than your best, you raised great sons—great men."

"Oh, Bea," she said, tearfully. "Thank you."

"You shouldn't have any doubts, Nola, but it's understandable with all that you're going through."

Nola sniffled. She had been doing a lot of doubting lately.

Beatrice wiped at her eyes. "Life is cruel. I never imagined that I'd see the day we'd lose either one of our children. Vann and his children live in Atlanta, Troy is gone, and Meika is being stolen right from under our noses. It just don't seem right."

"It's not," Nola agreed, wiping her cheeks dry.

"Isn't there anything we can do about Meika?"

"According to our lawyer, unless Cordelia is declared an unfit mother again, as biological parent, she stands a good chance of getting full custody."

"But you and Ron are the biological grandparents, don't you have just as much of a right to raise Meika, especially since Troy had custody?"

"Not according to Mr. Lipscomb. He says grandparents have no rights when it comes to fighting for custody of grandchildren against a biological parent. The courts would rather rule in favor of a parent with an abuse or drug or alcohol history, than give custody over to a grandparent. If Cordelia hadn't come forward, we would not have had a problem. As it stands, we're lucky to be getting visitation."

Beatrice's large breast swelled as she puffed herself up indignantly. "Visitation is your right."

"Visitation rights for grandparents are not etched in stone, Bea. Limitations are set by the sitting judge. In the final ruling, we could get a day a month; a weekend once a month; or zero days a month. It all depends on the judge's discretion. After what happened in court yesterday, I'd say that judge is hell-bent on giving Meika back to Cordelia."

"When are you going to tell Meika that she has to go live with Cordelia?"

"I'm hoping that I won't have to."

"Nola, you can't let it wait to the last minute."

"Maybe Cordelia will fall in a deep hole somewhere and break her damn neck before the twenty-fourth."

"You don't mean that."

"I sure do."

"Girl, you have to pray more. You have to believe," Beatrice said. She took hold of her left wrist with her right hand and rested them on her full stomach.

"I have been praying, Bea, and things aren't getting any better," she said, glancing past Beatrice to the Little League baseball and basketball trophies on the dresser. Some were Troy's, some were Vann's. They took turns giving them to Beatrice, they loved her that much.

"Nola, you haven't stopped believing, have you?"

She rolled her eyes back to Beatrice. "Let's just say, I'm . . . uh . . . wondering if God's on vacation."

"Honey, don't let Troy's death or what's about to happen to Meika make you lose faith."

That was it exactly. She was having a problem with her faith. If God wasn't on vacation, where was He? Like Vann, she wanted to know why God didn't step in to protect Troy's life. Why was He letting Cordelia take Meika from her? Why was He forsaking her, leaving her alone in an ocean of trouble to flap her arms and kick wildly to stay afloat? She was questioning God although she knew that it wasn't a mark of good faith.

She had to wonder. Nola threw back the covers. "I better get up before Ron comes and drags me out of bed." She swung her legs over the side of the bed.

"Nola, I don't want you to lose faith. I know it's hard right now, but God would never forsake you."

"Mama!" Meika called, scampering into the room. "Poppie say, when you getting up?"

A sense of timely reprieve came over her. When Beatrice started talking faith and religion, she usually ended up preaching. Until Troy's death, her faith had been just as strong as Beatrice's, and still she wouldn't say that she had lost it completely, though she had to wonder what God had in mind for her. Until she knew, she was full of doubt and uncertainty. She couldn't bring herself to believe that He wanted Meika to suffer the rest of her life at the hands of Cordelia; that was unfathomable.

Meika planted her hands on her sides. "Ma . . . maah! Come on."

"I'm coming."

Beatrice giggled. "Is she supposed to have her hands on her hips?"

"That's what she thinks," Nola said, standing. She stretched high and wide and yawned at the same time.

Beatrice again giggled. "What hips?"

"I got hips," Meika announced, patting her flat sides.

"Where? In your shoes?"

"No!" she said, her hands still on her sides. "My feet are in my shoes."

"Then your hips must have dropped off somewhere else. When you find them, I want to see them."

Frowning, Meika cocked her head to the side.

"Beatrice, stop teasing her."

"I'm not teasing our little princess. I just want to know where her hips are."

"Beatrice, leave her alone."

"Look Meika," Beatrice said, patting her thick hips through the opening on the sides of the chair. "These are hips."

Looking at Beatrice's wide hips protruding from the sides of the chair, Meika walked up to her and fell forward onto her lap, her elbows resting on Beatrice's mountainous thighs. With the sincerest look on her face, Meika said, "When my hips get big like yours, everybody'll see them then."

Doubling over, Nola snickered into her hands. "They sure will."

"That's not funny!"

"You asked for it."

Beatrice flipped one of Meika's braids. "Little girl, when your hips get as big as mine, they won't be called hips, they'll be called bumpers."

Nola burst out laughing.

Frowning, Meika looked at her. "That's not funny."

"No, it's not," Beatrice said sternly. "Go tell Poppie your mama is coming down in a minute."

Still confused, Meika straightened up. She looked curiously at Nola.

"Go on," Beatrice said, moving her along by tapping Meika on the backside. "We'll be right down." As soon as Meika was out of the room, she turned on Nola. "You know I'm sensitive about my hips."

"Well, you brought up the subject."

Frowning, Beatrice folded her arms high up across her large breasts.

"All right. I'm sorry for laughing, Bea, but you did leave yourself open for that. You're the one that called them humpers."

A little smile slowly began to replace the pout on Beatrice's lips. "It was funny, wasn't it?" she asked, beginning to shake as a hearty laugh exploded from her.

Nola fell back on the bed laughing. She felt better about facing Ron.

THIRTY

RON often said that *sorry* itself was a sorry word. It was a word that never rolled off his tongue as smoothly as the word *baby* when they made love; or as fluidly as the words *thank you* when she baked him his favorite coffee spice cake or massaged his often strained back. He would willingly do anything at all to make up, as long as he didn't have to utter the word *sorry.*

Nola had taken her time getting herself together before joining everyone in the dining room. Not surprisingly, Ron was very attentive, to the point of fawning—getting up to give her his chair, pouring her a glass of orange juice, and holding her coat for her to get into when they prepared to leave. He had no problem looking into her eyes when he gave her the details of what Detective Lopez was going to do to track down Troy's killer. Yet he wouldn't say that he was sorry.

While Beatrice thought Ron's actions spoke for him, Nola didn't agree. It was an easy way out of a verbal apology. However, Beatrice was right about one thing, they had too much to do for her to be sulking, they had to work together.

It was two-thirty by the time they pulled up in their driveway. Tailing behind Vann and Ron, she was alarmed when Vann suddenly opened the door and leaped out before Ron could come to a complete stop. Vann rushed back toward the street.

Nola had to jam on her brakes to keep from ramming into Ron. "What happened? Vann, where are you going?"

"Who me?" Meika asked from the backseat.

"No, Vann," she replied as Ron quickly got out of the car and he, too, walked across the lawn back to the street. It wasn't until Nola turned her head that she saw where they were off to—Detectives Lopez and Callahan had climbed out of their car at the curb and were approaching Vann. They were not expected and their showing up could only mean that they had something important to share. Easing her foot up off the brake, Nola put the car in park and shut off the engine. She glimpsed Ron, Vann, and the detectives as they started up the walkway. They had already started talking. Fumbling with the seat belt release, she tried to unbuckle herself. She wanted to hear every word they said firsthand.

"I wanna get out," Meika said, after failing to unlock her seat belt.

"Just a minute," Nola said, finally releasing her own seat belt.

"Nola!" Ron called, beckoning to her.

"I'm coming!"

In the few minutes it took her to hurriedly gather her and Meika's overnight bags and get Meika herself out of the car, Vann had unlocked the front door and was leading the detectives inside. Trying to close the back door, Nola dropped her overnight bag. She reached down to pick it up.

Ron beat her to it. "I'll carry the bags," he said, taking Meika's bag out of Nola's hand.

She let him, though she was surprised that he had come back for her. "Thanks," she said, not looking at him.

Meika skipped on ahead to the house.

Ron had both bags, yet he didn't start for the house. They stood facing each other. Nola kept her eyes low, looking at the suede-wrapped buttons on his jacket. When he said nothing, and since she felt a little awkward standing there, she started for the house.

"I'm sorry."

Astounded, she stopped walking and turned back.

"I was angry at Lopez and took it out on you. You were right to make me speak to him, Troy is more important than my anger."

"Yes he is."

"I'm sorry I hurt you."

Now she could look him in the eye and did.

"Vann and I had a long talk last night. It was good for both of us."

"That is good," she said.

"One of the things Vann said was that he learned a lot about love yesterday when he talked to you."

"Did he say that?"

"Yes. In fact, he said that he didn't truly understand what love was all about until your talk. I did hear some of what you talked about. I was in the kitchen."

"I know."

"Boy, Vann was mad as hell at me for putting my hand on you last night. He said he loved me, but if I couldn't touch his mother with only loving intentions, then don't ever lay hands on you again."

She was floored. What doubts she had that Vann might still believe that she didn't love him vanished completely. Her heart swelled with pride in knowing that Vann would go up against his father, the man he had always loved and admired, for her. Her own love for him and for Ron could not have been sweeter.

"Ron, you know Vann loves you just as much."

"Yeah," he said, beaming. "Even last night when he was angry with me, I knew. But I knew that back in January."

"He's changed a lot, hasn't he?"

"That he has, but the boy's getting too big for his britches."

She couldn't help but smile. "Actually, he's grown right out of them."

"If I had gotten up in my father's face, Vann would have never been."

Agreeing, she smiled. "I remember your father."

"Vann was right, though," Ron said, taking Nola's hand. "I have no business touching you any other way but in love. I'm sorry."

Her heart melted. She saw in Ron's eyes the man she fell in love with all those years ago. She tenderly touched his left cheek and kissed his lips.

Inside the house, Vann was wondering what was keeping his parents. Vann went back to the front door and stuck his head out as Ron dropped the overnight bags onto the ground and took Nola into his arms.

In the warmth of the sun on a chilly March day, they kissed; at first tenderly, then intensely, not caring what their neighbors might think, only caring that their love was felt from one to the other, soul to soul. It had been a very long time since that feeling had been there, and for the moment it was well worth savoring.

Approving wholeheartedly, Vann quietly closed the door.

THIRTY-ONE

MAMA, how come I always gotta go upstairs?"

"Because sometimes grown-ups talk about things that little ears don't need to hear. Now go on. I'll be up as soon as I can," she said, patting Meika gently on the behind to get her started up the stairs. "I'll order pizza for dinner, if you go play in your room."

"With extra cheese?"

"Gobs of it."

"Okay," Meika said, continuing on up the stairs. "When I get big, I'm gonna stay downstairs all day and all night."

Smiling to herself, Nola knew full well there were going to be those teen years when Meika was going to wish she could go upstairs to her room and hide forever. She waited until Meika was out of sight, then she joined everyone in the den.

"Now that we're all here," Vann said, glancing knowingly at Nola and Ron, "Detective Lopez was telling me that he and Detective Callahan went to the Property Office in Manhattan this morning and looked into the ownership of that house uptown."

"We do know who the owner is," Lopez said, "however, we're not at liberty to divulge the name of the individual."

Ron crossed his legs and laid his left arm across the back of his chair. "Detective, we can go to that same Property Office and get that same name ourselves, and if we do, what do you think we're going to do with it? Harass the person? Throw a noose around his or her neck?"

Lopez and Callahan looked at each other. "These are the facts," Callahan began. "The house is owned by a Mrs. Hortense Morgan, a widow, retired, age seventy-two."

"You got all that from the Property Office?" Nola asked.

"No, ma'am," Callahan replied. "We paid Mrs. Morgan a visit. She lives in the ground-floor apartment. Upstairs, she has two tenants. One tenant—"

"What are their names?" Vann asked.

Callahan glanced at Lopez, who right away nodded, giving him the go-ahead. "The only tenant you need to know about is a Victor Halihuston, who doesn't actually live in his apartment. According to Mrs. Morgan, he comes to the building approximately once a month, usually on a Saturday at the end of the month or the last days of the month, to pick up his mail and to pay the rent—he leaves a money order in her mailbox. She says he's a nice guy."

"Hold up," Vann said, leaning forward in his chair. "She has a tenant who only comes to the building one day out of a month to pick up the mail and to pay the rent, yet he doesn't use the apartment? She lets that go on and isn't suspicious of him? Where is he the rest of the month?"

"Those are my questions," Ron concurred.

"I'd be very suspicious," Nola said.

"I believe Mrs. Morgan has been worried for some time," Lopez remarked. "She stated that she questioned Halihuston, and he said he was staying with his girlfriend. Claims he wanted to hold on to his apartment in case things didn't work out between them."

"Does he keep any clothes in the apartment?" Vann asked.

"No clothes, no furniture."

"Naw, I don't buy it," Vann said, shaking his head. "It's too pat. It's a scam. He killed Troy."

"That's what it looks like to me," Ron agreed. "When are you going to arrest him?"

"It's not as simple as that, Mr. Kirkwood," Lopez said. "Each tenant has a separate, locked mailbox. Mrs. Morgan has not seen any of Halihuston's mail and can't verify that mail actually comes in in the name of Troy Kirkwood. However, she has seen mail mistakenly put in her mailbox addressed to other people that don't live in her building."

"You can get a warrant to go into the mailbox, can't you?" Nola asked, concerned that a locked mailbox would stand in their way.

"Not at this time."

"Why not?"

"Because of the Fourth Amendment," Vann said, standing. He began pacing with his hands in his pockets.

"That's right, ma'am," Callahan said. "We cannot secure a warrant without strong probable cause."

"You have that. Look at the credit report. That man killed my son."

"We don't know that. The credit card bills may be in your son's name. However, until Halihuston actually takes those bills into his hands and claims them as his own by opening the envelopes, we don't have probable cause."

"How are we going to know if he opens the envelopes?" Nola asked. "He might not open the mail until he gets where he's going."

"Exactly," Callahan said. "If we nabbed him when he took the mail out of the box, he could claim that the mail was put in the wrong box or was incorrectly addressed, and that he was planning to take it back to the post office. We can't arrest a man for that, that's why we need more to work with."

"Like what?" Ron asked.

"For one," Lopez began, "we'll have to stake out the house until Halihuston comes for the mail. At that time, we'll tail him to see where he takes it. If he does not go to the post office or drop the mail in a postal mailbox, we'll follow him to wherever he's staying, get that address, and then go for a search warrant. If the mail in Troy Kirkwood's name or any other name is found opened, then we have a case, even if it's for stealing U.S. mail, which brings in the feds."

"If Troy's mail is found opened, will this character be charged with murder?" Ron asked.

"Not necessarily," Lopez said. "Remember, we found no fingerprints or trace evidence to give us the leverage to point a finger at anyone. If anything, if we can get Mr. Stein to ID Victor Halihuston as being one of the men who came up on your son that day, we'll have more to work with in securing a possible indictment."

"That's more than we had a few days ago," Vann said, relieved. "What about the woman, Cookie?"

"We haven't forgotten her. If we're lucky, she's the girlfriend Halihuston lives with."

"I hope she's wearing red gloves when you find her," Nola said.

"It might not mean much. There's nothing unique about red gloves seen from a distance."

"When will you start the stakeout?" Vann asked.

"A week from this Saturday—the twenty-fifth. It's the last Saturday of the month. However, whatever Halihuston is looking for might not come on that day, there are five more business days left in the month. We'll be there every day after the twenty-fifth."

"You work at night," Vann said. "Suppose this character comes during the day?"

"According to Mrs. Morgan, Halihuston comes during the middle of the day, and during the day is when we'll be there."

"Good. However, I don't think we should wait that long," Vann said, beginning to pace again.

Lopez stood. "You'll have to," he said, taking a piece of gum from his jacket pocket and unwrapping it. "Most bills don't start coming in until the last week of the month. Thanks to you and your father, this is the first solid lead we've had on this case. However, we're going to have to bide our time to see if we can catch this fish with some hard evidence." He popped the gum in his mouth and glanced over at Callahan, who took that as a signal that it was time to go. "We'll be in touch as soon as we have something more."

"I'll see you to the door," Ron offered, standing.

"Thank you for coming," Nola said, looking at Vann and studying his face. By the grim look in his eyes, he wasn't satisfied. "What's bothering you?"

"I think they should start the stakeout today."

"People are creatures of habit, Vann. If that Halihuston person doesn't normally show up until the end of the month, it's a waste of time."

"People also change their minds and take different paths at times. We could be sitting back waiting for the end of the month and the fool shows up ahead of schedule. I wanna stake out that building starting today."

Nola sat back and folded her hands in her lap. "Vann, how do you sound? The 'fool' might show up, but the mail may not. Somehow I don't think that Halihuston person wastes his time going back and forth. He probably knows to the day when to pick up his mail. However, that's not the point, is it? You need to be there, don't you?"

He nodded.

"And no matter what I say, you are going to do what you want. Am I right?"

Vann rolled his tongue inside his left cheek. He saw no need to confirm what she already knew.

"Then I'll just say this. I don't want you out in front of that house by yourself. Take your father or one of your friends with you. And, I want you to call home every half hour."

"Fine. Anything else?"

"Yes. I want you to call Atlanta and talk to Michelle."

That was so far out of left field, it caught Vann right between the eyes. For a minute he looked at Nola but he could not read her expression, though he suspected that she knew that all wasn't right with him and Michelle. He turned away from her gaze and pretended to study the titles of the books in the bookcase. He hadn't spoken to Michelle in more than a week. He didn't know how to begin talking to her again. He had spoken to Sharice and Kareem several times and to his shame could not promise them that he was coming home anytime soon. The fact is, he didn't know if Michelle wanted him to come home. Maybe it was too late.

"I got a good feeling about this," Ron said, coming back into the den. "I'm putting in for vacation time. No way am I going to miss out on this stakeout."

Vann turned away from the bookcase. "I'm with you."

Nola looked at Vann. "That branch didn't fall very far from that tree, did it?" she quipped, getting up. "I'm going up to check on Meika. Once that killer is caught, we need to think about what we can do about Cordelia."

"Other than blasting her ass to Jupiter," Ron said, "I don't have a clue."

"I do," Vann said.

Stopping in the doorway, Nola turned back. "What do you have in mind?"

"Offer her money. That's all she wants anyway."

That hadn't occurred to Nola or Ron. They looked at each other like that idea might be plausible.

THIRTY-TWO

TIME slipped by regardless of whether or not Nola wore her wristwatch or whether or not she avoided looking at any other clock in the house; and the sun continued to rise in the morning and set in the evening, while the moon, full or otherwise, continued to appear in the night sky. With each passing day her heart grew heavier. A new day wasn't something she looked forward to. Mornings brought as much pain as the night before. As much as she hated to see another day end, Vann and Ron were rushing headlong into the day the stakeout would officially begin. Vann was like a caged tiger, ever pacing, always agitated. He went uptown to Eighty-eighth Street every day with Marcus, an old friend, but he never came home any less agitated. Nola wasn't about to say that she told him so, for she secretly hoped that Victor Halihuston would show.

Her timorous view of the passing days were filled with dread for the day Cordelia would ensnare Meika and change her life forever. She and Ron labored tediously over the pros and cons of offering Cordelia money in exchange for dropping her custody suit. In the end, the cons outweighed the pros. As Ron so aptly put it, "Since when can we trust Cordelia to keep her word or keep her mouth shut about us bribing her?" They could lose custody and visitation if the judge was ever told and Cordelia would have the money to boot. Cordelia's aim was to hurt them and taking Meika would do that. They were in a no-win situation and time was ticking on.

All week Nola served Meika all of her favorite foods; held her in her arms as often as every time she thought about her leaving; and slept with her every night while hoping that morning would never come. But it did, straight through to Friday morning, the day she feared most. She didn't have to open her eyes to see that it was daylight—she had never closed them from the night before. Throughout the night her mind had been restless not only because of Meika but equally because of memories of Troy's death on his birthday. Looking down at Meika sleeping like the angel that she was, her head resting on Nola's right arm, Nola could have easily been looking at Troy. He, too, had slept in her arms like this when he was a child. With the back of her left hand she stroked Meika's baby-soft cheeks. Her pain was greater knowing that she was not keeping her promise to Troy.

"Pst!"

She looked up.

Ron was beckoning her.

"What?" she asked softly.

"We need to talk."

"Can't it wait?"

"No, it's important."

Begrudgingly, she gingerly slipped her arm from under Meika's head and, easing off the bed, slid her feet into her oversized furry booties. Leaving her bathrobe behind, she went quietly out into the hallway.

"What is it?" she whispered, impatiently. She pulled the door up behind her.

"Did you tell Meika that she's leaving today?"

Feeling her throat tighten, she gazed blearily at him.

"Nola."

"I couldn't."

"We have got to—"

"Ron, I don't see why we have to tell her anything. She might not have to leave."

Ron saw the anguish on Nola's face. "Let's go into our room," he said, putting his arm lightly around her waist.

She glanced at Meika's door.

"She'll be all right."

She slumped against him. Her sadness filled every inch of her body. She wanted to cry.

He drew her closer.

His arm around her waist and the warmth of his body were comforting. She let him lead her to their room. They sat down as one on his side of the bed. She rested her head on his shoulder.

"We have to let her go," he said.

"Today is Troy's birthday."

"I know, but, babe, if—"

"Ron, we haven't heard anything from Cordelia. Maybe she changed her mind."

"Babe, don't fool yourself. Cordelia did not change her mind. She knows that she has a court order and she will be here at six P.M. sharp. That's why we have got to tell Meika."

"I can't lose Meika, Ron. I can't."

Squeezing Nola's waist lovingly, Ron knew that there was nothing he could say to make her feel better. The inevitable was going to happen and short of a natural disaster or Cordelia being hit by a bus, nothing was going to stop her from coming for Meika.

"Nola, five months will slip by before you know it."

"Five months will be an eternity."

"We'll get through it."

"And then? What happens after that?"

"We'll—"

"I'll tell you," she said, lifting her head off his shoulder. "That evil ass judge is going to give Cordelia permanent custody."

"If, and I'm not saying that it will happen, but if she gets custody, we'll still see Meika every weekend, and—"

"Ron, do you not remember what Mr. Lipscomb said? Cordelia could get our visitation rights overturned if she convinces the judge that we're causing her problems with Meika."

"That won't happen."

"Oh no? We didn't think we'd have to hand Meika over, did we?"

"No, but we won't cause any problems. Besides, I got a gut feeling that Cordelia is going to fail with Meika and Meika will end up right back here with us."

"What if her failure harms Meika?"

"It won't," he said, patting Nola's hand assuredly. "We'll watch Meika closely for any signs of abuse and we won't make a stink until we can prove it."

"In the meanwhile?"

"We'll just have to be very agreeable and go along with the program until Meika gets a little older. When she's twelve and can speak for herself, we'll go back to court and fight for full custody."

"My God, Ron. That's six years and two months!" she exclaimed, shifting her body sideways so that she could face him. "Cordelia could put Meika through pure hell during that time, and we won't be able to help her for fear that Cordelia will stop us from seeing her altogether."

"Well, we could give her some sort of balance on the weekends."

"Who's fooling who, Ron?"

"Nola, any time we have with Meika will benefit her."

"Not much. What we might try to undo on the weekends can in no way outweigh what's done to her five days a week. She'll be confused. She won't understand what's expected of her or us. If Cordelia hasn't truly changed, God knows how Meika is going to be when she grows up. What if she turns to drugs to dull her pain or to escape from all of us? Oh God," she cried, again letting Ron take her into his arms. "Ron, I promised Troy I'd take care of his baby."

"You're keeping your promise, Nola. It might not seem like it now, but one day, all of this is gonna be behind us. Meika is Troy's child and practically a clone of you; she'll be all right. Before you know it, she'll be grown and having her own babies."

In the midst of her tears, in the midst of her sorrow, Nola's shoulders suddenly started to shake, her sobs turned to chuckles.

Puzzled, Ron pulled back and looked into her face.

Throwing back her head, Nola's chuckles turned into a full, hearty laugh.

"Damn. You haven't lost your mind, have you?"

She laughed harder.

"Woman, you're scaring me."

"Aaaaa," she said, catching her breath and wiping away the tears that came first with her sorrow and then with her laughter.

"What are you laughing about?"

"What you said," she said, smiling. She kissed him on the lips, making a loud smacking sound in the process.

"What did I say?"

"You said Meika will be having her own babies. In my mind's eye I can't see Meika as a woman, but as a five-year-old tying red ribbons around a baby's neck, trying to teach it knock-knock jokes."

"That's some vision. I'm glad you can laugh about it."

"It puts things in perspective for me," she said. "A good part of who Meika will be has already been instilled in her. She's strong-willed and knows right from wrong. Cordelia won't be able to destroy her. Maybe on the weekends we can make a difference. I'll tell Meika after we come from the cemetery this afternoon."

"See, I told you. We can get through this."

"With a lot of prayer," she agreed, feeling a mite better.

"It won't hurt."

"You hungry?"

"I could eat something."

She started to get up. Ron held on to her, encircling her with both arms. He nuzzled her in the crook of her neck.

It felt good. She closed her eyes and went with the feeling. He kissed her tenderly on the neck.

Opening her eyes, she looked deeply inside him and saw his yearning. He kissed her tenderly, awakening her own desires. Leaning into him and closing her eyes again, she kissed him in turn as she began to feel, after such a long time, a surge of passion flow through her belly, enticing her to gently rub her breast against his side, making her nipples come to stark attention under her flannel nightgown.

Ron sensed the fullness of her breasts through his T-shirt and reveled in a sweet fullness of his own. Their tongues danced in a deep passionate kiss that sent tingling sensations through his veins. Letting his hand glide down her thigh to her knee and back up again, he slowly gathered up her gown until his hand touched her warm thighs. She sighed. He had no trouble removing her oversized flannel gown. Together they removed his T-shirt and boxers; together they climbed under the covers; and together, their bodies entwined, they became one intensely loving, rapturous being.

THIRTY-THREE

MEIKA never ceased to amaze Nola. Her innocence was her saving grace. At Troy's gravesite, Meika laid the yellow and white carnations she chose beneath his headstone and wished him a happy birthday. And as she had done before, she pressed Bobo's stitched black lips to the headstone in a dry kiss. She then kissed the headstone herself. Troy would have indeed been proud of his little girl. Meika asked, "Is Daddy gonna always look like he do in the picture at home?" Ron told her that he would, and that was the truth. Troy was ageless for all time.

From the cemetery they stopped off at McDonald's for a late lunch so that Meika could get her Happy Meal and a romp in the play area. Seeing her play, her spirits high, Ron and Vann figured it was as good a time as any to tell Meika that she was going to be living with Cordelia for a while. No time was good in Nola's opinion. Yet it had to be done, the time was close at hand.

Carrying a fresh napkin with her, the single minute it took for Nola to trudge several feet to the playground was like walking across the Sahara Desert—her mouth was dry, her breathing was shallow, and her legs were rubbery. Sitting down low on the bottom of the slide for a minute, she watched Meika play all alone in the colorful pond of plastic balls.

She tossed a blue ball at Meika. "You having a good time?"

"Uh-huh," she said, tossing a red ball back at Nola.

Smiling lamely, Nola caught the ball.

Meika's eyes glistened as she began tossing multicolored balls up in the air. The last thing Nola wanted to see was the light extinguished in Meika's eyes. She was thinking about not telling her, until she looked over and glimpsed Ron's face. She saw a reflection of her own pain. He nodded once, urging her on because, although he had volunteered to tell Meika himself, he would never be able to. As it was, he had had a hard time being with Meika the first day they found out that Troy was dead. He broke down crying and had to leave the room. No matter that he had offered to tell Meika, Nola knew that she had to be the one.

"Meika, baby, come over here next to me."

"Okay," Meika said cheerfully. On her knees, she waded through the balls, pushing them aside with her hands until she was at Nola's knee.

If she had been thinking, she would have brought her camera. Meika looked like a beautiful flower in a pond of beautifully colored balls of reds, blues, yellows, and greens.

"Mama, can we go to the cemetery and visit Daddy again?"

"Of course we can."

"Can I give him blue flowers next time?"

"You sure can."

"Good," Meika said, smiling broadly. Sitting back on her legs she dragged her arms back and forth in the balls.

Dear God, give me the words. She took a deep breath. "Meika."

Meika continued to play happily.

"Meika. Look at me, baby."

Meika looked up.

Meika's brilliance was blinding. Nola had to hold strong. "Um . . . Meika, for . . . for a little while . . . um, not too long, just for a little while. You have to go live with . . . um . . . Cordelia."

"I don't wanna go live with her," she said, tossing a ball up in the air.

"I know, baby, but you have to."

"No, I don't."

"Yes, baby, you do. But just for a little while."

Meika stopped playing. She looked into Nola's eyes. She froze.

"Honey, it'll be just for a little while, okay?" Nola felt her heart sink to her belly. The light in Meika's eyes was no more. That sweet smile was no more, and she was no longer playful.

Meika's mouth turned down. "I don't wanna go."

Nola pulled Meika up onto her lap and held her. "I don't want you to go either, but the judge thinks it best. She wants you to live with your mother, just for a little while."

"I don't wanna," she whined, throwing her arms around Nola's neck. "I wanna live with you."

"I know, baby," she said, struggling not to cry. "You'll still see me and Poppie every weekend, from Friday to Sunday. And when you come to visit, we'll have lots of fun. We'll go to the park, to the zoo, and guess what? The circus is coming back to town next week. We can go when you come to visit."

"Nooo!" she whined, beginning to weep. "I don't wanna come back to visit. I wanna stay with you."

"I know, baby, I know," Nola said, hugging Meika tighter. "But it's just for a little while. You can stay a little while for Mama, can't you?"

Tears washed over Meika's cheeks. "Nooo!" she cried, kicking out with her right leg. "I don't wanna!"

Nola closed her eyes to channel her strength. This was no time to give in to her own anguish, she had to stay strong. Opening her eyes, she kissed Meika once on each cheek. Then, using the napkin, she dried her face.

"Meika, we had a good time today, didn't we?"

Although she continued to cry, Meika nodded.

"We can have a good time like that every weekend, and for your birthday in May, we can have a big, big party with lots of pretty decorations and a giant cake, and all your friends will come. Wouldn't you like that?"

Shaking her head no, Meika's mouth opened wide, letting out a plaintive wail.

"Ooo," Nola said, looking to Ron for help. He had bowed his head and covered his face with his hands. Vann was looking at them but his eyes were glassy and his jaw was set. He, too, was of no help to her. The handful of people at the counter and a couple seated at a table nearby were looking at Nola, probably wondering what she had done to make Meika cry. They were of no concern to Nola as they couldn't help her. She started rocking Meika and rubbing her back. Her strong sense of déjà vu was not just imaginary, it was real, taking her back to the night they sat in the precinct, hoping, praying, waiting for word of Troy. And that same foreboding feeling of dread consumed her, warning her that this was not the best thing for Meika, but her hands were tied; either they do this, or lose her.

"Mama's gonna always be here for you, Meika. You can call me and I'll call you every day, okay?"

The promise of telephone calls meant nothing to Meika, she didn't stop crying.

This whole affair was devastating to Nola, a grown woman. It had to be beyond that for Meika. It was cruel of Cordelia to put her through this—to take her from all that she knew, all that she loved.

Ron brought over Bobo and Meika's coat.

Nola looked up at him. His eyes were glassy, his face was strained. Together they put Meika's coat on her.

"Let me take her," Ron said. He lifted her gently into his arms.

Being carried high up in Ron's arms, Meika, nuzzling her runny nose on his shoulder, gasped between her crying as he carried her out of McDonald's. Out on the sidewalk he began walking back and forth with her, trying to comfort her.

From her seat on the children's slide, with Bobo sitting on her lap and tears slipping down her cheeks, Nola watched Ron walk in the footsteps of many a mother who had to comfort a crying child. The glimpses she got of his face when he turned revealed that he was as tender and loving with Meika as he had been with Troy and Vann when they were newborns. In these last days, she had felt a renewal of her love for him; a rebirth of a love that had grown bland over the years from familiarity, from marital conflicts, and from passivity. She was glad that Meika was in his arms.

THIRTY-FOUR

PERHAPS she was being vindictive, perhaps she was simply being an absolute bitch, but Nola did not pack a single suitcase for Meika. In her small overnight bag she packed her toothbrush, her pink pajamas, a clean pair of panties, an undershirt, Bobo, and the telephone number—just in case Meika didn't remember. There was no need to pack anything more, she was coming back. With her broken heart straining to beat, Nola said good-bye to Meika in the kitchen and gave her, crying, over to Vann and Ron to give over to Cordelia as that was something she didn't have the strength to do or witness. Even as they closed the front door she could hear Meika's cries, which tore at Nola and made her give in to her own need to cry. In all her life she had never cried as much as she had in the last five months. It seemed a never-ending waterfall flowed through her, ever ready to spill out. Just this morning she thought she might be able to get through this; she was wrong.

Vann rushed into the kitchen. "We have a problem!"

"What's wrong?"

"Cordelia wants Meika's clothes."

"Too bad," Nola said, quickly drying her eyes. "She's not getting them."

"She's cussing up a storm out there, Ma."

She shot up out of her chair. "She's acting like that in front of Meika?"

"She says if she can't have Meika's clothes, we can't have her phone number."

"I got a word or two for her and I don't need her phone number to tell her either." Nola barreled out of the kitchen.

Right behind her, Vann suggested, "Maybe we should give her a few more things."

"Over my dead body!" she said, not bothering to grab her coat from the closet in the entryway on her way out the door.

"Ma!"

"I'll handle this, Vann," she said, stepping out onto the stoop. "You go get the video recorder out of your father's den."

"Good idea," he said, racing back into the house.

Ron was still holding on to Meika, who was still crying.

Cordelia glared up at Nola. "What am I supposed to do without her clothes? I'm telling the judge about this. You're supposed to give me her goddamn clothes!"

"Woman, let me tell you something," Nola said, starting down the steps to the walkway.

"Mama!" Meika cried, reaching out for her.

Ron started to hand Meika to Nola.

Nola put up her hand, stopping him. "Hold her! I need my hands free," she said, glaring daggers at Cordelia. "You claim you have the wherewithal to support this child, then do it!"

"I need her clothes!"

"Don't expect us to make it easy for you to be a provider. You're supposed to be a mother. Go out and buy her the clothes she needs."

"Mama!" Meika cried, again reaching out for Nola.

"Don't tell me how to be a mother! You're not the god of all mothers your damn self," Cordelia spat, taking one step forward. "The judge said—"

"The judge said, turn Meika over to you. She did not say I had to give you anything else from my house. You did not pay one penny for anything that goes on that child's back, you're lucky you're getting anything at all."

"That's the way it's gonna be, huh?"

"Damn right! Take your ass shopping. You need to buy her clothes, shoes, school supplies, and food. And if I even think she's not well taken care of, I will have your ass thrown under the jail."

"Try it!"

"You will not mistreat her. . . ."

"I'll have you locked up. All of you!"

". . . You will not abuse her or kill her spirit. If the court won't do something about you, I will."

Cordelia started moving in closer. "Is that a threat?"

"Is there any doubt?" Nola asked, stepping forward to meet her.

"You wanna take me on? Come on. You're bad. Come on."

"Nola!" Ron called.

Nola balled up her fist and charged.

"Hold up!" Vann said, rushing to step in between Nola and Cordelia. He held the video recorder in his right hand, though he hadn't begun recording. He raised his arm and held Cordelia at bay.

"Don't touch me!" she said, trying to push Vann aside. "Move!"

Nola started around the other side of Vann to get to Cordelia. "Let her go, Vann. I want her to put her hands on me."

"Nola!" Ron called again.

Vann blocked Nola with his back to her. Cordelia he faced.

"Get out my damn way!" Cordelia snarled. She slapped Vann hard across the face.

His head snapped back. Instinctively, he shoved Cordelia— hard.

"You hit me!"

Nola started after Cordelia.

"Nola, get over here!" Ron shouted.

Vann pulled Nola back. "Ma, you're not getting in a fight."

Crying so much that she now sounded hoarse, Meika began coughing.

Cordelia drew back her arm to strike Nola.

Vann grabbed her wrist, holding on to it like a vise. "Stop it!"

She clawed savagely at his hand on her wrist. "Get your god-damn hand off of me!"

The sting of her nails raking through his skin made Vann drop the video recorder to the ground. He whipped Cordelia around so that her back was to him. He yanked both her arms up behind her back.

"Ouch! Goddamnit!"

"Break it!" Nola said.

"Nola, get over here!" Ron ordered. He grabbed a handful of Nola's sweater. He yanked her backward. "Nola! What are you doing?"

She was breathing hard. "Trying to kill that witch!"

"Look at you, woman! You're acting like her!"

"Don't insult me."

"Mama," Meika cried, again reaching out for her.

"Take her!" Ron ordered.

This time Nola took Meika, freeing Ron to go over to Vann and Cordelia.

"I said, stop it!" Vann shouted into Cordelia's ear while squeezing both her wrists harder. He felt like he could crush her bones. He shook her. "Stop it!"

Ron stepped in. "Cordelia, calm down."

"Fuck you, you bastard!" she shouted back at Ron. Bent over, she struggled hard to free herself and, being unable to, she started screaming.

Meika's hoarse cries became screams.

"Goddamnit!" Ron said. "Vann, let her go!"

"Only if she leaves."

Trying her best to stop Meika from crying, Nola sat down on the steps. "It's all right. Meika, listen to me. You're making yourself sick. Stop crying."

Meika's coughing got worse. Nola began patting her on the back.

"Vann, let her go!" Ron ordered again. "We don't need this. Let her go."

Vann pushed off on Cordelia's wrists, shoving her, making her stumble forward. She caught herself from falling.

Rubbing her wrist she turned back. "I'm having you arrested!"

"I think I can do the same to you for slapping me. That's assault."

"Let's just all calm down here!" Ron shouted, stepping in between Vann and Cordelia. "Look how we're acting in front of Meika. Cordelia, why would you wanna upset the child like this?"

"I wasn't trying to upset her. All I did was ask for her goddamn clothes. You're supposed to give me her clothes."

"The judge didn't say that and I don't see why she would. This is only temporary and Meika is going to be here every weekend. I don't see any reason to hand over her clothes. You'll have to buy her some clothes, that's one of your responsibilities now."

Cordelia glared bitterly at Ron; she then looked past him at Nola cooing to Meika. She sneered. "Y'all think y'all so damn smart. We'll see who gets the last laugh. Give me my daughter!"

Turning cautiously away from her, Ron looked at Vann. "Go get her."

Nola gave Meika one last loving squeeze before she let Vann take her from her arms.

"Nooo!" Meika cried, trying to hold on to Nola.

"I'm sorry, baby," she said, taking her hand and kissing it. "I love you."

"I don't wanna go!"

Meika's cries tore Nola apart. "I'll see you real soon, okay?" she said, hating that they hadn't been able to do anything to spare Meika this anguish. All she could do was watch as Vann put her into Cordelia's arms, still crying, still trying to hang on to him.

"Mama . . . Mama!"

Leaving the overnight bag behind, Cordelia started off down the street. "Meika! Shut up!"

"Don't you talk to her like that!" Ron shouted.

Nola suddenly remembered the recorder. "Vann, tape her."

"Damn, I forgot," he said, looking around for the recorder. It was in one piece on the lawn. Quickly retrieving it, he turned it on, focused, and started taping.

Nola stood. "And the judge says this is best?"

Hollering, Meika squirmed and kicked.

"I said shut the fuck up!"

"Cordelia!" Vann shouted. "Keep talking to her like that, I'll kick your ass!"

"Fuck you!" Cordelia shouted back over her shoulder. Suddenly she put Meika down hard on the ground. She grabbed her by the hand. "You ain't no goddamn baby! Walk!"

"Look at that!" Nola couldn't believe it.

"I'm gonna kick her ass," Vann said, about to take off after Cordelia.

Ron held him back. "No. Keep taping."

"But, Dad—"

"We touch her, we make it bad for ourselves. She keeps that up, she makes it bad for herself."

Vann continued taping. "This is crazy."

"Insane!" Nola said.

"Our hands are tied," Ron said.

"Ron, this just isn't right."

"Nola," a woman's voice said behind them. "Are you all right?"

Still looking at Cordelia angrily pulling Meika behind her,

Nola didn't turn to see who it was. She knew it was Pam from next door. Nice enough woman though she was, she had a silly habit of asking stupid questions. Once she asked her, "You like gladiolus, don't you?" At the time she was in the backyard cutting a bunch to place them on the dining room table. She had been growing gladioli for at least fifteen years and Pam had to have seen them in her yard for as many years. She did not answer her stupid question that day either.

"Is there anything I can do?"

No longer able to see Cordelia and Meika, Nola waved her hand no and went back into the house, leaving Vann and Ron to contend with stupid questions. With a heavy heart, she trudged up the stairs to her bedroom and climbed into bed with her clothes and shoes still on, not caring, as she usually did, about the cleanliness of her sheets. Pulling the covers up over her head, she tried to block out Meika's cries and tear-washed face, but Meika's face was as real under the covers as it had been before her eyes only minutes before. She had known that it would be difficult, and, really, if Cordelia had taken Meika and gone on about her business without asking for the clothes, it would not have been so ugly. But hadn't all dealings with Cordelia over the years been ugly?

"Nola, the police are here again," Ron said from the doorway.

She yanked the covers down off her head. "Figures she'd call the police. We should've called them on her."

"They want us all downstairs."

"I don't care what they say, she's not getting those clothes."

"They're not just talking about clothes. Cordelia told them we held an unlicensed gun on her and that we have some cocaine in the house."

She sat bolt upright. "What!"

"That's what they said."

"That lying bitch," she said, bitterly, but then she got a good look at Ron. He was too calm. "What's up with you? Why are you so damn calm?"

"Because I know it's a lie. Come on. Vann is keeping them from searching the house because they don't have a warrant, but we need to be down there with him."

Nola angrily threw the covers back off her. They landed on the floor on the side of the bed. Leaping up, she sprinted past Ron and sped down the stairs into the living room where six policemen, Cordelia, and Vann waited.

She went right for Cordelia. "What the hell are you trying to do?"

An officer's arm shot out in front of Nola. "Step back!"

Cordelia smirked and folded her arms high across her chest.

Breathing hard, Nola stepped back only because the officer's arm was pushing her back and Ron had taken her arm. "You're a lying, lowlife bitch."

"Ma'am, calm down."

"Nola, we know she's lying."

"Ma'am," the sergeant began, "this lady says that she has a court order that states that you are to give her her daughter for a period of five months, and when she came—"

"We gave her her daughter, who did not want to go with her," she said, looking around for Meika. "And by the way, where is Meika?"

"She's out in a patrol car with one of the officers," Vann replied.

"Your granddaughter is safe," the officer assured her, "but this lady also says that she was assaulted and that a gun was pointed at her."

"That's a lie!"

"Ma'am, do you have a licensed or unlicensed handgun in the house?"

"No!"

"Do you have any drugs, specifically cocaine, hidden in a shoe box in a closet up in your granddaughter's bedroom?"

She looked at Ron. "I don't believe this."

"It's up there," Cordelia stated.

"How the hell would you know?" Vann asked.

"She's a damn lie," Ron said. "There have never been any drugs in this house and there never will be any drugs in this house."

"Everybody calm down. Sir, there's been a charge and we have to check it out."

"Not without a warrant," Vann said.

"A search warrant is in the works as we speak," the sergeant said. "We hate to inconvenience you folks, but we have to wait on the premises until the warrant gets here."

Cordelia smirked boldly.

"How would she know what's in this house?" Vann asked, pointing at Cordelia. "She hasn't been past the front hall in more than, what—three years?"

"That's right," Ron confirmed. "And she said these things are in a shoe box? How would she know?"

"She'd know if she broke in here and put them in here herself," Nola suggested, wishing that she could slap the smirk off Cordelia's face.

"Like he said, I ain't been past your front hall," Cordelia said, nastily. "I do know, though, that y'all always have drugs in here, and that y'all always hide it in Meika's closet."

Ron gasped. "You outta your goddamn mind?"

"Don't play all innocent, Ron, you know it's true. You gave a friend of mine some from up there."

"You crazy-ass, lying bitch!" he spat, bustling toward her.

All six of the policemen made a move on Ron at once, grabbing him and drawing his arms up behind his back.

"Hey!" Ron shouted, straining to pull his arms back down.

"Don't do that!" Nola shouted, trying to get to Ron through the horde of police officers surrounding him.

Vann leaped forward. "Get off of him!"

"Get back!" an officer said to Vann, his hand on his gun.

Reluctantly, Vann did.

"Let him go!" Nola screamed, grabbing for one of the officers.

"Hold up!" Vann shouted, pulling Nola out of the grasp of the officer who held on to her. "You guys are getting out of hand here."

"Sir, ma'am, do not interfere."

"You're hurting my husband."

Grunting, Ron kept trying to free himself.

Grinning gleefully, Cordelia planted her hands on her hips.

Vann held on to Nola, keeping her from going to help Ron. For himself he wasn't worried; he did not want them touching his mother.

"We'll let you go, Mr. Kirkwood, but you have got to settle down," the sergeant said, waiting for Ron to say that he would.

"Dad, stop struggling."

Ron immediately relaxed. He glared bitterly at Cordelia.

"Let him go!" Nola shouted.

"If everyone stays put, we will."

"We will. Just let him go," Vann said.

Cautiously, the officers released their hold on Ron and stepped back.

Ron's arms slid painfully down his back to his sides.

Nola immediately wrapped her arms around him and clung to him. "This is insane! This is not a police state! You-all can't barge into our house, accuse us of a crime, and—"

"Ma'am, we didn't barge into—"

"What do you call it?" Vann asked.

"You have no right to come into this house, accusing us of stashing drugs and guns just on her say-so," Ron said angrily, his glare fixed on Cordelia as she exaggerated the massaging of her left shoulder.

"Sir, I suggest that you do not make any sudden moves."

Ron pointed at Cordelia. "Get her out of my house! She has no right to be here."

"I ain't going nowhere until y'all give me Meika's clothes."

The sergeant looked at Cordelia. "Take her out," he said to one of the officers behind him.

"I want Meika's Social Security check for April."

"Get out!" Nola screamed.

"I hope y'all get locked up," Cordelia said, as an officer nudged her toward the door with his hand on her upper back. "It's a cold day in hell, Nola. Feel it?"

Vann shouted. "Get her the hell outta here!"

"Screw you, Vann!"

The officer nudged Cordelia all the way out of the house and closed the door behind them.

"Okay, folks. Calm down," the sergeant said. "What about these clothes she's talking about?"

"She's not entitled to those clothes," Vann said. "The court order says that she gets Meika for five months, it says nothing about us having to give up her clothes."

"My son, my husband, and I bought those clothes. No one can make us give that woman what we bought with our own money."

"That's a matter we have no jurisdiction over. Why don't you folks have a seat, we might have to wait awhile."

"Correct me if I'm wrong here," Vann said, eyeballing the sergeant. "You're here without a warrant, which means you have no right to be here."

"Sir, we did not force our way into your home. You voluntarily opened the door and let us in. The lady alleged that she was assaulted, which gives us the right to be here, and by law, the allegation of hidden drugs and unlicensed weapons, based upon information, gives us a joint right to be here to prevent you from disposing of or destroying pertinent evidence. However, we will not search your house until the warrant is in hand. So please, be patient. We will search the child's room, the closet in particular, and if there's nothing there, we're out."

"Oh Lord," Nola said, looking up at Ron. "I know she's low,

but why in the world would she lie and say that we had, of all things, drugs and weapons in this house?"

Vann flopped down in the armchair. "To get back at us, what else? She's a vicious bi—. Forget it."

"Let's just sit down," Ron said, putting his sore arm around Nola's waist and leading her over to the sofa. "This is crap."

"Shouldn't we call a lawyer?" Nola asked.

"We don't have to," Vann said, "we're not hiding anything."

"Oh Lord, poor Meika," Nola said, sitting down on the sofa. Then suddenly, she gasped.

"What is it?" Ron asked.

Covering her mouth, she gaped at him and then at Vann.

"Ma, what's wrong?"

Nola looked around the room. All the officers were looking at her. "Nothing. I was just thinking about Meika. Poor thing."

"She's in a lot of trouble," Vann said.

Ron sat back.

But Nola couldn't sit back, and she couldn't tell Ron and Vann what she had seen in the middle of the night more than a month ago—Meika coming back into the house with an empty shoe box. She must have thrown what was inside into the garbage out front. "Oh my God," she said softly. Cordelia must have had Meika bring the drugs and gun into the house when she came back from her Saturday visits. She must have told her to hide them in the shoe box. That's why Meika insisted on unpacking her own overnight bag.

Ron and Vann eyed Nola curiously while the officers began talking amongst themselves.

She tapped Ron on the thigh. "It's all right," she whispered. "What?"

"Don't worry," she said, winking at Vann. They were all right. There were no drugs or guns in the house—thanks to Meika. But how in the world did Cordelia get her to bring something like that into the house and get her to keep it so secret? Is that why Meika was in the bottom of her closet that day and wouldn't let her see inside?

She couldn't believe it. "Humph, humph, humph."

Both perplexed, Ron and Vann stared at Nola.

Ron laid his hand atop Nola's. "Are you sure you're all right?"

"I'm just fine."

THIRTY-FIVE

I T was ten o'clock before a plainclothes officer came with the search warrant. Oh, how Nola wanted to tell Ron and Vann that there was no need for their faces to look so troubled as the officers pulled everything out of the bottom of Meika's closet and from the overhead shelves. Nothing was hidden in secret places, in or out of her closet, and all the shoe boxes had shoes in them. The dresser drawers were emptied onto the bed and nothing besides little girl's undies and pretty little colorful socks and shirts and pants tumbled out. Nola went behind them, putting everything back in its place, her thoughts on Meika. Because of her, Cordelia's plan to get them in trouble failed. Nothing was hidden under Meika's bed, nothing illegal was stashed in her toy chest, nothing was found that a little girl shouldn't have.

The order also called for a search of Nola's closet because Cordelia said the drugs and the gun were hidden in a woman's shoe box. Like Meika's closet, her closet was clean. Finally, the search was called off. At the front door the sergeant said, "I didn't think we'd find anything here, but we had to check. I hope you understand."

"No, we don't understand," Ron said. "This isn't the Kremlin. How can you just search a man's house based on a crazy woman's say-so?"

"Normally we don't, sir. However, she alleged assault along with the drugs and a gun. We had to follow through."

"Next time, don't!" he said, slamming the door. "I hate that bitch!"

"My sentiments exactly," Vann agreed.

"This might work in our favor," Nola said, going off into the kitchen.

"I don't see how," Ron said as he and Vann also entered the kitchen.

Nola opened the refrigerator door. "Let's see what we can throw together for dinner."

"I'm not hungry," Ron said, sitting down at the table.

"I am," Vann said, "but, Ma, before you get started, why did you all of a sudden cool out? Didn't it bother you that they searched the house?"

"Nope. I knew they wouldn't find anything."

"I knew they wouldn't either," Ron said, "but I was fit to be tied. Damnit. They had no right."

From the refrigerator Nola pulled out a jar of mayonnaise and a jar of sweet relish. "Will tuna do?"

"Fine," Vann said, taking an ice tray from the freezer just as Nola put the jars on the table. "Ma, why were you gasping?"

"Because I knew why they weren't going to find anything."

"That's obvious," Ron said. "We weren't hiding anything."

"That's not quite true."

"What's not quite true?"

"I think there were some drugs and a gun in a shoe box in Meika's closet."

Ron gaped at her.

"No!" Vann exclaimed. He set the ice tray down in the sink.

"Vann, get the bread," she said, carrying a bowl with a fork, a spoon, and a knife inside it to the table.

"Forget the damn bread," Ron said. "How do you know that?"

Nola sat at the table. "Let me get the tuna together while I talk. Vann, get me three cans of tuna out of the cabinet."

Ron snatched the plastic bowl from in front of Nola. "If you don't tell me what you know," he said, "I'm gonna flatten this bowl."

She could see that he was practically breathing fire. "Okay," she said, relenting and telling them what she suspected.

They were both aghast.

"Oh, and something else. I went to Meika's room one day and she had the door closed. When I went in, I caught her crawled up in the corner at the bottom of the closet. I asked her what she was doing and she wouldn't tell me and she didn't want me to see what she had back there. That was the day I told her that Cordelia had been mean to Troy. That's why she was upset and didn't want to go home with her."

"That's why she threw everything out," Ron said.

"Yes. She said that she wanted nothing Cordelia gave her. At the time I thought she only meant the teddy bear. I had no idea that it meant more."

"I could kill her," Ron said.

Vann popped his left thumb knuckle. "I can't believe she'd give Meika that stuff and put her in danger. Suppose Meika had messed with the stuff and eaten it or played with the gun and shot herself?"

"I don't want to think about it."

"That bitch could have put us away for years," Ron said, gritting his teeth. "We could have lost everything."

"And," Nola began, "she would have gotten full custody of Meika."

"No telling how much cocaine she gave that child," Vann said.

Ron got up and went to the sink. "I could kill her," he said again, picking up the ice tray. The ice had begun to melt. He took a glass out of the drain and, holding the tray over the glass, slammed it down on top of it. Most of the ice landed in the sink, except for three cubes, which fell into his glass.

"Cordelia was always a conniving witch, Dad. Remember all the things she did to Troy?"

Ron took a can of ginger ale out of the refrigerator. "How could I forget? I could kill her."

"Meika saved our lives," Nola said, hoping to steer Ron away from Cordelia and what she had tried to do. It was only making him angrier.

"We have got to get Meika away from Cordelia," he said. "If that fool can get her hands on drugs and guns, Meika's in serious danger."

"Sounds to me like she's either dealing or using or both," Vann surmised. "The question at hand is, how can we use what happened tonight to our advantage?"

Ron popped open the can. "Who knows?"

"If we had the drugs or the gun as proof, we could take it to the judge."

"Well, we don't," Ron said.

"No," Nola agreed, "but I figure, if Mr. Lipscomb can tell the judge what happened, show proof of the police being called and that Cordelia was the instigator, she might reconsider her order. The only way Cordelia could possibly know that something was hidden in this house is if she either hid it here herself or told Meika to."

"That judge won't buy it," Ron said, filling his glass with ginger ale.

"Ron, if she says a child's best interest is her greatest concern, then she'll have to think twice about Cordelia. She can't sweep this under the rug."

Vann popped his fingers. "Maybe the videotape will sell her."

"We'll see, won't we? I'm calling Mr. Lipscomb first thing tomorrow morning," Nola said, taking back the bowl. "Ron, pass me the tuna."

"Ma, you stay home and speak to Mr. Lipscomb. Tomorrow morning, Dad and I are going uptown."

"Vann, please don't get in Detective Lopez's way."

"I won't. We're going to be parked in our own car up the

street where he won't even see us. I've already checked out the mailman's schedule. He hits that block anywhere between eleven and one. We plan to be there, already parked, at ten-thirty."

"Make sure your cell phone is fully charged," she said, looking over at Ron and pointing to the cabinet where the tuna was kept. "The tuna."

"I'm way ahead of you, Ma. I picked up a cigarette charger last week."

"Smart."

"You know me."

Ron handed Nola three cans of tuna. He sat down again. "Six months ago if anyone had told me we would be going through this, I would not've believed it."

"What a difference a day makes," she said, pushing the cans and the can opener toward Vann. And that was definitely true. So much had happened to turn their little corner of the world upside-down, she didn't know from one day to the next what was going to happen. She could only pray that she had the strength to get through it and that no harm came to Meika at Cordelia's hands.

THIRTY-SIX

LOPEZ and Callahan rolled into the block at eleven-fifteen; they drove past Vann and Ron parked on the south side corner behind an already parked car, diagonally across the street from the brownstone. Vann and Ron watched as Lopez parked several cars up on the same side of the street. Once parked, they could no longer see them.

"It's on," Vann announced.

"Nothing to do but wait."

And the wait was on. Vann hoped that the large thermos of coffee, the four lightly cream-cheesed bagels, and the two thick slices of marble cake they brought with them was enough. He had started to buy doughnuts but his father thought it a bit too clichéd. As it was, his mother had sent them off with a kiss and a remark about their being honorary detectives. Pulling him aside, she told him not to let his father dwell on Cordelia. He promised he'd do his best, and, at times, he had to stop himself from speaking about Cordelia and what she had done. He could kill her himself, but his life was too important to give up. He had to think about his children and his parents.

A half hour passed. Already they had seen the woman, with her son and daughter, they assumed they saw in the darkness on the night of their first visit. The woman's red shopping cart was loaded down with two large bundles of what may have been dirty laundry. Apparently, she was on her way to the laundromat. No one else had come and gone since.

"Dad, pass me a bagel."

"Boy, you hungry again? You had a big breakfast over an hour ago."

"Don't worry about how often I eat or how much I eat, Dad. Worry when I can't eat."

"Hey, I'm just surprised you still eat like you did when you were a teenager. You and Troy just about ate up half of every paycheck I brought home, and you don't look like you're even thinking about slowing down."

"Not one bit. Food is my passion."

"I see that," Ron said, reaching back in between the seats to the rear where he plucked the bag off the backseat. He handed it to Vann.

"Thanks," he said, opening the bag and sticking his hand inside. He felt around for a bagel, started to pull it out, changed his mind, and pulled out a piece of marble cake instead.

Watching Vann unwrap the cake, Ron shook his head. He didn't know where Vann put all the food he took in. Ron looked across at the house. "What if he doesn't show today?"

"Like Lopez said, I'll be sitting right here until he does," Vann said, chomping down on the cake, taking a good-sized chunk out of it. It was moist and sweet, just like he liked it. He chewed rapidly, enjoying every crumb. "Personally, I think we should hang around at least until six. It's conceivable that he could be held up somewhere."

"I don't have a problem with that, but we better call your mother by three or she'll make her way up here, mouth and all."

"That's why I brought my cell phone. I'll be calling her at two o'clock sharp, come hell or high water."

"I hear you."

Vann finished his cake while sipping on a half cup of coffee, hoping that he wouldn't have to get out of the car to find a secluded spot in a very public place, alongside a building or behind a big tree somewhere.

Which one of them looked at his watch the most Vann couldn't say, but they checked the time every time they saw someone pass through the block. They quickly ran out of small talk about Michael Jordan and his awesome talents—there wasn't anything to debate. They spent even less time discussing golf. It wasn't Vann's game.

Ron began looking at the inside of his eyelids soon after the conversation stopped.

Vann called home and got no answer, which was okay by him, he was not up for being grilled. Minutes later, he watched as two middle-aged men, who might have been renting the apartment on the parlor floor, came out and strolled toward Columbus Avenue. The lady with the two children returned from the laundromat. A half hour later she and her children went out again, most likely on another errand that a working mother could only get to on the weekend. There didn't appear to be a man in her life to share her chores or errands with. That was too bad. She looked like a good woman, a caring mother. Her children were well-dressed and appeared to be happy as they hopped and skipped ahead of her toward Amsterdam Avenue.

In Atlanta, at this very moment, Vann's own children were most likely out and about with Michelle, but he wondered if they were hopping and skipping, if they were happy. For the first time in their lives, he didn't know if they were, he had been gone too long. There was no doubt that Michelle was a good mother; and there was no doubt that she had been a good partner; and there should not have been any doubt that she would have been a good wife. When this was over, he was going to have to find out if she'd want him to come back home, because he was beginning to feel like he wanted to go back, and that was something he had to explore.

Ron began snoring lightly.

Vann took a bagel. He hated waiting. Waiting, whether it was on a supermarket line, a bank line, or in a traffic jam, was all the same to him—tediously boring. It wasn't in his makeup to wait for anything or anyone, and it would be his luck that the mailman would run late today. By two-forty-five, he felt as if his body had melded with the leather. Stretching out fully, he began to feel munchy. Making sure that Ron was sleeping soundly, he went for his second bagel. Taking man-size bites out of it, he popped the last piece into his mouth when, out of the corner of his eye, through the side-view mirror, he caught sight of the mailman bustling into the block from Amsterdam. He nudged Ron—harder the second time.

Groggy, Ron asked, "Huh?"

"The mailman."

Instantly awake, Ron quickly checked his watch. "Damn, he's late!" he exclaimed, looking at the mailman. "Did Hali-huston show up?"

"Nope."

They watched the mailman, a wispy young Asian, whisk from house to house pushing his mail cart, taking out bundles of mail, sometimes trotting up stone stairs, sometimes dashing into yards, methodically plopping mail in slots or mailboxes.

"That boy's moving," Ron said.

"That's because his ass is late."

Up one side of the street and down the other he went, never slowing down, never hesitating. He didn't pass up 112 and spent no more time there than he did at the other buildings. When he passed them by, even from where they sat across the street, not a bead of sweat dampened his brow. He was out of the block in minutes, turning north on Columbus, without a break in his stride.

"I don't think I moved that fast when I was a kid," Ron said, impressed.

"I'd like to see him do the two hundred meter."

"My money would be on him."

Vann's eyes hadn't left 112, nor had he forgotten about Lopez and Callahan parked up ahead of them. There had been no movement from them, leaving Vann to surmise that they, too, had brought victuals—probably those doughnuts.

"I tried to reach Ma a while ago, she wasn't home. Should I try again?"

Ron took his first bagel out of the bag. "Naw. If she was worried, she would've called us by now. Though I wonder where she got off to; I thought she'd be sitting by the phone waiting to hear from us."

"She probably went to see Mr. Lipscomb," Vann guessed, looking at the bagel in Ron's hand. "You gonna eat your other bagel or your cake?"

Ron looked at him in disbelief. "Here," he said, thrusting the bag at him.

"Thanks."

THIRTY-SEVEN

NOLA felt bad for Ron and Vann having had to wait throughout the day, well into the evening, to no avail. They came home tired from sitting, hungry for a hot meal, each in need of relief. Ron raced for the bathroom downstairs, Vann sprinted up to the bathroom on the second floor. Afterward, neither was very talkative as they gobbled down baked chicken and rice. Like theirs, her day hadn't gone too well. Mr. Lipscomb did not agree that they could use the fact that Cordelia had told the police that there were drugs and a gun in the shoe box in Meika's closet in their fight to get her back. There was no tangible proof as the drugs and the gun were both gone—nothing to work with. Simply hearsay. In addition to Meika being too young to say that what she threw away was in fact drugs, he thought that the judge might turn the tables on them and say that they were harassing Cordelia, and might even rule that they turn over Meika and her clothes, permanently. As for the possibility that Cordelia might be dealing or even back on drugs, he didn't want to bring that up again without a witness. Without a witness, it was supposition.

Again, a no-win situation, especially for Meika. Nola was worried sick about her. She wondered if Meika was sleeping through the night; if she was eating; if she was crying still; or if she felt that she and Ron hadn't protected her as they promised.

Since wondering left her with no answers and she saw no other way, she went in search of answers for herself. While Vann and Ron had been staking out Halihuston, Nola staked out Cordelia. Also to no avail. Cordelia never came out of the house; at least not while Nola was there, which was until four o'clock in the afternoon. What she couldn't understand was, why were all the cards being dealt in Cordelia's favor? Didn't they deserve a good hand for once?

Vann thought they did. Sunday morning, he and Ron snuck out of the house, before nine o'clock, leaving Nola sound asleep, thermos and sandwiches in hand, eager to get back to their stakeout. When she awakened, left with nothing else to do herself, she grabbed a thermos of hot tea and went back to her own stakeout across the street from the red brick house Cordelia called home. Ron would kill her if he knew. Within minutes of Nola parking, Cordelia came outside, alone. If she had glanced across the street, she would have seen Nola sitting, conspicuously, in her car looking back at her.

Too late to react by slumping down in her seat, Nola turned her head aside and prayed that Cordelia did not see her. She didn't look around again until she was sure that Cordelia had passed.

"I know she didn't leave Meika upstairs by herself," Nola said aloud. She watched Cordelia twitch her ass down the street toward the corner.

Opening the door, Nola started out of the car but, thinking better of it, pulled her leg back in and closed the door. She wasn't supposed to be there. Mr. Lipscomb had warned her to stay away, but there was another way to take care of this. She reached into her pocketbook for her cell phone and quickly pressed 911.

"Where's your emergency?"

"Operator, the woman upstairs has left her child, a little girl, alone in the apartment and she's crying."

"What is that address?"

"One-five-three-two Sterling Avenue in Brooklyn."

"Is there an apartment number?"

Oh shoot! That she didn't know, she had guessed upstairs. "It's a private two-family house," she said, playing it safe.

"How long has she been gone?"

"For quite a while," Nola said, continuing her lie, yet realizing that she was staying on the line too long. "Are you going to send a policeman there to check on that child or not?"

"Ma'am, no need to get upset with me," the operator said, sounding indignant. "I'm required to ask these questions. A car has already been dispatched."

"I'm sorry," Nola said, trying to sound contrite, "but I'm very concerned about the little girl. No telling what can happen to her in there all alone."

"Would you like to leave your name and telephone number?"

"No, but the little girl's mother's name is Cordelia Kirkwood," she said, quickly flipping her phone shut, disconnecting the call. A minute later, a patrol car moseyed into the block, intermittently stopping every few houses to check the addresses on the doors. They were making their way up the block so slowly, Nola wanted to get out and wave them on. At 1532 the car stopped. Two officers crept out of their car from both sides. One adjusted his nightstick in his belt, the other, who looked like a body builder—his jacket sleeves were straining from his bulging biceps—put his hat on his head. They took their own sweet time climbing the stairs to the door. If Meika's life depended on them, she'd really be in trouble. One of the officers rang each of the two bells. Nola held her breath as the officers waited for someone to answer. No one did. One of the officers took out his nightstick and tapped on the glass and iron door. Still, no one came. They seemed to be discussing what to do when they both looked down at the sidewalk. Nola looked, too, and was shocked—Cordelia had come back, carrying a small bag in her arm, and was talking to the officers as she approached the building.

This time Nola quickly slumped all the way down in her seat, bumping her knees under the dashboard. "Oww!" she whined, trying to straighten out her legs. The pain was well worth it if Cordelia were arrested for child neglect. Daring to raise her head enough to peek above the door, Nola saw that the policemen had gone into the house with Cordelia. Now, it was just a matter of time.

Sitting up, Nola looked anxiously from the windows on the first floor up to the windows on the second floor and back again at the door. How she wished she were the proverbial fly on the wall.

The door suddenly opened. Again she slumped, carefully this time, down in her seat. The policemen came out, without Meika and without Cordelia in handcuffs. Pulling the door up behind them, they both ambled down the stairs to their car, chitchatting, one even laughing. What had she told them to keep them from arresting her? If it was because Meika wasn't there, where was she? Cordelia had only had her two days, had she given her over to someone else already?

The door opened again. Cordelia stepped out onto the stoop, looking out, not smiling, yet not frowning, appearing to scan the street.

Nola practically threw herself across the front seat onto her side. Where was the cloudy overcast day when she needed it? The last thing she needed was to be seen spying on Cordelia, by Cordelia. Lord knows, Judge Fiske would enjoy rendering a final ruling in Cordelia's favor.

Nola heard the engine of what she thought was the patrol car start up. Just in case, she decided to wait a few minutes longer for Cordelia to go back inside. She heard the sound of a car pull off. She waited still. A crick began to creep into her side. She tried to pull it out by adjusting her position. It subsided at first then returned with a vengeance. She massaged her side although she knew that sitting up would be the only cure. After an eternal minute more, she very carefully raised her head and peeked out the window. The police were gone and there was no sign of Cordelia. Feeling that it was safe to sit up and get out of there, she turned the key in the ignition and shifted into drive, all the while stretching her side, working out the crick.

She didn't feel bad about calling the police. If anything, it was tit for tat. She wasn't too old to play that game. If she felt anything at all, it was shame for almost getting caught. Next time, she wouldn't sit smack-dab across the street from Cordelia's front door—that had been stupid. She pulled out.

CORDELIA STEPPED out onto the stoop as Nola drove off. Flipping Nola the finger, she spat, "Bitch!"

THIRTY-EIGHT

OTHER than numb butts and stiff knees, Vann and Ron had nothing to show for two days of staking out a mailbox that, in its metal gut, held the evidence that could point the finger at Troy's killer. They did not see Lopez on Sunday nor had they seen him so far today and surmised that he was not keeping his word to stake out the house, but that was okay, that's why they were there. Troy's killer was their concern.

For the third day in a row they sat, which prompted Ron to say as he lowered the window a few inches, "This has got to be the day."

Vann crossed his fingers. "Here's hoping."

At one o'clock, a different mailman delivered the mail. He raced through the block with long determined strides, lightening his load with every house he passed. After he left the block, Vann and Ron began hunkering down for a long wait when a sleek, white Mercedes cruised into the block and stopped in front of 112.

Vann shot up in his seat. Ron eased up slowly. They both watched the tall black man step out of the car. He was dressed head to toe in black leather—a full-cut leather bomber, sleek black leather pants that made his long straight legs look like leather-covered giraffe legs, a leather hat, and something Vann had once thought of buying for himself, a pair of riding boots.

"This has got to be him," Vann said.

"It's him," Ron said flatly, taking a piece of paper from the glove compartment and writing down the license plate number of the Mercedes. "You reckon he bought his clothes with Troy's credit card?"

"If not Troy's, somebody's."

Keys in hand, the man they assumed to be Victor Halihuston sauntered into the yard of 112 to the mailboxes. He dropped an envelope in one mailbox and then quickly unlocking another, removed a stack of mail and, while walking back to his car, leafed through it, not the least bit concerned about anything or anyone around him.

Vann's heart was pumping rapidly as he put his hand on the ignition key.

"Wait till he pulls off," Ron said, putting his own shaking hand on top of Vann's.

Vann let go of the key and clutched Ron's hand. Neither found it necessary to look at each other or speak. They knew what this meant and how they felt about it.

The Mercedes started moving.

Vann started the engine and quickly turned the wheel to pull out when a car came out of nowhere and stopped only inches from them. He jammed his brakes. "Goddamnit! What the—"

"If you get ahead of us, I'll have you both arrested for obstruction of justice," Lopez warned, leaning across Callahan, who was driving.

"You're letting him get away!" Ron shouted.

"Stay behind us. Go!" Lopez said to Callahan. They sped off.

Quickly pulling out, Vann asked, "Where the hell did they come from?"

"I don't know, but stay on their tail."

At the first stoplight, Vann and Ron both snapped on their seat belts. The light turned green. Gripping the steering wheel with both hands, with his heart in his throat, Vann rode Callahan's tail, tensely maneuvering in the maddening stop-and-go traffic down Columbus into Broadway to Fifty-seventh Street, through a caravan of yellow cabs hogging the streets, zipping in and out of lanes, then perilously inching past a parade of lunch-hour pedestrians who thought they were sacred cows crossing any- and everywhere at will, holding Vann at bay in the intersection and separating him from Callahan.

"Get outta the way!" he shouted out of the open window.

"Go to the left!" Ron coached.

Vann began inching left and had to stop abruptly to let a stray cow slip past before he could again catch up with Callahan. The way opened up once they passed First Avenue, taking them right into the FDR Drive south access lane, where he came up for air long enough to fill his lungs for the breakneck speed of the drive. The Mercedes, which he hadn't seen since they left Eighty-eighth Street, pulled smoothly onto the drive six cars ahead of them. One by one the cars ahead fed onto the drive merging into the flowing traffic. Callahan suddenly shot out, leaving Vann behind in the access lane attempting to follow Callahan on. With his chest practically against the steering wheel, his head halfway out of the window, Vann gripped the steering wheel tighter, ready to take off. Every time he crept up to pull out, he'd have to jam the brakes. Several cars sped past him, not giving him an inch, keeping him from getting on. Far up ahead he saw the tail of Callahan's black Ford Taurus disappearing out of sight. Gone!

"They're not letting me on!"

Half turned around in his seat, Ron watched for an opening in the oncoming traffic. Soon he saw their chance. "After the blue car!"

"I see it."

A black car sped past. The blue car sped past.

"Go!"

Vann floored the accelerator, propelling the car onto the

drive, taking it from zero to fifty in a split second. Immediately zipping across the middle lane to the third lane, then back to the middle lane, flicking his signal stick like a light switch, he drove that lane until he was tailgating the car ahead of him.

"You're too close!" Ron shouted, jamming his foot into the floor on an imaginary brake.

"I got the car, Dad!"

"I hope we don't get stopped."

"They'll have to set up a concrete roadblock to stop this car," Vann said, zipping again into the third lane, trying to keep his eyes on the road while trying to look far up ahead for Callahan's car. Contrary to his usual laid-back driving style, he was sitting so rigidly his back hurt. "I lost them!"

"Not yet. They didn't get off at Forty-ninth or Thirty-fourth."

"What's the next exit?"

"I think Twenty-third," Ron answered, craning his neck to look ahead, searching for the Taurus or the Mercedes. "Unless he's going to lower Manhattan, he's gotta be heading back into Brooklyn."

"Yeah, but we could have lost them."

Ron saw them. He pointed. "There's Callahan!"

"Where?"

"Middle lane, 'bout seven cars up."

"All right!" Vann shouted excitedly, striking the steering wheel with the ball of his right hand. He stayed in the third lane until he was neck-and-neck with the car behind Callahan. When he saw his chance, Vann sped up and shot into the lane, cutting off the car, making the driver abruptly cut her speed.

"Vann! Don't get us killed!"

He could see Lopez turn and look back at him. Callahan put his arm out the window and, waving his hand low, gave Vann the slow-down sign. Vann immediately let up on the accelerator, firmly touched the brake, then went back to the accelerator, this time with a lighter foot. Exhaling slowly, he relaxed his grip on the steering wheel and sat back as they zoomed past the Houston Street exit heading toward lower Manhattan.

Ron sat back and wiped the sweat off his forehead. "Remind me to get my heart checked."

"Yours and mine both."

The right signal came on on Callahan's car. He changed lanes. So did Vann. A distance ahead, looming far above, the sign "Brooklyn Bridge—Right Lane Only" confirmed that they were indeed going back into Brooklyn. Like elephants hanging on to each other's tails, a half-mile-long line of cars snaked their way into the Brooklyn Bridge exit curve.

"There's the Mercedes!" Ron said.

"I see it."

At first it was slow going onto the bridge, then the pace picked up once again. Vann spotted the Mercedes in the left lane, but Callahan didn't change lanes. Seeing his chance to pass, Vann put on his left signal and began flooring the accelerator.

"Don't!" Ron exclaimed.

Vann eased up on the accelerator and flicked off the signal. "Damn. Man, I feel like a kid following behind them."

"In this game, son, you are," Ron said, keeping his eye on the Mercedes. "They know what they're doing, stay behind them."

"Damn."

Once off the bridge, at Tillary Street, they made a left and drove down to Flatbush Avenue, where they made a right, and drove awhile until the Mercedes got into the left turn lane at Fulton Street. They took Fulton Street up to Lafayette Avenue, where the Mercedes made a left turn. The traffic light was still green. The two cars ahead of Callahan and Lopez continued on up Fulton, but Callahan stopped while oncoming traffic trailed by. The Mercedes proceeded on up Lafayette Avenue.

Vann came to an abrupt stop. He was up Callahan's tail,

their bumpers were practically kissing. He could not turn out. "What's he doing? Why doesn't he force the turn? He's letting him get away!"

Ron leaned forward, looking into Lafayette Avenue. "The Mercedes made a left three blocks up. Just lay back. Wait for Callahan."

Vann saw Callahan stick his arm out the window. As he had done before, he let it drop down against the door and waved his hand twice. "He's telling me to hold back."

The car behind Vann honked incessantly.

"Aw, shut the hell up!" he said to the driver in back although he did not turn around.

"Stay cool," Ron advised.

"Dad, I'm about to explode. If this is where this man lives, do you realize that he was damn near in our backyard?"

"Son, we live in a very small world."

"So small that it's scary."

The traffic light turned yellow.

"Damn," Vann said, striking the steering wheel, "we missed the light."

"The Mercedes turned three blocks up," Ron said. "I think that's South Portland. It can only go one way and it's a short block. Unless he parks, he'll turn into DeKalb. Hold tight."

"I am!" Vann snapped, more than a little annoyed that everyone was telling him what to do. Feeling like he was about to burst, he watched Callahan and the traffic light. Oncoming traffic stopped. Callahan began pulling into his left turn, and so did Vann—on red. Sure enough, Callahan made a left turn three blocks up into South Portland Avenue. Up ahead, the Mercedes was slowly backing into a parking space on the west side of South Portland down near DeKalb.

Callahan slid into a spot midway into the block and pulled up just enough to let Vann pull in behind him next to a hydrant.

Vann shut off the engine, but he couldn't shut off the

pounding in his chest. He was hyped. He was ready to confront Troy's killer. He put his hand on the door handle.

"No," Ron said. "Don't get out until they tell you to."

"Damn, Dad, I can't sit here," he said, closely watching Halihuston, who carried the mail in his hand into one of the houses.

"You have to. We don't want to blow this."

Vann settled back. "Fine." He began trying to figure out which house Halihuston went into. He slammed his hand on the steering wheel. "I can't tell a damn thing from back here!"

"It's all those gates and railings. It makes it hard to tell where one house begins and the other ends. Wait, here comes Lopez."

Vann unlocked his door and pushed it open.

"Don't get out," Lopez said, approaching the car, going right for the rear passenger door.

Pulling his door closed, Vann released the lock on the back door. He and Ron faced backward as Lopez slid into the backseat.

Lopez closed the door. "That was some driving you did. Need a job?"

Vann wasn't amused. "I have a job. What's up? Why are we sitting all the way back here? We can't tell which house he went into."

"I know the one."

"Which one?"

"You don't need to know that."

"That's great! I did all that driving, almost killing me and my father, just to not know?"

"You're lucky you know as much as you do. You weren't even supposed to be uptown. I could have ordered you away on Saturday and Sunday, but I figured it was a waste of time."

"If you saw us Saturday and Sunday, why didn't you say something?"

"What for? I decided to let you have your fun."

"Fun? That wasn't no goddamn fun! I wasn't racing behind a stock car. I was breaking my damn neck trying to stay on the tail of my brother's murderer."

"Let it go, son," Ron said, laying his hand on Vann's shoulder.

Vann abruptly faced forward.

"Detective, what happens now?" Ron asked.

"What happens now is you and your son let us do our job. We have to make sure that that was Victor Halihuston. If not, we need to ascertain who he is. We need to review the information we got from Mr. Stein on Cranberry Street; we have to check out the license and owner of that car; and, finally, we have to convince the judge of probable cause, in order to get a search warrant to search the suspect and his apartment for the mail. From this moment on, I am ordering you and your son to stay out of this block."

Vann stared at Lopez in the rearview mirror. "You can't make us stay away."

"Actually, I'm not even going to try. It's up to you. You want your brother's killer, you make yourself stay away," he said, locking eyes with Vann in the rearview mirror. "Mr. Kirkwood, please do not interfere with this investigation. At this point, you and your father can do more harm than good."

"I don't think so," Vann said. "If it wasn't for us interfering, you wouldn't have a suspect."

"Granted. However, Mr. Kirkwood, this part of the investigation is fragile. If everything, and I mean everything from A to Z, is not done according to the letter of the law, we can blow the whole case on a technicality. Unless you wanna see the suspect, the possible killer of your brother, walk, then I suggest, strongly, that you sit by the telephone—at home."

Vann dropped his head back against the headrest and closed his eyes.

"We'll wait by the phone," Ron said, looking at Vann. "Just

make sure you keep us in the loop. We need to know what's going on."

"I will," Lopez said, opening the door. "By the way, it shouldn't be more than a few days. It might be a good idea if you took a U-turn out of here about now."

Vann lifted his head. "Why?"

"Let's just say, I don't want you to get too curious," Lopez answered. He climbed out of the backseat. At Ron's window, he leaned down. "Assuming that this is our guy, you fellas did a good job tracking him down." He extended his hand to Ron.

At first surprised, Ron hesitated, but he took the hand offered and shook it.

Lopez went back to his car.

"You all right, son?"

"No." Vann started up the car. He waited for a car to pass before he U-turned out of the block and headed home, less than a mile away. He could not help but think that after the chase, he should have been able to confront Victor Halihuston; to put his fist in his face; to beat him within an inch of his life. Something. He should have been able to do something. He felt let down, depressed even, like the whole day had been for naught. He knew that he would not rest until he could look Troy's killer in the eye and let him know that the life he took was not his to take.

THIRTY-NINE

*P*OPPIE. *come get me, I don't like it here. Mama. Mama, I wanna come home."* The pitiful little voice trailed off into a mournful cry.

"Meika. Who you talking to?"

"Um . . . nobody."

Click.

Three times Nola had replayed that melancholy message; three times she cried; three times she could not believe that she was probably sitting in her car outside Cordelia's apartment while Meika was trying to reach her. She could slap her own self for missing Meika's call. She should have been home to speak to her, to console her.

Hearing the sadness in Meika's voice made Vann feel worse than he already did. "I wish I had let you guys take her and run."

"That wasn't the answer," Ron said, pushing back from the kitchen table.

Maybe it wasn't, but knowing that did not ease Vann's guilt for butting in. Suddenly he had a yearning to hear Sharice's and Kareem's voices. "I'll be back," he said, hurriedly leaving the kitchen.

Standing at the stove, Nola lifted the top off the pot and laid it upside-down on the counter. She picked up the spoon and began slowly stirring the pot of meat sauce.

"Where were you?" Ron asked. "Why weren't you home?"

She continued stirring.

"Nola, where did you go?"

She slammed the spoon down in the plate on the counter, splashing tomato sauce everywhere, even on the front of her blouse. "I was where I wasn't supposed to be, okay?"

"What!"

"Ron, I couldn't take it. I had to go over there. I was sitting outside of Cordelia's apartment trying to get a look at Meika!"

"Nola! Didn't I tell you not to go over there?"

She moved away from the stove. "Ron, don't start with me! I didn't know what else to do. I wanted to see Meika. I needed to know that she was all right."

"Nola, the child called because she's not all right. You should have been here to take her call."

"Please! I feel bad enough as it is," she said. The steam escaping from the pot drew her back to the stove. She picked up the spoon and angrily stirred the sauce before slamming it down again.

"You were wrong, Nola. What if something had happened to you out there?"

She slammed the top down on the pot, hurting her fingers. "Well, nothing happened to me, did it?"

"Nola, you are hardheaded. I can't tell you a damn thing."

On the other side of the kitchen door, Vann had been about to push it open when he heard the loud slam. He did not need to, nor did he want to be in the middle of this argument. He had butted in enough, but he did want to know what they were arguing about. He put his ear to the door.

Ron wasn't through with Nola. "You don't know who that woman's friends are. This time nothing happened to you, but what about next time? And, Nola, there had better not be a next time."

She felt herself swell. "There had better not be?"

"Ah, damn! Nola, don't go picking at my words."

She put her hands on her hips. "Ronald, don't tell me what

to do. And *especially*, don't tell me what to do when it comes to Cordelia. I want her ass. And as far as her friends go, I don't give a damn who they are. I will not back down. My only concern is Meika."

Troubled that he was partly to blame for Meika being with Cordelia, Vann felt that he had to step in—he had to mediate. He placed his hand on the door. He started to push the door open.

"Baby, you're not hearing me," Ron said.

Vann let up on the door. They weren't shouting anymore.

"I hear you, Ron, but I'm so worried about Meika."

"I'm just as worried about Meika as you are. But doing what you did, I have to put energy into worrying about you, too."

"You don't need to worry about me."

"Oh, no? Well, then, what about me? Don't you give a damn about me?"

Vann waited.

"Ron, what I did had nothing to do with you."

"That's not the way I see it. Nola, didn't you once tell me that when I don't call home to tell you that I'm going to be late that it worries you out of your mind that something could have happened to me?"

"Yes, but that's different."

"If you think about it, it isn't. With what's happened to Troy, now Meika, and, eventually, with Vann going back home, if something should happen to you, I would have no one," Ron explained, his voice tight.

Nola's arms dropped heavily to her sides. She slumped back against the counter.

"Why would you want to leave me alone, with no one?"

The stinging in her nose made her tear. "Maybe I shouldn't've gone over there. I'm sorry," she said, contritely. She went and stood in front of Ron. "I love you."

He encircled her waist and pulled her down onto his lap. They held each other. "I love you," he said.

She kissed him on top of his head. "I love you more."

They looked deeply inside each other. Yep. That loving feeling was still there. Their lips came together.

Glad that his parents' disagreement had ended with a declaration of love, Vann gave them a minute to enjoy whatever they were doing. Feeling as bad as he did, he did not want to spoil it for them. He had hoped talking to Sharice and Kareem would make him feel better, but he had not been able to reach them. He would try again later.

Vann slapped the door once with the palm of his hand to announce that he was coming in. He pushed it open. "It smells good in here. What's cooking?" he asked, not looking in their direction. He went straight to the stove and lifted the top off the pot. He inhaled the sweet herbal blend of tomato sauce and ground beef sautéed in onions and celery. He reached for one of the two loaves of French bread on the counter and broke off a large chunk. He dipped it in the sauce. Eating it, he savored its sweetness. "Mmm."

Nola and Ron slowly loosened their intimate embrace though they continued sitting, holding on to each other, not quite ready to part.

Ron looked at Vann devour the chunk of bread. "Good thing you bought two loaves."

Nola glanced over at the steam escaping from under the top of the second, larger pot with the water in it. "I know my son's appetite," she said, kissing Ron on the forehead. She also knew her son's moods, and he was certainly trying hard to cover up his depression. It was his eyes that told.

Ron let his hand linger on Nola's waist and slide down to her behind as she was getting up off his lap.

"The spaghetti will be ready in ten minutes," she said. She went to work opening the first box of dry spaghetti and then the second. "Vann, what were you doing upstairs?"

He dipped another piece of bread into the meat sauce. "Made a phone call or two."

She took a handful of dry spaghetti and, holding on to both ends, broke the bunch in two. She dropped the spaghetti into the boiling water. "Are you all right?"

"I'm fine," he said, going to the refrigerator. He opened the door and looked inside. "We got any wine?" He didn't see a bottle. He closed the refrigerator door.

Nola dropped more spaghetti into the pot. "Are you sure you're all right? You don't look too good," she said, using the fork to separate the strings of spaghetti to keep them from clumping together.

Vann sat. "Dad, please tell Ma I'm all right."

"The boy says he's all right, Nola. You mind passing me a piece of that bread?"

Buzzz!

"That's the bell," she said, handing the whole loaf of bread out to Ron.

"I'll get it," Vann said, getting up again.

She glanced up at the wall clock. "No!" she snatched the bread back out of Ron's hand. "Vann, you go get the plates down. Ron, you get the door."

"What difference does it make?" Vann asked.

"Let him get the door," Ron said, "he's younger."

She went and stood behind Vann. "Ron," she said, trying to signal with her eyes that he *had* to get the door.

Buzzz!

Vann started to look around at Nola.

She moved and pretended to busy herself at the counter.

It finally clicked for Ron. "Oh! I'll get it," he said, getting up quickly and rushing out of the kitchen.

"Vann, would you take down six plates?"

"Who's coming to dinner?" he asked, opening up the cabinet door.

"Family," she said, rushing back to stir the boiling, bubbling pot.

"Who? Cousin Beatrice?"

"Just a minute." She hurriedly stirred the pot until much of the bubbles settled down. "I hate mushy spaghetti."

Vann held the six large white plates in his hand. "Ma, who's coming over?"

"Vann!" Ron called from the living room. "There's someone here to see you."

"I'm not expecting anyone," he said, setting the plates on the table on his way out of the kitchen.

"Daddy!"

Smiling to herself, Nola snatched two pot holders off the counter and hurriedly lifted the pot off the stove over to the sink. She dumped the spaghetti into the colander sitting in the bottom of the sink. Running cold water full force over the steaming spaghetti, she reached over and turned off the stove. She quickly tossed the spaghetti once with the fork. Turning off the water, she raced out of the kitchen.

There was a big grin on Vann's face. Sharice and Kareem charged at him, almost knocking him over. They hugged him zealously, which he returned with as much ardor when he got his balance and wits about him. He kissed them feverishly all over their faces while feeling their love surge through him, invigorating him, reminding him of what he had been missing and of what he desperately needed to make his life complete—his family.

"I missed you guys," he said, lifting Sharice up into his arms. Kareem he hugged close to his body.

"We missed you, too!" Sharice said.

"What are you guys doing here? I just called y'all in Atlanta. How did y'all get here?"

"By plane," Kareem replied.

"Did we surprise you, Daddy?" Sharice asked, holding tightly to his neck.

He kissed her again. "Yes, you did."

Seeing Vann's joy, Nola smiled widely.

"Did you miss me, Vann?"

Vann looked toward the doorway. There stood the woman he had missed more than he would have ever imagined. He let Sharice slip easily out of his arms to the floor.

"Come, children," Nola said, taking Sharice and Kareem by the hand. "Grandma made you some spaghetti."

Kareem's eyes lit up. "Oh boy! U'm hungry, too."

"Let's eat then. Ron, I could use your help."

"Coming," he said, smiling and patting Vann once on the back as he passed.

"Grandma, where's Meika?" Sharice asked as the kitchen door closed behind them.

Left alone, Vann and Michelle held each other's gaze, neither saying what needed to be said to break the silence. Vann had much to say but knew not where to begin.

Michelle slowly unbuttoned her coat. Her long trim fingers lingered seconds at each hole as she pushed a button through. "Did you miss me?" she asked again.

"Yes," he answered, looking into her beautiful brown eyes. He saw the woman he had taken for granted; the lady who deserved to be treated with the respect she was worthy of; and the lover who yearned to get as good as she gave. He felt full of love for her and knew no other way to say that but to ask, "Will you marry me?"

Bringing her hands to her mouth, Michelle smiled as tears brimmed and emptied. Vann went to her. They came together, hugging and kissing deeply, drawing from each other and sharing the very taste and breath of the love they thought lost to them.

FORTY

UNTIL Vann held Michelle in his arms, he hadn't realized how empty his arms had been. Subconsciously, he must have missed her all along for many a morning he had awakened with a pillow in his arms held close to his chest, perhaps filling the void that had been left in his life and in his heart. Michelle had lost a few pounds since last he saw her in January, but still she filled his arms with her softness. Her tiny waist swelled into firm curvy hips and a soft round behind, which his hands gently caressed. He longed hungrily to feel himself inside her, to feel her sweet nectar come together with his own in a blissful undulating moment of ecstasy. But she said, "I want you, but I want to make love to you as your wife. Can you wait?" That he would, as she had waited much longer to be his wife than the few days he'd have to wait to be her husband. That he owed her.

It all felt right, but still, he couldn't believe that his mother had done this for him, behind his back, without ever letting a syllable slip. She had not only gotten Michelle to come to New York, but together, she and Michelle had lined up a minister and planned a wedding for Saturday. A wedding! Vann was clueless as to how that got by him. How did his mother know that he would propose when he didn't know himself? She had said as casually as she pleased when he asked, "I figured you were ready." She left him in awe of her intuition. If he had had any trouble believing that there was going to be a wedding, that trouble disappeared on Tuesday afternoon when he and Michelle went downtown to the Marriage License Bureau. That official piece of paper made it real for him.

Still, no matter how many ways his mother tried to explain that he had been telegraphing his change of heart about marriage, no matter how many ways he tried to figure out how he had telegraphed that to her, he was having a hard time coming to grips with the fact that she knew that he would ask Michelle to marry him. How did she know that he was ready, when he had only come to know that himself when he laid eyes on Michelle? Even when she told him that "a mother knows," and that if he stopped "intellectualizing his emotions" he would know that he was ready to marry the mother of his children, he was still stumped. There was no mention of her not liking Michelle. In fact, neither mentioned how she felt about the other and, at the moment, he thought it wise to not remind them that they were once distant. Admittedly, they had never argued, but they certainly had never been buddies. He watched in silence as the two of them, with their heads together, worked out the details of the wedding and went off shopping for a dress. At times, watching them talking, laughing, and planning, he could not help but think that that was the way it should have been all along, which is why he had conflicting feelings of anger that it had not been, and happiness that it was now. He needed to express those feelings to the one person who was most responsible.

Vann found Nola doing laundry in the basement. "Who are you and what have you done with my mother?"

Smiling, she closed the washing machine lid. "I am your mother," she said, pulling out the knob for the wash cycle to begin.

"But my mother never liked my woman."

"How do you know? Did you ever hear your mother say she didn't like your woman?"

"Ma, your actions spoke louder than your words." Vann sat on top of a heavy wooden picnic table. "You were cold to Michelle. We stayed in Atlanta because she was uncomfortable being around you."

That hurt. She sank down on the bench. "So that's why you didn't come home."

"If we lived in New York, we'd see you all the time, and seeing you would remind Michelle that you didn't like her. I didn't want her to go through that and I didn't want to have to stay away from you in order to keep peace in my home. Being in Atlanta made it easier."

"Look, the only problem I had with Michelle had to do with you and her getting together so young. I was worried about your future. No, I wasn't happy about you being in a committed relationship while in college, and, I guess, that's what came through in my attitude toward Michelle. But, Vann, how you and Michelle perceived that I felt about her never stopped you from getting together with her or stopped you from having children with her. Therefore, it should not have stopped you from marrying her. Why didn't you?"

"She . . . I . . . I had my reasons, okay?"

"Which were?"

"They're my reasons, Ma. But you? I know what you just said, but you, you couldn't even respect my decision to be with Michelle. You were so cold to her."

"That's not really true, Vann. I accepted your relationship with Michelle. I love my grandchildren. I'll admit that I never rubbed noses with Michelle, but I never went out of my way to make her uncomfortable in my house. Besides, since when has a mother's coolness toward her child's chosen mate been a determining factor as to whether or not they would marry? Vann, not marrying the mother of your children was solely your decision and had nothing to do with me."

"I don't know about that."

"Meaning?"

"Ma, if we hadn't had that talk a few weeks ago, I might be agreeing with you, but since we did, the more I think about it, I believe my not marrying Michelle had everything to do with you."

Nola drew back. She was beginning not to like this conversation any more than she liked the one two weeks ago. Was Vann again blaming her for the way he lived his life?

"Don't look at me like that, Ma. This is what I believe."

"How am I at fault?"

"Well, if you really want to know, for one thing, all these years I think I've been waiting for your approval, and since I never felt like you gave it, I never married Michelle."

"Vann," she said, unwilling to take the blame, "you've gone your whole life making your own decisions. You never sought anyone's approval for anything. You've always had your own mind."

"I sought your opinion on occasion."

"A rare occasion. You would ask your father and me for our opinions but, ultimately, your decisions were yours alone."

"Yes, but—"

"No. See, I believe it bothered you that I never said, 'Vann, marry that girl, she's the one for you,' but I also believe that you were afraid to sign that piece of paper that said that you were legally as well as emotionally committed to someone other than yourself."

"How could you say that, Ma? I've always been legally committed to my children and Michelle. I didn't need a piece of paper to tell me to do what's right."

"No, you didn't, and yes, you've always been responsible, but a marriage license means that you are not a separate entity unto yourself; that you cannot think about your own needs and wants without first considering the needs and wants of your wife—jointly."

"I've always considered Michelle's needs and wants."

"In that case, did she want you to come back here and stay as long as you have?"

Vann paused. He glanced at the vibrating washing machine. "Does marriage mean that I'm a prisoner? Because if it does, maybe it's not for me."

"Honey, don't say anything you might regret. Marriage does not mean that you are joined at the hip and cannot have separate interests and, at times, walk a separate path; it means that while you are pursuing those separate wants, needs, interests, and going down that separate path, you have to keep in your heart and mind how your wife fits in and how she feels about it, and what you'd have to do to make her still feel a part of your life, be it through conversation, sharing the experience, or, at times, inviting her into your separate world. Whether she wants to go along or not is her choice, but at least you extended an invitation."

Again Vann was in awe of his mother. Again she outexperienced him. "You sound like a marriage counselor. How do you know all this?"

"Honey, I've been married to your father thirty-three and a half years. Don't you think I should've learned something in all that time?"

"Postgrad work, huh?"

"The school of marriage is ongoing. As for yourself, you've been in school all along, you just didn't know it. You and Michelle have been living as a married couple, but you didn't put your nose to the grindstone and work at it like she did—being a woman."

"What does being a woman have to do with it?"

"We just work harder at our marriages than men do."

"That's sexist."

"But true. Vann, if you had worked hard at your relationship with Michelle, you really would have understood what being your wife meant to her, especially after having had your children. She feels used, unappreciated, and maybe even unwor-thy. All of these feelings were magnified when you stayed gone from her so long."

"I had to be here because of Troy."

"No, honey. You didn't have to be here this long."

"Are you saying that you didn't need me here?"

"Oh, we needed you. There is no question about that. What I'm saying is that you had a greater need to be away from your family."

He could not dispute that. He looked down at his hands. He popped his thumb knuckle.

Nola touched Vann's hand. She couldn't stand the sound of him popping his knuckles.

He stopped.

"Honey, I don't know all of what's been going on between you and Michelle, but you have to know that the relationship you two have is like a marriage. I can bet that you've had a lot of good times, but I guarantee you that you've had just as many, if not more, bad times. Marriage is work—sometimes pleasant, sometimes ugly and hard. However, if a couple works together and diligently, there could be plenty of sweet days."

"Have you seen a lot of sweet days with Dad?"

She smiled. "I've seen my share. But you should ask your fa-ther. Get it from a man's perspective."

"Maybe I will," he said, clasping his hands together. "Since I've been home, Ma, you and Dad have taken me on an odyssey of emotions that I never fathomed possible. I can tell you this. I feel like my love for you and Dad has been strength-ened. I love you both more every day and I can see why Dad loves you so much."

She felt her face glow. "I can see why your dad and I both love you. Vann, you're so special."

He smiled.

"We're proud of you. I hope you will always remember that. Plus, you have a fine family."

"Thank you, Ma. I can't describe to you what it was like for me to be holding my children and Michelle in my arms yesterday, other than to say, it was the height of euphoria. I'm wondering if this feeling is something that we men, at least some men, have been missing out on."

"Honey," she said, understanding Vann perfectly well, "women haven't cornered the market on love or emotion. We're just more open to it. We don't run from the idea of love or from the various emotions, good or bad, that love pulls out of us. In fact, we crave those emotions, more specifically the euphoric ones. Which brings me to this question. Vann, did loving Michelle make you feel vulnerable?"

He thought about it. "Maybe."

"How?"

"Well, in truth, I . . . I can't believe I'm about to say this."

"Trust me. Say it."

"Well, I kinda always felt like I could be hurt by Michelle because I loved her so much. I just never wanted to be hurt."

"Honey, you can't worry about that. You'll find yourself holding back in the relationship."

"I know, Ma, but Michelle knows everything about me. She knows my weaknesses, my strengths, my likes, my dislikes, my mind, and, really, she knows my heart. No one else on earth, not even you, Ma, knows as much about me, and because of that I felt that no one else could hurt me emotionally or financially but her."

"So you pulled away."

"I guess I did."

"Vann, let me ask you this. Do you feel comfortable leaving your wallet or your checkbook or your address book on the dresser at home?"

"Of course. Although Michelle did question me about the safe-deposit boxes I have for my clients."

"I'd question that myself if I didn't know about it," she assured him. "Other than that, do you trust her?"

He shrugged. "I guess I do."

"Then, honey, take it a step further. Trust her with your heart and your life. I trust your father with mine, and he surely trusts me with his. If you were ever wronged by Michelle, then you'd have reason to be wary, but until then, trust her and give her your love, unconditionally."

Vann nodded pensively. Michelle had never given him reason to mistrust her. She had been by his side through thick and thin and, if anything, he was the one who had let her down.

Nola patted Vann on the thigh. "I know you haven't had time to pick up a ring, so—"

"Oh, man!" He leaped down off the table. "Ma, I can't get married without a ring."

"You won't."

Vann bolted for the basement stairs. He looked at his watch. He stopped. He pivoted back toward Nola. "Damn."

"Vann," she said, calmly.

"It's too late. I'll have to try and pick one up tomorrow. Man, I hope Michelle doesn't get upset with me if I can't."

"Vann."

"I should've picked up a ring yesterday."

"Vann. Vann, you have a ring."

"Huh?"

"I want you to put my engagement ring on Michelle's finger."

He gaped at her. "Ma, are you sure?"

"Very. Your father gave me a new one for our thirtieth anniversary, but the first one has always been special. I want you to give it to Michelle. I want it to bring you both as much love as your father and I have had."

Misty-eyed, Vann went back and gathered Nola up in his arms. "I love you, Ma."

She kissed him on the cheek.

Letting up on his embrace, Vann wiped at his eyes. "Ma, I

need to tell you this. When Troy was killed, I felt like someone had cut off one of my arms. For weeks I felt like I couldn't breathe. I thought if I could find his killer and maybe hurt him real bad, I'd feel like I did something to avenge his death. Then I'd be able to breathe again, be whole."

Nola knew those feelings well. She glanced at the washing machine as it began to shake. It was in its spin cycle.

"Ma, on Monday, when Lopez made us leave the block after following that bastard from uptown, I felt so low, I felt like I had fallen into a bottomless pit."

"I can understand that. It was a huge letdown."

"Yes. I put so much of myself into finding Troy's killer, then chasing behind him, and to be so close, yet not close enough to grab him, was a downer. It felt so anticlimactic."

"I know."

"I actually felt sick, and it wasn't until I saw Sharice and Kareem that I felt better. My heart felt better, lighter. Ma, I'm really ready to be with my family. I'm ready to get married."

Nola pressed her lips together. She fought the urge to cry.

"I hate that Troy isn't here to stand up for me."

She nodded.

"See, Ma, that's the other reason I want his killer caught. He's taken so much from us. I want that bastard to draw his last breath sucking on a vicious dose of potassium chloride."

"I've given the death penalty a lot of thought in these last few months. I've had to do a lot of soul searching," she said. "I have no love for Troy's killer. When he killed Troy, I wanted him killed in turn. But I've been talking a lot to God and now I think that life imprisonment without the possibility of parole, at the very least, will satisfy me."

"Not me. His life for Troy's is the only vindication that will satisfy me."

"Honey, I've felt that way at times myself. I didn't like the feeling."

"That feeling, Ma, was the only thing driving me."

"Vann, listen to me," Nola said, taking his hand and holding it. "Considering that it was Troy that was killed, it surprised me that I didn't like feeling revengeful, hateful, and bitter. It was depressing. I could almost feel the hate eating away at my soul. Honey, I don't want you feeling that way."

"I don't. I want that bastard dead."

"Vann, a life will never bring back a life."

"No, but it will make me feel better. It'll be justice—"

"Vann—"

"Ma, let's not debate this one. This is how I feel. After having to pull Meika out of your arms to give to Cordelia, I can't feel any other way. Meika is Troy's legacy. His killer is our scourge. I want him dead."

FORTY-ONE

IT was a joy to be planning for Vann's wedding—it gave Nola something to do with her idle time besides worry about Meika. She was actually enjoying herself. March had been true to itself—it had charged in like a lion and had gone out like a lamb. The weather was warming up. Saturday promised to be bright and possibly ten degrees warmer, Meika was going to be home, and, like Sharice, she had a new dress to wear for the wedding that would make her look like a little princess.

Nola and Michelle had not planned a big wedding, just an intimate reception at Beatrice's. Nola was really enjoying Michelle's company and saw in her what Vann had seen all along—Michelle was rather nice and had grown to be a strong, self-assured woman. She was no longer the needy, obnoxiously clingy young girl of all those years ago who got on Nola's nerves every time she saw her lying all over Vann. Maybe that was the reason he had not married her early on. Perhaps he felt smothered. The woman that Michelle now was was every bit the woman Nola would have wanted her son to be with—time had done her justice. In all fairness, Nola had to accept some blame for holding Michelle's youthful weaknesses against her.

"Good morning," Michelle said. "Can I help you with breakfast?"

Nola closed the refrigerator door with her foot. "Michelle, come in. Have a seat." She set the carton of eggs and the butter dish on the counter.

Michelle strolled into the kitchen and sat down at the table, in Ron's chair. She straightened the place mat.

"Would you like some coffee?"

"I'll have some with my breakfast. What can I do to help?"

"Everything's ready," Nola said, sitting down herself. "I'm just waiting for everyone to get washed up. Did you sleep well?"

"Yes, thank you." Michelle straightened the fork and spoon on the place mat.

"Good."

"How about you," Michelle began, her eyes on the fork, "did you sleep well?"

"Well enough, thank you," Nola replied, realizing that all wasn't well between them. Now that they were not busy with the wedding, there was an awkwardness between them that begged to be aired. "Michelle, I've never liked the taste of humble pie, it can be quite bitter. The times in my life that I've had to bite into one, I've had to swallow it with a grin and a bitter dose of self-evaluation."

Raising her eyes, Michelle slowly entwined her fingers on the place mat.

"I owe you an apology."

Changing neither the expression on her face nor the look in her eyes, Michelle waited.

Nola realized that she and Michelle were not in sync as to which fork in the road to take. "Michelle, I've never opened up my home or myself completely to you."

Michelle slowly batted her eyes once.

It was obvious to Nola that Michelle wasn't going to help her. She was going to have to do this on her own. She took a deep breath. "One could say that I've been stubborn and selfish in that I thought very few women were good enough for my sons. Of course, Cordelia isn't good enough for any woman's son, except maybe the son of Satan, but that's another story. You were never anything like Cordelia, yet I stood in judgment over you for no good reason other than your youth. I was wrong."

Michelle closed her eyes.

Nola didn't know what to think. Maybe she was going about it all wrong. She began twisting her wedding band around her finger. "Michelle, you could have been vindictive and kept Sharice and Kareem from me, but you were wonderful to let them spend summers with us. I wouldn't blame you if you can't forgive me for the way I shut you out," she said, looking for any sign that Michelle was listening to her. She couldn't tell, but she pushed on anyway. "It's my fault that you and I have lost a lot of time. I can only hope that you will give me the opportunity to make it up to you."

Michelle remained quiet.

"Michelle."

Michelle slowly opened her eyes.

"Can we be friends?"

Glancing down at her hands, Michelle was pensive. When she looked up again, she was ready. "Mrs. Kirkwood, even before I met you, I'd heard so much about you. Vann talked about you and his father like you were his best friends— next to Troy. I was envious of how he felt about you. You see, my mother died when I was ten, so what Vann talked about, I envied. I craved a mother's love, a father's love. I don't know if you knew any of this, but I never even knew my father. I was raised in a foster home."

"I'm sorry, I didn't know."

"I wanted so badly to have a family like the one Vann talked about, parents like the ones he had, that I dreamed about meeting you," Michelle said, her voice strained. "Vann used to say all the time, 'I can't wait till you meet my mother and father, you'll love them. They're great.' I was excited. I was ready to meet you; ready to love you; ready to call you Ma, like he did."

Nola's shame embraced her like a blanket of snow. She

folded her arms tight, hiding her hands underneath, trying to warm them.

Tears rolled down Michelle's cheeks. "But when we met, you were so cold to me. I was devastated. I must have cried for a week."

Nola felt sick. Had she been that cruel, that cold to someone who needed her love?

"You have no idea how hurt Vann was. He wanted us to be friends. That's all the more reason I tried so hard to get you to like me," Michelle said, abruptly swiping away her tears. "But you never did."

Nola remembered the flowers that, for three years, came for her on Mother's Day, her birthday, and her anniversary, always separate from Vann's, always with a little card that read, "Happy Mother's Day; Happy birthday; Happy anniversary," followed by just her name, "Michelle." Nola never knew the sentiment behind the dainty script that graced those little white cards. When they stopped coming, shamefully, she hadn't missed them. Looking back, she remembered thinking that the flowers were an attempt to win Vann, not his mother.

"After a while," Michelle continued, "I gave up trying and let go of my dreams of having a close relationship with you. I gave my all to Vann and, eventually, our children."

Nola felt small. "Michelle, I never thought that I was perfect, but I always thought that I was kind. You've shown me that I've been unkind. That I've been insensitive and cruel. I am so sorry," she said, humbly. "Can you find it in your heart to forgive me?"

Michelle began to weep.

Taking another step in bridging the divide between them, Nola got up and closed the space that separated them. Michelle suddenly stood and threw her arms around Nola. They latched on to each other, holding on, bonding, ending years of misunderstanding and selfishness on Nola's part. The daughter that she had always wanted had been there all along, she just hadn't recognized her.

"Michelle, would you do me a favor?"

Relaxing her hold on Nola, Michelle pulled back just a little. She nodded.

"Would you call me Ma?"

Tears rolled down Michelle's cheeks. Her hold on Nola again tightened, affirming how she felt about that question.

FORTY-TWO

THERE was no time to finish eating their early lunch, no time to hang around a minute longer to be nagged by womenfolk trying to tell them to stay out of police business, as Lopez had also warned on the telephone. Vann was reminded that, as yet, Halihuston was only a suspect. To Vann, Halihuston was the killer, which is why he had to be there to see for himself that all their months of looking for a murderer were not in vain. Ron wanted to look Halihuston in the eye to let him know that he was not invincible, that he was going to pay for taking his son. For himself, Vann had to get close enough to Halihuston to damn him to hell.

Pulling into South Portland, Vann saw immediately that he had a problem. Policemen were everywhere. He had wanted to be there before the blue army arrived. He had wanted to get past Lopez's dramatic annoyance with their being there without an audience of policemen and curious neighbors. But the way things looked—six police cruisers, all empty, meant that Lopez was already inside.

Quickly double-parking behind the last cruiser, Vann and Ron raced to the house, where a young pimply-faced police officer stood at the entrance to the front yard, blocking them from entering.

"Excuse us," Ron said.

"Sir, unless you live here, you can't enter."

"We've been working with Detective Lopez on this bust," Vann explained.

"I don't know either one of you. Are you detectives?"

"Yes."

"No," Ron replied, tugging on Vann's jacket. "If you'll let us speak to Detective Lopez, he'll vouch for us."

The officer looked suspiciously at Vann. "The detective is busy."

At that moment Vann lost all patience. "I don't have time for this," he said, faking right and pushing left past the officer, shoving him hard enough to make him fall backward against the brownstone stairs, knocking the wind out of him.

"Vann!" Ron shouted. "What are you doing?"

"C'mon!" he shouted, reaching back and grabbing Ron's arm and pulling him along. They bustled across the yard to the open door that led to the ground-floor apartment. Inside the apartment, they pulled up short. Several officers, all standing around the room, stared at them. In the middle of the room, on a long white leather sofa, sat a white man and the black man they had followed from uptown. Both sat with their arms folded across their chests, looking bored and quite smug. Again, the man Vann suspected was Halihuston wore black leather pants.

An officer immediately approached Vann and Ron. "Who are you?"

Vann sidestepped the officer and sidled closer to the sofa. "Are you Victor Halihuston?"

"Sir, what's your business here?" another officer asked.

"Who wants to know?" the man asked, screwing up his lips like he smelled crap.

"The brother of the man you killed."

"Hey! Hey!" a lieutenant exclaimed, approaching Vann. "Mister, you can't be here."

"Man, I ain't killed nobody!"

The lieutenant looked at Halihuston. "Shut up!"

The officer who had been roughed up outside burst into the room. "Lieutenant!" he shouted, grabbing Vann's arm. "These men knocked me down after a direct order to stay out."

Vann yanked his arm out of the officer's grasp. "Get off me!"

All of the officers started closing in on Vann and Ron at once.

The young officer again made a grab for Vann.

Ron stepped protectively in front of Vann. "We have every right to be here. Where's Detective Lopez?"

The lieutenant held up his left hand. All the officers stopped advancing. "I'll ask you again, sir. Who are you?" the lieutenant demanded.

"Ronald Kirkwood. This is my son, Vann Kirkwood."

"Mr. Kirkwood, unless you're a cop or a suspect, you don't have a right to be here. This is a police matter."

"We're not going anywhere," Vann stated, stepping around Ron.

"Sir, then you're both under arrest for interfering with the police in the performance of its duties," the lieutenant said, raising his finger, prompting his men to move in.

Neither Vann nor Ron took a step back. "Don't even try to arrest us!" Vann said.

The young officer Vann had shoved snatched Vann's left arm and started wrenching it up behind his back.

"Get off me!" he shouted, twisting, following his left arm around, and with his right arm, came down with a hammer strike on the officer's arm, breaking his hold on him. Other officers fell upon Vann—one catching him around the neck in a choke hold while others latched on to his arms, immobilizing his upper body, forcing him to kick out wildly. Their struggle pushed Ron aside. A pack of blue coats fell on top of Vann.

"Take him down!" the lieutenant ordered.

Struggling harder to stay on his feet, Vann could feel his arms about to disconnect from his shoulders as he was lifted off his feet and slammed into the floor, chest first. "You bastards!" he blurted.

Ron was beside himself. "Stop it! Stop it!"

Two officers dropped down on Vann's back. Their knees jammed into his shoulders and spine, painfully disabling him. While unrelenting hands held his disjointed arms pinned up against his back, others pressed his head into the hardwood floor, smashing the side of his face in. His teeth cut into his cheek and if it weren't for his cheekbone, his eye would have surely been pushed back into his head. He couldn't breathe.

Ron yanked one of the burly officers that immobilized Vann's legs by the collar of his jacket, flinging him backward onto his butt. Going for another officer, a nightstick was suddenly thrown across Ron's chest from behind and yanked up to his neck, painfully cutting off his breath, and crushing his windpipe. Trying to pull the stick away from his throat, Ron felt himself being dragged backward.

Seeing nothing but the backs of all the officers caught up in the struggle, Halihuston and his partner eased off the sofa and, crouching low, slipped past and fled through the open door.

Vann could not move. He felt as if he were weighted down with cement. He could hear the ruckus around him and knew that if they were on him, they were also on his father. He didn't know what they were doing to him and it angered him that there was nothing he could do to help him. He struggled to breathe through the side of his mouth, though he was sucking in dust while slobbering saliva. If his lungs didn't burst first, he was sure his spine would crack. Gasping for air, he felt himself getting more lightheaded, he felt his heart pounding in his chest. Is this how he was going to die? If he died, would Michelle hate him for dying days before they were to marry?

"What the hell is going on out here?" Lopez asked, rushing out of the back room.

"These men are resisting arrest," the lieutenant explained.

Lopez caught sight of Ron's strained, pain-stricken face. "Let them go!"

"Detective, these men are resisting arrest!"

Lopez charged at the officers, pushing them off Vann. "I said, let them go! That's an order!"

Callahan rushed out of the back room also. He held a bunch of envelopes in his rubber-gloved hand. "Is that Mr. Kirkwood?" he asked, looking at the distorted, vein-popping expression on Ron's face. "You boys are gonna kill the man."

The officer who held Ron slackened in his hold on his neck.

Glaring at Lopez, the lieutenant ordered, "Back off!"

All at once the pressure of gripping, choking hands, sticks and knees fell off Ron and Vann, leaving each gasping for air, coughing, their throats scratchy, dry, and sore. Vann wanted desperately to massage his back and shoulders but he was unable to move. The pain in his arms, back, and shoulders wouldn't let him. Yet it was the pain that convinced him that at least he wasn't paralyzed.

Lopez could see Vann's head peek out from the slew of black thick-soled oxfords. "Move back! Give the man some air."

Still in a tight cluster, the officers began to back away from Vann and Ron, some mumbling to each other, others giving each other high fives.

Ron gingerly massaged his throat. "Goddamn bastards," he said, glaring dead into the eyes of the tall burly officer who had had him in a choke hold.

Vann began coughing as he struggled painfully to straighten his arms out, one by one, at his sides. He let each arm drop off his back to the floor. Trying to salivate, between coughs, to wet his parched scratchy throat, he rolled over onto his back and then, carefully bending his right arm at the elbow, reached for his throat to rub it.

"You hurt, son?" Ron asked, squatting down next to Vann.

He laid his hand on Vann's chest. "Do you need an ambulance?"

Coughing, his eyes closed, Vann shook his head once. He was in agony but he was not about to go anywhere.

Ron glared up at the officers. "I can imagine what you assholes do to real criminals."

Vann opened his eyes. "I'm gonna sue every one of you bastards for police brutality," he croaked.

"You were ordered to stay away from here," Lopez said. "I should have let them arrest you."

"We should have, because that threat he made is out of line," the lieutenant rebuked.

"Oh yeah?" Ron asked, rubbing Vann's left shoulder socket. "Wait till the Civilian Complaint Review Board hears from my lawyer. There will be plenty more threats you won't like."

"Mister, you had no business barging in on a police operation."

Vann sat up and, with Ron's help, got painfully up off the floor.

"You had no business ordering your attack dogs on us," Ron said, peering at the name on the badge, "Lieutenant McVicker. I am sure that the Civilian Complaint Review Board and *The New York Times* will want to know about a lieutenant who gives orders to his men to beat up on citizens."

Vann stood shoulder to shoulder with Ron. "You can kiss your pensions good-bye."

Lieutenant McVicker stepped in closer to Vann and Ron. "Don't threaten me," he snarled. "I'll—"

"That's enough!" Lopez shouted.

"You'll what?" Ron asked, sticking out his chest.

"I said, that's enough!" Lopez barked, pulling Lieutenant McVicker back.

"The suspects escaped!" one of the officers blurted.

Lopez whirled around and looked at the empty sofa. "Oh shit!"

A tidal wave of officers rushed for the door.

"Spread out!" Lieutenant McVicker ordered, starting out behind his officers.

Lopez reached out and clamped down on Lieutenant McVicker's shoulder. "You better find my suspects or I'll bring you up on charges myself."

Lieutenant McVicker cut his eyes down at Lopez's rubber-gloved hand on his shoulder. He stared at it. His lip curled up. "Move it."

"This is a comedy of stupid errors," Vann said.

Lopez did not remove his hand. "Don't fuck with me, McVicker. I would take down a goddamn grizzly if he tried to keep me from this collar."

Vann was impressed. He didn't think Lopez had any guts.

Stone-faced, Lieutenant McVicker spoke softly, "Another time. Another place."

"You got it," Lopez said, removing his hand, freeing McVicker to march past Ron and out of the house.

"I'll take a look around outside," Callahan said.

"No," Lopez said, "we'll stay here and continue the search."

"Oh! By the way, look at this," Callahan said, handing Lopez the torn-open envelopes and the plastic bag he pulled them out of. "Credit card bills and new credit cards in the name of Troy Kirkwood and a number of other people."

"Good man."

Vann's back straightened. "That's it. That's your proof."

"Thank God," Ron said.

Callahan paid Ron and Vann no mind. "In the bathroom back there, there's something dark splattered on the wall in the corner above the toilet."

Ron and Vann exchanged anxious glances.

"Could it be blood?" Lopez asked.

"Could be."

"That's it," Vann said, starting for the door.

Lopez shoved the plastic bag down inside his jacket pocket. "Where do you think you're going?"

"To find your suspects."

"Goddamnit, Kirkwood. I told you to stay home. You and your father charged in here like wild bulls. If you hadn't been so bullheaded, the suspects would not have gotten away. I'm—"

"That's your fault. You should have had them handcuffed and shackled."

"Kirkwood, before you tell me what I should have done, know what you're talking about. We had no solid evidence when we walked through that door. We had probable cause, which does not call for a man to be handcuffed or shackled. If the suspects get away, you have no one to blame but yourself. Goddamnit! Sit down! Both of you."

He moved slowly, but Ron sat on the arm of the sofa, while Vann, stubbornly resistant and sore, continued to stand where he was. Grimacing, he massaged his shoulder. "I'll stand, if you don't mind."

"You're a stubborn son of a bitch," Lopez said, turning his back on Vann to look at Callahan. "Put a call in to Forensics. Tell them to bring plenty of luminole, and—"

"What's luminole?" Ron asked.

"Don't worry about it."

"Man, don't dismiss him," Vann said angrily. "What the hell is luminole?"

Lopez set his jaw. He did not answer nor did he turn around.

Callahan, knowing the stubbornness of both his partner and Vann, answered, "Luminole is a chemical mixture that glows in the dark when it comes in contact with blood on a surface that appears to be clean."

"Yeah," Lopez conceded, his back still to Vann. "It's luminescent. It glows like a Christmas tree. Do you mind if we continue?"

"If Troy's blood and credit cards are here, then the case is sewn up," Ron suggested.

Vann twisted his lips in a mock snarl. "I doubt it. Next they'll say they need a video or an eyewitness to the murder."

Again, ignoring Vann, Lopez continued. "Make that call. Also, request that samples be taken of the spots for a DNA match, and get a uniform on the door."

"Roger that," Callahan said, taking a cell phone from his jacket pocket as he headed toward the back room.

Lopez turned to Ron. "Mr. Kirkwood *Senior,* I have work to do. I wish that you and your son would leave, but I know you won't without a fight. Believe it or not, I understand your wanting to be here. That's why I'm asking *you* to find chairs in a corner somewhere and stay put. Be cool."

"We'll do that."

"So that you understand me, Mr. Kirkwood. I'm asking *you* to make your son stay put."

Vann chuckled low and dry.

"I do not want him outside; I do not want him to go into any other room; and I do not want him to bother me. Can you do that?"

Looking at Vann, Ron recognized the defiant glint in his eyes. There was no doubt that Vann would not listen to him, much less Lopez. "I'll try," he lied.

"Do better than that. *Make him.*" Lopez did not bother to look at Vann before stalking off down the short hallway toward the staircase.

Vann waited until he could no longer see Lopez's feet on the stairs. "Dad," he whispered, "I have got to go."

"Just be careful."

"I will," he said, gingerly walking backward, watching for any signs of Lopez or Callahan. At the door he turned and stuck his head outside to see if the way was clear. He gave Ron a thumbs-up and stepped outside, again checking first to see if any policemen were around before he ventured farther out into the front yard. Trying to appear as casual as possible, he strolled to the gate. Out in front of the house sat the white Mercedes they had tailed from uptown. It was blocked by two cruisers, which explained why Halihuston hadn't taken off in it. Unless there was a second car, Halihuston was probably on foot. Even then, Vann knew that he would never catch up with them on foot. They had gotten too much of a lead on him. Besides, they could have run in any direction, leaving him with too many wrong directions to choose from.

From one end of the quiet block to the other, there wasn't a uniform in sight. In their wake, only a handful of people were curious or nosy enough to hang around on their own stoops waiting for someone to be dragged out in handcuffs.

"Damn," Vann said, undecided as to which direction he should go, yet determined to give chase. He looked toward Fulton Street, then toward DeKalb Avenue and at the cars that sped on their way toward downtown. Then his eyes locked on the entrance to Fort Greene Park. Like a magnet, the upward sweep of the park grounds disappearing high above the street held him transfixed.

"The park"—a voice sounding so much like Troy's ricocheted in Vann's head, snapping him out of his indecisiveness. Too much time had passed for him to run into the park from this side. If Halihuston or his partner had run into the park at all, he had a better chance catching up with them coming out on the other side. With that in mind, Vann dashed out of the yard, bumping into a woman he hadn't noticed coming down the street. The large Macy's shopping bag she carried dropped to the ground. He quickly grabbed her to keep her from going down the same way.

"Damn!" she said, clutching at the stylishly slanted black Stetson on her head. She glared angrily at Vann.

"Sorry . . . sorry!" he said, rushing off.

The woman adjusted the pocketbook strap slung over her right shoulder and across her chest. "Stupid ass!" she spat, flipping Vann the finger. Bending, she picked the large white shopping bag up off the ground.

Immediately starting the car and turning the wheel, Vann glanced into his side-view mirror at the same time to check to see if it was clear to pull out. What he saw and heard was a cruiser with flashing lights and siren careen into the block from Lafayette. Taking that as a definite signal to get going, he sped to the corner, never stopping completely before pulling out into DeKalb Avenue in front of oncoming traffic, leaving screeching cars and honking horns in his wake. He wasn't concerned about the cruiser following him; he knew where it was headed.

The woman looked around. "What's all these cop cars doing around here?" she grumbled. She went into the yard from which Vann had fled.

FORTY-THREE

VICTOR! Why is the door open?" the woman asked as she entered the apartment, passing by Ron, who was standing at the window looking at her. She sat her shopping bag down on the floor, pulled her shoulder bag over her head, dropped it onto the coffee table, and began to immediately unbutton her trench coat from the top. "Victor! What's going on outside? Do you know there are cop cars out front?"

Callahan hurried into the room. "Can I help you, miss?"

She stiffened. "Who the hell are you? Where's Victor?"

Callahan stepped in closer to the woman. "You live here?"

"Why? What business is it of yours?"

Four uniformed policemen came in from the outside. Callahan signaled to them, by holding up his hand, to hold back. The woman turned around and, seeing the policemen, gasped before looking back at Callahan.

Following orders, the officers stood just inside the apartment, their eyes on the woman.

"Miss, do you live here?"

"I ain't telling you nothing. Where's Victor?"

Dreamlike, Ron inched closer to the woman.

Sensing that someone else was in the room, the woman jerked around and, seeing Ron, again gasped, but she began to falteringly back away from him.

"I know you," he said.

"I don't know you," she said, nervously bumping into the arm of the sofa as she tried to move farther away from Ron. Her eyes darted from him to Callahan. "Where's Victor? Victor! Victor!"

"I do know you," Ron said, tensely, staring at the woman.

Continuing to back up, she tottered around the arm of the sofa. "You don't know me. I ain't never seen you before in my life."

Unwavering, Ron prowled behind her. He was certain that her face was more than familiar.

"Get him away from me!"

The four policemen started at Ron. Callahan again put up his hand, stopping them. He looked at the anguished fear in the woman's eyes as Ron slowly stalked her.

The sound of Lopez walking down the wooden stairs from the parlor floor broke through the strained silence, yet the woman and Ron held each other's gaze. Lopez walked into the room and, sensing the tension, held back and watched the woman. He caught on instantly that something important was about to happen. He waited for whatever it was to play itself out.

Ron reached out and snatched the hat off the woman's head.

She flinched. "Hey!" She tried to snatch the hat back. Ron held it out of her reach.

"God Almighty," he said, dropping the hat to the floor. "I do know you. You went with my son. She killed Troy."

Lopez began moving toward the woman.

"What's your name?" Callahan asked.

The woman stumbled backward, slamming herself into the wall. Shaking her head, her eyes bulging, she stammered, "I . . . I . . . didn't kill him. It was Victor! It was Victor! I . . . I . . . I tried to stop him."

Lopez and Callahan glanced at each other, then both zeroed in on the woman.

Tears rolled down Ron's cheeks.

"Mr. Kirkwood," Lopez said, "do you know this woman?"

Ron started to nod when the sparkling gold chain around her neck and what was hanging from it caught his eye. He stared at the large, man-size ring.

"Mr. Kirkwood, you gotta believe me. I didn't kill Troy! It was Victor. I didn't have nothing to do with it."

Ron continued to stare at the ring.

Lopez raced around the sofa. "Miss, 'You have the right to remain silent. Should you give up the right to remain silent, anything you say may be used against you in a court of law.' Do you understand your rights as they have been read to you?"

Callahan took out his notepad and pen.

The woman could not pull her eyes away from Ron. She began to cry.

Lopez shook her. "Do you understand your rights?"

She nodded quickly.

"Miss, who did Victor Halihuston kill?"

She cried.

"Who!"

"Troy! Victor killed Troy! I begged him not to. He was just supposed to talk to him, scare him. He killed him, he shot him. It wasn't me. I swear, it wasn't me."

"When?"

"I tried to save him. All I could do was make Victor take him back downtown so that he could be found. Mr. Kirkwood," she said, looking beseechingly at Ron, "you know I wouldn't kill Troy. I loved him."

"Liar! You killed my son!"

She cringed from Ron's scornful accusation.

Lopez put his hand on Ron to quiet him. "Miss, what is your name?"

"I didn't do anything," she cried.

"Her name is Valerie Lewis," Ron said. "She killed my son."

"I didn't. I swear to you, I didn't," she cried.

Callahan jotted quickly.

Trancelike, Ron reached out with his right hand toward Valerie's chest. She tried to shrink away from him, pressing her back into the wall, but the wall wouldn't give, it wouldn't swallow her up.

"Mr. Kirkwood," Lopez said.

Ron gently lifted the man's ring off Valerie's chest and, staring at it, turned it around so that the wings of the eagle swept around into the front to the sparkling diamond eyes. Raising his eyes and glowering at Valerie Lewis, Ron gripped the ring and yanked the chain from around her neck, scraping her skin.

She did not flinch from the burn. Sobbing, she covered her face as she slid down the wall to the floor, crouching into a tight ball.

"Is that your son's ring?" Lopez asked.

"Yes," Ron replied. He stepped back from Valerie. Slump-shouldered, he looked down at the chain dangling from his clenched fist.

"We'll need it for evidence."

Ron shook his head no.

Callahan, with his eyes, told Lopez to let it be. "Mr. Kirkwood, how do you know this woman?"

"She used to go with my son."

Callahan took note, Lopez looked down at Valerie.

She continued to cry.

Squatting down in front of Valerie, Lopez pulled her hands away from her face. "Miss Lewis? Do your friends call you Cookie?"

Glancing up at Ron, she quickly averted her eyes.

"Miss Lewis, are you also known as Cookie?"

"Yes!" she cried, pulling her hands back to cover her face.

"God," Ron said. He drew the chain through the ring. He threw it to the floor. "I hope you rot in hell."

Lopez picked up the chain. He beckoned to two of the officers. "Watch her," he said. "Handcuff her and sit her on that chair in the corner. Don't let her move an inch."

FORTY-FOUR

THERE were many more policemen on the street than Vann expected. They were everywhere—on the side streets, on the main roadways—some in cars, some on foot. So as not to draw attention to himself, he slowed up on Ashland Place before making his right turn into Myrtle Avenue where the north side entrances to the park were. At the first entrance he slowed to a crawl to see if Halihuston was anywhere in sight in the large playground area. There appeared to be only women and children. He sped up and pulled over and parked fifty feet outside the second entrance he came to. Young and old men alike sat on park benches and on the low wall outside the park—some talking, some shooting dice, some drinking beer, all enjoying the warm spring weather. Halihuston was not among them. Vann trotted into the second entrance but right away saw that it also led to the playground and the basketball court. Slowing down his pace, he glimpsed the teenage boys playing basketball and scanned the couples and single men and women strolling behind skipping, playful children along the path. No Halihuston.

He saw no need to continue on that path. Quickly backtracking, he ran to the third entrance several feet away. He stopped dead in his tracks. Off in the distance, far up on the hill at the foot of the park's columnar monument, two men were clenched in a fierce battle. A group of onlookers had gathered behind them and were cheering wildly. The hairs on the nape of Vann's neck shot up. He got a knot in the pit of his stomach. Even from that distance, he could see that one of the men was a white uniformed officer, the other a black man, dressed all in black as Halihuston had been. The officer was picked up and body-slammed down onto the ground, out of sight.

Vann forgot his pain. He took off like he was shot from a cannon. He dashed into the park, running headlong across the path onto the grass, thrusting himself up the steep hill on legs that hadn't moved that fast since he last played basketball back in college. The closer he got, he saw that the black man, without a jacket and wearing black leather pants, was indeed Victor Halihuston. He was at least twice the size of the small white officer he was astride. Yet no one made a move to help—grown men cheered.

Leaping over the squat wall that separated the hill from the flat monument area, Vann saw right off that the combatants were battling for the service revolver half holstered at the officer's left side when suddenly, *Boom!*

Panicked onlookers scattered.

A chilling scream exploded from the officer's throat while his face erupted into a red mask of excruciating pain, yet he continued to defiantly grip his revolver with all his might. Where the officer was shot, Vann did not know. He saw only that Halihuston was not shaken and was not about to release his hold on the revolver. Halihuston suddenly jabbed his knee into the officer's left arm and was only seconds from ripping the gun from his weakening hands.

Growling, Vann hurtled himself at Halihuston, ramming into him with the propelled force of his 190 pounds, knocking him off the officer and onto the ground on his back. Landing on top of Halihuston, Vann quickly tried to straddle him, but Halihuston rebounded with the speed of a panther, striking Vann with a hard right to the left side of his face, stunning him and at the same time throwing Vann off him with the upward thrust of his body. Vann grunted. In his daze, he wondered still why none of the men gathered around made any moves to help. He could hear them cheering Halihuston on like he was a boxer fighting for the title.

Sitting halfway up, his thigh bloody, the officer with his revolver in hand grabbed for his portable radio on his left shoulder. "Officer down! Officer down! North side of Fort Greene Park! Beneath the monument!"

Halihuston sprang to his feet and, having heard the officer's cry for help, kicked Vann hard in his rib cage, doubling him up into a fetal position. "You just like your punk-ass brother, motherfucker. You ain't shit!" He hawked and spit on Vann's pants, thereby dismissing him. He turned back to the officer, who quickly gripped his revolver with both hands. He pointed threateningly at Halihuston.

Holding on to his brutalized ribs, Vann didn't know which hurt worse, his temple, his ribs, his shoulders, his arms God, he was hurting. Off in the distance, he could hear the sound of police sirens. He took deep painful breaths. His dizziness began to subside and he was able to focus and fix his gaze on Halihuston, who was hovering over the officer. Pushing aside his own pain, he started straining to push himself up off the ground.

Grimacing sourly, perspiration running down his face, the officer, his hands shaking, his finger on the trigger, trained his sight on Halihuston's chest. "Get back! I'll shoot!"

Halihuston neither cowered nor turned tail. "White boy, I'm gonna put that gun up your ass and blow your brains out!" he threatened. He reached down for the gun.

Boom!

The bullet tore into Halihuston's left shoulder, hurling him backward, making him stagger from the impact. Bent-kneed, he stopped himself from falling.

The small crowd fell back, but not far.

"Oh shit!"

"Dag, man!"

"Shoot 'em again!"

Vann glanced at the officer. His face was bloody. His left eye was badly swollen. He looked like he was going into shock—more from having shot a man than from being shot himself. Vann wasn't worried about the officer, it was Halihuston who scared him. The bullet didn't bring him down, nor did it make him throw up his arms and give up.

The sirens grew louder.

Halihuston looked down at the blood pouring from the bullet hole in his shoulder, matting his black silk shirt to his body.

With the gun still in his trembling right hand, the officer quickly and painfully dragged himself up into a full sitting position, while Vann, getting up off the ground, readied himself to lunge if he had to. He could hear his pulse throbbing loudly in his ears. He and the officer both stared at Halihuston as Halihuston raised his right hand to touch his shoulder. He stopped a few inches away, then suddenly, snarling, baring his teeth, slowly drew his hand into a claw that snapped into a tight, vein-popping fist while glowering intently at the officer.

Although he looked like a deer caught in the headlights of an oncoming car, the officer, holding his revolver with both hands, extended his arms. "I'll shoot," he said, his voice weak and uncertain.

The crowd had grown larger and stood a respectable distance away. Loud, rowdy voices shouted, "Shoot him! Shoot him! Shoot him!"

Halihuston took one step forward.

The officer took a deep breath.

Halihuston lunged.

Vann, stepping outside himself, saw himself in slow-motion charge at Halihuston, ramming him in the side, pushing him down the wide, steep palatial stone steps and from the top, watched him tumble, head over heels, over and over, hollering at first, then grunting, until he landed at the bottom. His body was awkwardly twisted. One leg lay up on the step above while the other lay sprawled out to the side. The back of his head rested against the concrete landing.

Scores of policemen, closing in from all directions, some sprinting up the first two sets of steps toward Halihuston, all converged, all with guns drawn. The crowd that had rooted for Halihuston raced down the steps to see for themselves what the outcome of his fall was.

From around the sides of the monument and from the hill Vann had raced up moments earlier, throngs of policemen surrounded him. All dropped down into a three-point stance, revolvers in hand, pointing at his side, his back, his head.

"Get down on the ground! Get down on the ground!"

Vann slowly raised both arms above his head. He did not drop to the ground. He was not willing to lose sight of Troy's killer.

The downed officer lowered his revolver. "No! He's not the one! He saved my life."

Policemen began pulling out of their stance, holstering their revolvers. They rushed down to their fallen comrade. One shouted down the hill, "We need the paramedics up here!"

Lowering his arms, Vann never bothered to look at the policemen who had fixed their sights on him—he had not, even for a minute, been able to pull his eyes away from the sight of Halihuston lying still at the bottom of the steps, his body possibly empty of life. An officer crouched down and put his fingers on Halihuston's neck. Vann held his breath as the officer looked up and said something to the officers gathered around him before standing up. He was too far away to make out or hear what was said, but it looked, to him, like Halihuston was dead.

He felt weak in the knees. For months, he wanted Troy's killer dead, preferably by his own hands. Now that he had done it, he felt sick. He was sure that Halihuston had felt nothing but scorn when he killed Troy, and he saw how easy it was for Halihuston to want to kill that young officer, and if he had gotten his hands on the revolver, he would have used it, without hesitation, on him, too. The crowd's hunger to see a life brutally snuffed would have been satisfied. Strangely, it sickened Vann. He was disgusted. It mattered a lot that to save his own life and that of the officer's, he had to take an evil life, but he would never have imagined that he'd feel this bad.

"Sir," the young officer said behind Vann. "Thank you, sir."

Vann was about to say you're welcome, when he saw Halihuston feebly lift his right arm. He was alive. It was an odd sensation that fell over Vann. He dropped his head to his chest. He was relieved. He wasn't going to have to close his eyes every night with a death on his conscience. The unrelenting force that had driven him for months to track down Troy's killer was no longer inside him, it had vanished, leaving him weightless in his mind and body. "Thank you, Lord," he said, barely moving his lips, grateful for so much more. Halihuston had all but said he had killed Troy when he said, "You just like your punk-ass brother, motherfucker. You ain't shit!" Maybe life in prison would be a worse punishment by far than a hasty death with no pain.

"Sir, thank you," the young officer said again.

Vann turned and looked down at the officer and was surprised. It was the same pimply-faced officer he had shoved aside to get into Halihuston's apartment. His bloody thigh had been tied off above the bullet wound with a black leather belt. He lay on his back with a jacket under his head.

"You're welcome," Vann said, finally. He smiled. It was a great day.

He stood looking out over Brooklyn from atop the hill. He scanned the skyline of lower Manhattan all the way up to midtown from the twin towers of the World Trade Center to the

Empire State Building. It was a great city, but a little fast for his blood. Turning around and looking up at the monument behind him he realized for the first time that the lighthouse-like stone monument behind him, erected in 1908, with the large green lantern on top, was called the Prison Ship Martyrs' Monument. A martyr Halihuston would never be, but the prison part was so apropos.

At that moment, a short distance away, Halihuston's partner, Ivan Keller, was captured down on Flatbush Avenue about to go down into the subway.

ALTHOUGH VANN had played a pivotal role in capturing a murderer, Lopez was nonetheless angry with him. "Do you ever listen to anyone?"

"Not when he gets his mind set on what he wants to do," Ron had answered for Vann. And then he had smiled and said, "That's my boy."

Lopez had dismissed them unceremoniously and threatened to lock Vann up if he ever saw him in the precinct again. This time, Lopez didn't have to worry. Neither Vann nor Ron had any intention of stepping foot in his arena again.

Thursday evening Lopez called to tell them that the luminole had picked up blood splattering on the bathroom floor and wall. They'd know soon if the blood was Troy's, but Vann already knew. Troy's wallet, credit cards, driver's license, Social Security card, keys, and pictures of him and Meika were found stuffed in the hole behind the pedestal sink. No, Vann had no reason to go back to the precinct.

FORTY-FIVE

NOLA had worn a worry path in the carpet from the living room window to the front door. Ron's call had deeply disturbed her—Cordelia was either not answering her bell or she wasn't home. Nola was afraid of what it might mean. Friday night Ron and Vann had sat outside Cordelia's apartment until eleven o'clock waiting for her to come home. She never did. They called the police and were told what they already knew—there was nothing they could do as Cordelia was the mother and had temporary custody. "Take it up in Family Court," they were told time and again. Here it was, six o'clock in the morning, the day of Vann's wedding and he and Ron were again waiting outside Cordelia's apartment so that they could bring Meika home.

Nola was filled with anxiety, her heart ached. In the past few weeks alone she had been on an emotional roller coaster—escalating joy with the planning of Vann's wedding and the discovery of a daughter-in-law she had closed her eyes and heart to; sudden dips when she thought of Meika not being there to tell her knock-knock jokes, or lavish kisses all over her face; highs with the capture of Troy's killers; and devastating plunges upon learning that Valerie Lewis was in on Troy's death the whole time, that she was the one who set him up after she met with him at the Research Library. Troy had confronted Valerie about the credit card scam she was involved in with Victor Halihuston. He was going to turn them in. Valerie had known that Troy was taking Meika to the movies in Brooklyn Heights. Even if Valerie did not actually pull the trigger, she was as guilty as the other maggots. The prosecutor saw it that way, too. Halihuston, Keller, and Valerie Lewis were all held on first-degree murder charges, credit card fraud, and a host of other federal mail infringement charges. Halihuston alone was charged with attempted murder of a police officer.

When Nola should have been jubilant, she was in the grip of plummeting lows again because Meika was nowhere to be found. She felt sick to her stomach, and no matter whether she was emotionally high or low, she didn't know how much more she could take. Despite the fact that the sun was warmer and that the bitter cold sting of winter seemed to be behind her, she felt no warmer and hated that she was putting a damper on Michelle and the children's celebration.

Finally giving up her anxious watch at the window, Nola retreated to the solitude of her bedroom, shutting down, blacking out the world, hoping that neither dreams nor nightmares would dare intrude.

NOLA WAS pulled from her deep, protective sleep by Sharice's and Kareem's giggles outside her bedroom door. Thinking that Meika was home, she rose up "Meika!"

"See, y'all woke up your grandmother. Didn't I tell y'all to be quiet?" Michelle asked. "If y'all mess up your clothes, y'all can't go to the church with us. Go downstairs and sit down."

Nola sat up. "Michelle."

The door opened. Michelle was in her bathrobe, her hair was curled and swept up in back, her makeup was on. She wore diamond stud earrings and a single diamond pendant hung from a thin gold chain around her neck.

"I'm sorry, Ma. I told Sharice and Kareem not to wake you."

"Is Meika home?"

"She's not. I'm sorry."

Nola felt just about the way she felt the night Troy came up missing. She dropped her head back down onto the pillow. Was it never going to end?

"Vann and his father got back a little while ago, I told them you were sleeping."

"Did they find out anything about Meika?"

"They said the landlord saw Cordelia leave early Friday afternoon."

"Was Meika with her?"

"Yes."

"Did she have a suitcase?"

"Yes."

"Oh, God." Nola began to weep. Her worst fear was real. The harder she cried, the more she hurt. She didn't think she'd ever feel right again.

FORTY-SIX

For Vann, Nola mustered the strength to get out of her bed—it was his wedding day. She owed it to him to be there. Maybe not with bells on, maybe not with a broad smile, but with a mangled heart and tears for his happiness, Troy's death, and for Meika, who might be lost to them forever. Michelle was a beautiful bride in a soft shell-colored two-tiered knee-length dress, and Vann, his pain dulled by painkillers, was handsome in a black suit. He put Nola's engagement ring on Michelle's finger, and in turn Michelle put Troy's eagle ring on his finger, surprising him, making him teary. That was Lopez's temporary gift to them.

Vann and Michelle were married and were well on their way to seeing their future through the same eyes. They had wanted to stay past the weekend to console her and Ron, but Nola would not hear of it their lives had been on hold long enough. At the airport they said their teary good-byes and sent them off with a promise to visit them in Atlanta soon. That is, after they found Meika. Their custody case wouldn't come before Judge Fiske until August, as was originally scheduled, and until then they had, with Mr. Lipscomb's help, gone to Cordelia's employer. Cordelia had quit her job, and what family they could track down wouldn't say if they knew where Cordelia was. Every effort to find her left them disappointed, more angry, and hopeless.

In June, Vann was given a Certificate of Merit by the New York City Police Department for saving the life of a police officer. Ron stood in and accepted it in Vann's stead.

Nola went back to work to have something to do to fill her empty days. Ron was considering retiring early and talked of moving to Atlanta to be close to Vann. She liked the idea at once, which surprised even her. Atlanta was not a place she had ever considered moving to, although the warmer climate was appealing. The only drawback was that she didn't want to leave the only place Meika last knew her to be. If Meika ever got away from Cordelia, if she was ever able to call, Nola didn't want Meika to find her gone. For her peace of mind, Ron promised to keep an investigator looking for Meika, no matter how long it took.

Every time she thought of Meika becoming a teenager, becoming a woman without her, Nola became depressed and had to crawl into herself until she could face the world again. She prayed that enough of Troy was in Meika to make her strong, to make her the woman of substance and morals he would want her to be, and not the conniving, selfish woman that Cordelia might school her to be. Most of all, Nola prayed that Meika would not forget Troy, her, or Ron, for their love was forever hers.

Ron understood her depression because he was sometimes depressed himself. He didn't play his records anymore, nor did he golf. Most days after work and weekends he watched television or rented movies. Sometimes Nola joined him, but he had his days when he locked himself away in his den to mope and bemoan his loss—their loss. Rarely did she intrude when Ron wanted to be alone. He, too, had a right to nurse his own pain, in his own way. When they came together, they comforted each other with assurances that one day they'd see Meika again.

On Meika's birthday, Nola bought her a doll, clothes, and

learning toys. Ron bought the biggest doll he could find and together they wrapped all the presents and at the end of the day, put them all in Meika's bedroom. They had both cried that beautiful hot May day, but after that Ron shut down and spoke very little of Meika. He said, "It tears me up to keep talking about her." Nola left him alone and talked mostly to Beatrice when she had to talk, often repeating over and over the cute things Meika used to say or do—things that never failed to warm her heart.

Vann called often to see how they were doing. His life was good, Michelle was expecting, they were happy.

IN FAMILY Court, because Cordelia had skipped, and after viewing the tape Vann made of the day she picked up Meika, Judge Fiske granted them full custody of Meika in absentia. Little good that did them. After five months there was no word of her whereabouts—her trail was cold. The reports they received from the investigator said as much. Using the computer, Vann was able to determine that Cordelia was not working anywhere in the country—her Social Security number was not active on anyone's payroll and Meika wasn't registered in any school district in New York City.

Nola vowed that she would never give up looking for her grandbaby. That was her promise to herself, to Meika, and to Troy.

FORTY-SEVEN

MEIKA was nine now. Nola thought about her all the time, although she no longer bought her presents—it was too depressing. Everything they had bought previously that Sharice could use, they packed and shipped to Atlanta along with everything else they were taking with them. Since Vann and Michelle had another son, Ron made her give Meika's clothes, toys, and bedroom set to the Salvation Army. Meika was too big for any of those things. It had been difficult watching what was once a part of Meika's young life trucked away.

Nola turned down Beatrice's invitation to stay overnight; she wasn't yet ready to say good-bye to the home she and Ron had raised Vann and Troy in. Their last night in New York should be there, the memories were sweetest there.

With their bed gone, they were sleeping in Ron's den on the old nubby, brown twill sofa bed that they dragged up from the basement. Nola could feel the metal springs and the unyielding frame through the lumpy thin mattress. It hurt their backs and made them shift every now and then to ease their discomfort. Yet they fondly reminisced about the early days of their marriage in a one-room apartment back when the sofa bed was the first piece of furniture they could afford to buy.

Alone in the house they had scraped and saved for, memories of laughter and tears were just as dear. Drapeless windows, bare walls, bare wooden and carpeted floors with varying shades of colors from the fading sun, dirt, and furniture that rested on them took nothing from the essence that filled the rooms. They ate Chinese food, they listened to music on an old radio on which the clock and the alarm no longer worked.

Riiing!

She looked at Ron.

"It's on your side, you get it," he said. "It's probably Beatrice calling for the hundredth time anyway."

Riiing!

Nola leaned over the side of the sofa and picked up the telephone. "Hi, Bea."

"Nola . . ."

She winked at Ron.

"I told you so," he whispered.

". . . I'm cooking you and Ron breakfast before you pull out in the morning, so get here by six so you have time to eat and talk awhile."

"Thanks, Bea, we'll be there."

"I don't know why you don't sleep over here tonight, that house must feel empty and cold."

"Not really," Nola said, softly. "It doesn't feel empty at all, and it's really quite warm. I'll see you tomorrow, okay?" She clicked off the telephone and hung up before the conversation ruined her mellow mood.

"Didn't feel like talking, huh?"

"No. I just wanna be alone with you and our house."

Riiing!

Nola sucked her teeth.

"You know she can't bear the thought of you leaving."

Riiing!

"In eight months, she and Roosevelt will be following right behind us. So it's not good-bye."

Riiing!

"Answer it."

"I'm disconnecting it after this," she said, picking up the receiver. "Yes, Beatrice."

"Not Beatrice, Mrs. Kirkwood, Detective Lopez."

"Oh," she said, looking at Ron. "Detective Lopez, how are you? It's been awhile."

Ron leaped off the bed and turned the volume down on the radio sitting in the corner of the room.

"Yes, it has. How are you and Mr. Kirkwood?"

"We're just fine. My husband is right here. Would you like to speak with him?"

"What does he want?" Ron mouthed, sitting again.

She shrugged her shoulders.

"No, it's you I called to speak to."

"Me? The case is closed. They were convicted. Did they escape?"

"Of course not. Mrs. Kirkwood, this is about another matter. Today there was a drug bust down in Cobble Hill, near Red Hook. Did you catch it on the news tonight?"

"No, I didn't," she said, glancing up at Ron. Again she shrugged her shoulders.

"It was a pretty big bust."

"That's great. This city needs to keep as much drugs off the street as possible."

"Drugs?" Ron asked, puzzled.

"Yes," Detective Lopez agreed. "Mrs. Kirkwood, there were several arrests made in that house."

"That's great," Nola said again, wondering what concern it was of hers.

"One of the women arrested was Cordelia Kirkwood."

Nola's mouth fell open.

Ron tapped her impatiently on the leg. "What?"

"Cordelia was arrested!" she shouted. "Are you sure?"

Ron bolted up off the bed. "They got Cordelia?" he asked, reaching for the telephone.

Pulling the receiver back out of his reach, Nola slapped at his hand. "Are you sure it's her?"

"It's her all right."

Ron again reached for the receiver. "Let me speak to him."

She slapped his hand harder. "Where's Meika? Where's my baby?"

"He found Meika?" Ron asked, excitedly.

"She's right here with me. It's almost like old times."

"Oh my God . . . oh my God," Nola cried.

"Where is she?" Ron asked, impatiently. "Is she all right?"

"Mrs. Kirkwood, I wouldn't let them take her to Children's Protective Services. I knew that you had been looking for her."

"Oh my God! Bless you. Ron. Ron. They found Meika. They found her."

Ron was crying; he was pacing. He wanted to leap to God and give him a big kiss.

Nola's own tears crested and poured from her.

"Mrs. Kirkwood, Meika has been asking for you. Hold on."

"Oh my God. Thank you . . . thank you."

"MAMA?"

READING GROUP GUIDE

The questions and discussion topics that follow are intended to enhance your group's reading of Gloria Mallette's *Promises to Keep*.

1. Even though Ron and Nola's relationship is strong, Troy's death exposes some of the weaknesses in their marriage. What do they come to realize about each other and about their relationship after their son's death?

2. Troy was a man who never found the right woman. His relationships with Valerie and Cordelia seemed doomed from the start and ultimately destroyed him. What attracted him to women like Valerie and Cordelia? How do good people get mixed up with bad people?

3. Cordelia has never been a good parent to Meika, and when she returns to New York, Nola will do anything to stop Meika from seeing her. Is Nola right to treat Cordelia as she does? At that moment, does Cordelia have any rights to motherhood left?

4. As Ron and Nola struggle with the loss of Troy, their grief and anger nearly consume them. Only after Vann forces them to confront their pain do they begin to move on. How does he help them deal with Troy's death? Why aren't they able to turn to each other?

5. In their detective work, is there ever a time when Vann and Ron go too far?

6. Troy's death is all the more traumatic for his family because he was murdered. Does the resolution of his murder make it easier for his family to heal? What would have happened if the case had remained unsolved?

7. Nola tells Vann that no mother is truly satisfied with her son's choice of women; is she right? Do mothers find it hard to approve of their daughters-in-law? How do Nola's opinions of her son's relationships affect his choices?

8. One of the first reactions Vann, Ron, and Nola have about Troy's death is that they failed to prevent it. How hard is it to overcome this kind of guilt, even when it's unjustified? How hard is it to accept the loss of a loved one?

9. Why does Ron hurt Nola outside the police station?

10. For most of her first five years Meika grew up in a loving home with her father and grandparents, but once she leaves with Cordelia she disappears into a life filled with deceit and drugs. What do you think happens to Meika? Was the love of her first five years enough to get her through the next four?

11. Since childhood, Vann has felt his mother loved his brother more. Nola feels that she always loved them the same but that Vann rejected her mothering. Are they both right? Is this lack of understanding common between parents and children?

ABOUT THE AUTHOR

GLORIA MALLETTE is the author of the national bestseller *Shades of Jade*. Gloria and her husband, Arnold, are longtime residents of Brooklyn, New York. She would love to hear what you think of *Promises to Keep* and can be reached via e-mail at gempress@aol.com.

STRIVERS ROW

Strivers Row is online at www.striversrowbooks.com!

Strivers Row online is your guide to African-American literature from Random House. We take our name from the Harlem neighborhood that flourished and gained prominence during the Harlem Renaissance, and that same spirit of creativity and promise drives our Strivers Row imprint. Welcome to the neighborhood.

The Strivers Row e-newsletter

Our free e-mail newsletter is sent to subscribers and features sneak peeks, interviews, and essays by our authors, upcoming books, special promotions, announcements, and news.

To subscribe to the Strivers Row e-newsletter,
send a blank message to:
join-rht-afam@list.randomhouse.com
or go to www.striversrowbooks.com

The Strivers Row Website

Check out the Strivers Row website at www.striversrowbooks.com for:

- The Strivers Row e-newsletter
- Reading Group Guides
- Exclusive author profiles, interviews, and essays
- Sample chapters
- Links to author websites and chats
- News and announcements
- A full list of current and upcoming Strivers Row titles
- Other African-American books from Random House
- And more!

Questions? E-mail us at atrandom@randomhouse.com